Hippolyte's
Island

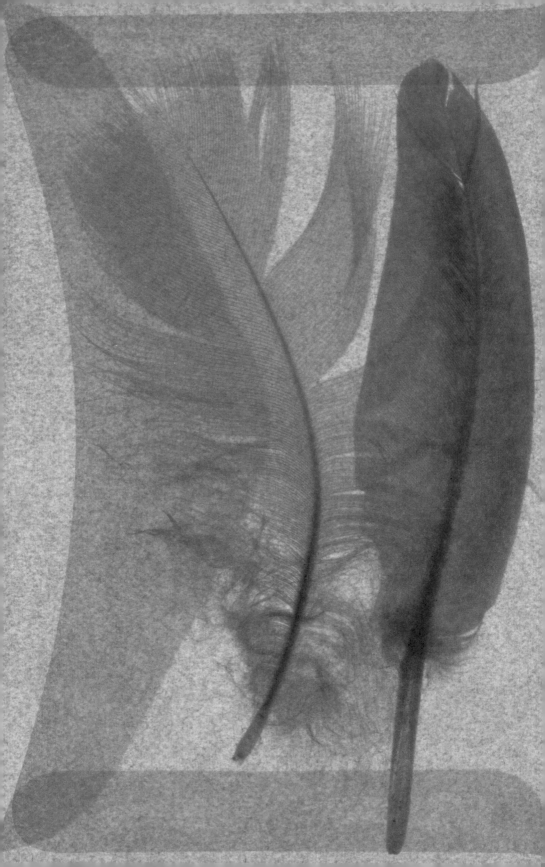

Hippolyte's Island

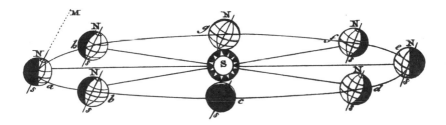

Barbara Hodgson

CHRONICLE BOOKS
SAN FRANCISCO

Design by Barbara Hodgson/Byzantium Books

All uncredited archival images are from Byzantium Archives. Every effort
has been made to trace accurate ownership of copyrighted text and
visual material used in this book. Errors or omissions will be corrected
in subsequent editions, provided notification is sent to the publisher.
Credits and acknowledgments are continued on page 282.

LIBRARY OF CONGRESS CATALOGING-IN-PUBLICATION DATA:

Hodgson, Barbara, 1955–
  Hippolyte's island : an illustrated novel / Barbara Hodgson.
   p. cm.
  ISBN-0-8118-2892-1
  I.Title.

  PS3558.O34345 H56 2001
  813'.54—dc21   00-050839

Printed in China

10 9 8 7 6 5 4 3 2 1

Chronicle Books LLC
85 Second Street
San Francisco, CA 94105

www.chroniclebooks.com

TO MY FATHER

PART ONE

SOUTH

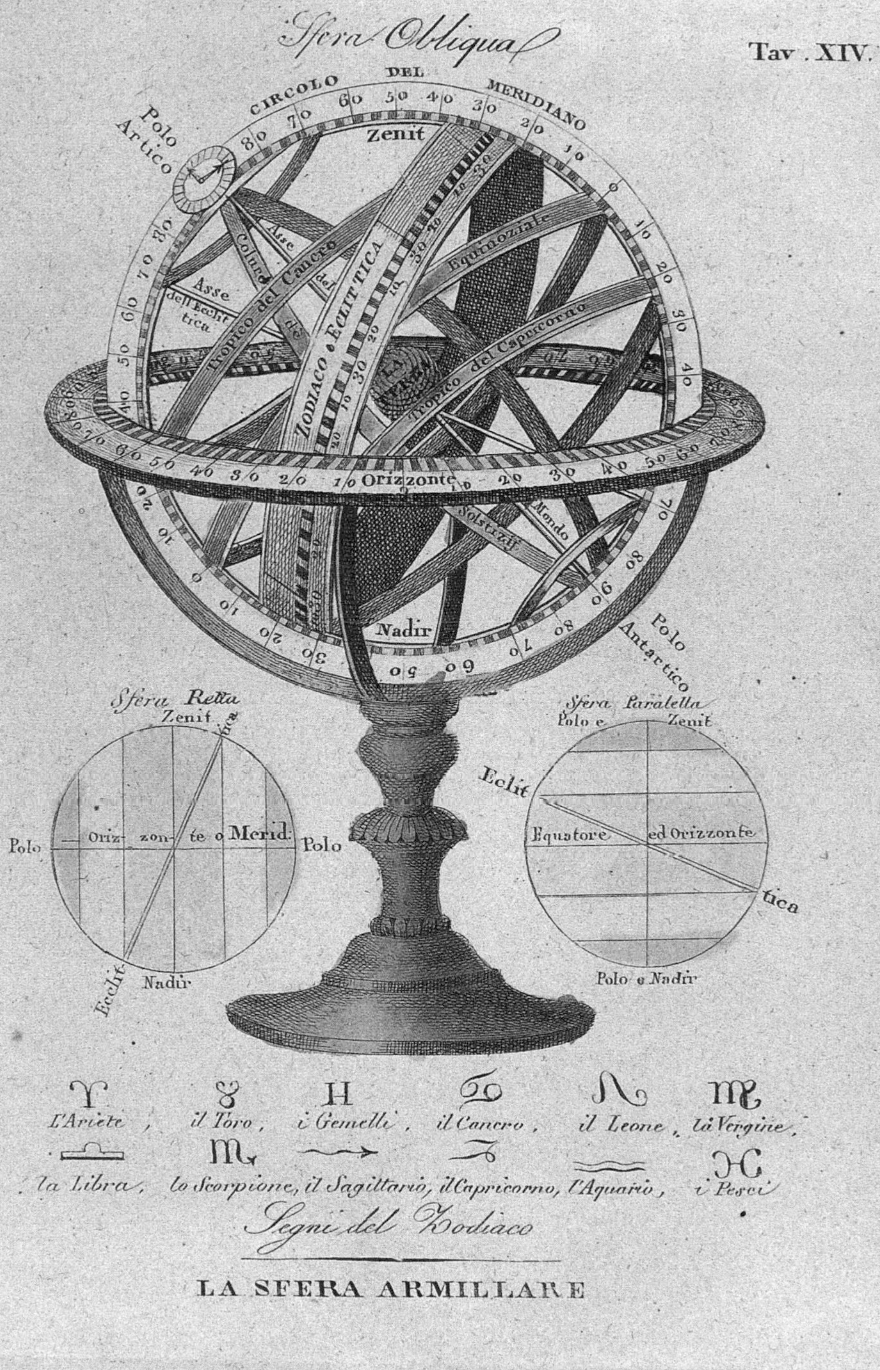

One

HEAVY STEPS CRISSCROSSED OVERHEAD. From his prone position on a saggy old couch, Hippolyte tracked them, watching the ceiling tremble faintly with each footfall. A chunk of plaster fell on his face. He brushed the powder off his skin and grinned. More plaster fell, and the resulting patch became an intriguing dried-out lake bed. He caught his breath. Where in the world is that? he mused.

This new feature was emerging in a ceilingscape that had already undergone much geological activity. Above stretched a coastline of stains, a three-dimensional terrain of bulges and flakes, charting years of slowly encroaching water damage. Beginning in the East, appropriately at the window, a voyage round this head-over-heels expanse followed a string of long fjords of dampness. Thin tentacles crept out from these inlets, the rivers that seemed to feed them. Continuing to the North, the eye navigated tufty patches of trial paints—spackley beige, rippled cream, stalactite eggshell—pigments applied by a previous owner who had reasoned that new color might disguise the damage, but who gave up, preferring, in the end, to suffer a loss rather than expend labor. Over to the West, the journey continued through the remains of the upstair tenant's overflowing bathtub. A spectacular deluge, this event had produced craters, cauldrons even, of heaving beams and drywall that flowed down the wall and into the closet.

The floor had its own geography—a splash of red wine here, a dent from the fall of a hammer there, the varnished golden wood rubbed rough and slivery white in paths of hard-booted heels and toes. Swollen and blackened tidal pools, ditches, and hummocks, legacies of the already-mentioned bath.

4

Hippolyte saw in the ceiling and the floor reminders of places he yearned to visit, so over the two years he had owned the apartment he had added his hand to its evolving contours by vigorously writing in names and filling in missing details. All features were subjected to his labeling frenzies: a wide split above his head that was reminiscent of the Don just before it emptied into the Sea of Azov, green mold creeping out from the wall that exuded the humid Caspian marshlands, a staggering Gobi Desert where efforts to dry the damp had resulted in crackling, blistering paint.

The small apartment was not as much of an anomaly in rain-soaked Vancouver as one might imagine. Plagued by shoddy building practices, the city was filled to the brim with inhabitants of such apartments who had no affinities with maps or movement, who despaired of similar features in their homes. Not so Hippolyte Webb. He had plastered nearly every available square inch of his walls with maps—maps with corners curling, fragments of maps reconstructed into mythical landscapes, maps adorned with precious cupids pink from the exertion of harnessing the winds. Of these his favorites were those with vast territories labeled *Terra Incognita,* unknown land, at least unknown at one time.

His apartment—in its own way as lost and forgotten a corner of the world as any he could ever hope to find—was perpetually overwhelmed by piles of atlases and gazeteers stacked precariously on the floor and by others threatening to slide off the warped and groaning shelves too narrow to support their burdens. Perched on the edge of the ancient couch that he shared with heaps of yellowed and brittling newspapers, Hippolyte was consumed by the forests, deserts, and mountain ranges hidden between the covers of these cherished books, the urge to tear them open and fly directionless through their pages irresistible. Home barely long enough to change his clothes, here he was yearning to leave again.

He loved this point in travel, the very beginning, the moment when the decision to go hit his heart and his gut, when the whirl of topography careening through his brain burned his feet, when the fine lines of maps tangled themselves around him like a net and drew him up and away, when his mind traveled the world before he even walked out the door.

But which way should he go? It had gradually dawned on him that the world had gone all screwy, and, though he couldn't put his finger on when it had happened or why, he knew that all of his certainties had been yanked out from under him. It was as if he had awakened from a deep sleep suddenly aware that the seasons had slipped unaccountably, giving way to the winter equinox, the vernal solstice. This was the year of warm spring rains in December, searing heat in April, falling leaves in June, and Arctic winds in September. Longing to find a land where the seasons had revolved to resemble those he remembered, he closed his eyes, and one by one, plucked the petals off that delicate compass rose, the rose round which navigators glide and sailors whisper. Round which even dolphins hold their breath. West, North, East, the cardinal petals fell.

There had been a time when he had thought he could go only West. That had all changed overnight, and he remembered exactly when; it had been last winter, during a stay in Bukhara. It was his second visit to that city, and he had decided to go back simply because he couldn't remember a thing about his visit made ten years earlier. On this trip he became disoriented—he blamed the inexplicable, suffocating heat—and found himself standing in front of a familiar doorway. It was a heavy wooden barrier, ornately carved and adorned with a medieval lock, like any of hundreds of doors in the residential quarter. Lost in reverie, he raised his arm to pound on it, but the iron fist of recollection stopped him just in time and brought him to his senses. He remembered that the door gave passage to a house that he had been forever barred from entering, the house of a woman he had unwisely fallen in love with. Subsequent westward trips to other destinations prompted the similar disturbing sensation: that he had gone so far that he was doing no more than retracing his own steps and was mistaking old memories for new. And since he was resistant to North's magnetic pull and was perpetually at cross purposes with East, there was no alternative; he decided right then and there to turn the world on its axis and head south to find his bearings.

Accustomed to crossing meridians and marking his existence by degrees of longitude, Hippolyte was enthralled by turning perpendicular and confronting latitude. This simple 90-degree shift, dismissed without thought in the past, was now seductive, tantalizing. South beckoned with the promise of places he'd never before heard of, places with names resonating isolation, places long ago forgotten. But it couldn't be just any South. Too many other explorers had already been, and he had sworn long ago to never give in and follow them.

He stood up suddenly. Newspapers slipped to the floor, joining others that had fallen some time previously. Two long steps took him over to the far wall where an old globe hung from the ceiling. He unhooked it and flung himself back on the couch, unleashing another cascade of papers. As he wiped its dusty surface with his sleeve, he discovered that it had dried out and was threatening to come apart at the equator. Ignoring the damage, he drew a bold, black line straight south, adhering strictly to his chosen direction. From Vancouver, the line made its way down to San Francisco and out into the Pacific Ocean, where it ran its watery course uninterrupted—except for the equatorial split, at which point he paused and seriously contemplated the possibilities of falling through—until it hit the polar shores of the Antarctic.

On this particular globe the snowy terrain of the South Pole was colored an optimistically warm and sunny yellow, though Hippolyte doubted that it would ever be anything other than cold and bleak. But as formidable and distant as it was, it had attracted more than its share of men who sought to lose themselves in the process of finding the undiscoverable.

In addition to the Antarctic, there were the Pacific islands on either side of the line: Tahiti, the Marquesas, and Pitcairn to the west; Easter, Juan Fernández, and the Galápagos to the east, respectively tempting visions of white sands and palm trees or isolated pockets of myth and adventure. But which one of these famous isles hadn't already been trampled upon or rhapsodized over?

West had been so easy. When he first began traveling sixteen years ago—he rapidly counted the time on his fingers—West had literally pitched him through Russia, Northern China, Mongolia, Kazakhstan, the Ukraine, Poland, Germany, France, and back home to Canada. Those three years spent circumperambulating the globe at the 49th parallel merely whetted his appetite for travel, but destitution threatened to stop him in his tracks. Then two employed but restless pals who had money in their bank accounts and were ignited by his stories proposed launching a travel magazine. The result was *50° North*. Because travel was hot yet underexploited, the concept caught fire, and the three of them reaped a considerable profit when they sold out a few years later to a large San Francisco publisher. It was this money that had since allowed Hippolyte the luxury of choosing when and where to travel, though he'd lately sunk too much of it into the apartment that did little more than serve as storage for his maps and books.

He thought of his life since that first momentous trip. An explorer by instinct and a self-taught natural historian by profession, but by no means by discipline, he had worked as a travel consultant, a botanist, and a linguist, but most of all he wrote. From his pen flowed detail and curiosity for a world full of contradiction. He was enticed by the emptiest of lands, the ones that lacked any signs of human presence, and was equally seduced by those so densely packed with life that they were the very hearts of humanity.

Hippolyte whirled his globe, watching the pinks, greens, yellows, and blues blur into a palate of erratic colonialism. Each spin further jeopardized North's increasingly fragile hold on the Southern Hemisphere, which was now hanging by a small paper hinge straddling Sumatra and Borneo. After halting its demented wobbling, he cradled the Antarctic in his left hand and tore at the seam with his right, liberating both halves from each other. In its newfound freedom, the world offered endless possibilities for a traverse directly south. He shifted South America to the west and redrew the line. It skimmed the Amazon, then sped through the South Atlantic. At 50° South it passed over three barely noticeable dots located midway between the Falklands and the island of South Georgia, then slammed once more into the Antarctic.

What was South offering him? A hell of a lot of water and ice, for all he could see. At least, West was land, *terra firma*. He rotated the bottom half again and again, then flipped the globe over so that the South Pole was now at the top. This reversed aspect gave the appealing illusion that the area he was considering was somewhat south of Antarctica. He carefully retraced his second line back towards the equator, pausing at the three unidentified spots. Why not try for a place that didn't even warrant a label? *Why* weren't they labeled?

Eager to find out more about them, he tossed aside the mutilated globe in favor of a dog-eared school atlas dated 1892. In his possession since he found it languishing in a garbage bin some twenty years earlier, the atlas still reeked of decaying vegetables and damp cigarette butts. Laboriously inscribed on the flyleaf—possibly at the behest of some prissy schoolmarm—was "March 12th, 1895, Perfection comes from small, daily sacrifices," a sentiment that provoked his impatience. Many of its cheap, thin pages had been torn, then crudely repaired with strips of Scotch tape that flaunted the fingerprints of whoever had tried to mend it. Bits of the tape—no doubt shriveled and desiccated long before Hippolyte was born—fell out each time it was opened. Other pages were forcefully scribbled upon in soft black pencil: nonsense names like Pindobar, Tunafed, and Bruzistan replaced Arabia, the Yukon, and the Urals. Vehement, random lines made by sharp pen nibs plowed haphazardly through the pages yet managed to convey the idea of the bombing of a crudely drawn Christmas tree or a house or the moon. Whole topographical features had been effaced by the constant pointing and rubbing from the tip of some grubby child's finger as he was doing whatever it is children do with maps. Hippolyte liked to think that the boy—and it was no doubt a boy, judging from the drawings of things being blown up scattered throughout—was trying to get a fix on where he was, as that's what Hippolyte himself had been doing at the age when he too drew pictures of explosions.

Overlying the destruction wreaked by the anonymous child were Hippolyte's own scrawls. He never planned trips with current maps since their landscapes were stained by huge cities and bisected by too many roads. Arrows, exclamation marks, circles, dates, mileages, all the specifics that he needed in order to devise yet another getaway could be found on the pages of the atlas. Now turning to South America, he realized that for all these years, his travels had favored the regions ravaged by the child's hand, that they'd both left the Southern Hemisphere unexplored. The map of the South Atlantic was so pristine that Hippolyte was prepared to regard the flawless page an omen and to get the hell back to familiar territory when he noticed smooth sailing between the Falklands and South Georgia, with not a hint of the three islands so enticingly speckled onto his globe.

He opened another atlas, this one from 1924. Again there were no traces of the islands. The maps papering the walls were no help, either; those bearing any semblance of reality were of only northern lands. Hippolyte dragged from behind a bookcase portfolio cases bursting with loose maps. The first yielded India, China, Russia; another, Africa, the Middle East; another, pre-WWI Europe. Finally he found the folio he was looking for. It was stuffed full of maps of South America, bought—found?—so long ago he couldn't even remember where they came from.

The real treasure here, the 1676 John Speed map of the Americas, lacked even the Falklands. The sight of this map swept Hippolyte up in an obsession of eclipses and heavens, of coastlines rendered delirious by the imaginative mapmaker, of rivers that had no sources, of islands that faded off into infinity. The danger of maps possessed him now; he caressed the rag paper, thick between his fingers and still bloated with the earthly colors daubed onto its landforms. Hippolyte recalled buying this map in a moment of intoxication with the sheer extravagance of its creation. Lacking sufficient cash, he'd offered to top off the contents of his wallet with his walking boots and watch. He'd left the shop, the precious map snugly rolled up in its cardboard tube, oblivious to the absurdity of his stockinged feet.

An 1851 Tallis map of South America, with its delicate coloring and charming vignettes, showed the Falklands and South Georgia but ignored the space in between. It reminded him of another in the series, a map of North Africa, and a wild goose chase that had taken him as far south as he had ever been. Someone, perhaps the engraver, perhaps the mapmaker, had marked "P. Hilsborough" onto Morocco's coastline, a short distance south of the city of Agadir. Finding no trace of this feature either in the country itself or on any other map, he had tried to uncover the secret of Hilsborough: had he been a self-aggrandizing apprentice in Tallis's company, or was the name—ludicrous considering the country to which it was appended—a means of trying to catch out would-be map plagiarists? His lack of success still rankled. Enough of this, move on! he cried out, dropping the maps at his feet. The next sheet, a pre-1850s *Black's General Atlas* South America map, also failed to provide the necessary detail; however, its corresponding "Chart of Magnetic Curves" of the world showed three unmarked dots.

"Magnetic Curves" gave him an idea. He turned to the opening pages of the school atlas and its double-page Mercator's projection of the world. Here he found not only the presence of the islands but, at last, their name: *Aurora Islands.* He'd had no doubt he'd find a name, but it gave him a jolt all the same.

Aurora.

The Auroras.

That he'd never heard of them was no surprise; there must be hundreds of islands that have slipped from public consciousness. He looked for them in the index. They weren't listed.

Further sifting through the South America folder produced a small but exciting Italian map from 1833 with *I. dell' Aurora* inscribed next to five rather significant islands and an 1877 French map with three distinct islands labeled *Is. de l'Aurore.*

In twenty minutes he'd sifted through a total of twenty-five maps: three from the 1800s with the islands named, four from the same time period with the islands located but unidentified, and eighteen, spanning three centuries, that ignored them completely.

Hippolyte swept more papers off the couch and stretched out again. Wouldn't it be amazing, he mused, to discover a forgotten island? Or even better, as it was in this case, a bunch of them. When was the last time an opportunity came along to actually find something that had slipped out of existence?

He gazed at nothing in particular, lost in his imagination, until a hole in his sock caught his eye. The sight of his toe sticking through the frayed wool was an unwelcome reminder of the general cloud of neglect engulfing him. It was always like this, when he was between travels, between lovers. He really ought to live with someone, he thought. Then he might feel inclined to spruce himself up and keep the place tidy.

But the desire to share his life temporarily obscured two small but important details, one of which was having enough time for reading. This was never an issue when he and a new inamorata first stepped over the threshold of temporary monogamy. But as weeks dampened novelty and reestablished habitual customs, he would ease back into his pages, selfishly ignoring the small voice in the corner when it selfishly tried to recall his focus back to the world of more important things like dinner conversation or shopping. Not that some women didn't share his passion for reading, but they believed there was a time and a place for it. None of them would consider squandering whole days and nights on it any more than they would consider sacrificing nightingales on the altar of love.

Besides, he couldn't start a new relationship now when he was on the verge of departure. This detail was more pressing and instantly rendered the whole notion inconceivable. He'd tried before, believing that if he explained the reasons for the transient arrangement then all would be well, but invariably ended up causing a disproportionate amount of distress. And probably more to the point, he had no prospects; opportunities to meet anyone new were limited severely by his continual absences. He ran his hand over the stubble on his chin, then pulled his socks off and stuffed them under the couch.

He reached out and sorted through the maps on the floor, grabbing the three that identified the Auroras. Questions raced through his mind as he studied the aged paper, engraved lines, and elegant lettering. If the Auroras did exist, then why had they been dropped off of some maps? If they didn't exist, why were they on these? Who found them? Who lost them? What was their modern-day status? For once, he regretted not owning a current atlas.

According to the 1877 map, the Auroras were located at 50° West and 56° South, exactly halfway between the Falklands and the remoter, more easterly island of South Georgia. The position of the five islands on the Italian map was vastly different, especially in light of its larger scale. Here they were placed farther east, between 332° and 336° West. West of where? What system of longitude were they using? Which meridian were they measuring from? The scale, too, was meaningless, specifying "Tuscan miles" and "French leagues." Spanish leagues he knew. American and English ones, too. What was the measure of a French league? Did scale even matter on a map of such appalling imprecision and inaccuracy? Inaccurate or not, though, it did display a great deal of confidence in the Auroras' existence, granting them tremendous space and detail. That sold him; they were definitely worth looking into more closely.

He sat up and frowned at the rain hitting the window. It was November; why wouldn't it be raining? Except it had been raining steadily since August, only now it seemed warmer. He was fed up with the weather, his restlessness, everything. It was time to leave again. He looked around the apartment and sensed it had already become a little emptier, that he'd already stepped partway out the door. Why not decide right here and now? Go to the Auroras. Find a new direction.

Albatross, sooty (*Phoebetria fusca*) uniform chocolate brown. Yellow strip or "sulcus" along lower mandible. Vagrant species on Falklands.

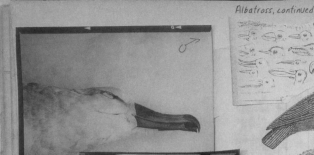

3

se .... Page 498.
iche et noire .... 499.   3. Le Pétrel cendré ....

Albatross, black-browed (*Diomedea melanophrys*)
— "Mollymawk" albatross. 2.5m wingspan, mass up to 4kg.
— underwing pattern with a wide dark leading edge.
— Yellow bill with orange-red tip, dark eyebrows.
— Ship follower
— Breeds in Falklands, Tierra del Fuego, South Georgia

whitechinned Petrel
(*Procellaria aequinoctialis*)
aka Shoemaker
— Largest burrowing petrel
- wing span 1.5m; 50cm. length
— v. dark with white chin
— Ship follower
Breeds in South Georgia and
Falklands and elsewhere.
Breeding season begins
mid-October, eggs hatch mid-January. Young ready to go Aprilish.
Smaller than the Giant Southern Petrel.

2

2. Le Fulmar .... 518.

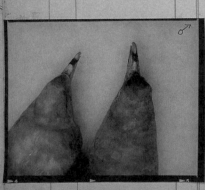

Fulmar, Antarctic or Southern or Silver-grey (*Fulmarus glacialoides*)
— 800g, 1.2m wingspan. Pale grey plumage with white head and black flight feathers. Looks like a gull, except for the nasal tube.
— Yellow bill, dark tip, eye and outline.
— Breeds Antarctic and South Georgia (Falklands? probably not)

Fulmarus   glacialoides

Gentoo (*Pygoscelis papua*)
orange, red bill, white flash
behind its eye. Large pops. at
S. Georgia, Falklands.

King (*Aptenodytes
patagonicus*) 2nd largest,
just under a metre high,
9-15 kg. Tall and elegant.
M, F take turns balancing egg
on their feet. Yellow stain at
the neck, yellow ear muffs,
underside of beak. Chicks
brown and fluffy. Breeding:
Eggs laid early Dec., by June
nearly full weight.

Magellanic (*Spheniscus mag-
ellanicus*) appears on the
Falklands. The only species
that visits S. America.
Donkey-like bray (aka jack-
asses). Underground nests.
Darwin calls them
Aptenodytes demersa.

Rockhopper (*Eudyptes
chrysocome*) smaller than
macaronis, have yellow
tassels that do not meet
between the eyes.
Three subspecies. Largest
pop. is on Falklands.

Macaroni (*Eudyptes
chrysolophus*) orange
tassels meet between
the eye. Aka Maccies.
Breed S. Georgia,
Falklands

Falklands:
  Mag.
  King
  Rock.
  Gent.

:: S.Georgia: Mac.
  Mag.
  King
  Rock.
  Gent.
  Ch.Strp.

1. Le Guillemot.
2. Le Macareux.
3. Le Macareux du Kamtschatka.
4. Le Pingouin.
5. Le grand Pingouin.
6. Le grand Manchot.

END OF SEVENTH V

1. Le Petrel damier...... Page

Two

HIPPOLYTE THREW HIMSELF INTO RESEARCH; he scoured histories and geographies, surrounding himself with titles like *Lost Islands, Oddities and Unexplained Facts,* and *No Longer on the Map.* His readings told him that hundreds of islands gracing legitimate maps had been, for one reason or another, left off of updates, disappearing, as it were, from the face of the earth. The South Atlantic alone, he read, was now missing Matthew, Saxembourg, Kettendyks Droogte, Diego Alvarez, Thompson, Grande, and the Auroras.

At last count more than two hundred islands around the world had been lost. Had they been submerged, eroded, or simply misplaced? Were they vanished fragments of demented sailors' imaginations or had they been erroneously positioned from ignorance? Had they been born out of deception, then killed off by survey? Were they blown out of the water by earth's belly aching? Perhaps they were just carto-graphic fantasies. If one were to think kindly of the mapmakers who gave them credibility, one might say it was because they were overly concerned for the wellbeing of sailors and littered the routes with make-believe obstacles to keep them all vigilant.

Who would mourn these lost or sunken bits of uninhabitable rock, anyway? The navigators who christened them were long since dead. Otherwise, there were only the sea birds, never known for con-stancy to any territory, and the cresting waves, left with nothing on which to vent their rage. And now there was himself; the Auroras became his passion.

He bought current marine charts and searched for even obscure signs of them. Anything would do: a higher-than-normal sea bed, the presence of an ocean ridge, a nearby island. His exhilaration hit a new high when he saw that the ocean floor rose from depths of 3200, 1300, 4300 meters to 366 meters at 50° West, approximately the correct longitude for the Auroras. Three hundred and sixty-six meters was still a long way down, but it was a start.

He studied shipping and air route charts to ascertain the possibility that the islands lay in what might be called a traffic vacuum, through which no vessel passed. However, though traffic was indeed light in the area, it was by no means non-existent.

Through his reading, he amassed proof that the earth could still hide parts of itself from the prying eyes that seemed to be everywhere these days: aerial and satellite photography, geographical positioning systems, radar, electronic mapping devices, all the instruments that intimately and thoroughly inspected the world's secret features, its dimples, crevices, and pockmarks. What was once seen from a vantage point on the surface, the summit of a mountain, for instance, and measured by eye, by hand, by pacing, was now diminished by accuracy and certainty. Press a button on a handheld whatever and know instantly where you are, especially relative to where you've been, where you want to go. Whatever happened to just being in a place and knowing it for what it is?

Hippolyte, one eye on the ground and one on the horizon, never lost sight of where he was or where he was heading. His bearings always in place meant that his discoveries were never without context. He almost believed that he was planted in the very soil he tread upon, that his roots reached down to the past. You could jab a finger at any point on any map, and, given that he'd actually been there, he could paint you the sky and the earth. And if he'd never been there, he could read the story of its map as if the cartographer had sat him down and had told him firsthand of the rivers, the valleys, the hills. His knowledge gave him the freedom to wander at will, to challenge the unknown, to lose himself.

He sighed as he considered the changing world. Mountain peaks, not so high anymore; distances across the oceans, not so far anymore;

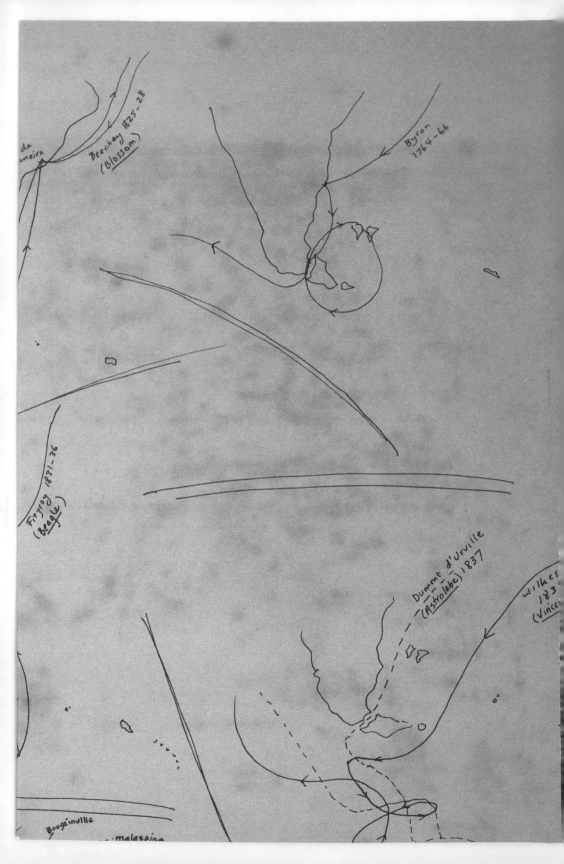

Beechey 1825-28
(Blossom)

de
aneiro

Byron
1764-66

Fitzroy 1831-36
(Beagle)

Dumont d'Urville
(Astrolabe) 1837

Wilkes
183
(Vince

Bougainville

malaseina

Auroras' place on maps for at least the next sixty years. In his account, Bustamente bemoaned the murky weather that clouded his view, the fleeting icebergs that cunningly disguised themselves as permanent landmasses, and the horrendous errors that crept into his readings—up to twenty minutes—of both latitude and longitude. The navigator despaired of ever finding the islands, writing "Everything conspired to disappoint us." His pessimism was short-lived, though. On the tenth day out, "the sight of one of them . . . came to release us from our state of continuous vigilance."

In another account, James Weddell, a British naval officer turned sealer who set out to find the Auroras in 1820 but failed, divulged his cynicism while admitting that belief in the islands was widespread.

Arrogant American sealer Benjamin Morrell, after hearing about Weddell, pretended to look for the Auroras, too. Maybe the word *pretended* was too harsh, but even to Hippolyte, new as he was to the history of South Atlantic exploration, much of what Morrell wrote did not ring true. This was not his opinion alone; skepticism rumbled amongst historians who specialized in the region, particularly when it came to his declaration that the route to the South Pole was ice-free and that he'd seen birds of paradise in the South Sandwich Islands. Morrell claimed to have sailed for four days to where the Auroras were supposed to be, then to have squandered twelve days staggering around the South Atlantic, giving up in disgust at the waste of time.

A fictionalized account, Edgar Allan Poe's *The Narrative of A. Gordon Pym*, disappointed Hippolyte greatly. Poe, that damned story writer, was no better than Morrell, helping himself to others' experiences and nailing the coffin shut on the question of the Auroras' existence, in spite of never having been anywhere near the place. Poe's character did, admittedly, concede that they may have once existed, but qualified this concession by adding, "we were thoroughly satisfied that . . . no vestige of them remained at present day."

Hippolyte put aside the books and wrote letters. He wrote to the British Admiralty, asking if they had acknowledged the Auroras on their marine charts. They sent him a photocopy of #357, "A Chart of the Ethiopic or Southern Ocean, 1808," with the tracks of Bustamente's survey, and a copy of #1240, "A Chart of the South Polar Sea, 1839," showing Weddell's attempt. The Library of Congress informed him that they had Bustamente's voyage on a Spanish map, #69028, "Carta Esferica del Oceano Meridional, 1800," but that he would have to go to Washington to see it. A letter to the Royal Hydrographical Society of Madrid, which had been referred to by both Weddell and Morrell, was returned, marked *Dirección desconocido.*

Excitement, ignited by the controversy—albeit one nearly two hundred years old—surrounding the existence of the Auroras, hurtled Hippolyte onto the next stage. He drew up schedules and routes and hunted down weather, tide, and wind charts. Calculating the best time of year to travel, he discovered that he was sitting smack dab in the middle of it. If he were to do this thing, to make this trip, he would have to start by the end of December—a scant six weeks away—or mid-January at the latest.

How to get there? With dividers, calculator, and detailed highway maps of the Americas at hand, he worked out overland distances, captivated by the idea of a road trip through Central and South America. The route, spread out over thirty mind-boggling sheets, was a study in mountains, seashores, rain forests, deserts, freeways, and urban sprawl. Red, black, and yellow roads snaked their way through altitudinal contours, each section jointed at towns and cities. Some highways—like those between Vancouver and Boise and on to Salt Lake City, Albuquerque, and El Paso—were dead straight and dependable; others—especially south of the Mexican border—petered out curvaceously into a series of dashes, then dots. The total distance to Punta Arenas in Patagonia averaged out at a whopping 11,960 miles. Even covering 300 miles a day—and how likely would that be?—he'd be looking at 40 days. After a realistic evaluation of the inevitability that he would become hopelessly distracted along the way as well as a serious review of the many flaws of his '74 Valiant, he reluctantly laid the plan to rest.

Hitchhiking or taking buses was out of the question with all of the equipment he'd need. Freighter trips appealed, but schedules and routes were convoluted and inconvenient.

He called travel agents and tourist bureaus, a process made all the more cumbersome because he didn't own a phone. (Or rather, he did own one, it just didn't work, since he had forgotten to pay months worth of bills during his last trip and had never bothered to go through the process of getting reconnected.) In no time at all, heaps of propaganda for cruises, tours, and charters to Patagonia, the Falklands, and the Antarctic swamped his apartment. He booked tentative flights on competing airlines from Vancouver to Mount Pleasant on the Falklands, via Santiago, and to Ushuaia, in Patagonian Argentina, via Buenos Aires. Spanish grammars were unearthed, and a Spanish radio station tuned to in the evenings when, for him, the darkness and silence of the night rendered foreign languages understandable.

With the logistics of getting to the South Atlantic under control, he turned to his 1906 Royal Geographical Society *Hints to Travellers*, ninth edition, mooned over the ad for the renowned but no-longer available Benson's Gold Keyless Field Watch, and perused chapters on meteorology, astronomy, and geology.

Hints reminded him to brush up on his natural history. "A week spent in study at the museum would not be wasted," it declared, meaning the British Museum. No, it wouldn't, agreed Hippolyte, if it weren't almost 5,000 miles away. Fortunately, the local university's zoology museum was an excellent alternative for studying the animal life that he would likely encounter. From the drawers of its small but gloriously idiosyncratic collection he was allowed to photograph birds of every size, color, and shape—the South Atlantic petrels, albatross, fulmars, prions, and skuas that a wise ornithologist had thought to preserve. He noted the sometimes huge, sometimes minute differences between these seabirds, measuring bodies and beaks. Birds stiffened into unnatural capsules, their wings drawn tight up against their bodies, their feet tied firmly together as if there were still a chance that they'd come to life, rise up on their scaly claws, and, if not take flight, at the very least run amok amongst the cabinets, blinded with cataracts of white cotton spilling out of eye sockets. While he padded about—birds cradled in his arms—from the drawers to the camera stand and back again, the strong scent of oily albatross and petrel feathers wafted from him. And he photographed the other birds that might have strayed onto his islands: falcons, vultures, owls, and even sparrows. For those animals not represented in the collection—the penguins, seals, and whales—books, dozens of them, filled in missing details: their Latin names, characteristics, habitats. With the photographic references and the notes, he created his own guide to the fauna of the South Atlantic.

On previous travels, although he'd identified plants and photographed them in the field, he'd never collected them. So, in order to quickly familiarize himself with the plants he might find on the Auroras, he made himself at home in the botanical museum, painstakingly drawing details of grasses, mosses, and lichens, frustrating himself with the intricacies of their infinitesimal features.

From zoology and botany it was a logical leap to the natural historians and artists from the famous Patagonian and Antarctic expeditions, including Wilson of the *Discovery,* Marston of the *Endurance,* and, of course, Darwin of the *Beagle.* Darwin's account of his voyage was filled with keenly phrased observations, but Darwin had nothing good to say about the Falklands. Spoiled, no doubt, by the abundance of the Galápagos, Darwin found the Falklands bleak, cold, and generally uninteresting. His opinion of the Auroras would probably have been even more dismissive.

Hippolyte was already acquainted with the process of collecting specimens but was astonished at the willingness of these early scientists to endure freezing temperatures and make do with jury-rigged labs. Even more amazing were the vivid sketches and photographs—many created under appalling conditions—that they brought back.

Books were all he had to make the South Atlantic real and so was crushed when the author of *Hints* reminded him that they were a useless burden and that "[he] had better at once abandon all idea of encumbering [himself] with them." To make up for the expected reference shortfall he meticulously copied indispensable and trivial information alike into his precious journals. The lifeblood of his work and travels, he certainly wasn't going to leave those behind.

Books aside, he had still to figure out how he was going to get to the Auroras from wherever it was he flew to. Once he got to the Falklands, or even Patagonia, he could conceivably charter a seaplane, but that meant hiring a pilot too, since he didn't know how to fly. Having another person involved wasn't out of the question, but it sure complicated matters and added to the cost as well.

Nothing he could think of got around his eventual need for a boat—though he didn't know how to sail either—so earnest letters went out to owners of charter boat companies in Chile, Argentina, and the Falklands, asking for prices, availability, advice. He read up on coastal sailing and on sailing the high seas, starting with weekend sailors and moving up to serious soloers like Chichester, Goss, and even, he regretted in hindsight, Donald Crowhurst, the British sailor who had gone mad while alone at sea. The significant differences between land expeditions, to which he was so accustomed, and ocean voyages, about which he was so clueless, were becoming painfully apparent. He turned again to *Hints* and to the chapter entitled "Scientific Outfit," hoping for some concrete advice on necessary gear. This manual, so reliable when it came to matters of the land, he had never before read with an eye to the sea, so it was with great relief that he discovered that the sections on sextants, chronometers, artificial horizons, and barometers also applied to ocean voyaging. Being familiar with the use of these instruments meant that he'd be a natural on the water. He was feeling better about the whole thing already.

The references to navigation in *Hints* prompted Hippolyte to visit the local sailing school, but his eyes glazed over the confusing list of the dozen or so courses offered. "Just sign me up for whatever's starting right away," he requested of the young woman handling registrations.

"What level?" she asked efficiently. Her name, according to the plaque on the desk, was Donna.

"What do you mean, what level? I just want to learn how to sail."

She nodded pleasantly—"Beginner!"—and duly registered him in a six-week course that covered how to read navigational charts and emphasized how to stay out of trouble. Donna—he found out that she was the manager's daughter—was particularly proud of the fact that the school offered GPS and all the newfangled things for which Hippolyte could care less; the early explorers found these islands with their eyes and their beautiful brass sextants and so would he.

"Just as long as the instructor talks about the old stuff, too," he said, "dead reckoning, astronomy, plotting positions." She nodded, concentrating on filling out the forms, not really listening to his chatter. "Oh, yes," he added, "and not to forget about sails, rigging, tacking, keels." He rubbed his hands in anticipation. All the questions he would ask! He started a list.

Learning to sail was one thing; paying for a boat and all the extra equipment it demanded was another. On top of air fares and living expenses, he was going to need a healthy amount of cash. Remortgaging the apartment wasn't an option; the banks had turned their backs on leaky apartments such as his. The balances of his bank accounts, the paltry amounts due in over the coming weeks from a couple of short travel articles, the values of the small wads of francs, pounds, marks he had stashed away here and there was just enough to see him through, though there'd be nothing to come back to, nothing to keep him going. He'd need more money sooner or later, and experience had frequently proved that just sitting around thinking about it wasn't going to make it materialize. So, he headed out to spend a wet morning huddled in the neighborhood phone booth—or, as he referred to it, *his* phone booth—to call all the travel and outdoor magazines he had ever had work published in and the others who had at some time or other held out hope for the future.

Someone was in the booth, a kid with a pocketknife, talking on the phone while engraving a gratuitous streak down the steel frame.

Hippolyte stood and watched for a moment, rainwater creeping along the brim of his hat and dripping down the back of his neck. Passersby glanced over, shook their heads, then rushed on with heads bowed low as though praying not to be caught disapproving of the boy's actions. Cowards! Hippolyte scowled. When he couldn't stand it any longer, he walked up to the kid, wrenched the receiver out of his hand, knocked the knife to the ground, told the voice on the other end, "He'll call back from the police station," and hung up. He hadn't managed to hold on to the boy, however, and sighed with relief as the miscreant hightailed it down the road. "It's my phone," Hippolyte yelled after the departing figure. "Go vandalize someone else's!" He picked up the knife and rolled it around in the palm of his hand. It was a snazzy little number, nice balance, but its stainless steel snap-action blade showed signs of neglect and disrespect. It was clearly intended for more noble deeds than its previous owner had been prepared to carry out. With a salute to the irony of stealing a knife off of a miniature thug, Hippolyte slipped it into his pocket and dialed the first number in his book.

He called *Dare!*, whose editor he got along with best, but was told that she had moved to *Inside,* a new interior design magazine, leaving him feeling betrayed by this rather wanton leap from nature to nurture. Her replacement was not answering the phone. He looked at his watch. Offices in Paris would be long closed, but it was worth trying *Hasards* anyway; the managing editor, a buttoned-up guy who lacked the imagination for risks of any kind, often worked well into the night. He got through and burned up precious phone credit on pleasantries all for a hazy promise that the editor would happily look at whatever was submitted, although there would be no money up front.

He then called *50° North* and spoke to the current editor, John Harada, who had a soft spot for the "old guys." John was intrigued with the idea of tackling 50° South and would think about giving him an advance for an exclusive article if he wrote a proposal. "As usual, Hippolyte," the young man said. "I don't need to remind you about these bottom-line publishers."

"I'll start on it right away," Hippolyte declared fervently, though the fever faded when the fee was discussed. "We were never such cheapskates!" he chastised.

The editor at *Far Corners* told him she was up to her "yin-yangs" with articles on sailing. "But it's not about sailing," he insisted to no avail, amusing himself all the while by wondering where yin-yangs were on a woman.

When he'd exhausted the magazines, he moved on to newspapers, a medium that he'd previously taken pains to avoid. The features editors shunted him over to the voice mail boxes of the travel editors, which spouted reassuring but vague disclaimers that all finished submissions would be looked at with sincerity. Another call to a newspaper-writing acquaintance yielded the disquieting information that a travel article might reap all of $50 to $150. So much for that idea.

Slumped against the wall of the phone booth, thumbing through the stack of business cards that he had accumulated through the years and that had somehow survived the move from wallet to pocket and from pocket back to wallet, he came across the name Jeremy Gould, a childhood pal whom he had run into again several years back at some media award ceremony in Toronto. Jeremy was now an editor at a publishing house, a big publishing house. Maybe he could make some money by writing a book!

"Mr. Gould no longer works here," intoned the receptionist. Hippolyte waited for her to volunteer more information but had to give up and ask where Jeremy had gone. "He is now the publisher at Rumor Press," she replied, as if Hippolyte should thank her for having made it possible for Mr. Gould to advance to such heights. And why not, he thought, maybe it was because of her.

"What do you think of this Rumour Press?" he queried. He'd never heard of it.

"It's a fine place," she confided, suddenly interested in talking. "You know, I wouldn't mind working there myself."

"What kind of books do they do?"

"Lifestyle . . ."

Lifestyle? What the hell was that?

"And biography," she continued, "adventure . . ."

"Adventure?" he perked up. "What kind of adventure?"

"Backcountry weekend driving with suvs, that sort of thing."

"suvs?"

"You know, sports utility vehicles."

Hippolyte was silent, thinking furiously.

"Jeeps, Land Rovers, Suzukis, *you* know." The receptionist was exasperated by his apparent ignorance. "Say," she said, "what's that noise I can hear over the line?"

"A truck just passed by," he replied, disconcerted by the change in subject. Since when had a Jeep become a sports utility vehicle?

"No, not the truck. There's something else; sounds like a kind of continuous fuzz."

"Oh, that's the rain."

"Do you have a window open? It's really loud."

"I'm calling from a phone booth."

"How come you're calling from a booth? You poor dear, don't you have your own phone? How can it be raining, there isn't a cloud in the sky! Ah, you're calling from Vancouver. I'd move to Vancouver if I could find a job." The receptionist clearly had her mind focused on moving, but was not so self-absorbed that she couldn't spare some feelings for him. "Do you have a book idea you want to talk to Mr. Gould about? He's wonderfully interested in all kinds of things, you know. Here, let me give you Rumor's number. It's in New York!"

"New York!" That was miles better than Toronto. "Thanks a lot!"

"Good luck," she yelled over the rumble of another truck.

Hippolyte checked the time, 2:14. That'd be 5:14 in New York. It had been pure luck to get the Toronto office before it closed for the day, but it was worth giving New York a try anyway. He stuck the phone card back in the slot and watched with dismay as the total flashed $0.15, and the card was spat out. A search through his pockets produced forty cents. He couldn't call collect, could he? He picked up the receiver and stared at buttons, then hung up, his mind racing furiously back through the past and to his old best friend, Germ Gould. Germ. He hadn't thought about that nickname for years! Hippolyte walked home, chuckling to himself at the idea of Germ, a publisher. He unlocked the door and drifted through the front room, blind to the stacks of paper obstructing his way, lost in reveries of imminent monetary salvation. Flopping down onto the couch, he proceeded to dream of how he'd spend the advance.

Hippolyte Webb
Box 21, Stn. A
Vancouver, BC V6B 1Z1

November 15, 1999

Jeremy Gould
Rumour Press
10 West 52nd
New York, NY 10019

Jeremy, how have you been? I was amazed to hear that
you're a publisher now. You'll have to fill me in on how
you got there. I bet you're surprised to hear from me,
especially after such a long time. I want to talk to you
about a book idea, a really great book idea. Remember me
telling you about my travels? Well, I'm ready to set off on
a pretty interesting trip, and I need some way to finance
it, so I thought of a book. You probably get 2 dozen letters
like this a day, but this one is different. I tried calling
you earlier to talk to you about it, and I suppose I could
wait and try again, but frankly, I'm just too excited. Look,
I'm heading off to the Aurora Islands. You've never heard
of them, I'll bet. Get an atlas out right now, before you
read any further and turn to the page that shows the South
Atlantic. Follow the Argentine coast down to Patagonia
then make a sharp right and head east past the Falkland
Islands towards South Georgia but stop half way. If the
lats. and longs. are marked, find 52°37'S, 47°43 1/2'W. Odds
are you'll be hovering over open waters and wondering what

Airfare $2000
Chile entry tax $50
YVR tax $10
Maps $120
accom. 30 x 10 $300
food: $20/day $800
Subtotal $3820

Equipment $2000?
boat? $$$$$
Gas, boat fees $1000?

the hell I'm talking about. But that's them! The
Aurora Islands. See my sketch; it'll show you
everything you need to know. The story of how they
got found and then lost is too long to include here,
except to say that nobody thinks about them anymore, and I'm going to put them back on the map.

My plan is to go there and rediscover them and then
write a book about my adventure. I'm not going to do a
Heyerdahl and recreate an ancient voyage; I'm just going to
rent a regular boat and make my way there as efficiently as
possible. While I'm en route, and once I find the islands, I'll
painstakingly document the geology and climate, the flora and
fauna; perhaps I'll even discover a never-before seen species
or two!

So, here I am, unashamedly asking you to consider my
proposal. I'm confident that if anybody can do this and write
about it in a reputable and convincing way, it's me.
However, the whole expedition, if
I may call it that, depends on
money. Isn't it always the same
old sad story? I'm really hoping
that you'll get as fired up as I
am. I'll call in a few days and--if
I can get through to you--pitch the
idea some more. Looking forward to
catching up,

Hippolyte

Hippolyte

Anyway, you can see it's going to take lots of dough

I can get you a detailed list if you want

48°W

50°

You

0°

The Auroras

50

Three

JEREMY LET THE LETTER SLIP OUT OF HIS HANDS as he sat back in his chair. He nodded his head to an unseen tune as a slow, contented smile broke across his face. What a good idea. One man against the elements. Damned good idea. Lost islands somewhere in the harsh and lonely South Atlantic. Why not take it on? His smile widened.

At Rumor for two years, he'd become accustomed to feeling sorry for himself; no one seemed to appreciate his style. His proposals baffled the editors and positively frightened sales and marketing, creating a situation where, in order to get a book through, he had to exercise his prerogative as publisher. This lack of compatibility got him thinking about why he'd been hired in the first place. When he was in the process of being headhunted—a process so heathenly cannibalistic that it was a shock to him that anyone dared to openly acknowledge the word *headhunt*—the hiring company made a big deal of his exquisitely trimmed beard, his unpeggable Canadian accent, his bilingualism. "They want someone who looks and sounds good," they told him, "foreign-like." But not too foreign, of course. And he was young, too. Only thirty-four when he was hired, he was younger than any senior staffer at Rumor. He had jumped into the work with blind enthusiasm, dreaming of capitalizing on his maverick status, but in truth no one took him seriously. At best, they allotted him the same concessions they'd give a nephew of the boss; at worst, they treated him like a company mascot.

Before coming to Rumor, he had always thought it a natural progression for an editor—like him—to become a publisher. Though no one seemed to appreciate it, he had a firm handle on the book business, a solid grasp of content and trends, and an acknowledged fast track to talented writers. But—and he'd be the first to admit it—he had a severe mental block when it came to commercial publishing; he just didn't understand the books the others wanted to publish. The daily process of slamming against the brick wall of safe titles shoring up Rumor's list was wearing him down.

Within the last year he had found himself an ally, though he was still far from breaking through the impasse. Marie Simplon, a no-nonsense editor with a classics background, always sympathetic to his ideas, had firmly supported his suggestion for a book on historical ecological disasters. The result, *Blunders of the Past,* written by an erudite and photogenic history professor, was now on best-seller lists across the country, inching its way toward sales of half-a-million copies. Opponents were temporarily silenced by that brilliant success, even though it was considered a fluke. Since then, he had worked with Marie on several unorthodox proposals, and he knew he could count on her for this one too; he could feel it.

Marie really should have been hired as the publisher here, he thought, with a twinge of guilt. She instinctively understood the ins and outs of the company and could play the game with both the big-money boys and the most demanding of authors. Jeremy had dissected her magic many times; he studied the authority that emanated from her regal deportment and marveled at her ease, her memory, her knowledge. In short, he worshipped her. She should have her own imprint, he decided, and resolved to suggest it if she backed him up on Hippolyte's idea. Would they get along, Hippolyte and Marie?, he wondered, then decided that it didn't matter; Marie would be the one person capable of controlling Hippolyte's chaotic energy.

Good old Webb. Jeremy picked up the letter again and chuckled at the enthusiasm spilling off the paper. He hadn't changed a bit from the looks of it. Memories of Hippolyte his boyhood friend now crowded into his thoughts. Hippolyte as scalliwag, Hippolyte as know-it-all. Particularly Hippolyte as leader. Jeremy remembered the time Hippolyte had led him on an exploration of freshly excavated basements in a nearby housing development, a novelty that greatly attracted the kids in their small, stagnant town. Somehow the ladder they had swiped, the only means of escape from the ten-foot-deep pit they were investigating, had disappeared—restolen, it turned out, by a notoriously nasty brat who had nicknamed himself Genghis—and they'd been left stranded overnight. When Jeremy failed to appear at his curfew time, his mother had hit the roof. Hysterical, she had called the police, the fire department, every last one of the neighbors. He learned after the fact, and to his intense shame, that she had threatened to sue the school, the municipality, even Lois the telephone operator who wasn't getting the connections through fast enough.

Mrs. Webb, on the other hand, sure of *her* son's ability to find his way back home, advised Mrs. Gould not to worry, then went to bed at her usual 11 o'clock and slept peacefully through the ringing phone and Mrs. Gould's incessant banging at her front door. When her alarm went off at 6:45 A.M., she got up, packed Mr. Webb off to work, had a leisurely shower, then made a huge breakfast of pancakes and bacon, stuff that Hippolyte and Jeremy loved.

A search party of sleepy citizens, their trousers drawn up hastily over their pajamas, had been assembled, but the two mischief-makers managed to get themselves out of the hole before they were discovered. Assured of a neutral welcome at the Webbs', they sneaked in at 7:30 and ate like the famished adventurers they were. Once the plates were licked clean, Mrs. Webb phoned the police and called off the search, phoned Mrs. Gould and appeased her as well as she could, then sent a glum-looking Jeremy home to face the music. The three of them cooked up some cock-and-bull story about falling asleep in the woods, which no one believed. Meanwhile, the construction workers searched high and low for their purloined ladder and quizzically examined footholds that had been skillfully carved into the clay wall of the pit.

The ingenious means of escape had been Webb's idea, but then he'd been the one with the carving knife. All Jeremy had had was a plaid handkerchief and a wad of chewed gum. Jeremy first wanted to yell for help, but once he'd been shushed, had settled for crying. He cried a lot when he was young, Jeremy recalled with no little sense of shame. This pathetic habit led to his hideous nickname, Germ, on account of the way his nose inevitably ran whenever he became weepy. That was one of the things that he had loved—loved? yes, damn it, loved—about Hippolyte: he, at least, bless him, had never called him Germ to his face.

What had happened to their friendship? Why had they ever drifted apart? It must have been university. Jeremy—a lackluster student through high school—had shocked everyone by effortlessly pulling off a stunningly high grade point average, whereas Hippolyte's academic career had been meteoric in the worst sense of the word, burning brightly before extinguishing itself and falling into oblivion. Hippolyte, unfocused and impulsive, had, in his ambulatory manner— slightly hunched, hands in pockets, trousers bagged at the bum, and always whistling out of tune—peregrinated from one department to the next, one faculty to another, racking up an impressive number of courses but a paltry number of credits. There was no question of him ever graduating. And then one day he just didn't show up; he'd packed a bag, hitched a ride out to the airport, and took the first flight with seats available for indigent standbys. The next he was heard of was three years later when a magazine article about his wanderings arrived in the mail. Since then there had been occasional postcards, less frequent phone conversations, and a chance meeting in Toronto a couple of years ago. This wasn't how good friends should treat each other.

Jeremy dug a tissue out of his pocket and blew his nose. Yup, Webb's idea was great. It had guts, something that was missing in the parade of books that marched across his desk. He picked up one that had been dropped off that afternoon, the newly released biography of an enraged Bulgarian peasant who had been considered in last year's Papal canonization list but who was then inexplicably passed over. A bio of a non-saint? Who wrote this trash? Flipping the book open to the flap, he saw that it was the brother of the managing editor. It made him feel lousy to see Rumor's name on the spine.

That settled it. He'd move heaven and earth to get Hippolyte ·
some money.

December 7, 1999

Dear Hippolyte:
I cannot tell you how knocked out I am by your idea. Even though
my editors will string me up, I'm going to go out on a limb and
make you an offer for this book. It's obviously too early to discuss
specifics; however, I can appreciate that you are trying to raise cash. I
will crawl further out onto my limb and offer to send you an
advance on the advance. I'm not doing this just as a friend but as a
publisher who sees really strong book potential in both you and
your travels. Let me know as soon as you are ready to talk detail, and
I'll get you working with Marie Simplon. She's a wonderful editor
with a varied background, including a strong interest in classical
mythology. Can you start before you leave for the South Atlantic?
    Call me, please! You'll have to keep in touch now, Webb. And
you know, I haven't been this excited about a book for ages.
Yours,

Jeremy
cc Marie Simplon

WINDS AND SAILS

Mainsail — Genoa
No 2 jib
No 1 jib
Storm jib

Head
Mast
Luff (front edge)
Batten
Mainsail
Leech (aft edge)
Tack (bot. forw. corner)
Clew (bot. aft edge)
Gooseneck
Foot (bot. edge)
Boom

✓ Compass
Lead and line
Patent log
✓ Parallel Rulers
✓ Dividers
✓ Binoculars
✓ Watch
Stop watch
Barometer
✓ Pencils
✓ Deviation card
Charts
✓ Flashlight(s)
✓ Batteries
Tide Tables
Log Book

Circular deviation card

Cook, Peter. The Complete Book of Sailing. GV 811 C565 1977

Bowditch VK 555

true wind   apparent wind

wind caused by boat moving

True wind   Points of Sailing   wind

No go

Close-hauled

Close reach

Beam Reach

Broad Reach

jibing

wind

tacking

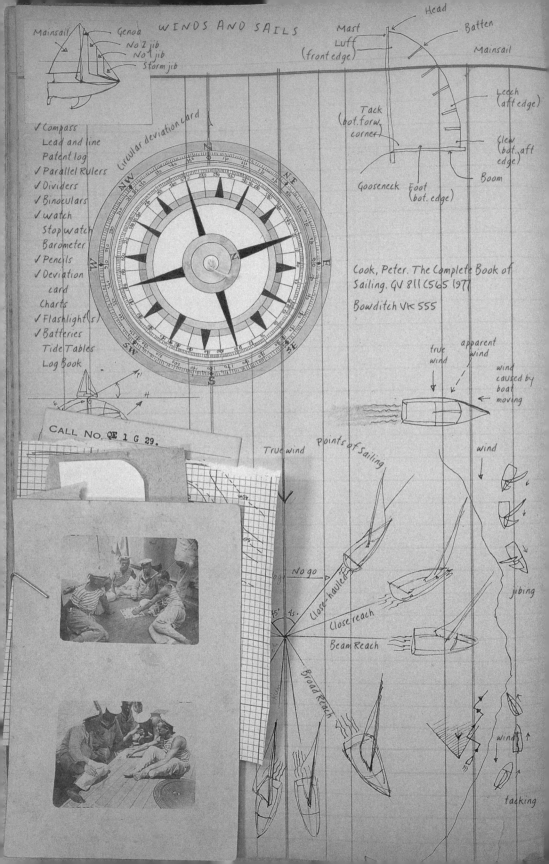

BEARINGS

Homework for next week

① Position by transit bearing and angle

A House #1
B House #1
Lighthouse

Boat goes North 20°, sees 2 houses A & B — angle at same time to lighthouse is 80°. Find boat's position. I hate these kinds of problems.

Northern Hemisphere

② Position by bearing & angle

Boat is going North 20°, sees lighthouse A and flagstaff F. — angle is 80°. Find boat's position

③ a Open bearings or running fix

Boat is steering 000° at 8 knots sees lighthouse L at 050°. After 45 minutes the lighthouse is at bearing 110°. where is boat when 2nd bearing is taken?

Southern Hemisphere

③ b

Boat is steering 140° at 10 knots sees lighthouse A at a bearing of 100°. Boat then sails for 1/2 hour through a current set 248° at 2 knots — lighthouse now bearing 030°. where's boat at taking of 2nd bearing? Have we learnt currents yet?

Is boat going along BA?

Cyclone paths and circulation of winds

③ c

Boat is heading 090° at 12 knots. Lighthouse T at 050°. After 40 min. T at bearing of 330°. Allow for current set of 090° at 1.5 knots. Find position of boat at time of taking 2nd bearing.

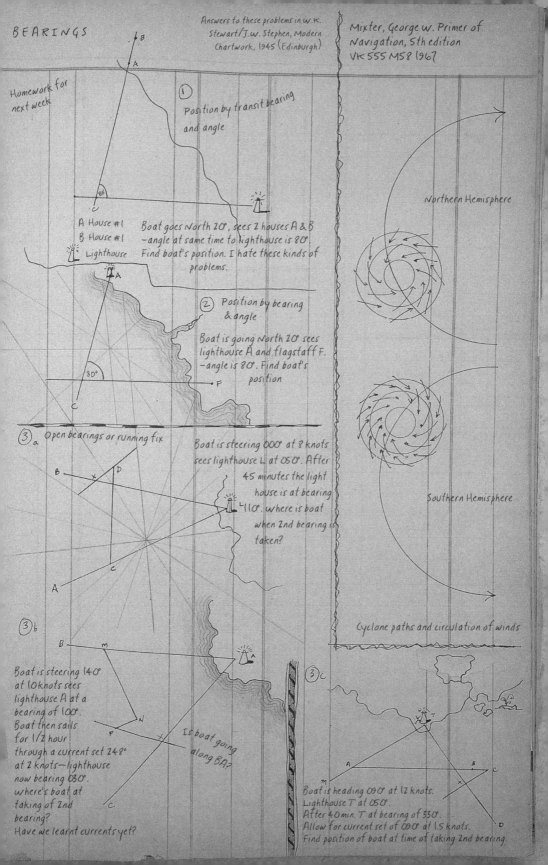

Four

Hᴀ́ᴘᴘᴏʟʏᴛᴇ ǫᴜɪᴄᴋʟʏ sᴋɪᴍᴍᴇᴅ Jᴇʀᴇᴍʏ'ꜱ ɴᴏᴛᴇ. Money! He then peered into the envelope, shook it, looked in it again, turned the letter over several times in disbelief, crammed it into his pocket, grabbed his coat, and was about to rush out to call Jeremy when the darkened skies informed him that it was too late. Why couldn't Jeremy have just sent the check now? Why did he have to write first to say that he would be doing it? Letters and promises were all well and fine but money was handier. Hippolyte looked at his watch for confirmation that it was as late as it seemed and remembered his sailing course. He slipped on his coat and hurried off to class.

Though he'd had severe doubts when he first walked into the class-room, the sailing course was proving worthwhile. Classes were normally held in the sailing club's building overlooking one of the pleasant city beaches close to Hippolyte's apartment, but because of repairs, they had been temporarily moved to the junior high school up the hill. Low ceilings, crackly fluorescent lights, and cramped school desks evoked nothing of the sea, so the navigational instructor pinned sea charts and boat pictures onto the classroom walls. Eight to twelve students attended the course, depending on the weather and what was on television that night. There were only two other males; Hippolyte hesitated to call them men, what with their faces sprouting more pimples than hair. When the instructor asked everyone why they wanted to sail, these two admitted that this was an obligatory course required by their juvenile detention rehabilitation program. The other students had their own reasons: one middle-aged woman had inherited a boat and was taking the course to posthumously spite the relative who had willed it to her, another had a profound fear of water, a third was going through a rocky divorce. Three young women, all in first-year university, had independently dared themselves to learn to sail. A young Chinese woman, whose grasp of English seemed elusive, couldn't find the words to explain why she was there. Two women said they simply had to get out of the house.

The instructor's name was Margarita DeVries, though she had introduced herself to the class as Marge, a waste, Hippolyte thought, of a beautiful name. "You know it means *pearl* in Latin?" he asked. She didn't. "By way of Greek, *margarites,*" he added. "Like you, it's got a connection with the sea, *Mar*-garita, from *mare*. Marge is closer, probably, to *margo, margino,* an edge or border. Wouldn't you rather be a pearl?" He took to calling her Margarita, to which she expressed delight.

Years of exposure to a raw reflecting sun had etched this engaging woman's skin with a premature yet becoming network of fine lines. The sharp bridge of her nose led to tight, yet not pinched, nostrils; her lips were set firm, almost without definition; her eyes squeezed narrow day or night, as though the clarity of the distant horizon was too intense. Sailing had eroded most excess from her face and deftly sculpted that which remained.

Winds, crueler, stronger ones, had also shaped her body, filled her sails. It rounded her torso and dictated her way of standing, with legs slightly bowed, feet firm against the ground. She made him think of rolling decks. "I could get seasick looking at you," he told her. He put his ear to hers, "I can hear the sea!" She laughed, and with her laugh he really almost heard the cry of gulls, the spray of water, the crash of surf.

Winds had split and shredded the ends of wispy brown hair that barely scraped the tops of her shoulders. The perfect length—her hair was—for the constant attention she paid to it, for if her fingers were not untangling or smoothing or braiding, one could clearly envision her seaworthy hands craving ropes and knots and settling on this poor substitute, then a hunk would be chewed upon as though it were a stalk of salty kelp.

That she was fascinating to watch did not prevent him from paying attention to what she had to teach. Margarita clearly lived what she taught and relished the task of loading him down with advice, never once allowing mockery of his plans to creep into her voice.

Hippolyte began shaving again, he did his laundry and wore clean shirts, and he brought his purchases to class for her approval: global compass, navigational protractor, parallel ruler, stopwatch, deviation card, drafting set. She admired the objects, all the while fretting over his lack of sailing experience and pushing him even harder to learn to plot courses, read winds, and manage boats. Although she approved of his insistence on using the traditional sextant, she impressed upon him the importance of taking a modern backup, to have even a basic GPS receiver and to know how to use it.

With all of his questions, his what ifs, his how 'bouts, Hippolyte dominated the classes. The other students settled back in their chairs, tolerating his interruptions, pleased to be overlooked during Margarita's weekly exams when she demanded solutions to seemingly incalculable problems involving declinations, logarithms, and tangents. Hippolyte always leapt to answer, often before his pencil even had a chance to touch the paper, and his usually daring but usually incorrect responses would lead her on her own tangents, taking the heat off of everyone. He relished her vocabulary drills; they reminded him of spelling bees, and he worked harder to please her than he'd worked for any of his grade-school teachers—beautiful young women with hair like angels and names like Miss Thompson and Miss Wright—whom he'd loved and idolized with boyish abandon and trust.

Margarita badgered him about his choice of boats. "You need a boat that can venture out on the open seas, but not something that you can't handle by yourself," she cautioned. "What arrangements have you made?" she'd ask every single week and would chew the ends of her hair when he admitted that not a single boat charter company had answered his letters of inquiry. "Call them, then," she insisted, "get this sorted out immediately!"

Then out on the water itself, her advice flowed while she showed the class the ropes. "This fifty footer," she yelled to him over the luffing sails, pointing to the boat they were on and that the students were trying hard not to swamp, "is a treat for you all; we don't usually get such a grand vessel. But you should look for something smaller, say around thirty feet. Some sailors think that a small boat is too cramped and unsafe, others that a large boat is too unwieldy. Of course, you'll get all kinds of conflicting opinions. Listen to them all, then make up your own mind. But imagine handling something this size all by yourself. It would be difficult for many of us."

At that moment, as a wave crashed over the bow, Hippolyte honestly doubted he could handle a five footer.

"Did we have to do this on a windy day?" one of the students howled. This was Donald, one of the "delinquents," as he called himself. He generally found most demands inconvenient, but this time all heads, Hippolyte's included, nodded in agreement.

Margarita trimmed the sails in revenge and the boat skittered across the swell. "Look at the ads in the boating magazines. You'll see examples of sloops, ketches, and . . . quick—anyone!—tell me the difference between a ketch, a cutter, and a yawl."

The Chinese student, Cindy, who hadn't yet uttered a word in any of the classes, who was fortunately life-jacketed and safety harnessed, leaned over the side and delicately threw up. Margarita watched her, judging, then let out the sail and reduced the heel; the speed fell back, for which she was rewarded a wan but grateful smile. She continued her lecture, "A keel boat is more stable in rough seas, unless you get swamped. How many miles do you calculate you'll have to sail? Four hundred, right; is that both ways? Ah, just one way, so eight hundred miles total. You'll need an engine, of course; you won't be able to manage sailing the whole time. Do you realize how much fuel you'll have to take with you? Look to see how broad the beam is. The broader, the better, more cumbersome perhaps for maneuvering, but harder to tip. Make sure it's equipped with radar, a radio, a sounder. Food and water; make lists. Buy all you can in advance;

you might not be able to purchase necessities at your point of departure. Water will be a problem; it always is. In temperate climates, sailors are advised to reckon on five gallons a day. Maybe you'll get away with less, but don't underestimate! A self-steering vane is invaluable. File a copy of your itinerary with the boat owner, the harbour master. Plan to keep in frequent radio contact. Where are you departing from? The Falklands? Argentina? Chile? You should at least know *that* by now! What's the shipping traffic like through there? How will you cope with being by yourself, being on watch, getting enough sleep?" Suggestions mixed with questions streamed out in relentless cascades. At the close of the day, as they neared the dock, she called out instructions for sails, rigging, fenders, lines. Drenched students swung themselves over the side, proudly showing off their throws and hitches. Others stowed equipment and wrestled with life jackets. Hippolyte threw himself into the work, imagining himself alone.

In the end, both he and Margarita had to admit that six weeks of instruction could not replace the years of experience that most sailors had before they set out solo. "Are you sure you won't take someone with you? I feel responsible. I shouldn't let you go alone!"

"Come with me?" he smiled at her; he almost meant it.

"Sure," she laughed, sounding as if she almost meant it.

The last evening's class disintegrated when the three university students, who had developed a giggly conspiratorial friendship, produced a bottle of red and a bottle of white wine, a quantity of plastic cups, and several bags of potato chips. They toasted Margarita, they toasted their newly acquired sea worthiness, they toasted Hippolyte's voyage; the bottles were eventually emptied, as was the classroom, except for Margarita and Hippolyte. Margarita's bantering agreement to join him lingered in his mind. Here was someone, finally, whom he could just about consider. Should he ask her seriously? He pondered the question, but couldn't shape the words. There was too much to think about. If she were even free to go.

42

As he thought, he talked. Talked more than he'd ever done with anyone. About anything. He wouldn't let her leave the classroom, let her go home. He allowed no breaks in his conversation, no place in which she could assert a friendly goodnight. She sidled, at last, to the door, stood at its threshold, opened and shut her mouth, nodded, smiled. She couldn't have had any idea at all of what was racing through his brain, but appeared more aware of him than ever before. Then finally, hand on switch, she turned out the lights. He picked his way round chairs and tables, guided by her figure, a silhouette in the hall light.

They left the building together—the rain had stopped but the night air was filled with a fine cool mist—and walked to the bus stop. Margarita glanced at her watch, explaining apologetically that the gesture was automatic, since her bus rarely kept to any schedule. Hippolyte waited with her, silent now, overwhelmed with his new idea.

"Do you take this bus?" she asked him.

"No, I can walk home from here," he replied.

"It's late; you don't have to wait," she said. "It was terrific having you in my class." She frowned and hastily added, "Call me when you get back. Please." She wrote out her number. "I'll be anxious to hear how it went."

He could ask her now, he thought. But he still wasn't sure.

The bus came. "Ten," he read aloud, as if the number held the key to its destination.

"Goodbye," she said, climbing the steps. But Hippolyte boarded the bus, too.

He sat down beside her. "I'll ride with you till your stop." He stared shamelessly at the other passengers, then scanned the advertisements. "Why don't they display maps of the route?" he wondered. She shrugged.

The bus stopped, passengers got off, more got on; it stopped again, and again, as it made its way through town. It filled to bursting, bodies pressing into him, pushing his shoulder, arm, leg, against hers. After crossing a bridge, it traveled along a wide quiet street that suddenly burned with light and the congestion of pedestrians who sought the still-open and busy shops and cafés. She pulled the cord and stood up.

"Well, here's my stop," she announced brightly. He was in her way. She held out her hand. "Goodbye, Hippolyte." He got up to let her pass, then followed her down the stairs, down onto the street.

"I haven't been over here at night in ages, you know." He looked around as if he'd just stepped into a new city.

Together they walked down the street, gazing into windows, Margarita purposely delaying, Hippolyte accepting the delay. She paused for a moment when they came level with a grocery store, one of those popular with the urban crowd, staying open late to sell organic granolas, precious olive oils, emaciated yet perfectly shaped heads of lettuce.

"Come in here for a sec." He followed her unquestioningly to the dried-foods aisle. She'd already grabbed a basket for him. "For your trip! Look at the choice." She pointed to soups in cups, casseroles in pouches, stews in bags.

"Couscous," he picked up a pouch, read the label, "semolina, lentils, carrots, potatoes, onion, cornstarch, natural flavor, sea salt." He put it back, chose another brand: chicken noodle soup, "wheat flour, liquid whole egg, dehydrated chicken meat, salt, potato flour, monosodium glutamate, chicken fat, hydrolyzed plant protein, cellulose gum." He made a face and replaced it.

"Do you like couscous?" she asked.

"Sure, but—"

"Chicken or beef?"

"I don't know. Chicken, I guess."

She plunked three packets in the basket. "Split pea soup?"

He stared at her.

"Do you like pea soup?"

"Yes, I like pea soup. Margarita?"

"Potato leek?" Her voice was suddenly loud, shrill almost.

He wanted her to come with him. She tossed three more packets into the basket and continued to scour the shelves. He remembered putting his ear to hers and hearing the sea in her. She'd told him that no one had ever done that before.

"Margarita? Would you—"

"Hippolyte," she cut in, suddenly turned round to face him. She couldn't have come even close to picturing the immensity of his question, but answered it all the same. "There's—someone—." Though she didn't put into words the faceless figure, sitting, waiting for her, she had made him real all the same. He now sat between them. Some man, waiting like a reef, patiently, hazardously waiting for her. She dropped the basket and fled.

SCALETTA PROFILE.

Toll. page 280.

Difficult Precipice by which we ascended

Steep hill as her head

PROFILE VOLCANO.

on VI.

De Seve, Del.

LE L.

20

Five

FREEZE-DRIED SOUP joined growing piles of equipment, as Hippolyte tried to slip back into the contentment of traveling alone. See how complicated another person can be? became his saving refrain. His planning, neglected during the intensity of trying to learn to sail, reignited him. Field guides, binoculars, specimen boxes, a flashlight, a meteorological kit, and a plant press were bought as were vials for sand and gravel, glassine envelopes for feathers, teeth, and seeds.

Everything that he would encounter would have to be recorded; to that end, he found a compact red hardcover book with heavy-weight grid paper that would be perfect for keeping his boat's log, a small plastic-covered binder that would do for his survey notes, and he had already started several blank ledger books that would suffice as his day-to-day journals. He had his camera overhauled and bought countless rolls of film, then was struck with the idea of taking instant pictures and rushed around experimenting with Polaroid cameras and adapter backs. He splashed watercolors over acres of paper, trying to recapture any control he had ever had over the medium. Pencils were sharpened then dulled in practice sketches; the garbage bin overflowed with wads of abominable attempts.

He placed a compact geological chisel and a snub-nosed hammer onto the stack and then took them off again, concerned about the weight. *Hints'* chapter on geological specimens was emphatic about their usefulness, so they went back on. Because they exuded visions of perilous cliffs and razor-sharp rocks, he included a medical kit stuffed with gauze, tweezers, bandages, and antiseptic creams, items that he had recklessly spurned on trips gone by.

He hauled bags, totes, backpacks, and crates out of storage, selected a limp blue duffel and a small tan suitcase, then spent several delightful hours rediscovering the treasures that he'd stowed in them at some forgotten moment in the past. Photos of complete strangers, door knobs from houses in Prague, a chalkboard, and a wind-up rabbit in overalls that smoked real cigarettes were but a few of the items that made their way back out into the open. Baffled by where to put these things, he left them where they lay. His duffel, a once-snappy bag that had suffered many tears and scrapes, now endured the indignity of his clumsy repairs. The suitcase, no longer blessed with functioning locks, had to be lashed with cord.

With the luggage merely adding to the desperate condition of the apartment, Hippolyte escaped into reading. History books spawned more history books all full of the allure of Cape Horn, the Straits of Magellan, Patagonia, and the South Pole. Explorers who had braved the South Atlantic but who had nothing to do with the Auroras strayed across the pages: Ferdinand Magellan and Francis Drake in the sixteenth century; John Narborough and Antonio de la Roche in the seventeenth; William Dampier and James Cook in the eighteenth.

All through this period of intense activity, regret for Margarita still troubled; where was her advice, the whiff of saltwater that blew in with her presence, her way of instilling, with her sharp gaze, a longing for the sea? Her suggestion to study boat-for-sale ads was but a pale substitute. Even so, he bought boating magazines studded with pictures of yachts with names like Corsair, Sovereign, Catalina. He hung out at the local marina and engaged the owners in boating chitchat, cornering them as they scraped their hulls, as they stowed their sails, as they walked to their cars. A tidy sloop with the unlikely name of *Biscuit* caught his eye, and he asked the owner, a tanned, lean man in his sixties, how long it was.

"Twenty-eight feet," was the reply.

"Do you sail by yourself?" Hippolyte asked.

"No, me and my wife."

"Do you find it large enough?"

"Most of the time. 'Cept when she's in a bad mood. Wife, I mean. Not boat."

A woman, also tanned and spare—almost the man's twin, in fact—poked her head up from the galley. "He means, except when *he's* in a bad mood." Then she chuckled and disappeared again.

The owner pursed his lips in mock disapproval, but the crow's feet curled around his eyes with pleasure. "She's snarky today because I'm going to make her redo the deck, since it's finally stopped raining for a minute. Look at that, will you." He gestured to the varnish that was peeling away like nail polish.

His wife popped back up. "I'm sure your friend won't object if you scrub the foredeck while you talk." She smiled at Hippolyte and tossed her husband a brush. A minute later a pail of sudsy water appeared.

"My name's Roger, by the way," he held out his hand.

"Hippolyte."

"That's Jean." He jerked his thumb toward the cabin.

"Pleased to meet you," came a distant but clear voice.

"Got a special interest in boats?" Roger asked.

"I'm trying to decide on what kind of boat to sail in open waters."

"That's a big question." He ducked and peeked down into the galley. Jean was not in sight. "Here, let's go around and ask some experts." He slipped off and they tiptoed down the dock.

Roger introduced him to owners of small boats who advised him to think big and those with big boats who urged him to think small. They showed him where their hulls were rotting and where their masts had cracked. They talked of the endless work, the alarming drain of money, and the worry of storms, vandalism, and amateurs. And they told him, as they looked away from the land and out to the water, that they loved their boats and wouldn't dream of giving them up. Their talk was reassuring but did nothing to quell his fear that he would fail to find a suitable boat, nor his fear that he would and then would have to prove to himself that he could sail it.

Taking the plunge, Hippolyte resolved to try to sail from Stanley, on the Falklands, though he still had no means of getting from the Falklands to where the Auroras were supposed to be. He settled on a travel agency, a firm in Stanley, to help him finalize his plans, but the agonizingly slow process was made worse without a phone. The agent went wild with all his changes of dates, his drive to get the lowest fares possible, his hesitations over itinerary, her inability to contact him instantly. Every time he assured her that he had no more changes, he'd make one more. Every time she assured him that there were no more charges, another tax or fee would materialize.

Once he committed to depart on January 31st and had tickets in hand, he dutifully drew out his route in the 1892 atlas, the three-hour flight from Vancouver to Los Angeles, the four-hour layover, the thirteen-hour stretch between L.A. and Santiago, Chile, the hops from Santiago to Puerto Montt and Puenta Arenas, and finally Stanley. Unable to resist the idea of stopping en route, he had arranged to have some days in both Santiago and Puenta Arenas, then changed his mind to extend the time, then changed it again to make the stopover on his return, then went back to his original plans when the agent pointed out the penalty for revising the tickets.

Wherever he stepped, some fragile instrument got underfoot; maps and books became coasters for coffee cups; to sit down was to hazard an uncomfortable reminder that space was at a premium and that it was time to start packing. But packing scarcely made a dent in the jumble. Although the duffel was forgiving and accommodated far more weight than it could support, the suitcase was an utter failure and had to be replaced by a large wooden crate. Into this went the boxes that would protect delicate specimens. He added a small backpack to keep with him on the plane for equipment that he couldn't afford to lose, and at one point it seemed that he had crammed almost every-thing into it.

Distracted, Hippolyte would make cups of coffee or even cook meals and amble with the mug or the plate from the kitchen only to discover something already prepared. Unfinished dinners, usually in the form of toast and egg—sometimes scrambled sometimes hard-boiled, always, in the end, congealed—dotted the place like islands.

His social life, not brilliant to start with, was seriously disadvantaged by his single-mindedness. Friends would occasionally knock on the door, checking to see if he was still around. He'd whisk them into the chaos that was his apartment and regale them with routes and suppositions on why the islands disappeared and ask them their opinions. Sometimes they'd try to be helpful by bringing printouts of the latest annoyingly elusive and unbelievably erratic Internet weather forecasts. Other times they'd be just plain obstructive and tell him he was losing his mind. If he remembered he'd offer them cold coffee or warm beer.

His apartment had become, more than ever, a compact but confusing foreign country, crying out for a guide or at least for a map of its own. Claustrophobic and intimidating, no one but Hippolyte could bear to stay in it for more than a few minutes.

"Come out for coffee, Hippolyte," a former girlfriend pleaded. "Get away from here; you're going crazy!"

"But I have to show you this book," he protested. "I'll make you coffee. As long as you don't want milk."

He knew she couldn't drink coffee without, and now she was backing out the door. "I thought you didn't like possessions," she said, pointing an accusing finger at the accumulations sprouting like weeds. It had been the sore point that had split them asunder.

Hippolyte was confused. "But I don't."

She looked around, her mouth hanging open. "What about . . . ?" Then gave up.

He followed her finger, her eye, and watched her retreat. What about what? These things weren't possessions; they were the stuff of study. No one else would value them; they didn't count.

His sensible mother, who had always refused to set foot in his apartment—on the grounds that her sanity would be compromised if she did—insisted that he visit her at least twice a month when in town. To this end she served up a reasonable-sized dollop of light-hearted mother guilt and profited from his usually spontaneous appearances by extracting as much information as possible about his plans, thereby allowing her to keep her records of his travels up to date. This trip, however, stymied her. Nothing he said could convince her that a lost island was a legitimate destination. Hippolyte had never seen his mother's faith in him waiver and regretted, in hindsight and for the first time, telling her. The empty South Atlantic was the main stumbling block, but even after he carefully, reassuringly penciled the islands into her atlas, she still couldn't accept it and erased them over and over until the printed blue of the ocean faded back to the white of the paper. At last he ended the line that delineated his route at the Falkland Islands and spoke no more of the Auroras.

January 15, 2000

Dear Hippolyte:
I'm happy to enclose a $20,000.00 advance for your proposed book of exploration. I know it's not a hell of a lot of money, but please don't think that it's because Rumor lacks confidence in your project. This is a rather unorthodox situation and took a lot of explaining. It's a good thing I'm the publisher! It goes without saying that I wouldn't do this for someone I didn't believe in; it's not just because you're a friend.
I envy you, Webb. Good luck.

Jeremy

Twenty thousand dollars! Hippolyte immediately grabbed a pen, endorsed the check, and rushed to the bank. As he stood in line, he realized that he and Jeremy hadn't agreed on an amount; they hadn't even discussed the subject, but here was Germ coming through way beyond expectation. Hippolyte was ecstatic, so much so that he had failed to notice that the check was made out to Polite Webb. The ensuing argument with the teller over the name and his right to deposit the money into his account was made even more annoying in light of the fact that Hippolyte had been coming to this same bank for the last five years—off and on to be sure, but still his constancy spoke of a certain loyalty—and had dealt with the same teller for much of that time. He had even spurned automatic teller cards in hopes that his efforts would save jobs. But he was far too happy to let the bank get in the way of his triumph; he cajoled the teller into depositing the check into his account, gave her a hug, and ran off.

At last the day of departure. He weighed the duffel and finally and absolutely removed both chisel and the hammer. He was off.

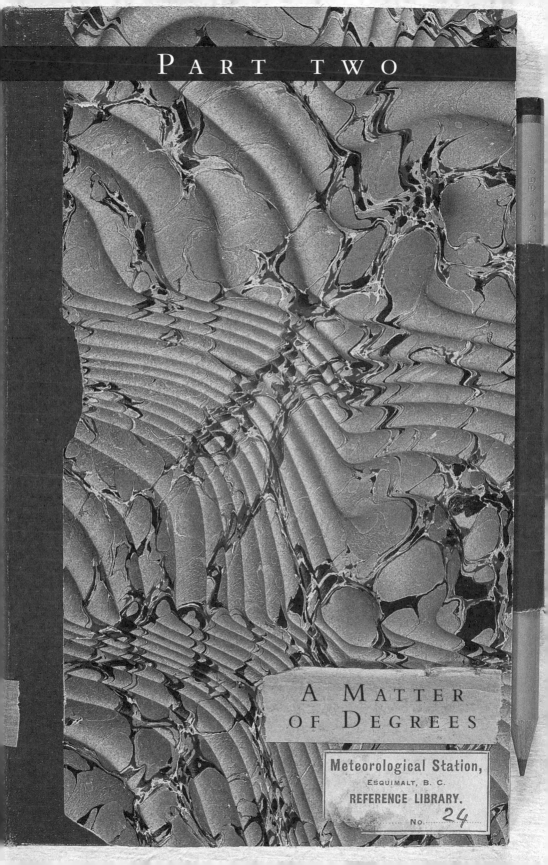

PART TWO

A MATTER OF DEGREES

LOG OF THE Southern Saracen

From: Stanley Harbour
Towards: the Auroras

Date: Tuesday, 15 February 2000

Hours: 1030

Knots: 5   Fathoms: ?

Wind Direction: wnw 340°

Force: 3 / Breeze

Barometer: 29.98

Temp. Air: 16°C   water: 13°C

Latitude: 51° 41'S

Longitude: 57° 40W

Remarks: cirrus 3/10, unlimited visibility

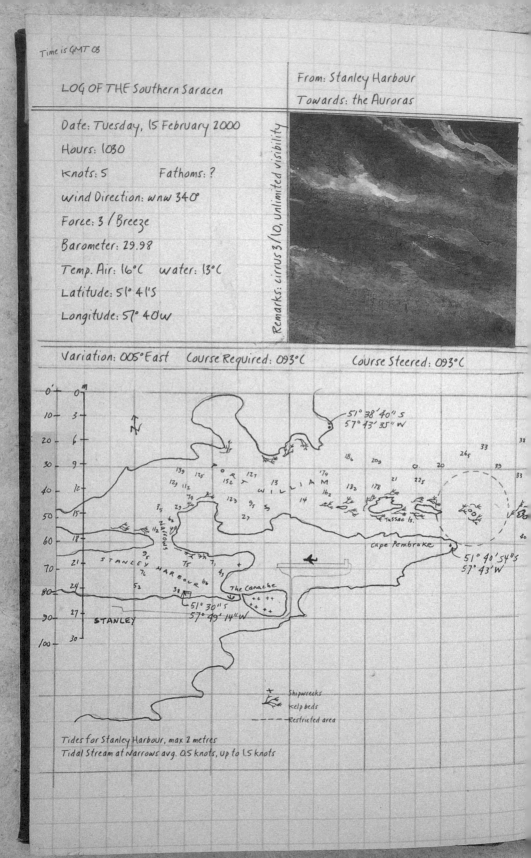

Variation: 005° East   Course Required: 093°C   Course Steered: 093°C

51° 38' 40" S
57° 13' 35" W

PORT WILLIAM

Tussac Is.

Cape Pembroke

51° 40' 54" S
57° 43' W

STANLEY HARBOUR
Narrows

STANLEY

The Canache

51° 30" S
57° 49' 14" W

+ Shipwrecks
кelp beds
--- Restricted area

Tides for Stanley Harbour, max 2 metres
Tidal Stream at Narrows avg. 0.5 knots, up to 1.5 knots

How's this for fate? I bust up an old globe, draw a couple of haphazard lines following some cockeyed version of South and end up on a leaky tub in the antipodean fringes of the South Atlantic. I could fill my book with what I don't know about boats, the sea, sailing. But I'm not going to do that. Instead, it will be about land, that's my place, and I'm heading for land—land they say doesn't exist. The question is, Doesn't exist anymore? Or never existed? Three specks sighted by observant, brave, intrepid, gullible, lying, hallucinating, vainglorious, reckless, spiteful eighteenth-century explorers. About to be rediscovered by an updated version endowed with pretty much the same characteristics.

I've set my course for 52°37'S, 47°43 1/2'W. If they're out there, I'll find them, these three little dots called the Auroras. Firmly anchored onto so many maps. Tangible evidence of a belief that no one ever had much faith in. Who can resist a place that's known but not known, that is but isn't? I can't.

Commerson's Dolphin

Peale's Dolphin

Hourglass Dolphin

Spectacled Porpoise

Pygmy Right whale

Minke whale

Sei whale

Blue whale

Killer whale (orca)

Fin whale

Alnoux's Beaked whale

Six

THE PROBLEM OF THE BOAT HAD BEEN SOLVED. Sort of. It had taken
Hippolyte a solid week of negotiating to arrange the charter of a
dilapidated sailboat from a morose sailor who had washed up in
Stanley some three months previous. Peter Givens, an unsettled,
scarcely employed mechanic from the U.K., was in the process of trying to sell his boat and settle on the Falklands. He had placed an ad in
the local weekly's classifieds, but there had been no takers. The tub, for
that's all it was, hadn't been moved from its mooring since he'd
arrived, but a much more ancient neglect was evident. Its owner cared
only if it floated or not; that it did was good enough. It had brought
him some 7500 nautical miles, from Portsmouth through the Bay of
Biscay, across the equator, down along the coast of Argentina against
the Falkland Current to the Falklands themselves. As he himself put it,
his boat was a diamond in the rough, a workhorse to be proud of. So,
rather than waste time scraping down the hull or overhauling the
engine, Peter instead scrutinized Hippolyte's every gesture, from his
attempted sailor stance to his way of squinting into the breeze.
Hippolyte could feel Peter's sharp disapproval; even his clothing—the
new yellow rubber boots, the pile vest, and rainproof anorak—was not
passing muster.

Hippolyte soothed his own doubts by inwardly criticizing the
boat: it stank of fish; its equipment was dated; the engine, a sturdy two-
cylinder, ten-horsepower Volvo, wheezed rigidly, threatening to seize
up; the radio cord was frayed—great! he thought, bare wires exposed
to salt air should work terrifically. Slimy algae and barnacles, visible
along the waterline, clung tenaciously to the hull and would do noth-

ing to improve speeds. The grommets on the sails were a mere breeze away from tearing off the canvas. Line ends were unraveling, a travesty even to Hippolyte's untrained eye. Mold inside the galley icebox spoke volumes about the frequency of its use. But enough! At least it had a radio, radar, a sounder, an engine. It was exactly what Margarita had recommended: a thirty-foot sloop, single masted by definition with a full keel. Adequate for keeping lubbers like him out of the water, it would have to do.

Peter was far from content with the arrangement; for a start he had scorned Hippolyte's request to charter it. "She's for sale, not for let. Buy 'er if you want to take 'er out," was his first response. A cool £40,000. But negotiable.

"Not on your life," Hippolyte declared. Non-negotiable. "If I wanted to own a boat, I'd get one in Canada where it would be half the cost and in perfect condition."

"Then you'll have to find something else, won't you?" Peter appeared unfazed at the loss of opportunity. Their conversation took place on a short dirt and gravel mole at the Canache, a harbor just outside of Stanley. Ostensibly protected from the wind, on this day a hard-blowing southerly was driving rain into Hippolyte's face with seemingly unprecedented force. But then, he had no experience of this kind of wind. Peter, on the other hand, was specially built for wind. His sturdy legs were planted far enough apart to give him complete resistance to the buffeting blasts; his tightly shorn, curly brown hair barely ruffled, the cigarette that never left his lips was motionless as though cemented on.

"Can we go somewhere more sheltered?" Hippolyte yelled, gesturing to the boat moored at the end of the mole. He was losing his voice.

Peter made a face and didn't budge. The gale was causing him no discomfort; his back was bearing the brunt of it.

"How many buyers have inquired?" Hippolyte shrieked.

"Why, several."

"Any actual offers?"

"A couple."

"Serious?"

"Definitely."

"Why isn't it sold then?"

"Not serious enough, I suppose."

"Not a lot of sailors here on the Falklands, I see."

"Nope."

"How long are you going to tough it out?"

"Till I run out of do-re-mi."

Hippolyte had struggled against the wind into town and to the aroma of baking cakes and cookies in the bed-and-breakfast where he was too well fed. His subsequent visits were on less nerve-wracking days, allowing him calmer chances to chip away at Peter's resistance. The rumor mill revealed that Peter had received only a couple of inquiries when the ad first appeared and no offers whatsoever. He was living with his parents, native Falklanders, who had moved away some years earlier and then returned for their retirement. He had applied to stay permanently and was currently working on a scheme to take tourists out on the boat, though he hadn't quite managed to come to grips with all that would entail. Hippolyte pointed out that his chartering of the boat would be a step in the right direction and that he would freely and shamelessly endorse the boat and Peter's tours. And it would give Peter a much needed injection of cash.

Hippolyte had told no one on the Falklands about the purpose of his trip, not Peter, not the travel agent who had helped him book his trip (and who was in the process of rescheduling the return flight), nor the lady who ran the bed-and-breakfast. He wanted neither their opinions nor their scorn. Lying unashamedly, Hippolyte told everyone that he merely intended to explore the waters round the Falklands.

One night, about four days after his arrival, despondent that he'd made no headway with the boat and frustrated that Peter was his only lead, he dropped in to one of the smaller pubs, determined to drink his way to a solution. All the tables were taken, but an old man immediately welcomed him to his.

"No sense drinking on your feet," the man scrunched his eyes up and vigorously scratched his temple. "What brings you here?"

"Beer," Hippolyte replied.

"Don't get cocky with me!" the man snickered, always ready to appreciate a smart ass. He rubbed the side of his burled nose.

Hippolyte looked around cautiously, making sure that Peter wasn't tucked away in some corner, aware that he was about to go against his better instincts. "I'm here," he announced, "to find the Auroras." He watched the man's pale eyes, glittering with the transparency of age. Had he found a wise old man who would tell him everything he needed to know?

The man nodded, seriously considering Hippolyte's statement. "Never heard of 'em," he finally admitted and took a thoughtful sip. "What are they, anyway?"

"Islands." No point being too disappointed, thought Hippolyte; it had been a long shot.

"Islands, did I hear you correctly?" A faint Scottish accent was breaking through. "Well, you've come to the right place!" He turned and spoke to the room. "Chap here's looking for some islands." The men at the next table burst out laughing and dragged their chairs over.

With the Falklands consisting of some two hundred islands, the admission elicited no more than its fair share of teasing and jokes. He was fed a tale of a shipwreck involving a Spanish galleon and a treasure. Or, wait, was it an American sealer and a ransom in furs? But no one could tell him the name of the ship, and they couldn't remember when it was supposed to have been wrecked. Speculation went on through the evening; new arrivals were drawn into the discussion; Hippolyte produced his map and much was made of it; suggestions for boats were tossed about.

"Used to be lots twenty, maybe thirty years ago," a voice cut through.

"Sure, but where are they now?" someone else countered.

"Sold off, I expect. Not much of a market, is there?"

"There surely is, don't you know what boats are going for these days?"

"I know a man with one in storage."

"You mean Johnny Page's old scow?! Get off with ya."

"I'll talk to Peter for you," the old man finally offered.

"You will?" shouted Hippolyte over the competing noise. Then he gasped, "Don't tell him where I'm going!" The man promised, and they drank to the success of his adventure.

That negotiations with Peter were concluded within a week was due more to the timely interference than to Hippolyte's persistence and desperation. Even so, Peter had remained stony faced and unmoved until the week's end when he raised both his hands in not-so-mock surrender and said, "You win, Mr. Webb. Take my bloody boat." The capitulation was not as spontaneous as it seemed; Peter, in the intervening days, had scrubbed down the hull and had mended the sails.

As Hippolyte loaded supplies, Peter scratched his head over the quantities of food, water, propane, and fuel (no purist, Hippolyte planned to use diesel, not sail, whenever necessary) being loaded onto the boat. He supplemented the twenty-five-gallon water tank with sixteen one-gallon jugs, and, in addition to the thirty-gallon capacity of the fuel tank, added six five-gallon canisters of diesel.

Hippolyte had calculated and recalculated his water and fuel needs, working out times, temperatures, knots, head winds, distances, but even the most optimistic figures confirmed Margarita's assertion that he couldn't bring enough. Where fuel was concerned, he'd have to sail as much as possible to conserve a sufficient amount to realistically get him back. This wasn't worth worrying about, he repeated constantly, like a kind of mantra, many sailors have no engine at all. With regards to water, well, he could always rig up a system to collect condensation or rainwater. And there might be fresh water on his Auroras. He smiled to himself at his presumption.

Sextant, barometer, binoculars, camera, and chronometer were all loaded under Peter's hawklike gaze. "You know how to use one of these?" he asked, fingering the sextant. "I've almost forgotten, myself. I've *got* GPS, you know. And what is this, if you don't mind telling me?" He picked up a complicated-looking device, a forked wooden pole with a ball attached to it by a series of wires.

Hippolyte was on his knees, stowing gear under the bunk. He craned his neck to see what Peter was holding. "It's a Brooke's Deep-Sea Sounding Apparatus."

"I *have* a sounder, you know!"

"Deep-sea?"

"Of course not! What boat short of the navy does? What crank sold you this little miracle?"

"I made it myself. Based on Maury's description."

"Who?"

"Have you never heard of Matthew Fontaine Maury?"

"Yeah, of course I heard of him. What of it?"

Suddenly a *soi-disant* expert on everything oceanic, Hippolyte was in danger of getting out of his depth. "I mean, this is a sounder that Maury recommended."

"Think it's still 1850, do you?"

Hippolyte tried again. "Of course, your sounder will give me accurate readings in shallows, but this allows the bottom to be sampled as well as giving the depth. And I didn't know that I'd end up with such a well-equipped boat," he added diplomatically.

"Your line can't be more than—let's see—fifty feet. You call that deep?! Besides, if you want to sample the bottom, just use the lead line; I have one of those, too. This is ridiculous." Peter's words rippled sarcastically under his breath. The prismatic compass, the folding survey rod, the telescoping tripod, and the chain, too, came under scrutiny. "There's already a compass on board. What'll you measure with these?"

"Land. What else? I mean, I plan to survey a couple of islands."

"You're planning to do topos? What for? The islands have been mapped already, properly, with proper equipment. By trained surveyors." He flipped open the compass and took a reading on one of the wrecks dotting the shoreline. "Just how do you intend to do this by yourself, anyway?"

Hippolyte shrugged; what could he say? He was curious about the answer to that question himself. "It's an interest of mine, I guess. I'm a writer; I like data, statistics, you know, tide levels, altitudes, circumferences of islands. Nothing serious, really, but it adds a certain something, I don't know, truth or reality, or something like that, to my articles. By the way, is the log electronic or mechanical?"

"Mechanical."

"Has it been calibrated recently?"

Peter lost patience. "Calibrate it yourself, if you're so worried."

The empty boxes, the shredded packing paper, the books were also considered and disapproved of. "This paper stuff, you know, it won't last out a day, what with the salt spray and the humidity. And you get a wave come over and you'll be swimming in the cabin. You and all this crap." He thumbed through the log that Hippolyte had already started. "Why are you writing this out by hand?" he asked. "They have pre-printed ones. You just fill in the details. I could give you one if you like." Hippolyte made a grab for the book, but Peter began scanning it more carefully.

"What's this name? *Southern Saracen*? Is this another boat? But it's today's date. My boat's called *Seaspray* in case you hadn't noticed."

Hippolyte reddened. Peter's deft hand was on everything. "Is it unlucky to change the name of a boat? I haven't done it permanently; I haven't scraped *Seaspray* off the side or anything like that. It's still your boat, your name. It's just a whim." He was mortified at being caught out at something so absurd. He grabbed the log, stuck it in his pocket.

Peter dropped the issue of the name and went on to dismiss the down sleeping bag. "The down'll bunch up into useless little clumps and the nylon'll freeze your nuts off; wool blankets is what you want." *The Sailor's Guide to Knots, Hitches and Splices* fared no better: "You need a *book* to tell you how to tie a knot?!" And the packets of freeze-dried stews elicited an explosion: "That's not food!"

Hippolyte went below to stow his food, including a whole box of tinned condensed milk. He couldn't stand the muck but had read that these little tins provided much-needed solace to many a solo sailor. Seemingly out of the blue, Peter yelled down to him, "What'll you be doing with this?"

"With what?" Hippolyte asked, not looking up. When Peter didn't answer, he glanced around to see the boat's owner leaning over the gangway, chart in hand, frown on face.

"What's that you've got?" he asked, squinting to read the title.

"South Georgia. It's an island nine hundred miles away, in case you didn't know."

At least that map was harmless, Hippolyte thought; it didn't have the course to the Auroras plotted on it. And how had Peter gotten his hands on it anyway? It had been rolled up tight in the map holder. You sneak!, he felt like yelling. But didn't. Instead he joked, saying, "I have one of Tahiti, too; but I'm not going there; I happen to like charts." He pulled out his travelers checks and suggested paying another installment on the boat rental fee. The distraction worked like a charm; Peter didn't ask to see the chart of Tahiti—which was fortunate since it didn't exist—and Hippolyte was able to relieve him of South Georgia and shove it out of sight.

"Weather ahead sounds interesting." Peter looked up at the skies as he pocketed the checks.

Hippolyte's heart sank. He'd thought of everything except the weather forecast. "I forgot about that," he admitted. "What's it look like?"

"How's your stomach?"

"Good. I think. Haven't put it to the test. How rough?"

"Rough enough. Later today, force six, winds from the North or thereabouts." He nodded at the sky and pursed his lips. "See the clouds?"

Hippolyte blinked in assent. His own gestures were rapidly truncating to match Peter's. Pretty soon they wouldn't even have to use words.

Peter looked sideways at him. "Cirrus."

Hippolyte chewed on his lower lip. *Cirrus* from the Latin, to curl, curly. Indicative of what meteorologically? Think quick: big fluffy *cumulus,* from the Latin for heaps, accumulations, rain ahead; *cumulonimbus,* heavy black clouds, thunderheads. Cirrus for? For what?

Peter's impatience broke in. "Rougher weather coming. Don't anchor too close in, though, if you're not in a proper harbor. There aren't too many of those around. You got the frequency for the weather updates?"

Hippolyte nodded.

"Where do you plan to drop anchor tonight?"

Hippolyte had the answer ready. "Lively," he replied, referring to a small island to the south.

Peter nodded. "Heading for Sea Lion?"

"Yup."

"Register your itinerary?"

"My itinerary? With who?"

Peter sighed. "The Harbour Master."

In fact, Hippolyte had duly registered his departure and had paid the clearance fee; his passport had been stamped and his estimated return date acknowledged, but because he was heading outside of territorial waters, he hadn't been asked for his route. He told Customs and Immigration that he was heading to South Georgia and doubted that anyone would be the wiser if he didn't make it that far. He prayed fervently that Peter would not drop in and ask to see his non-existent itinerary. "Right. The Harbour Master," he said out loud. "Of course. I've registered with them." Was there really any point in all this lying?, he asked himself. Would it do any harm to tell Peter where he really was planning to go? Yes, it would, he decided; it was too late now, in any case. "If I stay out longer, I'll radio in. Is that okay?"

"You've got my only radio, so you'll have to send me messages via the Harbour Master. HF 4066.1 Kilohertz—same frequency for the weather—and 2182 Khz. That's during working hours. VHF Channel 16 or 10 anytime. Keep channel 16 clear, except in an emergency. You have to radio for clearance to leave."

Permission to depart granted, Hippolyte pried Peter off of the boat and onto the jetty. He leaned against the wheel and contemplated the boat's unhappy owner. "You wouldn't happen to have a couple of spare blankets, would you?" he asked.

Peter sauntered over to his Land Rover and dragged out three worn, gray ones. He, in turn, leaned against the vehicle, his head tilted at an angle, considering the boat, Hippolyte, the shorelines securing the boat, as if he were trying to picture what was wrong. He came back and handed over the blankets. "Thought you might need them," he admitted. "People always forget about blankets. When did you say you'd be back?"

"Four weeks."

"They'll check up on you if you're not back by then."

Hippolyte was quite interested in this detail. "How?"

"If you don't show, they follow up on your itinerary and check with the islanders. See if you've been. Where you've gone. They told you to contact the residents at the various islands you're going to, didn't they?"

They didn't of course, because he wasn't going to any islands. "What makes you think that this will even be an issue?" Hippolyte evaded.

"I don't know. You strike me as a chap who doesn't pay attention to details, like dates, I suppose."

"Let's say that I didn't return in time and didn't radio in to let anyone know. Are you saying that they'd send out a search party?"

"Not send out a search party, but certainly ask people: islanders, fishing boat crews, FIGAS pilots, you know, to look out. Depends how late you were. Depends how bad the weather has got. Then of course, I would always alert them if I thought you were in trouble."

"How long would you wait before you alerted someone? I mean, what if I forgot; I'd hate for all that bother."

"And what if you sank my boat? Or what if you crashed on a reef? Think on it, man. Imagine you're sharing a pointy little rock with a sea lion who's got his eye on either you or one of those packets of dried flakes you've managed to salvage. Only, you'd be easier, because he wouldn't have to soak you in water and heat you up, would he? And you wouldn't want someone keeping an eye out for you?" He paused. "I'd wait a couple of days."

"Five."

"Are we bargaining?"

"Sure. Don't go to the authorities unless you haven't heard from me five days after I'm due back."

Peter squinted at Hippolyte's earnest face. "This is the damn craziest thing I've ever heard of. Four."

"Okay, four. It's a deal." They shook hands.

Hippolyte took his place at the helm, and feeling every bit a South Atlantic sealer with feet tucked into his scuff-proof boots and with a sou' wester hat stored charmingly but needlessly on his head, he ran through the start-up procedure. "One: activate the fuel pump; two: key in ignition; three: pull out, what?—clutch; four: key to start position; five: run vent fan; six: key to run position; seven: key to turn over!" The engine spewed a cloud of blue smoke. With all of the things to do, he'd forgotten "eight: cast off"—his quickly scribbled checklist was stuffed in his pocket, somehow too embarrassing to refer to what with the rigorous inspection. Fortunately Peter had already released bow and stern lines and was tossing them onto the deck.

Peter scowled at Hippolyte's wave as he stood there on the gravel, his hands in his pockets, pensively eyeing his property. "We think we're the Queen, do we? Goddamned lubber!" he said aloud to no one in particular, then yelled, "Take care of my boat, eh!?"

Hippolyte waved again as he pointed the bow west to Stanley Harbour proper. He shot forward with a lurch. "Take care of my boat!" Peter shouted louder, this time making a megaphone with his hands. Then he looked around as if desperately searching for a kayak, a canoe, anything that he could grab to go and reclaim his precious vessel. He semaphored frantically. "I forgot to tell you about the dinghy!" Hippolyte dashed a mock salute to the diminishing figure on the jetty, then changed course, heading northwest towards the

Narrows and Port William. Tears came to Peter's eyes and flowed down his cheeks as he stamped the ground impotently. "DAMN IT, MAN!" His cry must have blasted the eardrums of the gods, but for Hippolyte it was only the faintest of sounds. "BRING BACK MY BOAT!"

We call this line zero.

Davis's Quadrant F,G = 30° arcs
Backstaff vane c, d = 60° arcs Longti vane
A = horizon vane

Set 'B' at even degree, less 15° or 20° than zenith distance, turn to sun, look through 'C' and 'A', raise or lower till shadow of upper edge of 'B' falls on 'A', then raise or lower 'C', till horizon appears through 'C' and 'A'.

P = pole

ABFQ = rhumb line desc. by ship

PA, Pb, Pc, etc. = meridians

AL, Bk, Cp, Og, etc. lines of lat.

East   17 Feb. 2000   0100 hrs.   North   West

Equation of Time

Sirius

Antares

			Can't identify:	
1. Aldebaran	9. Acrux	A. Orion	Lepus	
2. Rigel	10. Achernar	B. Canis Major	Columba Noachi	Corvus
3. Betelgeuse	11. βCentauri	C. Argus	Pisces Australis	Ara
4. Sirius	12. Rigel Kent	D. Eridanus	Musca	Grus
5. Procyon	13. Antares	E. False Cross	Chameleon	Pavo
6. Pollux	14. αCentauri	F. Southern Cross	Hydra	Apus
7. Castor	15. Spica	G. Centaurus	Crater	Corona
8. Canopus	16. Alphard	H. Scorpio (better seen in late March)	Monoceros	Australis
	17. Regulus	I. Hydra	Cetus	Dorado
	18. Leo		Phoenix	

CONSTELLATIONS OF THE
SOUTHERN HEMISPHERE.

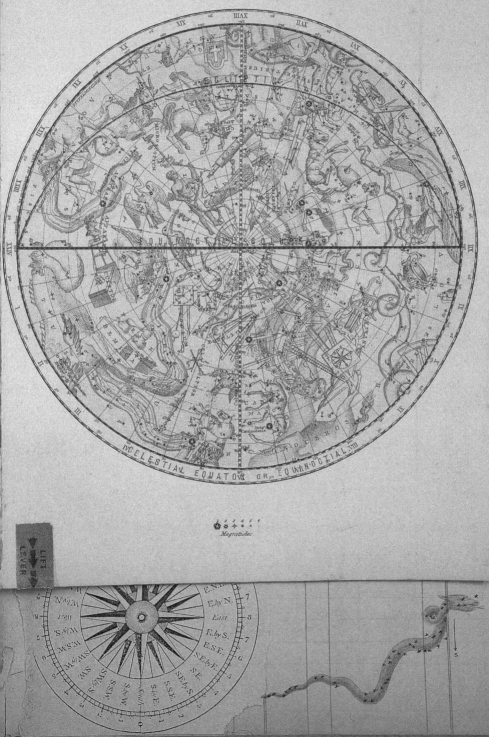

Magnitudes.

Seven

LOG OF THE *Southern Saracen*
From: Stanley Harbour   Towards: The Auroras
Date: Thurs., 17 Feb. 2000   Hours: 1200
Knots: 6   Fathoms: ?
Wind: NW 322°   Force: 5 / Fresh breeze
Barometer: 30.14   Temp. Air: 13°C   Water: 12°C
Remarks: Scattered light cumulus 2/10. Unlimited vis.
Lat: 52°00′S   Long: 54°08′W   Var: 003°E   Course: 098°C

Two days out, steady as she goes. Nothing between me and the Auroras except birds and waves and birds and waves. I've never been so sick in my life. Waves and birds. If I watch the horizon, I feel better. Marginally. Tell yourself that, Webb. Watch – the – horizon. Up and down, side to side, rolling, heaving. I've got nothing left in this poor old gut o' mine.

Impossible to be scientific. Pencil goes down to the paper at a half a knot, paper comes up to the pencil at two knots, nib gets smashed. Sharpen the lead. Hey! Take that knife away from that guy, he could hurt himself! Oh yeah, the knife. I wonder what the kid is using now. Uzi, probably. What an ape. No, not ape, not fair to apes. God, I feel drunk! Lurching all over the cabin, heaving over the side. I stink.

Didn't someone tell me about pills? Why didn't I buy pills? I'd give my soul for a Gravol. Someone once said drink seawater before you start; he said, whoever it was, that it'll keep you right and ready. Nothing more revolting. Someone else figured that the best cure was to go lie down under a tree. I'd go for that.

Paper's already sticking together, and it hasn't even rained. My fingers are so cold; they've stopped working properly—aren't bending at the hinges—can't get the damn pages apart. Everything, me included, is rotting from humidity. Sextant won't focus properly, and even if it did, I can't see straight to work out my position. Should be grateful for the GPS.

So far, wind's generally from Northwest, but gusts seem to come up from all directions. Wind-speed readings from the masthead anemometer threw me until I figured out that you have to take boat speed and mast movement into account. I'd rather defer to Beaufort; it gives me something in common with the woman who reads out the radio weather forecast. Squawwk yourself! Albatross just flew across the bow. Big fellow, but then, that's the way they make them.

Hours: 1930   Knots: 4
Wind: N?   Force: 3 / Gentle breeze
Barometer: 30.16
Remarks: Accumulating cumulus 5/10. Unlimited vis.
Here's the weather report, read by my lovely companion; I will transcribe her words of wisdom: 1930 shipping report for 2200 to 1000 open waters tomorrow: synoptic: low pressure 150 nm SE Falklands, occluded front, wind 5 to 7 over east, visib. good gen., sea state v. rough, rain and showers die out later. Missed the rain. Outlook next 24 hrs. Strong north, mod-rough, fog poss. w. good to poor vis.

Hours: 2340   Knots: 4
Wind: NW 316°   Force: 3 / Gentle Breeze
Barometer: 30.16   Remarks: Dark.
Estimate that I've come 150 miles, averaging 3 knots, though I'm fairly skimming along now. It's a strange sensation to be slicing through the water in the dark with no idea what's ahead or what's been left behind. It rather takes your breath away. At this rate I'll arrive in a total of 6 days. I'm going slower than I hoped, and yet there's an exhilarating sensation of speed. Curious to see how fast I can make this thing go.

II. To find the Difference of Latitude between two Places

RULE. When the latitudes are both of the same name, that is, both North or both South, subtract the less from the greater, and the remainder will be the *difference* of latitude. But when one is North, and the other South, their sum will be the *difference* of latitude.

EXAMPLE I. What is the difference of latitude between the Lizard and Cape Finisterre ?

Latitude of the Lizard ...	49° 58' N.
Lat. of Cape Finisterre	42 53 N.
Diff. of latitude	7 5
	60
In miles	425

EXAMPLE II. A ship from latitude 3° 10' S. arrives in latitude 2° 26' N. : required the difference of latitude made good.

Latitude left	3° 10' S.
Latitude in	2 26 S.
Diff. of latitude	5 36 S.
	60
In miles	336

II. With the Latitude left and the Difference of Latitude, to find the Latitude in.

RULE. When the latitude left and difference of latitude are of the same name, their sum gives the latitude in ; but when they are of different names, their difference is the latitude in, of the same name with the greater.

EXAMPLE I. A ship from the West end of the Island of Madeira, in latitude 32° 48' N., sails North 520 miles* : what latitude is she in ?

Latitude of Madeira ...	32° 48' N.
Diff. of latitude 520 m. =	8 40 N.
Latitude in	41 28 N.

EXAMPLE II. A ship three days ago was in latitude 2° 48' N., and has since then sailed South 426 miles : required her present latitude.

Latitude left	2° 48' N.
Diff. of latitude 426 m. =	7 6 S.
Latitude in	4 18 S.

* When the difference of latitude or longitude is given in miles or minutes (') it is to be divided by 60, to reduce it to degrees and minutes (*see* p. 6).

I never considered sailing at night. For some reason I had this idea that I'd be putting in at harbours, even though I knew none existed. The number of errors I committed last night! Forgot to turn on the navigation lights, left full sails up—honestly don't clearly remember switching from the motor to the sails—that's how cloudy my memory of yesterday is—didn't organize flashlight, chart. Tonight's all right. Turned stern and bow lights on, left masthead lights off to better see the stars. I must acquaint myself with these southern constellations, these jumbles of still nameless, featureless stars. My God, it's cold. The kind of night you want to wrap yourself around a warm body.

The sky was putting on an amazing show: bright, huge stars, twinkling fiercely in a code only they could understand. Whether it was a trick of atmosphere, a gift of the utter blackness, the nature of South, or a combination of all three, the Milky Way revealed itself exquisitely. Now, more than ever, Hippolyte understood the sensation of reaching out to touch the stars, of tugging on the visible cord that they are all strung along and sweeping them down around him and watching them dance upon the rise and fall of the waves.

He had managed to get several charts of the southern constellations before he left. One of them was printed with fluorescent ink that glowed in the dark, a mini-galaxy in its own right. He started his survey with Orion, the Hunter, whose well-defined belt drew the eye in an arching sweep east and upwards to Sirius, then directly above that star to the constellation Argo, the ship Argus. To the west was the star Achernar, at the mouth of the sinuous constellation Eridanus, the River. The Southern Cross, an unexpected beacon, was unmistakable with a trail of two bright stars, Rigel Kent and ß Centauri, trailing like the tail of a kite.

There was no lack of choice words overhead. With zeniths, nadirs, and azimuths at his command, it's no wonder he thought of Arabia. A veritable shimmering of a thousand nights lit by Eltanin, Rastaban, Sadr. And there were words enough and more to fill the Greek and Roman skies: horizons, eclipses, galaxies, meridians, and constellations, not to mention Polaris, Hydra, or the trembler Sirius, all the alphas, betas, and gammas that illuminate the hours of darkness.

Hippolyte's love for language and names had developed early in his life; he spent hours tasting words and experimenting with pronunciations, weighing an emphasis here, altering an ending there. He thought of the amusement that his own name gave him, though he hadn't always found it entertaining. At the age of five, he discovered, while reading a children's edition of the Greek myths, that he'd been saddled with a girl's name. "If you had to give me a dumb name, why didn't you get it right?" he stood with his book open to the authoritative page, appealing plaintively to his father. "HIPPOLYTUS or HIPPOLOCHUS is for a guy, not HIPPOLYTE."

"Go ask your mother," replied his father, who should have been more understanding.

"It's a French name." His mother dismissed his unhappiness with what he believed was faulty logic.

"Where did the French get it?"

"I don't know, but THEIR men don't have anything to worry about. And besides, it says here," she pointed to the exact paragraph, "that Hippolyte was an Amazonian with tremendous diplomatic qualities. Look, she offered to give Hercules her . . . her belt when he needed it to satisfy his ninth labor. You should be proud to share a name with such a person."

"But it says *here* that Hercules killed her anyway. Why didn't you call me Hercules? And it doesn't say 'belt'; it says 'girdle.' That's stupid, what would Hercules want with her girrr-dle." Only a child could dismiss women's underwear with such contempt.

"It's the translation. *Girdle* in this case means *belt*." Afterwards Hippolyte told people matter-of-factly that their belts were really girdles and dryly cited Mother as his source.

Anyway, Hippolyte had a son by Theseus—at least according to one version—whom she named Hippolytus. This none-too-savvy young man had spurned the attentions of the love-sick Phaedra, who, to complicate matters, was his stepmother, and who, because of him, hanged herself, but not before leaving her husband (Hippolytus's father) a suicide note in which she claimed that Hippolytus had raped her. This spurious bit of slander reached Theseus, who conjured up one of the handy curses that Poseidon had given him, causing the seas to spew forth a raging bull to frighten Hippolytus's horses, which then dragged him to his death. Hippolyte looked across the deck to the now-calm waters and shuddered; no wonder Poseidon felt like an enemy. Hippolytus, later exonerated by his idol, the primly chaste goddess Artemis, fled to the heavens and shone in northern skies as Auriga, the Charioteer.

Hippolyte and his mother returned frequently to the issues surrounding his name.

"You aren't named after the Greeks," she stressed. "It was your grandfather's name; it was good enough for him."

"How do you pronounce it?" he asked over and over.

"Hip-o-lite," she invariably replied. "You should know. You've heard me say it a million times."

"I think it should be High-*pol*-ee-tay," he would declare.

"I-po-leete would be possible. That's how grandmother pronounced it."

"And what about great-grandfather? How did he pronounce it?"

"I never did hear him say his own name," she admitted.

"Maybe he was too embarrassed."

"Shush."

The French legacy thrilled him more than he'd ever admit, especially when he discovered that Hippolyte *à la française* had produced a geologist-archaeologist-paleontologist, a painter-photographer-gardener, a historian-monk, a thinker-critic, a documentarian-historian, and a physicist. He was particularly happy with the multiple paths that most of these I-po-leetes took.

But what did his schoolmates call him? What kind of nickname could be dreamed up from Hippolyte? Kids gave Hippo a whirl, but that was a flop, as he had been a skinny child. The same held true for variations like Flippo and Blippo. Of course, they couldn't just call him

Hippolyte. No, their usual choice was Webb or Spidey, as in spider web. Or Web-foot. Or Duck. He got called Quack a lot, too. And Duck Tail. Brash newcomers might try Duck's Ass, even Waddle, but only once; school-yard fights put an end to that. Hippolyte thought about how Jeremy's check had been made out to Polite. Now that would have been classy.

As a boy, Hippolyte had been a magnet for all the children who had ever caught a glimpse of their own recklessness; they aspired to his instincts and treated him like a Nelson. But as all generals find, he was hoisted so high above the ranks, he was ultimately alone. Or would have been if it weren't for Jeremy. Germ was his shadow; a kind of Lord Nelson's valet; a considerate, unfussy—except when he cried—companion, so attentive and so close that it was a surprise they drifted apart.

The cold and the damp crept into his bones; he zipped his collar tight over his chin and yanked his toque down over his ears. The blackness curled around him, nestling him deeper into the night. He wasn't ready to give up the air and the stars, and furthermore, he was onto his favorite topic: names. He was convinced that most people don't realize there's so much in a name. Take the editor that Jeremy has proposed, Marie Simplon, as an example. Marie—though a common enough name what with all its variations, Mary, Maria, Marietta, Mariel, Marion—conjures up thick, wavy, raven locks and a passionate demeanor. Passionate and demeanor didn't sound right together; they canceled each other out. He was going to have to be more careful choosing his words now that he was writing a book. How about passionate looks? Appearance? Image? He'd buy a new thesaurus first thing. Thesaurus: from the Latin for *treasure* or *treasury,* from the Greek *thesauros.* Any connection to Hippolytus's father, Theseus? Back to Marie. Passionate features? Passionate presence? He was already looking forward to meeting her. And Simplon. A pass in the Lepontine Alps 6590 feet above sea level, more than a nautical mile. The thrill of climbing the Simplon Pass gave him goose bumps; climbing always did. The thought of Marie was giving him goose bumps.

At some point in his past Hippolyte had memorized the heights of the various passes in the Swiss Alps: St. Gotthard's (6900 feet), Théodule (11,000 feet), and Weissthor (12,000 feet). And the mountains! His memory climbed to dizzying altitudes before falling back to sea level with a decided thump. There was no getting around it, he thought as he surveyed the relentless flatness, this water business was hard to get used to.

He looked at his watch: 1:30. He had to catch some sleep. Still, it was difficult to tear himself away, to abandon the watch and the security of seeing what was ahead, even though traffic through this area was almost non-existent. Shivering, he took a last look at the black seas around him. Fish, here and there, broke the surface, then disappeared, leaving a phosphorescent glow of white lace. The thermometer read three degrees centigrade. No wonder he was cold.

With a tap of the compass and a slight nudge of the wheel to correct the course, he went below. The tight confines of the bunk could barely contain his broken dreams. He flung out his arm, a subconscious response to a vestigial desire invading his sleep, but instead of drawing a warm body to him, he slammed his hand against the side of the hull, and awoke in screaming pain.

NAVIGATION

MEASURE OF LE[NGTH]

12 Inches	= 1 Foot.
3 Feet	= 1 Yard.
2 Yards, or 6 Feet	= 1 Fathom.
220 Yards	= 1 Furlong.
8 Furlongs, or	
1760 Yards, or }	= 1 Statute Mi[le]
5280 Feet	
3 Miles	= 1 League.
6080 Feet	= 1 Nautical [Mile]

SURVEYING AND CHART MEAS[URE]

100 Fathoms, or }	..... = 1 Ca[ble]
600 Feet	
10 Cables, or 6000 Feet	= 1 M[ile]

MEASURE OF TIME

60 Seconds.........	= 1 Minute.
60 Minutes	= 1 Hour.
24 Hours	= 1 Day.
7 Days	= 1 Week.
28, 29, 30, or 31 Days	= 1 Month.
12 Months	= 1 Year.
365 Days ,........	= 1 Year.
366 Days	= 1 Leap Year.

1 Hour = 60 Minutes = 3600 Seconds.
24 Hours=1440 Minutes=86400 Seconds.

Code	Bea[ufort]	
---	Sca[le]	
0	Cal[m]	
1	Lt [air]	
2	Lt [breeze]	
3	Br[eeze]	
4	Mo[d]	
5	Fre[sh]	
6	Str[ong]	
7	Mo[d gale]	
8	Fresh gale	Mod high waves, tops b[reak] blown by wind
9	Strong gale	High waves, heavy foam, sea 41-47 rolls, spray interferes w/ vis.
10	Whole gale	Very high waves, sea white, heavy 48-55 rolling, v. low vis.
11	Sto[rm]	Ext. high waves. Lose sight of 56-63 small-med-sized ships.
12- 17	Hurri[cane]	Foam and spray fills air, waves 64-118 [?]5 feet plus, no vis., sea com-pletely white

Tides: Stanley Hbr

13/02	0142: 1.4m / 0738: 0.6
SR 0549	
SS 2022	1417: 1.4 / 2008: 0.7
14/02	0233: 1.4 / 0844: 0.6
SR 0551	
SS 2020	1530: 1.3 / 2056: 0.8
15/02	0336: 1.4 / 1010: 0.6
SR 055[?]	
SS 2018	1657: 1.3 / 2207: 0.8

°T=Degrees True
°C=Degrees Compass
°M=Degrees Magnetic
nm = nautical mile
Kn=Knot (=1 nm/hour, not
knot/hour!)
m=metres (for depths
& heights)
fm=fathom
(1 fm=6 ft or 1.8 m)

2		
3	[?]4	= 1.64
4	[?]2	= 2.19
5	[?]0	= 2.73
6	......	= 3.28
7	......	= 3.83
8	......	= 4.37
9	......	= 4.92
10	......	
100	......	

1 Mi[?] [?]39[?]
1 Cen[?] [?]393[?]

f4 29

Eight

LOG OF THE *Southern Saracen*

From: Stanley Harbour   Towards: The Auroras

Date: Fri., 18 Feb. 2000   Hours: 1200

Knots: 5   Fathoms: ?

Wind: Variable, 280 to 290°   Force: 5 / Fresh Breeze

Barometer: 30.12   Temp. Air: 11°C   Water: 10°C

Remarks: Cumulus 6/10. Unlimited vis.

Lat: 52°10′S   Long: 52°56′W

Var: 000°E   Course Req: 098°C   Course Steered: 097°C

Goddamn hand hurts like hell. What on earth did I do to it? There's a big rip across the knuckles; needs some gauze and a bandage.

Granola for breakfast, with tinned milk. Instant coffee, with tinned milk. I'll get through this stuff if it kills me. I've scrubbed the decks, those birds'll shit anywhere; scraped mold out of the fridge, looks like 5-year-old Stilton.

I know what I miss, it's music. It never occurred to me to bring any tapes, a cassette player. I tried tuning in to a music station but fretted about running the battery down. Daytime's not so bad though, like today! With the breeze, the sails up and full, the rigging was slapping against the mast for all the world like a mad Flamenco troupe! If I closed my eyes. Wild clapping, shoe stamping, whirling! Flashes of red satin skirts, polished black shoes! Olés, palms slamming against guitar boxes, driving rhythms. The deck alive—swarming—with these unexpected but welcome visitors. Speaking of visitors, a couple of persistent ship followers, Cape petrels, have landed on the deck in order to give me a good scolding. I haven't exactly been tossing them delicious tidbits; perhaps that's what they're in a snit about. One even dropped down onto my head and perched there, swaying back and forth, picking up one foot after the other, preening its wings, probably dropping fleas or nits all over my hair.

Hippolyte squandered hours staring at the albatrosses and petrels as they circled round or passed by. They made him feel small, these huge birds with their wings that spread across the sky. The time he had spent at the zoology museum, nostrils clogged with down and fingers slick with albatross oil, were paying off; he could distinguish many of the different species, but was shocked at how ambivalent he was at first towards these living examples. He hated them. With their too big beaks, their too intimidating shrieks, their bodies the size of tanks, colossal webbed bat-wing landing gear, they were nothing like their brothers and sisters in the museum, who were, at that moment, snoozing peacefully, eternally, in drawers, their dangerous claws safely roped together.

Diomedea exulans, melanophris, chrysostoma, epomorphora, chlororhyn-chos. Albatrosses all, wandering, black-browed, gray-headed, royal, yellow-nosed. His constant companions kept a kind of shiftwork watch over him; when one went, another replaced it. Diomedea from Diomedes, the brave citizen of Argos, tamer of horses, friend to Odysseus. War-hungry, a hero of Troy, but that didn't stop him from turning tail and fleeing Zeus when the going got rough. There wasn't much of a welcome for him when he returned home: his wife had been duped into unfaithfulness, and to make matters worse, his fellow Argives kicked him and his men out of town. He lived in exile in Italy but one day vanished. Poof. Like magic. And his comrades, the men who fought at his side at Troy, became gentle albatrosses.

First and foremost, there was *exulans,* the wanderer. A god of a bird that took its name so seriously it could circumnavigate the globe on the dip of a wing, hitchhiking on currents. What were flights of 10,000, 20,000 miles to this restless one? *Exulans.* From *e, ex:* out of, from; *exul* or *exsul:* banished person, wanderer.

Then there was *Diomedea melanophris:* the black-browed albatross. *Melan,* Greek for black as in melancholy; *ophrys* for brow. Smaller than the wanderer, the dark eyebrows and wings stood in stark contrast to the white body. A graceful scavenger and pleasant company, Hippolyte would have considered it a good omen if one were to adopt him for the duration of the voyage.

His favorite of all the birds, though, was Willie the Wilson storm-petrel, *Oceanites oceanicus.* Barely larger than a sparrow, Willie fearlessly skimmed the surface of the water, almost running along with his little feet tapping against the swell. Edward Wilson, the naturalist who had died during Scott's fateful voyage to find the South Pole, had had a soft spot for him, too. As Hippolyte watched the tiny storm-petrel playing with the spray, he felt a profound sense of loss at Wilson's senseless death. He chuckled. "I'm getting maudlin. It's the solitude." But he couldn't help thinking about this man who, along with other hardy souls, had traveled to the Antarctic when it was truly a feat. He had trekked hundreds of miles in unbelievable conditions in order to learn; he had crammed sketchbooks full of albatross, petrels, penguins, seals, and whales; he had been the glue that had held the men together.

"Now I know I'm getting carried away," Hippolyte said out loud. "Okay, I only know him from his work, but you can read a lot into the way a guy draws and writes. You can read humour and patience and generosity. How did I get on to Wilson? Oh yes, Willie, the storm-petrel. Here, a small offering to *Oceanites oceanicus* and to you, Wilson, and your spirit flying along with this brave little bird. It's only a paltry sketch, but I hope you like it all the same."

From: Stanley Harbour   Towards: The Auroras

Date: Sat., 19 Feb. 2000   Hours: 2130

Knots: 4   Fathoms: ?

Wind: NNW 290°   Force: 3 / Breeze

Barometer: 30.11 falling slowly   Temp. Air: 7°C   Water: 10°C

Remarks: Sunset 2012

Lat: 52°22′S   Long: 51°13′W

Var: 001°W   Course: 097°C (corrected 002°)

Can't miss the weather report. How are you this evening, my dear? My pencil is ready: 2135 shipping report for 2200 to 1000 open waters tomorrow: synoptic: moist, mild stable air mass, wind 5 easterly over east, thunderstrms poss., visib. v. poor improving, sea state mod. to rough. Outlook weakening northeast, sea state mod., good vis. Good night. Until tomorrow. Storm tonight? It looks okay, but will heave-to, just in case.

Heaving-to sounded like an easy technique in the classroom, but he'd never gotten a chance to practice it on the water. Just point the bow into the wind, I think, he said out loud, before turning to face north-northwest. Something didn't feel quite right, so he went below and consulted his manual. As he read up on the maneuver, he marveled at how he hadn't bothered to use it before, especially before trying to cook a meal. Following the instructions, which explained that he would be balancing the rudder and the sails, in effect "stalling the sails," he backed the headsail to windward then eased the mainsail out to the opposite side. The boat refused to lie close to the wind, so he shortened the jib. Then shortened it some more, then finally reefed it. The finicky work occupied him for a full hour, but when he was done he looked up at the mainsail proudly and shook his head in bemusement. Though the wind was holding steady, the clear, starry sky had never seemed so benign.

LOG OF THE *Southern Saracen*

From: Stanley Harbour   Towards: The Auroras

Date: Sun., 20 Feb. 2000   Hours: 0510

Knots: 4   Fathoms: ?

Wind: NW 330°   Force: 3 / Breeze

Barometer: 30.10   Temp. Air: 9°C   Water: 10°C

Remarks: Cumulus 8/10. Visibility 2 miles?

Lat: 52°22′S   Long: 49°30′W

Var: 001°W   Course: 098°C (corrected 002°)

Got underway an hour ago. Didn't sleep much what with fiddling with the sail to keep hove-to. Thunderstorm didn't materialize, neither did fog; I may be out of the forecast area. I just wasted a good four hours, sitting almost in one place, well not quite; the leeward drift appears to have been quite considerable. Some catching up to do.

It looks like I've come 314 miles. I'm very close to Bustamente's position of 52°37′S, 47°43½′W and should be in sight of the Auroras in about 70 miles.

The day dragged out interminably. The little preoccupations of the previous days—mending, scrubbing, reading—no longer distracted him; Hippolyte couldn't concentrate on a single thing aside from his islands. He hung over the pulpit whenever he could free himself from the sails, staring out into the distance. His chart became pale and creased with the erasures of courses and alternative courses plotted upon it. He raised the binoculars to his eyes every five minutes, then refused to believe the emptiness before him. So he rubbed at the glass, first carefully with its special lens cloth, then afterwards with his finger, his sleeve, with whatever was handy. Birds cruised overhead, shrieking at him to pay attention; except for brief glances of annoyance, he ignored them.

LOG OF THE *Southern Saracen*

From: Stanley Harbour   Towards: The Auroras

Date: Mon., 21 Feb. 2000   Hours: 0900

Knots: 4   Fathoms: ?

Wind: NW 325°   Force: 3 / Breeze

Barometer: 31.10   Temp. Air: 8°C   Water: ?°C

Remarks: Cumulus 6/10. Vis. 2 miles?

Lat: 52°34′S   Long: 47°52′W   Var: 001°W

Course: 098°C (correction of 001°)

About 5 miles from est. position.

Hours: 1245   Knots: 3 to 4

Wind: NNW 330°   Force: 4 / Mod. Breeze

Barometer: 30.10 holding steady

Temp. Air: 11°C   Water: 10°C

Remarks: Cumulus 8/10. Visibility 2 to 3 miles

Lat: 52°35′S   Long: 47°40′W   Var: 002°W

Still nothing, though the wind has picked up and the whitecaps are increasing in frequency.

Within the space of five minutes, Hippolyte looked at his watch at least ten times before he could convince himself to go make something to eat. And once below, he found a dozen reasons for rushing back up on deck. The howl of the rising wind, an uncanny pocket of silence, the dull thump of something hitting the hull, the flap of the canvas, any excuse. Finally sufficiently vexed with his scattered agitation, he forced himself to concentrate on lunch. Unable to commit to actually heating up anything, he nibbled dry crackers and picked at the last of the cheese—a tasteless processed Edam that could have lasted for a century had he brought enough. Determined to take a proper break, he shed his outer gear and tried sitting down, but his feet and legs wouldn't stay still, so he stood up and reached across the table to his jacket, drawing the South Atlantic chart out of its pocket. This he unfolded for the thousandth time. He ran his finger along his route, stared up at the hatchway, then got up, put his waterproofs back on, and went topside. He'd managed to stay below all of fifteen minutes.

Hours: 1352   Knots: 5
Wind: NNW 335°   Force: 4 / Mod. Breeze
Lat: 52°38′S   Long: 47°38′W   Course: 102°C
Either Bustamente was wrong, or my calculations are out. Well, no, they aren't out, or at least, not by much; have to admit I've been using the GPS, so max. 100 metres out. Put the blame on Don José, otherwise I'd be able to see them by now, even if they were nothing more than flat, low reefs. No change in the appearance of the water.

Hours: 1440   Knots: 4
Wind: NNW 335°   Force: 4 / Mod. Breeze
Lat: 52°38′S   Long: 47°40′W   Course: 190°C
I'll head south for a couple of miles, then turn back if there's no luck.

Hours: 1552   Knots: 4
Wind: NNW 335°   Force: 4 / Mod. Breeze
Lat: 52°40′S   Long: 47°42′W   Course: 210°C
Goddamn it. Where are they? Could I have been wrong?

Hours: 1705   Knots: 4
Wind: NNW 330°   Force: 4 / Mod. Breeze
Lat: 52°39′S   Long: 47°43′W   Course: 280°C
It's a big ocean; I know they're out here somewhere. Patience.

Hours: 1820   Knots: 3
Wind: NNW 330°   Force: 5 / Fresh Breeze
Lat: 52°36′S   Long: 47°44′W   Course: 340°C
Wind has picked up even more, lots of spray from the whitecaps and some large waves. Not breaking over the boat yet, though. Really working the sails.

Hours: 1910   Knots: 3
Wind: NNW 330°   Force: 4 / Mod. Breeze
Remarks: Cumulus 6/10. Vis inc: 5 miles?, starting to get dark
Lat: 52°35½′S   Long: 47°45½′W   Course: 038°C
Winds are slightly calmer, moderate breeze. Waves have subsided. No
sign yet.

Hours: 1950   Knots: 3
Wind: WSW 245°   Force: 5 / Fresh Breeze
Lat: 52°35½′S   Long: 47°44′W   Course: 110°C
I should hold this course for a while instead of zigzagging like I have
been. I could be miles off.

Hippolyte saw it coming just before it hit: the freshening wind—
strong though manageable—swung clockwise and turned into a
venomous gale-force gust out of the Northeast at 20 degrees. The
sails whipped over to starboard—he barely escaped having his head
demolished by the boom—and the boat was knocked down danger-
ously close to the rail. Instinct told him to drop the sails as quickly as
possible, but it was also nagging at him to try to right the thing by
hiking off the port rail. Which was more important? There was no
time to weigh the options, the crashing canvas was so terrifyingly
insistent. He gathered his wits and was about to take down the sails
when the wind suddenly died. As quickly as it came up, it disappeared,
without leaving even a wake. The *Saracen* righted herself, her sails
sagged and she bobbed about, her bow drifted listlessly to port.
Stunned, Hippolyte looked around in disbelief, then saw, over the
stern a short distance behind him, a black spot on the darkening horizon. It was land.

Nine

Hours: 2055
Wind: sw 230°   Force: 4 / Mod. Breeze
Lat: 52°36′S   Long: 47°43′W

I've done it. I've done it! It's got to be the Auroras! How can I get off this tub and get on land? Why didn't I get Peter to show me how to launch the dinghy? I'm going to go crazy sitting here.

Anchored about 75 feet off a narrow, sloping beach in what could optimistically be called a harbour on the west side of an island. I'd get closer but it looks like there are reefs. Can't tell if there's one island or several, but this one seems fairly large. It's impossible to determine its north/south extent, and the rise of land is high—I'd guess about 100 feet. The height makes me all the more disturbed about how I missed it in the first place. I've checked and rechecked my positions, and I swear my course took me right over what I see in front of me. I wasn't even messing around with the sextant; then I could understand my mistake. I know there's some error in the GPS, but even making allowances for that, this doesn't make a whole lot of sense. That sudden wind must have dragged me miles off course in the short time it blew.

All that aside, though, just for now, approaching land this way, not being able to tell if this is a small body of land or a large one, I marvel all the more at early explorers, to whom almost everything was unknown.

Hours: 2112

The boat was drifting, so just wasted an hour dropping the second anchor. There's quite an art to this anchor business, it seems, but they're

90

holding firm now. How are you supposed to weigh anchor, anyway, with both of them stuck in the seabed?

I wish I knew how to get that dinghy down; it's frustrating sitting here, writing these feeble notes. I'd feel safer if I knew that the anchors really had a hold on the bottom. I hope I don't get shoved toward the shore. This spot could hardly be described as sheltered. Temperature has dropped to 6°C, though it feels warmer. Barometer is falling.

Hours: 2125
Nothing but static on the radio; battery levels are OK; the wires must have finally given out.

Hours: 2130
Still no radio. Looks like my weather lady will stand me up tonight.

LOG OF THE *Southern Saracen*
Anchored at the Auroras
Date: Tues., 22 Feb. 2000   Hours: 1630   Fathoms: 6
Wind: Variable sw to w   Force: 4 / Mod. Breeze
Barometer: 30.11   Temp. Air: 11°C   Water: 10°C
Remarks: Clear. Unlimited vis.

This is splendid. This is the Auroras! It's not Shag Rocks or any other kind of rock. It's full-sized, legitimate islands!

Have to write this all down so it makes sense. Got up this morning at 0900, groggy and muddled. I thought I'd be up hours earlier, but I guess I needed a good long sleep. Tell the truth, I feel as tired as if I hadn't slept at all.

Still some kind of interference on the radio, reception mostly static, a few distorted words pop through now and then. I lowered the dinghy late last night—only takes brute strength—so I was off by 0945. Blasted thing leaks like a sieve—filled with a good 2 inches over the distance of not more than 75 feet. Peter could have mentioned it,

91

you think! Ran it up onto the beach, then savoured the sensation of stepping onto glorious white sands. I have no idea if I'm the first human being to ever land here, and frankly I don't care, but that I'm here now seems nothing short of miraculous. The penguins, who I doubt have ever seen such a creature as myself, came hop-waddling over and crowded round like children sniffing out bonbons. I got a jab in the leg from a curious beak but nothing serious. Gentoos, in a colony I'd checked out on the Falklands, knowing human beings for the obnoxious intruders they are, tended to either watch cautiously from a distance or trundle away. Here, there's no such knowledge, so they are intensely interested; as I cleared a path through, I felt like bowing my head to the left and to the right and saying, "Excuse me, ladies, gentlemen."

I should be approaching this more scientifically.

Size of the island: Approximately 3 miles north south, 1.5 miles east west. Walked the length in 3 hours but stopped frequently. The width I traversed in an hour, delayed because of massive tussock grass.

Maximum height: 120 feet, to be confirmed.

Shoreline characteristics: The island slopes up gently from the west and reaches a narrow plateau (less than half a mile in width) before dropping off to a dramatic scarp face along the eastern edge. The north end is pointed and has a moderate drop-off to jagged rocks and reefs. The south drops more gently than the north and is characterized by flatbeds of rock heaved out of the sea. Very cataclysmic. Very sobering.

Waves break quite fiercely off of both north and south tips, especially where the rocky faces indent, forcing the water to eddy and swirl. The winds whip spray up to the tops of the cliffs. Where I was able to descend to the lower rock shelves, I found them slippery, treacherous really, and it was tough to maintain balance even out of the wind.

Vegetation: There's a considerable amount of tussock grass, probably much like the Falklands used to be. Many different kinds of lichens, but I'm no expert; they just look different. There are mosses, too, but same thing, can't tell one from another. Yet. Just wait till I'm finished. No trees, of course. No shrubs, either. Reminds me of what Captain Cook wrote about South Georgia, something along the lines of "Not a tree was seen, nor even a shrub big enough for a tooth pick." He could have been writing about this island.

Tidal pools: Many along the west shore, accumulating between slabs of granite that rise out of the water from the west and slope up eastwards. No anemones or starfish, but lots of mussels, seaweed. No drinking water so far.

Animal life: Rockhopper penguins with the yellow/orange plumes, one large colony mixed with a small number of macaronis; one magellanic colony burrowed into the tussock; two gentoo colonies, including the welcoming committee, one of which is infiltrated by four kings (three adults and a chick). Nesting black-browed albatross, petrels and skuas, fulmars, king shags, gulls, storm-petrels, maybe vultures. Sea lions, small group of 4 or 5 individuals; fur seals, large colony. Elephant seals scattered in several bunches of 20 to 30 males. No bugs so far, or evidence of rodents or other land mammals.

But there's another far more important detail. There are two additional islands: one to the northeast, also fairly large, and another farther north, quite small. Bustamente was right; there are at least three Aurora islands.

Anchored at the Auroras
Date: Wed., 23 Feb. 2000   Hours: 1615   Fathoms: 6
Wind: w 270°   Force: 5 / Fresh Breeze
Barometer: 30.10   Temp. Air: 6°C Water: 9°C
Remarks: High cirrus 4/10, lower cumulus moving in 2/10.
Sunrise: 0608   Sunset: 2001

The Auroras are definitely made up of three main islands and numerous small reefs or shoals. The positions of the tiny outlying bits of land change from hour to hour, so they may be icebergs, although that doesn't seem completely reasonable given the season. Or does it? I must read up on icebergs; perhaps summer is their season to migrate north. The seas are so rough, I haven't had a chance to get up close enough to look at them, and it's hard to get bearings. The largest island—the one I'm on—is the most westerly and the farthest south. It's the only island that seems to sustain any significant vegetation. A narrow channel— perhaps a half mile at most—separates it from its nearest neighbour to the northeast. This second island is much lower, and, except for the side facing the first, most of it is no higher than about 45 feet. Numerous reefs guard its eastern shoreline. The third island, or large reef to be more precise, is directly north of the second and is separated by a channel approximately a mile wide. It, too, is low, perhaps 40 feet, perhaps a bit less, at its highest elevation. It's probably regularly submerged by high tides.

Since icebergs calve in summer, seeing them would makes sense.

High seas, not high tide, could be the explanation for my missing the islands initially. If the sea was running high on the 20th (which I didn't notice because I was so focussed on finding the islands), *and* if my position was a bit off, then I easily could have missed them. I noted on that day that the winds were a moderate breeze, force 7. That explains it; force 7 is large, breaking waves, except . . . except moderate breeze is only force 4. I made a mistake. There was no gale on the 20th. Damn. Come up with another explanation.

Hippolyte attempted to circumnavigate each of the islands, but, because of the reefs and the tides, couldn't bring himself to sail between them. The fickleness of the current through the narrow channel between the largest island and the second one was frightful. The water surged in, then unable to escape, changed its mind and raced back the way it came. Getting from one end to the other would take the undivided attention of an expert sailor skilled in precise timing. These were not exactly conditions favorable for surveying. There was no place to land; the sides of both islands rose straight out of the water, offering nothing—not even a shred of vegetation—to hang on to. Only the outer coasts, that is, the west side of the west island or the east side of the east island, offered any refuge. The northernmost island didn't even count; almost always partly submerged by heavy spray, it was more often than not too dangerous to approach.

Whole hours passed unnoticed in the contemplation of his islands' treasures. Little or no tact was necessary to watch the penguins. He'd sit down near the colonies, inching his butt onto flat, mossy stones that might have been so placed just for his convenience, and focusing on them through the lens of his camera or re-creating them on paper with the nib of his pen. As if he were the first person on earth to do so. Occasionally he'd laugh at his naiveté, then at the sight of some newly observed penguin antic—a chick, running full speed towards the wrong parent, its beak open, its flippers askew, for instance—he'd fall back under their spell.

The calls of the penguins, except for the donkey-braying magellanics, defied description. He would listen, then write down his impressions: "Rockhoppers discuss with a kind of chattering sawing; the gentoo's urgent warbling trill, accompanied by a puffing in and out of the upper chest, punctuated by sneezing and hissing, at times disintegrates into the hee-haw of the magellanic; the kings converse in low hushed tones, barely audible to anyone outside their circle, until some overwhelming sentiment unleashes their vocal chords and they raise their beaks to the sky and trumpet their regal certainties." And reread without knowing what the hell it was he had tried to describe. And so would start again, and again, limited by his capacity to render sound into word, would fail.

Elephant seal noises, of which there were many, were easier to classify. Easing their not inconsiderate three-ton larders onto the beaches, the huge male seals groaned in pain from the mosquito pecks of the tiny tussock birds and snarled when one of their own dared move. Listening to them roll incontinently against each other on whatever beach they happened to wash up on was as entertaining as watching them. The snortling, snuffling, fartling sounds were pure Rabelais.

He could never believe just how close he could get to all of these animals, how trusting they were, so he shot off hundreds of photographs as he crept nearer and nearer, wasting, it seemed, miles of film.

Senecio
candicans →

Valeriana sedifolia
? Azorella selago
✓ Bolax gummifera

✓ Empetrum rubrum
Myrteola nummularia
Gaultheria microphylla
Pernettya pumila
Baccharis magellanica
Gunnera magellanica
Oxalis enneaphylla
Viola maculata
Sisyrinchium filifolium
Enargea marginata
Leucheria suaveolens
Calceolaria fothergillii
Codonorchis lessonii
Primula magellanica
Cortaderia pilosa
Hierochloe redolens
Blechnum penna-marina
✓ Blechnum magellanica

✓ Poa (Parodiochloa flabellata
Apium australe
Carex trifida
Luzula alopecurus
Senecio littoralis
Poa alopecurus
Agropyron magellanicum
Pratia repens
Aster vahlii
Rubus geoides
Rostkovia magellanica
Eleocharis melanostachys
schoizeroides

Rostkovia
magellanica
30-35cm

Drosera uniflora
Astelia pumila
✓ Senecio candicans
Poa robusta
Crassula moschata
Armeria macloviana
✓ Hebe elliptica
Chiliotrichum diffusum

5cm

Blechnum
magellanicum

Poa (Parodiochloa) flabellata

LOG OF THE *Southern Saracen*
Anchored at the Auroras
Date: Thurs., 24 Feb. 2000   Hours: 1025   Fathoms: 6
Wind: WNW 282°   Force: 6 / Strong Breeze
Barometer: 30.08 falling rapidly
Temp. Air: 9°C   Water: 9°C
Remarks: High cirrus 2/10, cumulus thickening 6/10.
Sunrise: 0610   Sunset: 1959

The most westerly, largest island is my home away from home. My beach, somewhat sheltered by an arm of low land that circles round from the north, is actually a fascinating microcosm of South Atlantic life, teeming with all kinds of interesting goings-on. There are four different kinds of limpets. I know, what's so exciting about a limpet? They're Aurora limpets, that's what! And clams and mussels, blue and ribbed.

At first I thought there were no freshwater springs, but I was wrong. About 300 feet south of here there is one barely perceptible trickle that drains redly into the sea. It's responsible for a couple of pools, puddles really, that the penguins have successfully fouled. Tried drinking from where the water emerges; however, there's a strong peat taste that matches the unhealthy ochre colour. If I had a test kit, I'm sure I'd find a billion particles of something to the cubic inch.

The lack of fresh water reminds me how ill-prepared I am. If I had known the things I know now about being at sea, I never would have done this. I take so much for granted on land; taking *anything* for granted at sea is certain doom. I completely misjudged clothing, water, paper, books, equipment. And fuel. If I could have stowed sufficient fuel, I wouldn't be so dependent upon sailing, but I have to make sure I can get back to the Falklands. I've also come to realize that having a moderately developed survival instinct is not good enough out here. Although it could be argued that any survival instinct at all would have warned me to leave that stupid globe alone. Here I am instead, caught in the solitude of my own mistakes.

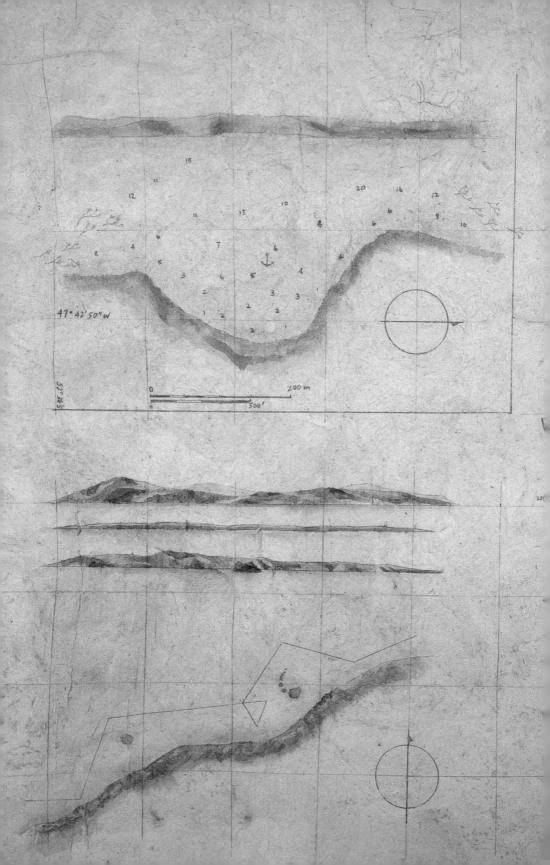

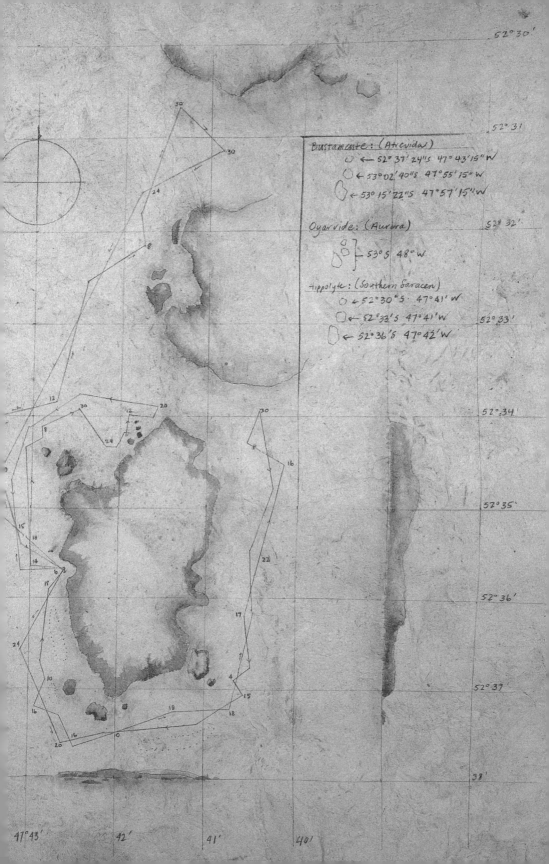

52°30'

52°31'

Bustamente: (Atrevida)
     ↙ ← 52° 37' 24"S 47° 43' 15" W
     ○ ← 53° 02' 40"S 47° 55' 15" W
     ○ ← 53° 15' 22"S 47° 57' 15"½ W

Oyarvide: (Aurora)

     ○○]—53°S 48°W

52°32'

Hippolyte: (Southern Saracen)
     ○ ← 52° 30"S 47° 41' W
     ○ ← 52° 33'S 47° 41' W
     ○ ← 52° 36'S 47° 42' W

52°33'

52°34'

52°35'

52°36'

52°37'

38'

47°43'   42'   41'   40'

Ten

LOG OF THE *Southern Saracen*
Anchored at the Auroras
Date: Fri., 25 Feb. 2000   Hours: 0830   Fathoms: 6
Wind: NW 324°   Force: 6 / Strong Breeze
Barometer: 29.20   Temp. Air: 6°C   Water: 9°C
Remarks: Thick low cumulus 10/10.   Sunrise: 0612? Sunset: 1957

Last night I was tempted by the Sirens to beach the boat. The sky looked hellish; I could feel a storm coming up. Logic told me to get on land rather than ride it out. So I raised the anchors—had enough sense to close the ventilators and clear the deck—then got as far as pointing the bow landward and opening my trusty sailing guide to "Landing on a Beach." It was encouraging: "Landing on a surf-bound coast is always a perilous operation, and one that requires great skill and coolness." I barely managed to read the next sentence, which advised the navigator to judge whether the waves were breaking before the shore or on the beach itself—well, *I* couldn't tell—when a really big wave hit. I was on my own.

Fortunately, the ebbing tide (not sure if it's really ebbing tide or just retreating waves) pushed me farther away, and I got a chance to pick up the sodden manual and find my place. I read on. I read that a boat coming straight in on a wave will have the bow depressed, giving any breaking waves a chance to force the bow under. It said I'd be better off backing in, stern first. Just try that yourself! By now I was quite far out and was feeling a hell of a lot better for the distance. It gave me a chance to think this through more rationally. Just what was

I supposed to do once I was beached? How was I supposed to get back into the water? Give the boat a nice shove? Wait for high tide? What if this was high tide? What time was all this happening, anyway? Must have been around 1930 hours. Let's see the tide chart. It's for Stanley; does it correspond? There certainly isn't one for the Auroras! Here. Feb. 24. Low tide. Anyway, the author of my book turned enigmatic, enthusing that "equal skill" would be necessary to get off the beach. Although I didn't understand the first part of the next sentence: "unless way can be kept on the boat." I sure understood the last part: "she will probably be thrown broadside on and capsize." Then I remembered: the keel! If I beached the boat, that'd be it, no more boat. I couldn't believe I'd forgotten that!

I dropped both anchors again, something I should have done first. Then I opened up my *Beginner's Guide to Sailing* to the index: Storms, 192–93, 202, 204, 210. Page 192: "The sailor who finds himself in the midst of a storm should make for safe harbor as quickly as possible." Thanks. Page 193: "Given that the storm is breaking while the boat is anchored offshore and that finding a sheltered position is out of the question, the sailor would be best advised to ride it out at some distance from the shore where the possibility of being driven onto a reef is unlikely. Ensure that all sails have been lowered, that the boat is properly anchored, and loose equipment and supplies are secured."

This was far better advice. I'm all set.

The wind blew something fierce all night and is still howling. A strong gale, at least force 9, with rolling seas, high waves, lots of spray. The proverbial "if I ever get out of this place" is going through my head like that insane pop song. If I ever get out, what? Go to church? Settle down? The wind's subsided a bit now, but still a gale, far too energetic for me to weigh anchor. Opening the hatch just resulted in an unwelcome shower of water. Oh hell, everything's soaked. Hey, fresh water! It's raining!

Hours: 0915

A tarp's now ready to collect the rain with the excess draining into a spare bucket. And the water jugs are outside, securely wedged, so they don't tip over. Unlikely much water will get into them, though; the necks are pretty narrow.

There's probably been more written about riding out storms than all the other things that happen at sea. Above all, it just plain gets on your nerves—the wind, especially, constantly trying to insinuate itself into every crack and crevice, to explode and destroy; its relentless painful bellow, like some stranger come in the night, banging at the door, supplicating, "Let me in, I need help, I mean no harm. Just let me in." And the boards bend and shiver like they're giving up, snapping; the stray lines whip about, adding to the cacophony; the tins I forgot to put away roll about in the galley, crashing from side to side. And the dinghy—its wood-splintering assaults on the starboard hull grinding into my brain—damage is going to be appalling. All this noise, apocalyptic, like the end of the earth, like a hellish crew mutinying. It could send a man completely mad. I can't let down my guard; I don't know what you're supposed to do in these situations. I know about taking cover in a rock shelter against the side of a mountain, I know about holing up in a tent in a desert sandstorm. That's land.

Water is dripping down the walls, from the rain and waves breaking over the side. The cabin floor, or whatever the hell it's called, is awash to the tune of a good 4 inches. I could bail; I could try to get the pump working—should have done that and pumped out the bilge when I first realized this was coming—or I could just go to sleep.

Hours: 1210
Wind: ?°   Force: 1 / Light Air
Barometer: 29.10 steady   Temp. Air: 6°C   Water: ?°C
Remarks: Thick low cumulus 10/10. Sunrise: 0612? Sunset: 1957
The wind has stopped; I think the rain's stopped, too. It's awfully quiet out there, not even the sound of the waves. I remember now, the floor is not a floor, it's a sole. Absurd marine talk. It's snowing!

LOG OF THE *Southern Saracen* ·
Anchored at the Auroras
Date: Sat., 26 Feb. 2000   Hours: 0940   Fathoms: 6
Wind: variable   Force: 2 / Light Breeze
Barometer: 29.42 rising   Temp. Air: 7°C   Water: 9°C
Remarks: Unlimited visibility, thin, high altostratus 2/10

Pump sputtered for a few seconds; will look at that later. Spent yesterday afternoon bailing. Can now walk in the cabin instead of wade. Fortunately, paper stuff was off the floor, otherwise there's nothing that can't be dried out. Wasn't such a bad day in the end; the air warmed up rapidly with the shifting of the wind from the west to the northwest, and the snow melted as it fell; there wasn't really a lot to begin with.

I've set up the tarp on shore and stored a few supplies—a lantern, fuel, water, some food—as a caution against future storms. I'm close to the gentoo colony (upwind!); they're very hospitable; they've already inspected the camp. I think they're looking for things to swipe.

Hardly a scrape where the dinghy plowed into the boat. Like I was imagining it all. There's a hell of a lot of water in it though, almost half sunk. That leak. I have to figure out how to fix it.

LOG OF THE *Southern Saracen*
Anchored at the Auroras
Date: Mon., 28 Feb. 2000   Hours: 0825
Wind: SE?   Force: 1 / Light Air
Barometer: 29.20 falling rapidly   Temp. Air: 5°C Water: 10°C
Remarks: Nimbostratus 10/10

Safe here under my tarp, watching the old weather. Something's in the air. It's cold today but deathly calm. The barometer continues to fall, and the clouds, having thickened and lowered impressively from last night's high cirrus, are really black. The air is heavy with moisture; it sticks to the skin, in the bones.

In the 15 minutes since I've been watching the sky, the wind has picked up and rain is starting to fall. Double-check the ropes holding down the tarp.

Everything is secure. The sea is quite rough now, whitecaps, even in my little bay. Farther out it's hard to say; visibility is practically nil. The rain's coming down in sheets!

Hours: 1038
Well, that was impressive. Thank goodness it's over. Barometer has stopped falling. Can't see much past the boat, the low clouds are that thick. I'll get back to work. So calm again, so quiet.

Hours: 1415
Wind: wsw 190°   Force: 8 / Fresh Gale
Barometer: ?   Temp. Air: 4°C   Water: ?°C
Remarks: Cumulus 10/10
The wind's come up again. It's subsided to force 8, but for what seemed hours it was stronger, a hurricane almost. I'm writing with my back to it; it's difficult to even hold the pen, but I have to get this down while I can still feel it. The wind blew so hard, it literally snapped the ropes holding down the tarp; it shredded the plastic sheeting, ripping out the grommets; it nearly whipped the skin off my bones. My eyes wrapped themselves around the sides of my head; my nose flattened; my teeth jammed into the roof of my mouth. Tears and snot streamed out of my eyes and nose. I couldn't see; I couldn't breathe. I was drowning in all that air.

I understand what it is to drown in an ocean, the sea, a bathtub. In water, the body itself is a willing accomplice, aiding and abetting through its own delusions of weightlessness and immortality. The weight of the water pressing in against chest, arms, thighs, abdomen, everywhere, replacing the nerves, transforming the body, a fatal illusion where the drowning one becomes the water in which he is drowning.

Air, on the other hand, at least this South Atlantic air, is an adversary. It has no names, as if in its wake its victims lose their powers to describe. Northeasterly, northwesterly, southerly, force 7, 8, 9. Its character deformed by its origins, its behaviour categorized by Beaufort. Its personality a mystery to be discovered only in the midst of struggle. It slashes and swirls; it fights. It claws its way up my nostrils and across my mouth, like a hand clapped firmly across my face. And it stinks, too. Stinks of seaweed and bird shit. And it fills the lungs, only it's worse than water. Water knows when to stop, but air keeps coming in, inflating the cavities till you have no choice but to burst.

I didn't come all this way by sea only to drown on land.

Hours: 1550   Fathoms: 6
Wind: NNW 334°   Force: 2 / Calm
Barometer: 29.85 rising
Temp. Air: 6°C   Water: ?°C
Remarks: Cumulus 8/10

This morning's tempest just about did me in. Still haven't got my breath back. I don't know if I would have been better off on the boat, or if I made the right decision to stay put. Maybe there wasn't any choice; it came up really fast, hit like a sledgehammer. Was caught about a half a mile from the camp and got drenched, not that there was much left of the shelter by the time I managed to get back. Serves me right for not knowing my meteorology! Worried myself sick about what was happening to the boat which was probably good 'cause it stopped me from worrying about myself. I've just rowed over to check it out, and everything seems to be okay. The dinghy's leak is worsening; I wonder how much longer I'll be able to use it. The clouds, which were dark and heavy up until an hour ago, are starting to dissipate. Bits of blue are brightening the sky. It's kind of hard to do anything right now.

Hippolyte's frustration with water grew; his knowledge of land was useless, his attempts to learn about the sea futile. A kind of wave, seen, memorized, identified—crests at so many inches, falls at such a rate—

disappears, never to be seen again. What use is this learning?, he asked as he looked out over the waves. What does color mean? The water turns from blue to green to gray to black and back again, as easily as the winds brush its surface. Indicative of what? The stain of oily brown that rings the islands is easy; that's giant kelp—*Macrocystis pyrifera*—slapping its tangled masses of stems and leaves and bladders against the sea's ceiling. But this slate gray over here must mean that something happening above is reflected like a mirror: a darkening cloud; a dulling, flattening sky. That azure there must mean something special is happening below: a change of the composition of the ocean floor, black rock giving way to white sand, perhaps? It smells so intensely blue, a safe smell, not like the terrifying reds where sheets of krill amass. "What am I missing? What can't I see from the deck of this boat?" he cried out loud in frustration. Is there a school of fishes darting about below like a herd of fat-tailed sheep? Or is the frigid polar current winding its way through the depths like a cold-blooded snake? And the black over there, in the distance, the black hole fringed by delicate white wavelets, the black hole that looks like the entrance to Hell. Does that mean the bottom of the sea is within reach, or is it a million miles away? Fathomless?

Sound the depths! There was a thrilling ring to that phrase. He flung his Brooke's Deep-Sea Sounder overboard. The bottom was always deeper than the length of his line. He hauled it back in and contemplated the water once more.

There were too many tides. Their ebbing flooding surges eroded his certainties, drained him of self. There were too many currents. Each stole his assumptions, creating in their undulating course a being once resolute, now awash with uneasy contradictions. The depths were too great; histories and prehistories had been swept away and sunk. Their cries from the deep were too faint, too cold, too sodden. Even when the surface is calm and inviting, the ocean is no better than a cunning false friend, luring you down into the always icy depths.

LOG OF THE *Southern Saracen*
Anchored at the Auroras
Date: Tues., 29 Feb. 2000   Hours: 0930   Fathoms: 6
Wind: Variable from the w   Force: 2 / Light Breeze
Barometer: 30.11 steady   Temp. Air: 11°C   Water: 10°C
Remarks: Mixed cumulus and altocumulus 4/10

Much better night. Calm. The storms really do seem to be over, at least
for a bit. The water's topped up again; I figured out an improved way
to cook meals by finally reading the instructions. You let the dehydrated flakes soak for a long time before heating them up. Saves fuel
and seems to pull a bit more flavour out of them. Better than the ined-
ible mush I've been enduring.

For some reason I brought an amazing number of boxes of crackers, which is funny because I rarely eat them. What's worse is these are
the brittle masochistic kind with no flavour whatsoever, not even salt.
I think you're supposed to stick something interesting on them, like a
nice fat cheese or big plump prawns. Olive spread. Parma ham. Nuts
and dried fruit would have been a much wiser choice; chocolate
wouldn't have been out of place either. And this broccoli soup I'm
cooking up now would benefit from a glass of that pleasant Chilean
Chardonnay. Cooled in the ocean to 10°C, surprisingly rich and thick
for a white, I can taste it just as it's about to trickle down my throat.
I'd have one glass at a time, diligently stretch it out over a few days. I
could get 4 glasses of about 185 ml each, or 5 at 150 ml, to a 750 ml
bottle; that way, if I'd brought 5 bottles, they would last from 20 to 25
days. There they are, with their embossed golden labels, lined up on
the shelves of the Stanley Co-op. I looked at them; thought about it,
for all of two seconds. What did they cost? Around £10, if I remember correctly. $24.00. Struck me as too expensive at the time; hah! a
mere bagatelle. I'd pay a hundred dollars for a bottle of wine now. I
don't even care what kind. There's some kind of austerity program
happening here, and it's hard to believe that I was in on the decision-
making process.

Chocolate reminds me of something. I did bring chocolate. Somewhere, there are a couple of chocolate Power Bars that I hid in case of emergency. This is an emergency. The ingredients sounded outrageous, but if there's chocolate in them, they can't be all bad. Where the hell did I put them?

The weight is sloughing off of me, and it's not like I have a lot to spare. I haven't shaved since the morning I left the Falklands, and I haven't combed my hair, either; I finally washed it yesterday morning. Took the bandage off my hand for the first time in days. Yech. I'll keep it off for now and let the air get to it.

But, as I said, things have improved. It's a shame that I've wasted almost two days, but look on the bright side, without the storms I'd be on my last container of water and desperately hoarding dew! I'll get back to work now. There's lots to do; for a start, these islands need a history. It's up to me to create one now that I've established their existence. My history will go back far before the first sighting by the *Aurora*, back to when they were formed. I'll chronicle the seas that have washed over them through the millennia, the vegetation that has taken root, the birds that migrate to their shores, the fishes that have swum round them. The climate, geology, biology. Their existence will be supported with facts and figures, undeniable proof that they are here and that I set foot upon them.

I'll establish a weather station; I'll collect specimens; I'll chart the contours of the land and show the rookeries where penguins nest, the concentrations of grasses, the beaches where seals wallow. My methods will be precise and thorough; my facts will be irrefutable.

I must start by naming each of the islands. At this moment only the grouping has a name. The Auroras. Named after a Spanish ship. Named after the Roman goddess of the dawn. Named after the fires in the polar skies. Aurora australis, southern lights, merry dancers.

These islands, these so-called "airy nothings," as Morrell called them, have appeared with great authority on maps from Spain, of course, and from Italy, France, Russia, and Britain: Las Islas de la Aurora, Isoles dell Aurora, Les Isles de l'Aurore, Kamni Avrory, the

Auroras. But Aurora alone is not enough, beautiful though it is; they're each different, they've each got their own distinct identity and secrets. This isn't a matter of a couple of rocks here; these are living places.

Because the Spanish first discovered them, the Auroras should have Spanish names. Aurora, Princesa and Atrevida, after the ships that spotted them, would be good. Aurora—Princesa—Atrevida. Atrevida. Doesn't sound much like the name of a place. What does it mean? *Atre, atra,* something to do with contradicting, crossing. *Vida,* to see? to be empty? No, life, of course. Crossing life. I could solve this pretty easily by looking it up in my Spanish dictionary. One of those indispensable books that I couldn't leave behind. Let's see. *Atre-verse, atrevido. Atrevido:* bold, impudent. Not so bad after all.

Okay, I will settle this for once and for all; the cluster is called the Auroras, the main island will be called Aurora, the middle, Princesa, and the smallest, Atrevida. Maybe with its feisty new name Atrevida will battle to stay afloat.

Then—if I'm going to do this history correctly—I could give them a succession of names. The Falklands, for example, underwent many changes: Islas de los Patos, Yslas de Sanson, Southern Isles, Hawkins' Maiden Land, Sebald Islands, Îles Malouines, Islas Malvinas, Falkland's Land, to name but a few. I'd continue to call the overall grouping the Auroras, but what could I change the individual islands to? Maybe, I'll take a cue from places with names like Cape of Good Success, Cape Circumcision and Inaccessible Island and be more descriptive, tell a bit of a story. Trouble is, nothing but weather's happened here.

Or I could name one of them after me. That's it; I'll make my name part of their secret history. That'd be just about the most conceited thing I've ever done in my life. Why not? Hippolyte's Island. Sounds all right. Sounds rather grand actually, no matter how you pronounce it: Hip-o-lite's Island; I-po-leete's Island; Hip-o-lee-tay's Island.

√Tonicia chilensis—Elegant
Chiton: the birds pick them up
and dash them on the rocks

√Barnacles: proper name?
√Limpets: Nacella concinna (slow-growing variety)
  √Nacella deaurata—Golden limpets
  √Fissurella picta: Key-hole limpet. Everywhere!
√Mussels: Not noted on map, very common
  and profuse: Mytilus edulis—Common blue
  Choromytilus chorus—Chorus mussel, v. large
    √Trophon geversianus—Gevers' trophon
      Incredible range of sizes and
      colours
        √Rough Thorn Drupe—
          Acanthina monodon

Fissurella picta

Trophon geversianus

adonto cymbola
magellanica

adelomelon ancilla

gevers trophon

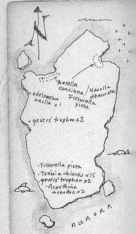

Nacella
concinna / Nacella
· adelomelon   deaurata
ancilla x 1   Fissurella
               picta
· gevers trophon x2

· Fissurella picta
· Tonicia chilensis x 15
  gevers trophon x2
  · Acanthina
    monodon x 2

AURORA

Acanthina
monodon

Skolithos: made by worm-like
animals which cause vertical
pipes. Lived in the sand on
the Devonian sea floor
(c. 400 million years ago).
Brachiopods (shellfish)
Plants: Lower Cretaceous:
    Pagiophyllum
     insigne
    Bellarinea
     barklyi
    Taeniopteris
     daintreei
    Cladophlebis
     oblonga

Hausmannia
   dichotoma
Phlebopteris
   dunkeri
Gonatosorous
   nathorsti
Ginkgo huttoni
Glossopteris
  sp, inc. indica

Diocroidium sp. Inc. odontopteroides, Verteberaria indica, Gunnarites sp. (Ammonite),
Cheiracanthus sp. Pecopteris sp. (below, right, resembles fern), Aporrhais (Tessarolax)
antarctica sp., Rotularia australis sp., Devonian
invertebrate fossils: Trilobites, Annelids, Cephalopods

Gastropods:
Bellerophon
(Plectonotus)
quadrilobata
Brachiopods: Derbyina
Lower Cretaceous
gastropods:
Inoceramus sp.
Pecten argentinus
Cyprina sp
Thracia sp
Spaera? Striata

ammonite

Eleven

THE STORMS HAD LONG PASSED and though the seas had continued high and the air, crisp, South was fulfilling its fair promise, presenting one beautiful day after the next. The ocean had relented and was almost placid; the sun, for a few hours at least, was surprisingly strong. The mercury crawled up to 10°C, an accomplishment that bestowed untold pleasure. With the lack of wind, it felt, if anything, twice that. The sun's rays beat down against his bare back, for he'd stripped his shirt off at the first hint of warmth. Accustomed to wearing as little as possible whenever possible, Hippolyte had been fermenting under all of the heavy gear: the flannels, the sweaters, the oilskins, the boots, and the life jacket (when he remembered to put it on). As the sun baked his skin, he filled out his log, taking advantage of the absolute stillness of the water.

LOG OF THE *Southern Saracen*
From: Around the Auroras   Towards: Aurora Harbour
Date: Thurs., 2 March 2000   Hours: 1430
Knots: 2   Fathoms: 6 to 10
Wind: None   Force: 1 / Lt. Air
Barometer: 30.10   Temp. Air: 10°C   Water: 10°C
Remarks: High cirrus mare's tails 2/10, lower scattered cumulus 3/10
Lat: 52°35′S   Long: 47°43′W   Var: 002°W   Course: 020°C

Have completed the first entire circumnavigation of my islands and managed—at low tide—to land on both Princesa and Atrevida. It's been a very successful day, so far, but I just realized, as I was coming along to where I'm now anchored, at the north tip of Aurora, that something has been eating at me. I map features, then can't find them again; I count birds, then they disappear. I don't know what it is, but I get the impression that I'm seeing things that aren't there.

He closed the book, glanced at his watch—2:38—stood up, and, hands clenching the boom, stretched luxuriously. You find days like this in paradise, he thought, not in the South Atlantic. He studied his lean frame, whittled by seasickness and Spartan meals. His appetite was back to normal now that he'd become accustomed to the rolling motion of the boat and had improved on his cooking. He stamped his feet on the cockpit's slatted, varnished boards, flapped his arms, rolled his head upon his stiff neck, flexed his fingers and toes.

The same rays that warmed him shone upon the smooth surface of the sea. He slipped his hand into the water, let the water caress his fingers; it too felt of—not heat, but a softly tempered coolness. The injury was healing in fits and starts; a long scab stretched across the knuckles. The submerged wound pulsed; he winced as the stinging salt water worked its way across.

The ocean temperature remained constant at 10°C. The air temperature was the same, and it was positively balmy. He stepped back, braced his feet unnecessarily against non-existent motion, and looked away from the island and out to the horizon. Sheer nothingness taunted him, and all the while the sun grew hotter.

Water struck the hull, slapping a rhythmic chant that harmonized with the boat's gentle sway. Little ripples erupted and sped along the surface away from him. He wanted to follow them, to see where they went when they disappeared. The sun's rays pushed against him as though they were hands urging him onward.

He shed his remaining clothes. His jeans and shoes joined the shirt doffed earlier. He tore off his watch, letting it fall, not caring where it landed. Then he dove into the ocean. He dove in unprepared for the shock of the cold lurking below. His muscles collapsed, his lungs screamed, his brain revolted, he nearly fainted. A frigid grip seized each part of his body—his head, his neck, his torso—as he sliced through the surface of the water. It tightened itself around him, like leather straps, squeezing so forcefully that blood and air were bursting to escape, to explode.

The painful understanding that he had just unleashed himself into an empty, lonely sea with no one around to save him was terrifying. Only a breath away from the Antarctic Convergence, here he was toying with the coldest, densest water on earth. He struggled to resurface, but he couldn't. He mouthed a soundless MOVE! Neither his arms nor his legs would obey. When he finally surfaced—how he had done so, he had no idea—he gasped to regain his breath. The reassuring serenity of the air settled upon him and calmed him. He turned to face the boat, but both it and the island had vanished from sight.

Panic surged again like a welling sickness. Round and round he whirled, a compass crazily demagnetized out of its 360° sweep. His dizzy spinning finally stopped and he took hold of himself, tried to rationalize the void surrounding him. He had to think it through.

He hadn't moved, so the boat must have drifted. But how could it have strayed in these calm conditions when it had held rock steady through the storms? And even if it had, he should still be able to see Aurora. He had turned so many times, how could he reestablish direction? Why hadn't he thought of the utter disorientation that such panic would induce? He looked to the sun, determined West, revolved 180° to face what would presumably be the way back to the island, then methodically studied the horizon in 30° segments starting from East. By the time he returned to 90°E, he was thoroughly discouraged.

Never had he felt such cold in his life. As he tread the water, he fluttered his arms and got a glimpse of his already pickled and pasty hands. Then, as his limbs quickly solidified, he thrashed about violently, urging the blood to flow faster. He reconsidered his situation. How fast does hypothermia set in? What are its first signs? He was probably on the verge of collapse. Disjointed thoughts crowded in: a comedy routine heard sometime long in the past in which God asks Noah, "How long can you tread water?"; the realization that he still had an old girlfriend's key in the pocket of the jeans now lying ownerless on the deck; the joy of receiving Jeremy's check, the despair that he might not live long enough to spend it all. He remembered that the apples onboard were smelling ripe and he must eat them right away, that water exerted a pressure of 60 pounds per square inch or was that per square foot?, and that he had coiled one of the lines counterclockwise and must recoil it first thing or it would be hopelessly kinked.

Think!, you idiot, he admonished himself. He couldn't be so far from the reefs that he wouldn't be able to see bottom at some point. The water was clear enough, but oddly, all of its residents had skedaddled. No signs of life, no fish, no lazily floating weeds or kelp, no blankets of plankton that usually obscured the water's surface. He was absolutely, absurdly alone.

If he dove down and established bottom, he'd be able to work his way back. Braced for a new onslaught of cold, shoving the threat of hypothermia to the back of his mind, he swam down as far as his strength could pull him, as deep as his lungs would carry him. But an overwhelming fear of depth forced him back to the surface. He took a deeper breath and tried again. Over and over he repeated the dive, the maneuver instilling in him the confidence that he would find his way back. But there was no bottom. How far out was he when he first dove off? Think! He resurfaced, sputtering air and water and confusion. Think harder! He'd been sailing south and had anchored off of Aurora's northwest tip. What was the distance from shore? Half a mile? No, it had to be far less than that. Two hundred, a hundred meters? Yes, around that. Three hundred feet. At his usual anchor seventy-five feet offshore, he'd figured that the bottom was some six fathoms deep. At how many feet per fathom? Six, right? That was already six times six, thirty . . . think! Brain's getting fogged. Thirty-six feet! It must be hundreds of feet deep here; no wonder he couldn't see bottom.

He looked to the sun and once again established East. He swam hard, counting his strokes, one two three four until it felt like he'd covered the length of a fifty-meter pool. He dove again. It all seemed so pointless, but what else could he do? The activity kept the cold at bay; his lungs grew stronger, allowing him to remain below longer, but each time he surfaced, he felt the transient heat of the day fade a little more, until the drop in temperature goaded him into trying harder. He dove again. And again. And again. How long had he been in the water? Time had lost its meaning, but it was passing all the same, still with no sign of the bottom or the boat or the island.

He wouldn't dream of giving up. How could he? Out of breath, with chest heaving, he left off scouring the depths and while submerged, rolled over in the water to contemplate the sky still glittering through the reflective surface. It was then that he saw the barnacled bottom of the boat hovering directly above him.

He shot up through the water. He suddenly became aware of fish darting about and of weeds clawing at his ankles, trying to drag him back down. Aware as well of a paralyzing frigidity far more intense, more deadly than that he had just been struggling against. The boat creaked and moaned as if terrified, too, of the thought of being abandoned in this empty sea. Its low keening was accompanied by another distant sound, a far more disturbing lament: Neptune's ugly daughters upset that he'd escaped.

Hippolyte hauled himself up the ladder and flopped shivering onto the foredeck, his face and his chest and his legs straining to soak up what warmth was left in the boards. His mind was a zero; he could do no more than give in to the gentle rocking and contemplate a small puddle of water by his right hand. He tried to sweep it away, to disperse it, but his fingers weren't moving. Couldn't think straight. The image of a blanket flashed by. Then it was gone. Out of breath, panic senselessly surged back now that he was beyond danger. The insanity of his dive ricocheted through his chattering teeth. A throbbing melody rolled perversely around his brain, and he opened his mouth to sing "The Mermaid's Song." His lips stretched across his teeth, his tongue arched, his throat tightened as he tried to expel the words: *Now the Dancing Sunbeams play On the green and glassy Sea Come with me and we will go Where the rocks of coral grow of co - ral grow* the words stuck like a soundless skipping record for he could make no sound at all *fol - low me followfollow me Far be - - low the Ebbing tides* He rolled on his back; water drained from his nostrils *Stor - - my winds are far a—Fol – low followfollow.* He coughed suddenly, violently, retching seawater onto the deck. He dragged himself up on one arm and rested his head in his hand. Ugh! What was in his hair!? Sound finally escaped, a pathetic scream. Berserk, he batted frenziedly at a clinging strand of kelp. When it was at last disentangled, he stared at the van-quished shred of plant in disbelief.

What happened out there? Whatever it was, it didn't make any sense. He raised his arm and focused on his wrist, searching vainly for the hour amongst the hairs and goose bumps. Of course, he'd taken his watch off before diving in. He crawled back to the cockpit and patted the heap of clothes he'd abandoned: there was his knife, his pen, his log. No watch. On all fours, he searched high and low. It was not to be found. He looked out over the pushpit towards the island, now clearly visible, the rays of the sun reflecting off the spray-soaked rocks. The low, bright light was hard on the eyes, making him squint.

That was it! The sun got in his eyes; that's why he couldn't see any-thing. It's worse out in the water, all that reflection. No, that wasn't it; he knew that wasn't it at all. A piercing flash struck out a dazzling Morse. Momentarily blinded, he inched towards it: his watch, nestled amongst coiled line. As he fastened it around his wrist, he blinked the dancing spots out of his eyes, then focused on the one to twelve, the second, minute, hour hands. 2:43 he read. Was that possible? Hadn't he dived in at 2:38? Did all of this just happen in a short five minutes? He shook the timepiece; its reassuring reliable workings ticked on.

He trembled and collapsed back onto the deck. What am I doing here? I hate the sea, he gasped. I hate seawater. It leaves you covered with a sticky, salty crust instead of skin. The brine mats your hair, blisters your lips, parches you. You look and smell like someone drowned. Perhaps you are. You gulp and swallow against your will. A bitterness born of salt, sulphates, magnesia, and lime coats the mouth, sucks the water from your inner core. Metals: lead, copper, silver; poisons: arsenic, mercury; and animal wastes: mucus, shit, decomposing bodies, churn your stomach. The seaweed tangles itself around your feet and pulls you down, the fish come and taste your toes and fingers. The toes and fingers that above the surface have a healthy glow, pulse with healthy blood, down here are nothing more than helpless white appendages, drained of life. The little fish nibbling—harmless, pretty—how can they be so mistaken; you aren't dinner, for God's sake! The carelessly floating jellyfish collide with your face, their oozing gummy surface revolting, Medusa's horrifying caress of slime. And if you think yourself lucky to touch bottom, think again; the spiny urchins viciously slice through your feet.

Then birds come and gloat, screeching in your ears, mocking your rootedness, your love of land. They dive at you and peck at you and try to force you to go back, to leave this place. They know you for the prey you are; they land on your shoulders, climb onto your head, using your nose and your ears and your bottom lip as purchase for their clawing feet; they deftly ignore your attempts to bat them off. Then they show their absolute disdain and deposit stinking excreta in your path.

The sun joins this battle against you. No longer a benevolent source of warmth, now a malevolent monster—even in these high latitudes—it sharpens its rays on the glassy surface of the water and burns out your eyes, scorches your skin. Then, as if recanting, it sinks too low in the sky; it gives up all pretense at heat and radiates a devastating cold. But it's worse without the sun, bad though that is. Without the sun, the winds are fiercer, the rains pelt harder, the mists are thicker; the elements conspire to stir the seas into a boiling, roiling cauldron to which you are at the mercy. If it had mercy to give.

There's more: here night falls darker than any night on earth. When you're alone, when you're afraid, forget the stars and the moons and the planets; their frail illumination is no match for the dark. Forget the tales of phosphorescence and Saint Elmo's Fire. Forget the comforting glow of home fires burning on the shore or of ships passing in the night with hearty hellos belting across the water. At 52°36′ South and 47°43′ West there's nothing. The feeble light from the boat's lantern conspires with the night, making it blacker if possible, deader.

How the land is different! When you picked up earth, you rolled it in the palms of your hands, you got it under your fingernails, it stayed with you and smelt of good things, of living organisms, of the promise of growth. It had substance, and when you flung it back to the ground, you could see it as it fell and know that a plant could take root in it, this clump of earth that you had held in your own hands.

Hippolyte shook his head. He was safe on his boat; breath had fought its way back into his saturated lungs. His swim hadn't been nearly as terrifying as his delirium. Enough self-pity! He had work to do, a lifetime, no, many lifetimes of collecting, measuring, classifying, surveying. Thinking of the land brought him back to his senses; he buried his vague uncertainties and let his book well up and confront him. Up to this moment he had no idea what he would write about. Sure, he'd already vowed to write a history of the islands, but now it was clear. He would immortalize them. There would be papers given, more books written, a reputation established. He could see himself being interviewed on radio, a newly inducted member of the Royal Geographical Society, presented with its highest honors at the same time. Given the Order of whatever it is they give to people who discover new places. They'd probably have to dust it off. The last person to ever do anything like this would have been, maybe, Thesiger? He was made Sir Wilfred for his explorations. Hippolyte shrugged. He didn't want a knighthood.

His notebooks would be jammed with astonishing facts. He'd start with the Aurora's tectonics. He'd find out why Morrell and Weddell sailed right over them, why they don't appear on any aerial or satellite photographs. He'd go back to the fossil record, the Mesozoic, the Paleozoic, even, and would find traces of tropical life from an epoch when *south* really meant *south*. All along he'd been secretly harboring regrets that it wasn't richer, lusher, hot even, but look around! Barren on the surface, but hiding a wealth of material, raw, unspoilt, unknown. He'd construct a natural history that would put Humboldt, Lamarck, Cuvier, even Darwin to shame. He'd discover a new species—why just one?—maybe several, maybe dozens: fish, shellfish, insects, plants, reptiles, why couldn't this be a new Galápagos? He'd be a latter-day Linnæan apostle, making major contributions to botany, zoology. He'd . . . He remembered the boat. He had a scant two weeks left. Ah, the hell with it, if Peter wanted it back, he could come and get it. No he couldn't, could he? Peter thought he was tootling around the Falklands.

Hippolyte shivered again, frozen to the bone. He drew on his jeans, his shirt, felt them rasp against the salty surface of his skin, his skin that was now so tightly drawn about him, it was as if it had shrunk. He raised the anchor and chugged back to his familiar harbor.

That night sleep was elusive. The memory of his swim haunted him, and he was racked with deep shudders; he was desperately swimming, trying to find his way, not to the boat, to where? More than once he threw back the blankets to go and rescue himself, but finally managed to lay the image to rest. The nagging question of how he had lost the boat would not go away. Adding to this disquiet was the constant worry about the floating hazards that could crash into the boat, about the storms that might arise from nowhere and tear him from his anchorage, about the sheer blackness that encircled him. Mingling with the disjointed tempest of his thoughts was the incessant and disturbing game playing of his restless aquatic neighbors, the waves, who licked the hull, squeezed the boards until they groaned, and rocked the boat the way a delirious mother enfevered by discordant rhythms might rock the cradle of an unloved offspring. Hippolyte lay taut and tense, poised to spring and tackle whatever barnacle-encrusted intruder climbed up out of the deep. He could see the creature, amorphous except for the powerfully built arms it used to hoist itself up and over the side. It would have a long white beard braided with limpets and mussels. The beard would be alive and pulsating with thousands of tiny krill, all frantically waving their minuscule feet, trying to stay afloat. Criss-crossed with rhumb lines, dotted with wind roses, this venerable trespasser would lure Hippolyte back into the deep with its promise of direction.

The deck creaked and creaked again. Hippolyte's head shifted step by step with the noise as it crept along above him. His eyes were wide open, unseeing in the absolute darkness yet taking all in. A muffled thud shook him out of his bunk and had him rushing to the bottom of the gangway. Except that he tripped, fell awkwardly against the instrument crate, and tore away the skin of his arm on the edge of yet another badly placed box. He roared with pain. He sat where he had fallen, trying to recover his wits, holding on to his injured arm with the hand that was only just healing. The raucous creaking had become furious, but it had also become identifiable, the result of a rising wind, not the footsteps of a briny miscreant.

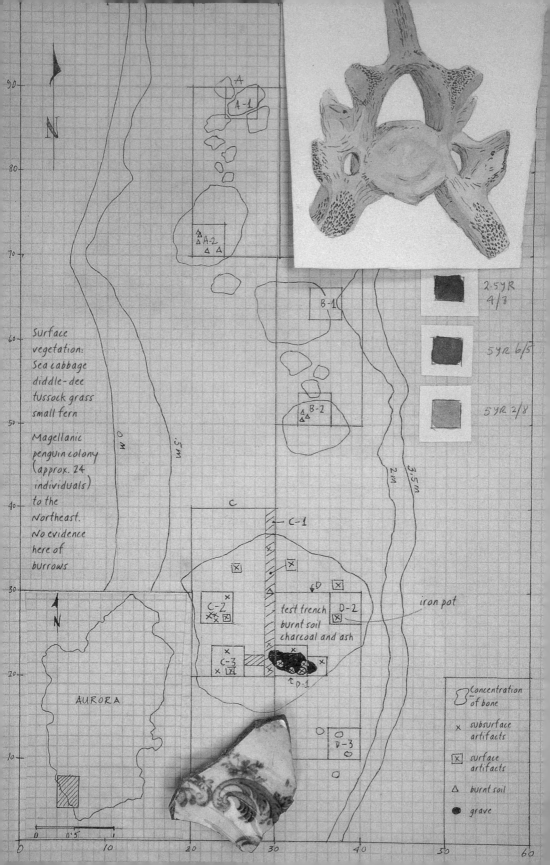

N

90

80

70

60 — Surface
vegetation:
Sea cabbage
diddle-dee
tussock grass
small fern

50   Magellanic
penguin colony
(approx. 24
individuals)

40 — to the
Northeast.
No evidence
here of
burrows

30

N

20   AURORA

10

0

A
A-1

△ A-2
△   △

.0 m   .5 m

B-1

△ B-2
△△

2 m   3.5 m

2.5YR
4/3

5YR 6/5

5YR 2/8

C
— C-1

⊠   ⊠

⌐D
C-2   ×   ⊠
×× ⊠   D-2
test trench   ⊠
burnt soil
× C-3   charcoal and ash
×⊠   iron pot

↑ D-1

○   D-3
○
○

Concentration
of bone

×   subsurface
artifacts

⊠   surface
artifacts

△   burnt soil

●   grave

0   0.5   1

0   10   20   30   40   50   60

Twelve

LOG OF THE *Southern Saracen*
Anchored at the Auroras
Date: Fri., 3 March 2000   Hours: 1120   Fathoms: 6
Wind: WNW 305°   Force: 3 / Breeze
Barometer: 30.06   Temp. Air: 10°C   Water: 10°C
Remarks: Clear, high cirrus 2/10
Lat: 52°36′S   Long: 47°43′W   Var: 002°W

"Hypothermia chills the core of the body and can kill within a matter of minutes." Dramatic yes, specific no. Let's see if there's anything
else here on the subject. Page 308: "Hypothermia . . . common after
immersion in water below 20°C." But 20 is warm! Or is it? "first signs
. . . intense shivering . . . uncontrollable . . . difficulty in speaking . . .
body temp. drops to c. 32–30°C., shivering decreases, patient becomes
clumsy, irritable, slurs his speech. Further heat loss leads to inability to
reason, loss of muscle control . . . slowed pulse, respiration. Temp. [at]
c. 27°C., victim loses consciousness, heartbeat becomes erratic . . . further drop in temp. results in death." [*Complete Sailing Manual*]

Finally found the chocolate Power Bars. Two of 'em. Ate one on the
spot. It tasted so good, but talk about working the old jaw. It gave me
an idea, though, while I was chewing away, so I softened up half of the
other one on the galley stove and plugged the dinghy's leak with it.
Covered the outer, exposed side with a skin of chewed gum.
Spearmint. Common sense says it'll all dissolve in the water, but it held
up on the row over here this morning. Got my fingers crossed.

Hum of a plane in the distance. What an odd sensation! I've just looked through the binoculars but can't see anything. Strange, there aren't any clouds; it should be visible. Hard time writing this, feel dizzy—maybe from staring too long at the sky—the ground is—seems to be—evaporating.

Can't hear it anymore. Bizarre. I literally felt the earth melt below me.

That fall last night has really given me a run for the money. I ripped a slice out of my upper arm and now have a shocking bruise to boot. Bled all over Peter's blankets. Was stuck to them this morning. Didn't realize in the dark just how gruesome it was. All bandaged up now, put back together. Hurts? Yeah, but who's going to kiss it better?

My notes are giving over and becoming a record of my clumsiness. And idiocy—I've run out of film! Ransacked the bags—nothing—how many rolls wasted on pictures of birds? What a disaster. Polaroids were used up days ago.

Speaking of birds, I'm watching petrels right now. Where the albatross soars, these southern giants swagger. They're also called stinkers, and they rip their prey out of the waters in big, bloody, smelly fights. Still, they're cautious, timid even, and have an astonishing sense of self-preservation, abandoning their babes at the slightest provocation. I took advantage of their absence once and approached the nestlings, who, unlike their mothers and fathers, made no move whatsoever to ruffle their comfort. They shift themselves, stretching already formidable wing, detaching tufts of soft baby feather with impatient beaks. Feathers and down, which I have collected samples of, exude that now-familiar petrel odour.

Hours: 1415

It's just come back, the plane, heading west this time. It's got to be down around 500 feet; the din is sensational. Damned if I can see a thing! I'm sitting on a rock alongside a sandy ridge on the northwest coast of Aurora. I trained the binoculars right at the heart of the sound, and there was nothing. No plane, no down rush of wind, but I waved anyway, in case whoever's up there can see me. When I put down the glasses, my hand went right through the stone, into air; I'm suspended in transparent fog. I can see down into the heavy swells of the water below me. What's keeping me from falling in?

The plane's gone again and the ground has solidified, closed up under my feet. But feels amorphous all the same.

LOG OF THE *Southern Saracen*
Anchored at the Auroras
Date: Sat., 4 March 2000   Hours: 1105   Fathoms: 6
Wind: NNW 320°   Force: 4 / Mod. Breeze
Barometer: 30.05   Temp. Air: 9°C   Water: 9°C
Remarks: Stratus 10/10. No visibility. In other words, fog

Yesterday afternoon, after I worked up the nerve to walk—legs shaking, weak, drained—I managed to row back to the boat and just went to sleep. A heavy, dreamless sleep. Didn't wake up until 8 this morning. So I guess that's what that was all about; I still haven't caught up with my sleep and I was hallucinating. That's what it must have been, sheer hallucination.

At any rate, no question of the islands disintegrating this morning! Very interesting day so far. Doing a metre-by-metre survey of the beach toward the southernmost tip of Aurora and found a piece of driftwood, on which I can just make out the carved initials G.T.; and the names Corona and St. John. There are traces of some sort of ochre paint or colouring over the carved-out letters, possibly constituted from the red soils at this end of the island. There might have been a date as well, but if so, it's been rubbed away. There is also an amazing amount of very weathered seal bone (too small for whale and too porous for land mammal), and I'm wondering if I haven't stumbled across a sealer's camp. If so, that means that someone else actually landed here at some point. I just reread this paragraph. Funny how you write something that is so important and when you reread it, it sounds as riveting as a trip to the grocery store. This is bloody staggering! I am very excited; it proves that the islands existed all the time when others were trying to find it!

Is there a logbook out there in some archive that records the finding of the island? If so, it would be a matter of me digging some more to find it. Speaking of digging, this is the perfect spot to conduct an impromptu archaeological excavation—some random pits—to see if I can find harpoons or knives, anything cast off by the sealers. Now, I didn't bring a spade or a trowel; I wonder if there's something useful hidden away on the boat. Man, this is an unexpected turn of events.

LOG OF THE *Southern Saracen*
Anchored at the Auroras

Date: Sun., 5 March 2000   Hours: 1315   Fathoms: 6
Wind: NNW 320°   Force: 4 / Mod. Breeze
Barometer: 29.98   Temp. Air: 10°C   Water: 9°C
Remarks: Stratus 6/10

I dug a test trench with a collapsible spade I found stowed in the hold and uncovered a layer of burnt soil mixed with charcoal and ash.

Another pit 2 metres farther inland yielded rusted bits from an iron pot. Estimating from the curves of the pieces found, I reckon that it was a significant size, a metre or slightly more, in diameter. A portion of a handle discovered nearby substantiates that conclusion. Several fragments of china were scattered about, as was a clay pipe stem. Could use another hand at this work! My injured arm is slowing me down. I'll pick up speed in a day or two. Maybe the phantom of one of the sealers will materialize and help me fill in the missing details!

LOG OF THE *Southern Saracen*
Anchored at the Auroras
Date: Mon., 6 March 2000   Hours: 1507   Fathoms: 6
Wind: NNW 310°   Force: 3 / Breeze
Barometer: 29.97   Temp. Air: 9°C   Water: 9°C
Remarks: Stratus 3/10

Unbelievable! Shouldn't have said anything about ghosts! Have just uncovered a grave. Man, this has put the bejeesus into the whole operation. Face it, Webb, you thought you were here alone! Not anymore, not with these bones, for Christ sake. His skull has been smashed in a couple of places; so has one of the femurs; I'll note those carefully. Some teeth, several phalanges are missing.

This puts me into a dilemma. Since I've run out of goddamn film, I can't take pictures. Idiot. I could remove some of the remains; the skull would be the most meaningful part. But what would it prove? Then the site would be tampered with, who knows, even ruined, for if and when I come back with a proper team to excavate. My best bet is to sketch it, try to pick up features that will help determine age and such.

On the other hand, if I did carefully document the position of the skull before I removed it, then carefully packed it, maybe I could chance taking it with me. Something's not right about this. What if I capsized the boat? What if I forgot it at an airport? What's the deal on taking this kind of thing through customs? Anything to declare? Just human remains, sir. I'd have to go through the Falklands, Chile, the U.S., home, that's four times the risk of getting caught and it being confiscated.

I must be bothered by the idea of dismantling this human being who has lain for decades, maybe even a century or more, undisturbed on an island that no one recognizes anymore. If only I hadn't run out of film, I wouldn't be sitting here arguing out this quandary; I'd shoot some pictures and be done with it. Let's get going and finish our work. Face it, we're not going to take anything.

SU...

DA...

H.C.

SSTA.   FORWARD   REVERSE   MEA...

① 1.9 cm

2.5 cm

② 2 cm   5y 2/8

0.6 cm

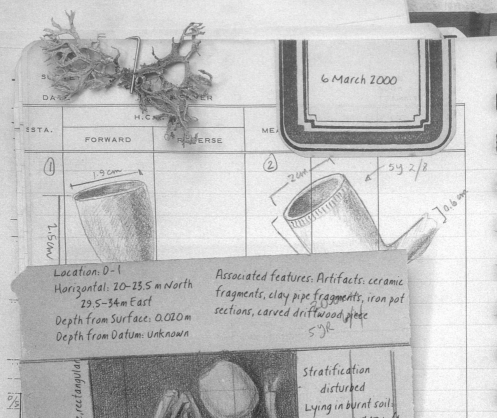

Location: D-1
Horizontal: 20-23.5 m North
    29.5-34 m East
Depth from Surface: 0.020 m
Depth from Datum: Unknown

Associated features: Artifacts: ceramic
fragments, clay pipe fragments, iron pot
sections, carved driftwood piece
5YR

Flexed burial
Head to west
Surface grave, rectangular

0/s
S
0.50S
0/s

Stratification
  disturbed
Lying in burnt soil:
  Munsel 5YR 6/4
Nearby: charcoal,
ash assoc. with iron
pot
Condition: missing
phalanges on left
hand, crushed
occiput, missing
upper left inscisor
and both 1st & 2nd
premolars. Otherwise,
good.
Age: ?, mature
Sex: Male probably

1m

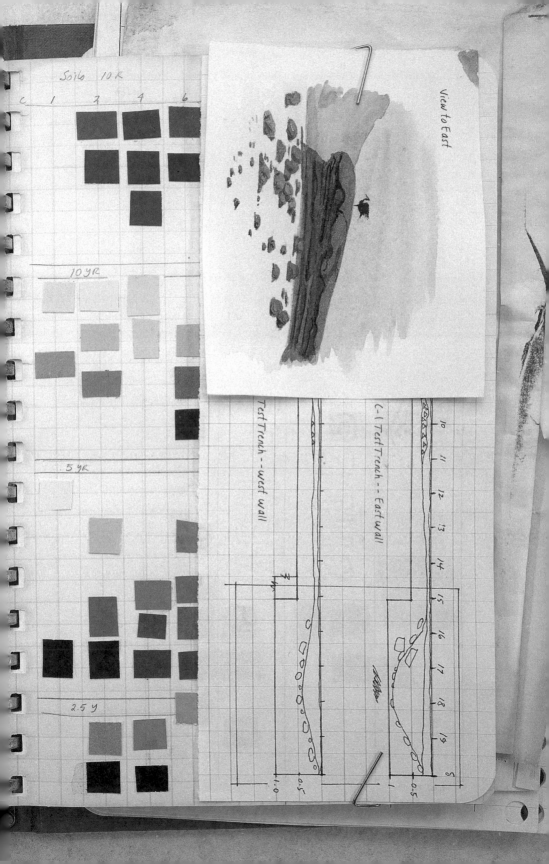

Soils 10R

| c | 1 | 3 | 4 | 6 |

10 YR

5 YR

2.5 y

View to East

Test Trench -- west wall

C-1 Test Trench -- East wall

10
11
12
13
14
15
16
17
18
19
5

1.0
0.5
0.5

LOG OF THE Southern Saracen   Anchored at the Auroras

Date: wed., 8 March 2000

Hours: 1515

Fathoms: 6

Wind: NNW 290°

Force: 4 / Mod. Breeze

Barometer: 29.42↑

Temp. Air: 8°C

Water: 10°C

Remarks: Cumulus 6/10

Intended to leave today but didn't get nearly enough done in time. Wind's been pretty fierce but looks to be dying down somewhat. Still have to backfill the trenches and complete notes on the excavation. Sunset's now at 1936 I can work outside till at least then and finish up the notes tonight. Sunrise tomorrow will be at 0634. If I get up at 0600, I'll be ready to launch the dinghy by the time it's light. Good grief, I've hardly collected any plants.

How can I leave?

1) Take down tarp, clean up
2) Find sample of diddle-dee
3) Finish sketches of plants (in case of customs)
4) Pack shells properly

Never did take any pictures of my "camp"

Prevailing wind

North

Low tide

High tide

"shelter"

West

legs from galley table

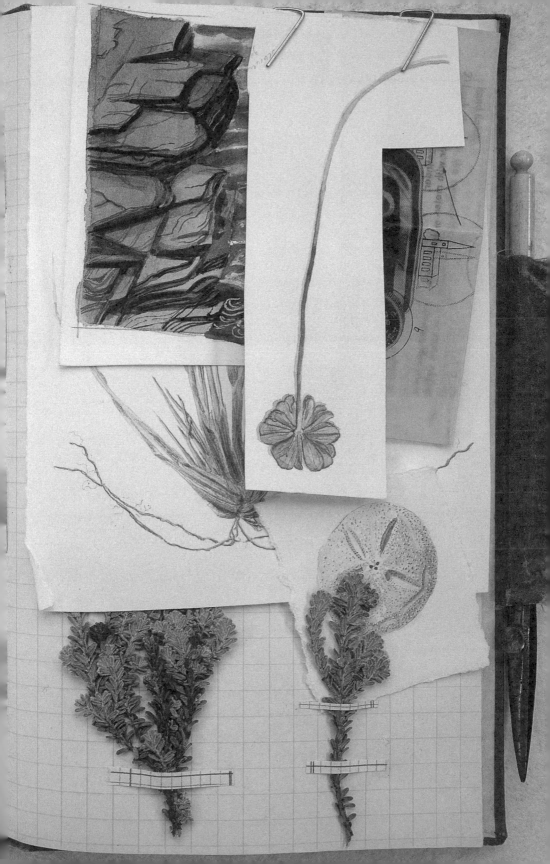

Thirteen

Fig. 186.

AN INEVITABLE DEPARTURE WAS DELAYED; the first time for a spell of brilliant weather too miraculous to waste on the open seas; the second due to northwesterlies at force 6, foolhardy and futile to attempt; and a third and final time, because of the last-minute fear that some corner lay unmapped or some plant remained unsampled. Then there were no more excuses, and he had to depart.

Hippolyte, a man who dispensed sentimentality grudgingly, if at all, wept the day he finally left the islands that bore his footprints— and his alone, now that others from long ago had been washed away— the islands that had satisfied his desire to find the unfindable.

The boat was loaded. The temporary camp, the emergency stashes of food and water cached here and there, had been retrieved. His traces had been obliterated. He could think of a hundred reasons to stay, but none, indeed the sum total of them all, could not match the one good reason to leave: the deterioration of the weather. He'd been noting with dismay not only the falling temperatures and the increasingly consistent strong winds but also the corresponding and rapid drop in hours of daylight. Darkness was closing in, squeezing dawn and dusk together at a rate of four to five minutes a day.

The gentoos, who'd accepted him as one of their own, bid farewell. They slid into the water and frolicked about as he rowed the dinghy to the boat. They were momentarily frightened away by the throb of the engine but soon came back, and once he was underway, sped alongside him, flashing in and out of the waves like flying fish, their backs arched like porpoises. He couldn't watch them enough, these carefree birds, so awkward and silly on land, so naturally playful and at home in the sea.

LOG OF THE *Southern Saracen*
From: The Auroras   Towards: Stanley, The Falklands
Date: Thurs., 9 March 2000   Hours: 1120
Knots: 4   Fathoms: ?
Wind: NNW 320°   Force: 5 / Fresh Breeze
Barometer: 30.06   Temp. Air: 9°C   Water: 9°C
Remarks: Heavy fog to the east. Clear to the west. Stratocumulus 8/10
Lat: 52°36′S   Long: 47°43′W
Var: 002°W   Course Req: 282°C   Course Steered: 281°C

Radio's still not responding. This is going to make for a difficult voyage back. Not only for getting in contact, but for navigation, too. And I have a feeling I let my watch run down at some point, though I've made adjustments, knowing from my tables when the sun rises and sets.

Well, I'm off. I've not done nearly everything I wanted to do. I have gaps in my collection of plants; I barely started on the geology; I didn't photograph everything I wanted and took too many photographs of things that don't matter. I didn't spend enough time on Princesa or Atrevida; I could have if I had really planned my attempts better. My mapmaking is faulty; I didn't think I'd have so much trouble doing it alone. And the excavation was left incomplete.

I tell myself, I've told myself a hundred times, I can come back. But looking behind me, now as I leave, I see that the mist has closed in, and my Auroras are nowhere to be seen. They have completely disappeared. What would happen if I slowed down right this very second and returned? What would I see as I neared the shore?

Would they be there, or would there be yet another world in their place?

As he set his course for Stanley, he couldn't help but turn and turn again to stare at the vacant bank of fog, like a wall expressly shielding him from his own discovery. He was out past the kelp beds and the reefs, and the way in front was clear, offering unlimited visibility westward, though the sky was overcast. With just over ten gallons of fuel remaining, there was enough to cover maybe a quarter the distance that lay ahead. He raised the mainsheet and unfurled the genoa, considering all the while the laborious tacking that lay ahead. For the first time since he had set out, he strapped on the safety harness.

The gentoos had long fallen behind, unwilling to risk such distance from their young. Alone again on the sea, he remembered his swim, his folly. He dragged the thermometer out of the water and checked the temperature. It was still 10°C. He leaned over and trailed his hand along the choppy surface. It was so cold. How could he have ever even entertained the idea of diving in, not to mention doing it? How had he survived? Swim in the South Atlantic! Indeed! As far as he was concerned now, it had never happened. He glanced over his shoulder again, the fog thicker than ever, and recalled frantically treading water, scanning the horizon for his boat and for his islands, stunned at their disappearance. He had never come up with a reasonable explanation for that moment. It even shook his own faith. And what about the inexplicable sailing over them in the first place?

He flipped through his logbook; was there not one single page that didn't make reference to some illusory incident? Maybe there were a few, but overall it was pretty damning. Well, he decided, there was no question of allowing anyone to read this. Maybe he should just dump it overboard immediately. He leaned off the pushpit and held it out over the water, but his hand shook at the very idea. Stretching out farther, he fought the desire to keep it, struggled with himself to submerge it in the boat's wake. He shook his head and drew back, book still in hand. How could he consider doing such a thing, to throw out this record of such a hard-won victory? Maybe I can't give it up, he declared, but from now on, I'll never admit it exists.

Hours: 1510   Knots: 3   Fathoms: ?
Wind: NNW 345°   Force: 5 / Fresh Breeze
Barometer: 30.06   Temp. Air: 9°C   Water: 9°C
Remarks: Stratocumulus 4/10. Unlimited vis.
Lat: 52°35′S   Long: 47°37′W
Var: 002°W   Course Req: 282°C   Course Steered: 280°C
Word is, if it takes 4 to 6 days for a reasonably fast boat to sail to South Georgia from the Falklands, it takes twice as long to get back.

I've got to try to get that radio working. Maybe if I take it apart, something will be obvious: a wire shredded even more than the rest, a loose switch, a bad connection.

It's working now; I just switched it on. The usual static but otherwise it's okay. Now I'll be able to hear my weather lady. I've missed you, sweetheart.

LOG OF THE *Southern Saracen*
From: The Auroras   Towards: Stanley, The Falklands
Date: Fri., 17 March, 2000   Hours: 0830
Knots: 6   Fathoms: 38
Wind: ?°   Force: 2 / Calm
Barometer: doesn't matter anymore
Temp. Air: 11°C   Water: ?°C
Remarks: Stratus 10/10
Lat: 51°39′50″S Long: 57°43′W   Variation: 005°E

Mainsail's reefed, gen is furled, switched to diesel, heading for the public jetty in Stanley. Just past the line that stretches from Volunteer Point to Cape Pembroke, I've radioed in position and ETA. What a good boy I am. Hope the Harbour Master relayed the message that I sent to Peter yesterday to meet at the Canache. I'm supposed to dig up £30, but I wonder if I can get away without paying, since it's Peter's boat and he's a resident here. There should be a yellow pennant around somewhere that I'm supposed to fly. What'll they do to me if I don't?

Stanley's in sight.

"Unusual flag, Mr. Webb. I don't believe I've ever seen one like that before." The customs agent contemplated the yellow boot hanging from the mast. His eyes strayed to Hippolyte's bare feet. "You can take it down now and put it back on; I presume you do have another one somewhere. You're all cleared, by the way." He stamped Hippolyte's passport and wrote out a receipt for the £30. "I understand from Mr. Givens that you'll be proceeding to the Canache."

"Word gets around."

"Oh, yes, it does indeed." The agent stepped back onto the jetty. "By the way, Mr. Givens seems to think you were due back last week. No business of ours, but he was rattling the cage a bit. Rather concerned about his boat, I suspect. Goodbye, then." He walked away.

Hippolyte started up the engine, cast off, and headed east, not looking at all forward to Peter's welcome. A few minutes later a mud-spattered Land Rover, parked at a resigned tilt, came into view. As he neared the gravel jetty, the jeep's door opened. Peter emerged and strolled down to the end of the embankment, casually motioning for Hippolyte to raft alongside a sailboat already moored at its head. Limbs slack, one could hardly call him anxious. Hippolyte conscientiously flipped the fenders over the port side, tossed out the bow line, waited for Peter to secure it, then tossed him the stern line. He hesitated before stepping onto the neighboring boat.

"The owner's in Stanley," said Peter, hands in pockets, gesturing with a nod for him to cross. He pointed his nose at the boat, a sparkling fifty footer, "She's off to the Mediterranean in a couple of days."

"How're you doing, Peter?" Hippolyte asked, tiptoeing over the neighbor's foredeck.

He shrugged. "I see you've decided to come back, after all."

"Why wouldn't I?"

"You're a touch tardy, don't you think?"

"Lost track of time."

"You said four weeks; you lost a whole week?" He looked at his watch, and revised, "Ten days?"

"Just five days. I had a struggle getting back; that took up the rest."

Peter seemed content to drop the subject. At least for the moment. "Everything okay?"

"Yup."

"Glad to hear it." He sounded anything but, then sighed and arched his back, as though stiff from sitting waiting in the Land Rover for the last week and a half. "How about the dinghy?" He allowed a slight smile, almost as if happy at the memory of having failed to tell Hippolyte of its problem.

"It leaked, but otherwise it was okay. Why?"

"Nothing. Just that I forgot to tell you that about the leak."

"I plugged the hole. It's fine now, but you might want to have it looked at. I doubt my repair will last much longer."

Peter stepped onto the boat and with Hippolyte crossed over to his own. He checked over the dinghy, reassuring himself that it was secure, then ran his fingers along the hull to the hole. He crouched down to inspect it closely. "Is this tar?"

"Nope."

"Resin?"

"Nope." Hippolyte was grinning.

"I give up. What did you fix it with then?"

"Gum and a chocolate Power Bar. I knew those things had to be useful for something."

Peter looked at him with a touch more respect, noting the inflamed scar. "What did you do to your hand then?"

"Bashed it. It's healing."

"Looks pretty ugly."

"It's the knuckles." He closed his fist tight. "Every time I flex my hand, it opens up again. See?" New blood oozed from the edges of the scab.

Peter made a face. "Get it looked at, for pity's sake."

They started unloading gear. "Do you want any of this stuff, Peter?" Hippolyte asked. "The water canisters? The leftover food? Condensed milk?"

"Whatever."

"I'll get your blankets cleaned."

"Forget it."

"No, I need to. Had an accident and bled all over them."

"Your hand?"

"No, my arm. I tripped in the dark." He rubbed the spot; it was still slightly swollen and very sore.

"Accident prone, aren't you? Anything else happen?"

Yeah, said Hippolyte to himself, I lied to you and went east instead of west, I found three islands that are said not to exist, I withstood a pounding that I'll never forget, I took a swim and lost your boat, I dug up a dead man. "Nope," he replied.

"Had a party out looking for you." Peter was picking his way back across the deck, precariously balancing the duffel and a cardboard box. "What's in this bag? It weighs a ton."

"You did? Why?"

"Did I mention that you've come back late?"

Hippolyte did not respond.

"Got Fisheries air patrols to keep their eyes open." Peter dropped the box onto the jetty. Dust flew up.

"Careful with that stuff, Peter. Thanks." The bag landed a second later and rolled a few feet down the slope. Hippolyte winced. "But not a special search or anything?"

"No, nothing special. Thing is, though, when I asked them to have a look for you, they checked their records and told me they'd have a look next time someone was heading out towards South Georgia. We had quite a discussion over that. Seems you never intended to go dallying around the islands."

"Sorry, I should have told you." Hippolyte guessed that the plane he heard must have been them. So, if they saw him, they would have seen the Auroras! That would be further confirmation. As soon as he could ditch Peter, he'd call them up and find out what the pilot reported. "They must have seen me then?" He handed Peter another box. "Careful with this one; it's got plant specimens in it." Peter took the small box gingerly with both hands and with exaggerated care minced over and dropped it onto the pile. The dry smile slipped across his face a second time.

"Are you pulling my leg?" asked Hippolyte, catching the fleeting grin. "Did you really request a search?"

Peter became serious again. "Yeah, Mr. Webb, I did. I am not, as you say, 'pulling your leg.' "

"You're taking it awfully well."

"I guess I don't see the point of dwelling on it. You're back again, aren't you? You're not likely to go out and do this again, are you? And you're old enough to know better than to have done it in the first place, and I don't think me nagging at you like a stricken mother is going to give you any more sense. And yes, the pilot saw you out there, on your my bloody boat, happy as a clam, doing your Queen Victoria wave. Hand me that box." He snapped his fingers impatiently.

Hippolyte frowned. They saw him on the boat? Then that must have been another time, though he couldn't recall hearing more than the one plane, let alone waving at it. "When did you talk to them?" he asked.

"I dunno, around the second, I think."

"You promised you'd wait till I was late. Four days late, remember?" Peter ignored the whining as if admitting the worthlessness of his promise.

They loaded up the Land Rover and drove into town. "I have a buyer for her," Peter announced.

"Great!" Hippolyte forced enthusiasm, but inwardly his heart sank. She'd been his refuge, his land through all of his quarrels with the sea, and he'd forgotten to say goodbye to her. He'd have to go back out and take proper leave. Perhaps it was better that way anyway, to do it in private, away from Peter's caustic watch. "My having her out didn't cause you any problems with the deal?"

"No, as a matter of fact, it was the best thing. As soon as you left, this chap, a slacker really—he'd been stalling all summer, I'd given him up for a no-count months ago—anyway, he panicked when you took off. Nutter'd thought she was going to be around forever, that he'd be able to get the old girl for a song. Got some barmy idea about taking tourists out on her." Peter guffawed. Both men sat silent for a few minutes. Peter geared down and swerved around a tight corner. "Not that it's such a bad idea," he amended, a circuitous way of conceding that he himself had had the same plan. "Just that he's going to be a bit cramped, don't you think? I'd a done it myself, if she'd been fifty, sixty foot," he continued. "What'd'you guess he'll be able to charge? What do they get where you come from?" Hippolyte was amazed to hear the flood of words pouring out of this hitherto silent man who didn't wait for an answer. "I expect he'll be wanting somewhere about fifty, a hundred quid a person! A day! We already signed the papers! He's pissing his pants afraid that you're not coming back!" He glanced over at Hippolyte and winked. "Let's leave him stew a bit longer, shall we? What'd'you say to a pint?"

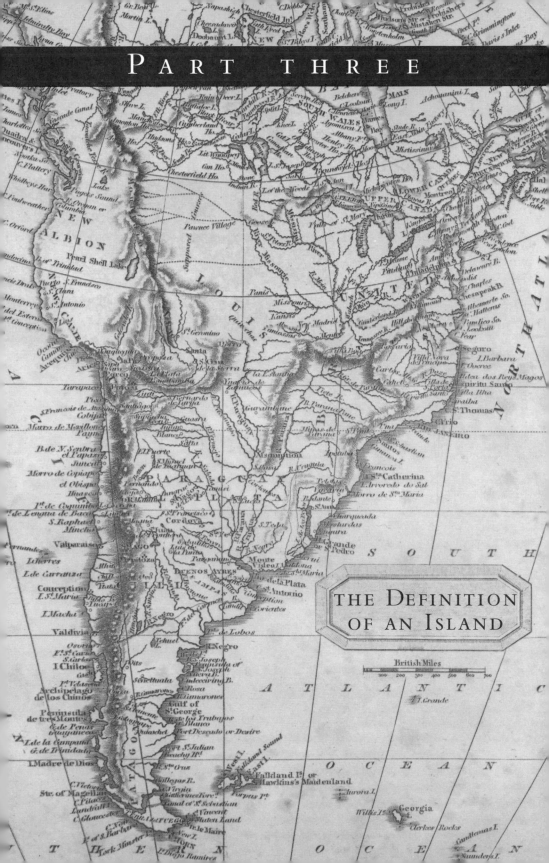

PART THREE

THE DEFINITION
OF AN ISLAND

How I Found the Auroras

by Hippolyte Webb

This book, like my explorations, has set its own
course, which it will follow, with me or without me. I
provide mere ballast, nothing more. It is a search for
past hopes and an astonishing journey to a land
thought to be beyond recall.

By no means a fantastical undertaking, it is
nevertheless comparable to such imaginative works as
Jules Verne's Journey to the Centre of the Earth,
H. Rider Haggard's King Solomon's Mines and James De
Mille's A Strange Manuscript Found in a Copper
Cylinder, not because it conjures up an unknown world
teeming with incredible inhabitants and exotic, even
dangerous, flora and fauna--it doesn't--but because,
in this day and age, the simple concept of lost or
undiscovered lands is fabulous.

It all begins with maps of bygone centuries, upon
which vast territories were labelled "Unknown Land."
Provoked (and not for the first time!) by this
mysterious and compelling phrase and certain that
Unknown Land could still be visited, I scoured these
maps for possible destinations. It was during this
search that I noticed and became intrigued by places
that had been identified, charted and named but that
are now forgotten. To my delight, I found many--
islands, mountains, deserts--scattered around the

next page

globe and in their pursuit could have travelled to any
and all corners of the earth. But an irresistible urge
pointed me south. So, armed with my compass, which
tells me the here, and my watch, which tells me the
now, I set out to confront a modern-day "Terra
Incognita." In doing so, I rediscovered the Aurora
Islands.

First reported by Spanish navigators braving the
treacherous waters of the South Atlantic in the 1700s,
the Auroras were observed again and again through the
last half of that century. Surveyed in 1794 they were
assured of immortality through placement on maps by
1800. In the 1810s and 20s, they came to the attention
of sailors, who hoped to find untapped colonies of
lucrative fur seals. Attempts by Captains Weddell,
Morrell, etc. failed to relocate them, and eventually
belief in their existence began to falter. They were
finally left off official charts by 1850, although they
remained on decorative editions and school atlases
until the 1890s. Controversy surrounding them,
however, did not die out and rumours persisted well
into the twentieth century of these elusive islands in
the South Atlantic.

Painstakingly documented and filled with maps, plans,
charts, drawings and photographs, all conclusively

next page

proving the existence of the Auroras, this book will
raise new hopes for other such discoveries. I stopped
at nothing to ensure that details were checked and
double-checked, that facts were corroborated with
modern scientific understanding, that sufficient data--
in the form of botanical and zoological as well as
geological specimens--was retrieved in order to allow
others to analyze and confirm my observations.

My journey was fraught with many challenges, but
overcoming doubts that I was embarking on anything
other than an extraordinary voyage was not one of
them. Here is my story.

Manuscript enclosed

Fourteen

MEMO
April 11, 2000
To: Marie Simplon, Editor   From: Jeremy Gould, Publisher
Marie:
Have a look at this submission from a potential new author,
Hippolyte Webb. He's got a fantastic story about being shipwrecked
on an island in the South Atlantic. Given the success of "extreme"
travel accounts in the past couple of years, I think we should give
this one a shot. Let me know what you think.
J.

MEMO
April 20, 2000
To: Jeremy Gould, Publisher   From: Marie Simplon, Editor
Dear Jeremy:
Regarding this Hippolyte Webb thing. Can we meet?
Marie

"Do you mean to say, that in your rush to get a book on—what did
you call it? 'extreme travel'?—you didn't actually read it?" Marie, sitting
across the table from Jeremy, fanned through the mass of loose, dog-
eared papers dividing them. The tone hovered on accusatory; the face,
though, was gently sarcastic.

"This is a book with rare potential." Jeremy leaned forward and
took possession of the pages, proudly accepting responsibility.
"Hippolyte Webb is an explorer, naturalist, cartographer. This book

147

will really put us on the map." He paused, waiting for an acknowledging chuckle, but Marie was now occupied drawing big xs and NOs on her notepad and hadn't caught his feeble pun. Or had chosen not to acknowledge it. With her eyes focused on destructive doodling instead of on him, he could continue with even more assurance. "However, it needs your fine touch to turn it into something really publishable."

"Do you have any idea what it's about?" Her voice was calm now, level; Jeremy sighed happily, his flattery had worked!

"Hippolyte Webb has voyaged, single-handedly, to a remote island in the South Atlantic and he has written about it."

"What has he written?"

"You've read it yourself. You don't need me to tell you."

"I would like to hear from you, what you understand this book to be about."

"Oh. Before I forget. Victoria asks if you're free for dinner Saturday."

"Jeremy!" She threw her head back and laughed. Then groaned.

"Okay, okay," he beamed at her expectantly, as though waiting for her to rephrase the question. She responded with her own expectant look.

"Okay, Marie." He submitted. "It's about his being shipwrecked."

"Shipwrecked," she repeated flatly.

"And icebergs? And—" fizzled out.

She shook her head in disbelief. "I'm glad we're the same age, Jeremy. It means that I don't have to treat you with any respect. In fact, if you didn't sign my paycheck I'd call you names." She drew the pile back towards her. Stained and mangled top sheets had been ripped from a coil-bound notebook. Spearing them with her pencil, she waved it in his face. "This is not only dreck, but I will get a disease if I touch it. Look! Is this coffee or what?"

"I admit it needs work," he shrugged.

"A lot of work. Too much." They both stared at the offending manuscript. "You could always turn it down," she suggested, erasing any hint of levity.

"I think we should take it on."

"Refuse it," she urged. "It won't be the first time a manuscript's been rejected, you know."

"But I *want* to publish it. You can edit it, rewrite where necessary."

"Oh, please don't make me whine, Jeremy. It's not that it's badly written—at least there are complete sentences—it's that it's full of lies. It's fictional. The whole thing is a fabrication!"

"How do you know?"

"Read it! He's not a sailor, yet he sails single-handed through heavy seas and finds islands that have been missing since 1794? Come on! I'll bet you I could prove it," she snapped her fingers, "just like that. Ten to one they're not on any satellite photographs. In fact, I happen to have a book of such photos with me now." She flipped the book open to a marked page. "Here!" She circled the South Atlantic with her finger. "There's nothing. Absolutely nothing."

Jeremy was silenced, but only momentarily, "Don't you see? Your inquiring mind is what makes you the perfect—"

But she interrupted, not caring to listen, "Or, if this empty ocean's not good enough for you," the book was shoved aside, "I'll get in touch with people he mentions, like the boat owner Peter Givens, if he exists—I bet you he's never even heard of our Mr. Webb—or I could write to—" She was ripping through the manuscript and scribbling furiously at the same time, a list of names: the Admiralty Office, the Falkland Islands Harbour Master, archaeologists, historians, geographers. She paused, then added *psychologist* followed by *delusions???*

"You'll have to fix it then, Marie; make it real."

"I won't. Tell him to go away, Jeremy. Take his little lies and this nasty paper and go away."

"I can't."

"What do you mean you can't? It's done every day." She put down her pen. A thin film of shame coated Jeremy's face. "You've signed it on, haven't you?"

"Sort of. You still have to work out the details."

"I get it; you've paid him an advance."

"A small one."

"How small?" Taking a stab, guessed, "Two thousand dollars?"

"Not quite that small." His nervous hands knotted the ends of his tie into a tight bun. "Is this so very important?" he demanded. She stretched across the table, freed the tie, smoothed it. The turmoil between them subsided, and into the revived calm he blurted, "Okay, twenty thousand."

She sat back with a thud. "Whew! That takes care of one question. That's how he could afford to rent a sailboat for a month. Anyway, I see your position. You know, it's not my place to tell you how to run your business, but I can't rescue this. It'll have to go to someone else. Could you leave that thing alone for a few minutes?"

Jeremy dropped the tie, pulled a handkerchief out of his jacket pocket, and commenced rolling it into a tube. The action somehow roused his confidence. "I gather that your main problem is credibility. Why? Because you think that it's not possible to find a lost island these days? I do. Look at those guys who found the missing city in the middle of the desert, you know, in the, where was that? Yeah, Empty Quarter. And everyone said it was impossible to find anything new on the earth anymore."

"Urbar," she announced, then revised, "No, Ubar."

"Ubar! That's right, and what's the name of the movie star fellow that found it, Fines? Randolph?"

"It wasn't a movie star. It was Ranulph Fiennes."

"Same thing, he's pretty good looking, eh? Isn't that the kind of thing women go for?"

"Jeremy, would you please tell me what planet you're on today? Besides, scholars knew of Ubar's existence; they just didn't know exactly where it was."

"Hippolyte's good looking, too. His picture could be on the jacket." Jeremy felt himself blushing; his eyes watered, and his nose ran, but he rattled on through swipes at his handkerchief, his own voice resounding ridiculously in his ears. "This could really break out, wide audience, young, old, men, women. Handsome hero, stranded on a desert island, I mean not a desert island, but you know what I mean, and within spitting distance of Ernest Shackleton! We could call it *Endurance Revisited* or *Stranded in Shackleton's Shadow.* Did he take a dog? Damn, he better have; those dogs onboard ships are irresistible! Well, he—you—could always write one in."

"How do you know so much about Antarctic expeditions, Jeremy?"

"Oh, I don't know a thing about the Antarctic! Marie! You know that. That's why you have to be the editor! And, anyway, why couldn't there be a lost island? Why couldn't one man find it again? It's a modern-day Robinson Crusoe story with Darwin and Scott and Livingstone rolled up in it. It's got everything: adventure, high seas, trekking, disaster! Webb's like Burton; he's been all over the world; he speaks at least five languages, four of which I've never even heard of. I don't care if it has been faked! It's too good to pass up. And YOU are going to make it work!" He glared at her, his stab at authority overtaking him. "Please!"

Fifteen

MEMO
April 25, 2000
To: Marie Simplon, Editor   From: Jeremy Gould, Publisher
Marie:
Thank you for agreeing to work with Hippolyte Webb on his book tentatively entitled *How I Found the Auroras*. The title is obviously a loser and will have to be changed. I've decided to remain closely involved with this project, so please feel free to count on me for feedback. And do keep me posted on your progress.
J.

Marie Simplon, Editor
Rumor Press
10 West 52nd
New York, NY 10019

April 25, 2000

Hippolyte Webb
Box 21, Stn. A
Vancouver, BC V6B 1Z1

Dear Mr. Webb:
Re: Manuscript submission entitled *How I Found the Auroras*
It is my pleasure to inform you that Rumor Press has accepted your submission. There are questions that need answering, though, before we can finalize the deal.

The first concerns scheduling. We are anticipating a publication date of September 2001. However, there is a significant amount of work still to be done, and I wish to ascertain if you are willing to work with me on revising the manuscript. I also want to know how flexible your own schedule is. To meet the deadlines we need a finished ms. with supporting material ready to go to editing around November 2000. Is this feasible for you?

The second question has to do with the illustrations you are hoping to include. Your cover letter mentions maps, photographs, and "specimens." Could you be more specific? Do you see this as a mostly text-based book with a section of illustrations, or do you envision a heavily illustrated book? I'm afraid that neither your submission nor your conversations with our publisher give me much to go on.

Lastly, our publisher speaks highly of you, but I must admit I know little about your background or of any previous publications. Could you please send me your C.V. and a telephone number where I can reach you during the day? A fax number and/or e-mail address would be helpful as well.

Yours sincerely,

Marie Simplon

Marie Simplon
cc: Jeremy Gould

April 28, 2000
Dear Ms. Simplon:
Thank you so much for your letter. I'm <u>alarmed</u> about your reference to revisions.
Yours truly,

Hippolyte Webb

Hippolyte Webb

May 8, 2000

Dear Mr. Webb:

Re: *How I Found the Auroras*

Thank you for your letter of April 28. I understand your concern,
but revisions are a natural part of the publishing process. We can
discuss specifics in detail, if you still wish to pursue publication. In
the meantime, please let me know when I can expect the answers to
my questions. Feel free to call me at ext. 112.

Yours sincerely,

Marie Simplon

Marie Simplon

cc: Jeremy Gould

May 12, 2000

Dear Marie:

I can't fathom what changes you'd want made. The discovery
is the discovery. I can't make it more exciting, and I
wouldn't want to make it any less so. I can't tell you the
total number of pictures as I have no idea how many more I
will have accumulated by the time we are ready to go to
press. I'm not a painter, so I have no illustrations, but
there are rough sketches and photographs and you could
arrange for someone to take pictures of my specimens that
I brought back. I have at least 40 maps of South America
and the South Atlantic, 20 of which show the Auroras. I
also have a terrific portrait of Edgar Allan Poe, which I
would like to see inserted somewhere in the book. A copy
is enclosed.

Yours,

Hippolyte Webb

Hippolyte Webb

*Sorry, couldn't find Poe; I'll try to put
him in my next letter. H*

May 18, 2000

Dear Mr. Webb:

Re: *How I Found the Auroras*

You really mustn't be too concerned about the idea of revising. We simply need to address tense, grammar, pacing, chronology, style, and balance. It's a normal part of the process, and most authors, even those with many books to their credit, undergo at least some editing.

I'd like to outline the stages we go through to put a book together. I'd prefer to do this by telephone or in person, so I could answer any questions you might have, but lacking your phone number or your presence, I'll try to give you a brief summary here.

As your editor, I will be responsible for ushering your manuscript through the house. In all respects you'll be working with me or via me. This brings me to your submission, much of which is typed or handwritten. This was acceptable at one time, but now a manuscript is normally submitted on 8 1/2 x 11 paper, input to our specifications, using a compatible word-processing program. I will send you a spec sheet.

As the author, you are responsible for providing—at your own expense—all illustrative material in reproducible form. When I refer to illustration, I'm not just speaking of a drawing or a painting; it is anything visual, whether it be a photograph, a chart, a map, whatever. You'll receive a list of our technical requirements shortly.

When you send me your revised ms. (along with a disk), I will hand it over to the copyeditor, who will read it thoroughly, checking for spelling errors and for errors of fact or inconsistencies in the chronology. We will send the ms. back to you then for your comments and changes. Usually a number of issues are raised at this point, fresh eyes having had a chance to read it. The copyedited ms. then goes to design and production and then to press. You need to be available to review page proofs at various times throughout these last stages.

If you have any questions, please call me. And please don't forget to answer the questions in my first letter. I have enclosed a copy in

case you have misplaced it. I would also appreciate having your phone number!
Yours sincerely,

Marie Simplon

Marie Simplon
/encl.
cc: Jeremy Gould

June 1, 2000
Dear Marie:
Jeremy knows I don't have a computer. Didn't he tell you?
So, I don't know about redoing the manuscript on disk.
Also I don't have e-mail. I just looked up "C.V." in the
dictionary. Did you know that "Curriculum Vitae" means
"course of life" and was adopted as a designation for
résumé in 1902? Résumé, on the other hand, has been in
use since 1804.
Yours,

Hippolyte

Hippolyte
PS If I'm responsible for paying for photographs, then
I'll take them myself.

Curriculum Vitae

Hippolyte Webb

Address: Box 21, Stn. A   Date of Birth: I'm 36,

Vancouver, BC   is it better if I seem

V6B 1Z1   older or younger?

TRAVEL

2000 (that is, currently): I travelled to the Aurora Islands. I
called several magazines, asking them if they would be
interested in articles about my trip, but they either turned
down the idea or couldn't give me a sufficient advance. This
takes care of the last of '99 and the first of 2000.

1999: Three months of planning to go to the Auroras, various
short, free-lance assignments, recovering from and writing
about Tannu Tuva (see 1997).

1997 and 1998: Temporary resident of Tannu Tuva just
north of Western Mongolia. I wrote a number of articles
about the distinctive regional flora.
See publications below.

1995 to 1997: I wrote a series of articles on the specialized
flora and fauna inhabiting the littoral of the Black Sea.
These were published in scientific journals in Britain,
France, Russia and Turkey (my own translations). I can
supply you with the names of the journals if you wish.
Otherwise, see below for more accessible articles.

1992 to 1994: I was working for a travel agency type place--
sorry I forgot their name--they arrange excursions to out-
of-the-way regions--doing preliminary legwork to the hot
spots that some tourists scramble to get to first. So I was
in Kazahkstan, Georgia, Azerbaidzan setting up contacts
and scouting out places to stay. I wrote several articles
for the magazines listed below, as well as for Far Corners,

continued--

but that was about it; at that point it was more important to try to stay alive.

1989 to 1992: Miscellaneous travel and articles for 50° North.

1987: Co-founder of 50° North Established at the end of a round-the-world walking tour at that latitude. I was called the contributing editor (which means main writer; I don't know a thing about editing) until '89. Sold in 1990; continue to write for them.

PUBLICATIONS

1998 and 1999: Journal of Thule Studies (August 1998) (with translations). I wrote others, but they were lost when the horse I was riding foundered in a bog. Things went downhill from there, so I never got the chance to tackle them again. A profile of my trip was featured in 50° North (October 1998) (reprinted in the All-Asia Guide for Scholars and Researchers, 1999). Fodor's or Frommer's, I can't remember which, asked me to do a chapter on Mongolia for their Asia guide, but I refused, since they wanted write-ups on fancy hotels and restaurants. That would have taken up about half a page!

Here's the Poe I promised to send—H

1997 and 1998: Somewhat accessible versions of the flora and fauna analysis of the Black Sea littoral were published in the magazines Natural History (October 1997), Naturwissenschaft (January 1998) and Botanik Bügun (also January 1998). Travel articles were written for several popular travel magazines: Back-pocket Traveller (U.K.), Landescape (Germany), Hasards (France) and Dare! (U.S.).

June 8, 2000
Dear Mr. Webb:
Re: *How I Found the Auroras*
Thank you for the C.V. We need to get moving on this as there is a
lot of work ahead. I don't want to delude you into thinking that the
next year and a half is going to be anything but difficult. Since you
are unable to be more specific about the number of images you
foresee being included in the book, we have decided to limit it to
two 16-page inserts, comprising about 32 images, black and white
only. The book we are proposing will be hardcover, 6 x 9; we will
aim for 224 pages (including the 32 pages of photographs). Now
please, call me—collect, ext. 112—so I can discuss the conditions of
the offer with you in person, so to speak.
Yours sincerely,

Marie Simplon
cc: Jeremy Gould

June 10, 2000
Dear Marie:
I've started taking photographs; I've enclosed a few, so
you can get an idea of what I'm doing. What do you think
of How I Found the Auroras as a title? I'll call you
tomorrow, no, Monday.
Yours truly,

Hippolyte

June 12, 2000
VIA COURIER
Dear Mr. Webb:
Re: *How I Found the Auroras*
Good to talk to you. As a result of our conversation, I've put
together the formal offer; you'll find it enclosed. Please get back to
me by phone as soon as possible on this.
Yours sincerely,

Marie Simplon

Marie Simplon
cc: Jeremy Gould
encl.

June 14, 2000
Dear Marie:
I'm glad I was able to talk to you today; the wording in
the offer is quite confusing; thanks for steering me
through it. I was surprised that you don't like my title,
having seen it written on all of your letters. Here are
more pictures.
Yours truly,

Hippolyte

Hippolyte
enclosure

June 18, 2000

Dear Marie:

Re: <u>The Daring Adventures of Hippolyte Webb</u>

How does that grab you? Jeremy mentioned that daring adventures are hot right now.

   Here is the contract, signed and witnessed as instructed. I've made a bunch of changes on pages 2, 3, 5, 6, 7, 8 and 10 and have initialled them. I know we settled on the amount of money, but on reflection it's nowhere near enough. Don't you agree? And I'm pretty broke right now, so I'd rather have it all at once instead of waiting for dribbles. Also, why would Rumour get anything if another publisher takes it? (I've crossed that paragraph out.) It seems to me that's between me and them. And the same with movies, so I crossed that out too.

   I hope it's okay that this is a collect package. You'll find three boxes: the first official installment of my specimens, or "illustrations," as you call them.

Yours,

Hippolyte

Hippolyte
enclosure

MEMO
June 20

To: Marie Simplon, Editor   From: Jeremy Gould, Publisher

Marie:

Having now read Hippolyte's response to the contract, I can certainly understand your concern. I will talk to him and try to make him understand.

J.

June 20, 2000

Dear Hippolyte:

You can be a real pain in the butt sometimes. For Pete's sake, quit acting like a prima donna and sign the bloody contract. There's a *clean* copy enclosed. And get a phone.

Yours sincerely,

Jeremy Gould

/encl.

cc: Marie Simplon

June 26, 2000

Dear Marie:

Here are the new copies. I've duly signed them like the good boy I am. Are you talking to me again? What did you think of my specimens? Take care of them please; it's not easy to find giant squid tentacles in North America. I'm on my knees, begging your forgiveness!

Your never more recalcitrant friend,

Hippolyte

MEMO

June 30, 2000

To: Jeremy Gould, Publisher   From: Marie Simplon, Editor

Dear Jeremy:

Here's a present. Your author says the boxes contain giant squid tentacles. As you seem to have plenty of space in *your* office, YOU can take care of it.

Marie

June 30, 2000

Dear Mr. Webb:

Re: *The Auroras*

Thank you for the boxes of specimens. They are currently stored in a safe place until such time as we need them.

Regarding the title, we are now tentatively working with *The Auroras,* although we are concerned that it may be confused with the celestial phenomena of the same name. I'm afraid that we had to decide against *The Daring Adventures of Hippolyte Webb.* The general consensus was that it sounded too much like a children's story.

Could you please give me a phone number where I can reach you?

Yours sincerely,

Marie Simplon

Marie Simplon

cc: Jeremy Gould

Sixteen

MEMO
June 30, 2000
To: Jeremy Gould, Publisher   From: Marie Simplon, Editor
Dear Jeremy:
Attached are two letters you should read.
M.

June 16th, 2000

Mr. & Mrs. Arthur Givens
Stanley, Falkland Islands

Marie Simplon, Editor
Rumor Press
10 West 52nd
New York, NY 10019

Dear Miss Simplon:
Thank you for your letter of April 21st, and please excuse me for
having taken the liberty of opening my son's mail. Your letter sat on
our sideboard for weeks while my wife and I pondered what to do
with it. You see, our Peter joined the crew of a scientific expedition
and is presently in the Antarctic, and he was never a one for keeping
in touch. I'm not sure why it is <u>so</u> important for these scientists to
go to the South Pole in the middle of winter, but jobs are hard to
come by, so we can't complain about him having work, can we? I
can help you on one matter: Peter sold the <u>Seaspray</u> just a few short
days after Mr. Webb returned. Our one regret is that he never took

us out on it. We'll certainly let him know your letter is waiting for him. I'm sorry that we can't help you with your other questions; we didn't have the pleasure of meeting Mr. Webb.

With my best wishes,

Arthur Givens

Jules McGovern
Hydrographic Dept.
British Admiralty Office

13 June 2000

Dear Ms. Simplon

Re: Your letter of 21 April 2000

Please excuse my tardiness in responding to your inquiry. I have read through the portion of the manuscript that you sent and sympathise with your predicament. However, Mr. Webb's fictions are so transparent you should have no qualms about rejecting his work, or, at the very best, churning it out as a novel of some sort.

The Auroras, along with other false islands, made their way onto maps through oversight. They were officially removed from Admiralty Charts in 1853, but unfortunately persisted on others. You'll not likely find them on maps published after 1900. Furthermore, sea traffic regularly traverses the section of the South Atlantic where the Auroras were said to be. Yachts, fishing boats, BAS vessels would find themselves in deep trouble if the Auroras appeared suddenly out of nowhere! As you know, James Weddell, the Antarctic explorer, conducted a search in 1820 and attributed the previous erroneous sightings to the presence of icebergs. Whether or not this is a plausible explanation is of no matter. The fact is, they simply don't exist.

American Benjamin Morrell, who plied the South Atlantic a few years after Weddell, wrote "A Narrative of Four Voyages" about his so-called quest for the Auroras. In his case, his fabrications were designed to prove their non-existence. That Mr. Webb is trying to prove their existence makes him no less a liar. Bookstores and libraries are filled to the brim with dubious accounts of exploration; please do not insult us readers by adding Mr. Webb's trash to this heap.

Yours sincerely,

Jules McGovern

Jules McGovern

MEMO

June 30, 2000

To: Marie Simplon, Editor   From: Jeremy Gould, Publisher

Marie:

Re: McGovern: Ouch!

Givens' letter is very encouraging, don't you think? Please work with Hippolyte for as long as you possibly can. Would you do that for me? Let's give it two months, see how it's going and decide then. That would make it Wednesday, the 30th of August. Okay?

Thanks, J.

July 5, 2000

Dear Mr. Webb:

Re: *The Auroras*

I've noticed that you haven't written an introduction for your book. I'd like to flag this now, so that you can get started on it. Have you resolved the issue of a computer yet? I plan to send you my notes regarding revisions of the first draft shortly. Also, can you supply me with a bibliography? Were you able to contact any first-hand sources, such as the Hydrographic Office of the British Admiralty? Do you have a phone?

Yours sincerely,

Marie Simplon

Marie Simplon

cc: Jeremy Gould

10 July 2000
Dear Marie:
Here goes:

Introduction

A decision to travel to the unknown is not one made
lightly. When I began planning my voyage to the Auroras,
I knew that I would be facing many difficulties, my own
natural doubts notwithstanding. My background as a
dedicated traveller gave me the conviction and the ability
to surmount the obstacles facing me.

My resolve to make all the world my home came at a
young age. My mother swears that I had my passport
application filled out by the time I popped out of the
womb. Neither of my parents travel, but both have been
great supporters of my ambitions; my mother by
encouraging me, my father by not discouraging me. A guy
could not hope for more.

Globe trotting is not conducive to a stable family life,
so even though I'm now in my mid-thirties, I have never
married, and honestly doubt I have any children.
Advertising for the perfect companion amongst the pages
of a book is perhaps unorthodox, but if there is anyone out
there who, after reading this account, feels she could live
my kind of life, kindly get in touch with me via the
publisher.

I write copiously while on the move. If I didn't, I
would immediately forget all but the most trivial details.
I write with whatever means available. I usually travel
with a portable typewriter, but for the most part prefer to
make my notes by hand. My favourite pen is a Micron
permanent black 010. But anything will do. I have never
taped a conversation and would feel uncomfortable
proposing the idea.

I speak, with various degrees of fluency, English, Spanish, German, Turkish, Mongolian. And French. I taught myself to read and write Arabic, because I am in thrall to the shape of its letters; they're addictive when they unravel their cursive selves. Arabic's sinistral flow is perfect for cryptic memos composed of transliterated English words.

Cyrillic letters were the stuff of childhood secret codes, thus I can also read and write Russian and Greek but cannot speak them fluently. I can also write some 70 Chinese characters. I wish I knew more; writing Chinese is like laying down the foundation of an empire of words stroke by stroke.

I rarely let on when I am conversant in a language, as the opportunities to eavesdrop are far greater when you are perceived of as virtually deaf and mute. I have consistently discovered so much more--about life, politics, danger--through judicious and conservative use of language than I ever have by admitting understanding.

Travel is an unknown quantity, and I prefer it that way. To that end, I take chances, sleeping whereever (but preferably NOT in hotels--Santiago and Stanley being notable exceptions), sharing rides in taxis or trucks rather than renting cars, eating whatever looks intriguing. I lost a passport once, and was shattered, but found it again.

There's a bibliography at the end of the manuscript. You'll find two more names below; could you tack them on for me, please? Thanks.

Hattersley-Smith, G. "The History of Place Names in the Falkland Island Dependencies." British Antarctic Survey, Scientific Reports, No. 101, Cambridge: 1980, p. 80.

Murray, G. The Antarctic Manual. London, 1901.

Laws, Richard. Antarctica: The Last Frontier. London: Boxtree, 1989.

July 14, 2000

Dear Mr. Webb:

We're getting nowhere. Are you planning to come to New York anytime soon?

Yours sincerely,

Marie Simplon

Marie Simplon
cc: Jeremy Gould

Seventeen

RUMOR'S LOBBY COULD NOT have contained Hippolyte and his gear
for a moment longer. The door had opened with a bang, and he
whirled in, carrying his burdens—his long-suffering duffel bag and the
large oak crate—easily as if they were picnic baskets. He dropped this
cargo in the middle of the room. While he waited for the receptionist to call Marie, he bounced on and off the chairs and over to the desk.
"She's not exactly expecting me!" he confided. While the receptionist
clung to the phone, waiting for a response from Marie's office,
Hippolyte perched on the coffee table, tipping magazines off of
it. Scooping them up and tossing them onto a side table, he upset a
potted plant. It hadn't been watered for weeks, so the dry soil and
vermiculite were broadcast across the carpet. As he bent down to
sweep up what he could, the receptionist, who, until now, had been
stunned by the sheer energy ricocheting off the walls, flapped her
hands, in an incoherent effort to get him to stop. She replaced the
receiver and hastened over to where he was squatting just as he stood
up. He knocked her over, but she had the good grace to land in a
chair. They burst out laughing.

Marie, on her way to another office by way of the lobby, paused to
watch the spectacle unfold. This looks like something to stay well out
of, she thought, and wondered why one man alone, and a weedy one
at that, had been given such large items to deliver. The receptionist
looked up and almost shouted in relief, "Miss Simplon, this is Mr.
Webb!"

Marie stared at the delivery man who was grinning at her and sticking out his chest. Why was the receptionist introducing him to her? Mr.

Webb. Oh, God, Hippolyte Webb! Her mind raced; had he told her he was coming? What was she supposed to do with him? She had meetings all day! She kinked her mouth into a rough approximation of a smile and stretched her hand out in a poor excuse of a welcome. "Mr. Webb," she said. Hippolyte, who was holding the clump of potting mixture, thrust out his hand in return. "Hello, Marie," he began. The ball of dirt fell onto the carpet between them. They both looked down at the little pile at their feet, their hands frozen in midair. Marie could see the staticky white vermiculite already clinging to her shoes. Hippolyte's boots, she noticed, were dusty.

He roared with laughter; tears rolled down his cheeks. The receptionist snickered into her hands. Marie, not finding anything funny about the situation, scoured the room for something with which to sweep up the mess. Hippolyte grabbed the plant's pot and cursorily brushed the dirt back into it.

Marie managed to get Hippolyte out of the lobby and led him down the hall to her office, ignoring the luggage left lying in the way. "I'll just leave you here for a moment," she told him, as they entered her office. "Take a seat. I've got to go postpone some meetings."

As Marie once again passed by the lobby, she watched the receptionist cautiously circle around the crate, the way one might reconnoiter a U.F.O. It was a formidable object: two feet wide by two feet tall and three or so feet long. Many coats of thick varnish gave the impression that it was encased in amber, complete with bubbles and preserved insects. After first inspecting her expensively painted fingernails, the young woman contemplated its rusty handle, disapproval furrowing the skin of her otherwise smooth face. She tugged down on her short skirt, but being of that flattering spandexy-type material, it automatically sprang back to its preordained length. She bent over, grabbed the hook, and gave the box a pull. It didn't budge. She rechecked her nails for damage, gave her skirt another twitch, braced her feet, locked her knees, and yanked again. Still no luck. Giving up on the box, she attacked the duffel bag with the toe of her polished shoe, poking it as if it might emit a loud and dreadful smell along the lines of a fish store at the end of a hot day. She nudged it again, this time with even less certainty, as though she expected it to growl or squeak or scuttle under the coffee table.

Marie, mesmerized by this performance, suddenly realized that she had never learned the receptionist's name. Being the third young featureless woman to have taken the seat at that desk in less than a month, no one had tried to find out what she was called, as it was assumed that she'd not be there much longer. Judging by the sour look on her face as she tried to deal with this mess in her lobby, they could have been right. Marie watched her pick up the phone and wait, impatiently tapping the desk with her already mentioned fingernails. After only a couple of rings she slammed the receiver down, called out to no one in particular, "I'm leaving the desk for a minute," then noticed the editor standing in the doorway.

"Oh, Miss Simplon! You startled me!" She blushed a deep red. "May I speak to you about these things?"

"Ask Mr. Webb to move them aside; I'll be over in production for a few minutes and then with Mr. Gould, if he's in," Marie replied as she turned to leave, bumping right into Hippolyte, who was standing behind her.

"Pardon me!" she exclaimed. "How long have you been there?"

Hippolyte grinned. He turned to the receptionist and gave her a sad-sweet smile of such warmth and intimacy that Marie suddenly felt as though she were intruding. "I'm sorry, Janice," he said. "Are those things getting in the way? Marie?" He included her in the smile. "Do you mind if I take a minute to move my stuff? I was so excited when I got here, I guess I just left them without thinking."

Marie wondered how he knew the receptionist's name already; Janice's scowl evaporated as though she had never been annoyed with him. Hippolyte picked up both box and duffel, winked, and walked back down the hall.

When Marie returned to her office a half hour later, frustrated because she hadn't been able to locate Jeremy, she discovered Hippolyte astride the box, his arm wrapped around the pliable, grinning publisher who had settled on the outstretched duffel. "Look what I found! Lurking in the hall!" Hippolyte shouted. The two men, exploding with camaraderie, overwhelmed the office. Marie considered Jeremy anew; on his own, his presence had never commanded much attention and now, although still overshadowed, he almost pulsated with audacity. Seemingly feeding off Hippolyte's radiant energy, it was as if he were suddenly poised to leap into his old friend's world, readily abandoning his own. Hippolyte eventually unlocked him, and he subsided back into his former self, melting out of the office, leaving Marie and Hippolyte and the question of just what she was supposed to do with him.

Hippolyte hauled himself up off the crate, kicked the bag aside, and dropped down onto a chair. "More of my specimens," he said, pointing to the box with his toe, "the illustrations for the book," he clarified. "I'll show them to you later. Now, whenever you're ready, about that title!"

The air was alive with the aroma of something indefinable, something other than pleasant, and in gut response, Marie could sense pain, or at least discomfort, steal across her face. She had noticed that Hippolyte himself smelled a bit, which was surprising as he was quite nicely dressed. Casually rumpled, but stylish, his was a disarray not bought in some trendy camping store. Studying him, she realized that his clothes, though well cut and of superlative material, showed wear and were too large for his lanky frame. In fact, he looked as though he had slept in them; more than that, he reminded her of an unmade bed. And he had grass in his hair. When he lapsed from grinning or talking, his face relaxed into that rather beguiling smile. She had to admit Jeremy was right; with the smile and his prematurely weathered boyishness, Hippolyte was good looking.

"I haven't had a shower in a couple of days," he admitted, out of the blue. "And hauling this stuff around," he kicked the bag again. "I probably stink to high heaven, sorry about that."

"Where are you staying?" she asked, rearranging her face into a more neutral expression. "And for how long?"

"The park near here. Central Park. It's really big!"

"You're staying near Central Park?"

"No, I'm staying *in* Central Park. Do you think I could afford to stay in a hotel in New York? Do you think I'd want to stay in a hotel that I could afford in New York?"

"But, how? I mean, what do you sleep in? Aren't you afraid? Do they let people do that?"

"It's not a question of whether or not *they* let people do that, it's a huge place, easy to hide. I doubt it's dangerous. Most people who hang out in parks at night are doing the same thing, saving on accommodation, sleeping in the great outdoors instead of in cockroach-infested dives or paying out every cent they've got. However, I wouldn't suggest that you do it. Rats, you know!" Then he shivered in a semblance of horror. "But back to the title. Any new ideas?"

"We've many things to concern ourselves with before we need bother with the title, Mr. Webb. For instance, how long are you planning to stay?"

"Aw, don't call me Mr. Webb, Marie. My name is Hippolyte."

Marie hated this point in the editor-author relationship. She preferred to abstain from the first-name basis with any author but knew it was inevitable that the formality be dropped at some point. Trouble was, these days, this came sooner rather than later; authors wanted their editors to be their friends.

"Yes, of course, Hippolyte," she replied. "As I was saying, let's not worry about specifics; we have some far more fundamental issues to address." The smell, she decided, was not Hippolyte but an organic emanation leaking from the bag. "What's in there?" she asked, pointing to it, vowing to get it as far away as possible as soon as possible.

"Plants, maps, don't worry, I'll show you, but the title first; I can't think clearly about the book unless I call it something."

"Then make up a title. We're calling it *The Auroras*. When will you be going back?"

"I don't want to sound pig-headed, but I have to call it by its real name, otherwise I won't think of it as real."

"Mr. Webb, Hippolyte, please. The title will come to us eventually, and we'll all be happy. Keep a list of ideas."

"Speaking of ideas"—he was now patting his trouser pockets—"can you recommend a good thesaurus? I need to expand my vocabulary." He was now combing through his wallet, so engrossed in a search for something, that he didn't seem to expect an answer. He scratched his head, then dragged the bag over and opened it. A powerful odor of rotting plants invaded the office. Marie overcame her disgust and watched him rummage through its contents. In it, she could see books, small boxes, cloth bags, and a couple of boards sandwiched together. Finally he dragged a much-revised handwritten list out from the pages of a worn red hardcover notebook. He crammed the book back into the bag and smoothed the rumpled paper out on the desk. "Here," he announced proudly. "My list!"

She persuaded him to forget about the titles only to be faced with a barrage of personal questions. "Where are you from?" "Where were you born?" "Why do you live here?" all of which she avoided, with the excuse that they had to stick with the book.

Under normal circumstances at a first meeting with an author, she itemized the things that she liked about the work, followed by the things she didn't. But with Hippolyte's submission she couldn't think of a single compliment that wouldn't sound facetious or fatuous. So she dove straight in to the manuscript, which had become a plague of paper infesting her desk. "There's no real order in here," she told him. "You move erratically from history to your trip and back again. Also, there are numerous references to the geology, botany, and zoology that aren't given any context. You've made a stunning discovery of a seal-hunt site and a human skeleton, yet you barely accord," she hunted through the papers, "here it is, chapter twelve. You hardly give it even this one chapter. And to start with, it's not exactly clear how you got to the islands. We need to work through this chronologically, leading up, as you do, to the discovery of the site, but with a greater emphasis on the impact of what it means."

She pushed the first chapter over to him. "I have some questions here," she said, and began to list them. "Let's start with your description of planning for the voyage. I don't get any sense of the process. How long did it take you to get everything in order? You've specified three months in a letter, but this detail is missing in the manuscript. When did you first become aware of the Auroras? Exact dates will help create a tension leading up to your departure."

"You'll have to read my journals!" From a small backpack that she hadn't previously noticed, he pulled out several dog-eared books. *"Voilà!"* he crowed. Selecting one and opening it at random, he proudly offered it to her. "This sort of thing?"

She hesitated; the pages that he'd chosen were a mess, a hodge-podge of taped-on photos, rubbed-out sketches, scribbled notes. "Go on, take it; there's nothing personal," he insisted, mistaking the source of her reticence.

She deciphered the thorough list of equipment scrawled down one of the margins and skipped to the next page, absorbing references to supplies, schedules, dilemmas. "These details will help make the trip more believable." She stopped abruptly; had promised herself she would avoid words like believable, fake, lies. But he didn't appear to have noticed.

They flagged pages until the journal fluttered with yellow tags. "What else?" he asked.

"The structure. What would you think of organizing your entire adventure into dated, daily entries?"

He hauled another book out of his duffel. "I have survey notes! And maps!" File folders materialized. "And photographs! I'd have more," he apologized, "only I ran out of film."

Thank God for small mercies, she thought, as glossy black-and-white prints of penguins, grasses, and geological features slid across the surface of the table and plastic boxes of transparencies landed on the desk. Her expression was not hard to read, she was clearly aghast by what she had unleashed. "Is there anything else?" she asked. Might as well get the worst over with.

"No, that's it," he said with a shake of his head.

"Is one of these the ship's log?" She fanned the pages of the survey book.

"No." He dug around in the duffel some more and pulled out a small box. He opened it and arranged its contents—bird bones and wave-washed stones—in parade formation across the floor. "Specimens!"

"Did you keep a log?"

"Yeah, but I lost it."

"That's a shame. What was that other book you had out earlier?"

"What?"

"That red book?"

He stared at her for a minute, then shrugged his shoulders. "Nothing to do with this," he replied.

She dropped the subject; the invasion of her office was alarming enough without inviting more. Where the loose sheets of his manuscript had provoked horror—their order was illogical, their appearance unspeakable, their content incomprehensible—compared to this new deluge, they were at least manageable. "How do you keep track of everything? Why don't you just use one book so that everything's chronological? Is one of these books your log?" Instead of replying, he busied himself in the task of marking pages, turning down corners, jotting in margins, and scribbling on the backs of photos.

August 30th, Marie promised herself, picking up the crumpled list of titles from her desk, only until August 30th.

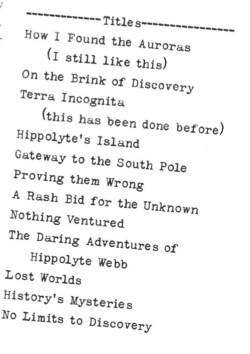

-----------Titles-----------
How I Found the Auroras
(I still like this)
On the Brink of Discovery
Terra Incognita
(this has been done before)
Hippolyte's Island
Gateway to the South Pole
Proving them Wrong
A Rash Bid for the Unknown
Nothing Ventured
The Daring Adventures of
Hippolyte Webb
Lost Worlds
History's Mysteries
No Limits to Discovery

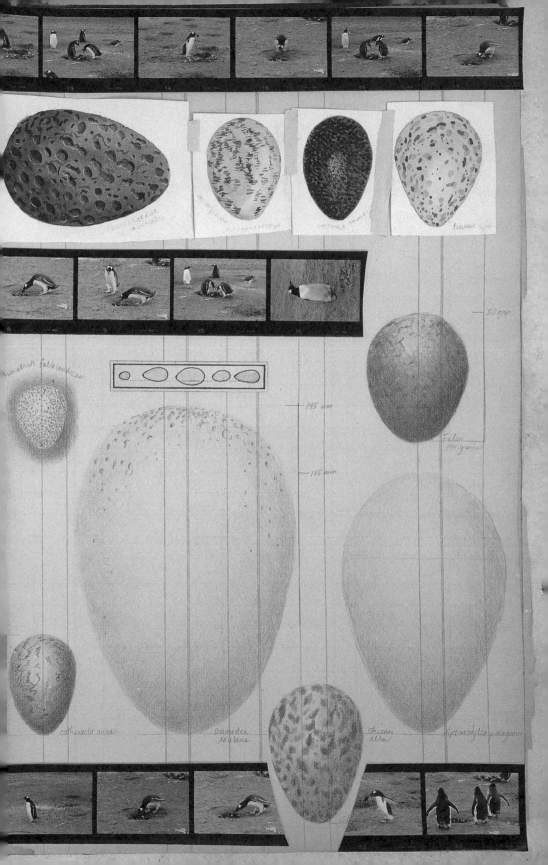

Phalacrocorax australis

Phoebetria melanophrys

Diomedea exulans

Laurus scoresbii

50 mm

145 mm

115 mm

Charadrius falklandicus

Falco peregrinus

Catharacta skua

Diomedea exulans

Chionis alba

Aptenodytes patagonicus

SOUTH AMERICA

Geo. F. Cram,

ENGRAVER AND PUBLISHER

SCALE OF MILES

0   50   100   200   300   400   500

Population   36,061,000
Area, square miles   7,196,158

SOUTH GEORGIA

Pickersgill I.   Royal Bay

Eighteen

JEREMY AND MARIE HAD RESOLVED not to let a Rumor author, no matter how tenuous, sleep rough in the middle of Manhattan, even if it pleased him. To assuage their feelings of responsibility, Hippolyte allowed a measure of shunting and was spirited off to Jeremy's Brooklyn home, where he energetically cross examined his friend about Marie. Jeremy proved most reluctant to discuss his editor's private life; his wife, Victoria, however, had no such scruples. From her, Hippolyte learned that Marie had been married briefly. Unfortunately, Victoria was an inadequate gossip; she had no idea why the marriage broke up, nor if there was a current love interest.

After staying for a week, Hippolyte escaped the publisher's sedate household, and landed back in Marie's court. He was enchanted by her futile efforts to find him alternative accommodation, particularly since she kept him at arms length in their day-to-day dealings. So when she invited him to her apartment for dinner, he considered it remarkable that she was going to allow him into her home, to sit at her table and eat her spaghetti, drink her wine. The evening would give him a chance to learn more about her. She was as unfathomable and unknowable as the Auroras first appeared. And as such she had become a natural focus of pursuit.

From the moment they met, Hippolyte had been ecstatic; Marie was just as he had imagined. So at odds with the cold austere office décor, she didn't belong, but clearly had no idea. For a start she was too tall for the low ceilings. Not that she was any taller than he was, but she stood proudly, made herself look imperial. When he first saw her in Rumor's lobby, he had automatically straightened himself up. And she seemed to use more horizontal space than most, more in fact than any human being deserved. She commanded a wide berth, won by a long stride and broad, sweeping gestures. Her unruly black hair demanded to be touched, weighed, and given its weight in gold.

She hadn't bothered to try to constrain her physical appearance, to shrink into her allotted space, to manacle her hair, but she had adopted the dress code. On that first morning, she had worn a conservative dove gray business suit that could have been bought out of a catalog for all it had to do with her. Dark earth colors, he wanted to cry out. Dark olive green! Do you have any idea how beautiful you'd be in dark green! But he held his peace and smiled. And today she was wearing that suit's prudent sister, an equally nondescript beige of which, for the moment, she had at least discarded the confining jacket to reveal an uncomfortably geriatric blouse.

"We have to take a subway!" she exclaimed when she realized he intended to bring his large wooden crate with him.

"That's okay," he replied, "it's not heavy."

"But then it's a long walk! Besides, what do you need it for?"

"In case we get a chance to go through the stuff in here."

"We can do that tomorrow. Leave it!"

"You say that every day. I'll bring it. I'll be fine."

So they took the subway, then walked the four blocks to her apartment. On the way, Marie paused beside a late-model Japanese compact and grabbed some handbills that had been stuck under its windshield wiper. "My car," she said by way of explanation. "It's a miracle it hasn't been towed yet."

Her apartment was old and small, a warren of closet-sized rooms sprouting off a narrow hallway. Squeezed into the tight corridor were bookcases loaded down with double-stacked softcover novels and hardcover biographies. While Marie started dinner, Hippolyte stashed his box in the living room, then immediately made himself at home, rooting through the shelves, setting aside titles that interested him, until he realized that all of the books were arranged in alphabetical order, according to author. He shivered at the excessive organization and jammed the books he had removed into a free space on one of the higher shelves. Due to its cumbersome size, an atlas had defied categorization and was wedged between a bottom shelf and the floor. Upon freeing it—nearly unbalancing the whole unit in the effort—he wrapped his arms around it and trotted out to the kitchen, trailing dusty webs.

At the sight of him and the atlas, Marie shook her head. Her "There was a reason—!" was punctuated by a dull thump, then by another, then by an onrush of thumps as slithering paperbacks could be heard plopping onto the hallway floor. Hippolyte sped out, and seconds later the noise abated. He returned, wiping his hands on his trousers, ignoring the tight set of her mouth.

"Wine?" he asked cheerily and poured them both a glass from a bottle sitting out on the counter. Then he cleared a space for the atlas.

Marie interrupted him. "I reread the first five chapters today; they still need work, but at least the chronology has been established."

"You don't want to talk about work right now, do you?" he countered.

"We have to keep plugging away. It's time you tackled some specifics, like sailing."

"Let's leave the book for awhile," he pleaded. "I'd rather hear about your background." He sipped some wine, a tentative sampling, then looked appreciatively at the glass in his hand. "Except that I have to say one more thing. When I was on the boat I literally dreamed about moments like this; I'd forgotten to bring any alcohol; no beer, no brandy, no wine—" He broke off and laughed. "You're going to think I'm a boozer!" He laughed again, not caring, and swallowed deeply. "Where were you born?"

By leading her through the atlas, Hippolyte eroded some of her reluctance to talk about herself and convinced her to trace her family's tracks from the French Alps to Manchester, England, to Philadelphia, and at last, on her own, to New York. She admitted a smattering of

French, an awareness of Italian. He barely suppressed a triumphant yell that he'd guessed right about her origins.

"You see," she snapped, "nothing noteworthy," and refused more discussion, citing meal preparations as her excuse, rejecting Hippolyte's offers to set the table or toss the salad. Hippolyte took the atlas over to the table and opened it to South America. "No Auroras," he announced. When Marie sat down, he poured more wine but kept one hand wrapped around the cold green bottle as though it were about to vanish.

"Speaking of the boat," she regressed, "I want to know why you haven't written about sailing."

"I have."

"Not much."

"But the book's not about sailing; it's about my discovery."

"I'd still expect more detail. You're an amateur sailor who braved the South Atlantic; why wouldn't you be proud of your newly acquired ability? I'm surprised there aren't more notes about how you handled the sails, the winds. Didn't you have to—what's the word?— I'm not a sailor either—is it tack? Sailors are always talking about tacking. And they constantly refer to halyards, masts, rigging, and such. There would be a greater sense of reality if you were to provide more nautical references. Didn't you keep a log?"

"Of course I did." He had skewered an orderly procession of tomato, green pepper, and radicchio onto his fork and was absorbed in admiring the colors. "It's the olive oil that gives them the glow," he said, then shoved them into his mouth.

"You haven't shown that to me yet, have you?"

"I told you I lost it. You should eat; your food's getting cold."

Strands of pasta were hanging awkwardly from her fork; she set it onto her plate and asked, "Did you lose it during your voyage? After?"

Hippolyte shrugged. "Just after. Do you want to see a neat trick?" He neatly caught a tidy portion of spaghetti by twirling the tines of his fork against the plate.

Marie ignored him. "That must have been devastating. Have you tried to reconstruct the entries?"

"Why are you fixated on the log, Marie? Most of the information is in my journal and survey book. It's no big deal."

"Okay. I have another question. How on earth were you able to learn sufficient sailing and navigation skills so quickly?"

"I took a course."

"One course? Was that enough?"

"Appears to have been." He was now stripping the label off of the bottle.

"You must have had an extraordinary teacher."

"I think so." The label freed, he started picking at the remains of the foil collar.

"Learning about sailing could be written in as part of the challenge. Discuss your shortcomings, your fears, why you chartered a boat. Include more terms and describe more incidents at sea. As it stands, your manuscript reads as though sailing the vessel single-handed was incidental." His face was blank, unconvinced. "Think of it this way," she persisted, "there's a huge audience for sailing stories. It would expand your readership. And make the book more interesting. I wish you still had your log. Could you rewrite portions of it?"

He absently dug a pencil out of a pocket and began sketching onto the still-open page of the atlas. "I will think about it, but honestly, there are sailing books galore." A sailboat took shape, crude but unmistakable. "Sailing doesn't interest me, Marie. The boat was a means of getting to the Auroras. That's all. Besides, I mention weather, the time spent sailing. I write about sea life, birds, loneliness. And you realize, I hope—I've never tried to disguise this—that I did resort to the engine whenever I could. It was a hell of a lot simpler to power it up than to hoist the sails. There! A sailing term!" As Marie watched open-mouthed, he continued drawing sails and masts and arrows across the South Atlantic. "Oh, sorry," he said, when he realized what he was doing. "It'll erase, I hope." But she grimaced all the same.

"I get the impression that you sailed more than motored, though."

"Only because I didn't bring enough fuel. I couldn't bring enough." He tried to obliterate the marks with the pencil's eraser but managed only to blur the lines into a gummy, smeary mess.

"Please leave it alone, Hippolyte. Didn't you enjoy the sensation of sailing? Once you got used to it?" She reached over and shut the atlas.

"Sure, why not?" He brushed the eraser crumbs into the palm of his hand, looked at them quizzically, then stuck them in his pocket. "Skimming across the water is a gas. When you're in control. But I wasn't, at least not often. Usually something else was in control, and I didn't like that feeling one bit. It was damned frightening, in fact. Looking over the side and not even being able to see down into those terrible depths, to truly consider your possible destiny as a surface for barnacles, knowing all the time that the depths are there, are real, and there's no safety net to stop you from sinking. There's just creaky boards between you and the bottom of the sea four thousand metres below, and what's keeping them from splitting?" He closed his eyes against the thought. "I don't want to emphasize that. There's no point; dozens of genuine sailors have already covered this territory, quite admirably."

"Be that as it may, I want your description of getting to the Auroras to appear convincing. How would you propose to do that?"

Hippolyte rubbed his scalp. He'd gotten his hair cut and was reacquainting himself with the shape of his head. "Isn't it believable?"

She hesitated, then revised. "Come up with a neat way of depicting it."

He frowned. "There's all my calculations. I can reconstruct those. Anyone could check them and duplicate the course I set. This is good sauce." With his fork, spoon, and a slice of bread, he scraped every molecule of food off of his plate. "Do you like to cook?"

"Not particularly."

"I do when there's a reason. I could cook for you."

"Hah! The kitchen's too small for you. Furthermore, to tell the truth, I've got a lot of work to do. I can't afford any more interruptions. Sorry to be so blunt, but your book is taking up a disproportionate amount of my time."

"Well, that's honest." He laughed. "I should be working harder and bothering you less."

"Basically."

Dinner finished, she barred him from the kitchen, not allowing him to wash the dishes or snoop through her cupboards. She parked him in an easy chair in the living room, tuned the radio to opera, and thrust a magazine into his hands; there he sat docilely, trying to shut out a messy soprano strangling the airwaves.

Figures she'd grab hold of the logbook. Just like a terrier with a rat. He could make up a new log and pretend that he'd found it. That way the issue of the islands disappearing wouldn't be raised and it would satisfy her sailing obsession. It was worth thinking about.

He fanned the pages of the magazine, then tossed it aside. He stood up and opened the drawer of a small teak desk. Income tax form, receipts, car license renewal application, a parking ticket, a steel pica ruler, some pens and pencils, a couple of stamps, paper clips. He slid the drawer shut.

More shelves held reference books and a preponderance of paperback novels, mostly orange spined. The only vegetation in the room was a dried-flower arrangement; the couch did not fold out into a bed. There were no pictures on the walls. He wandered down the hall, sneaked a look in her room. Here were books stacked high next to the double bed, others spread out on the unslept-on side, papers scattered helter-skelter on the carpet, two alarm clocks, a complete absence of frills and stuffed toys. The coast was clear, so he stuck his head into the closet packed full of awful gray and brown suits. Did she have nothing to live in? He pushed aside hangers from which rigid shoulder-padded blouses hung. Dresses, all with sleeves to the wrists, collars above the collar bone, hems below the knee; shoes that daren't show toes, never mind the cracks between them; no trousers at all, no saggy baggy sweaters, nothing to cut loose in, or run in, or just plain forget oneself in. Since staring at the dead jackets and skirts wasn't going to bring them to life, he closed the closet door and headed off to check out the bathroom.

Hippolyte spent a moment scrutinizing himself in the reflection of the mirrored cabinet. Finding nothing new in his face, he yanked open the door and looked inside. Where were the birth control pills, the prescription skin creams, the anti-aging lotions? What about stress pills, sleeping pills, wake-up pills? He snapped the kid-proof cap off a bottle of Aspirin, took a pill out, and bit into it. Aspirin, no mistaking that. A bottle of rubbing alcohol, dull nail clippers, unisex stick deodorant, a soft-bristle toothbrush, anti-cavity toothpaste. He resqueezed the toothpaste at mid-tube, forcing half the contents back to the bottom, then shuffled through a pile of little soaps from hotels in San Francisco, Savannah, Toronto, Guadalajara. There were no signs of male guests: no spare toothbrushes, no face cloths mono-grammed in masculine script, no bottles of Aqua Velva, or man-size razors.

He'd been hoping to find some giveaway to a lighter, more friv-olous side of her nature, like a copy of *1001 Bathroom Jokes* or one of those ghastly bath bombs filled with rose petals. Nothing made him scuttle faster than a new flame trying to entice him into a bathtub filled with this absurd compost even if it did smell nice. A rustling at the door made him look around. With a start he realized that Marie had been watching him.

"I'm looking for soap," he said.

She turned away. "It's late; I think it's time you left."

He picked up soap that had been sitting on the counter and waved it. "Can I have a shower before I go?"

She looked him up and down and rolled her eyes. "Oh, for Heaven's sakes," she sighed, "of course, have a shower." She withdrew into the hallway, then stopped and turned around. "It's ten-thirty. I'll put a blanket and a pillow on the couch. But it's just for one night." She shut the door behind her.

Hippolyte stood in the hallway, rubbing away at his hair with a damp towel. His shirt was unbuttoned and hung out of his trousers; he hadn't bothered to put his socks back on. He stared at her now-closed bedroom door, thought about trying to see if it was locked. But the shut door was clear enough. He'd been hoping that the invitation to stay extended further, but knew it was too much to expect. She'd given him no sign, no signal that could even be misinterpreted.

He turned out the hall light, then sat down on the floor outside her room. Her light was out; there was no telltale glow coming from under the door. He imagined her lying in bed thinking about him, thinking about this man outside her room, this man who would be much better off inside her room. He imagined her tossing and turning, trying to decide if she should get up and invite him to join her. He shifted a bit, hoping to make the floorboards creak. There was only silence; the boards were tightly lodged and damnably discreet. He curled up like a faithful mutt and lay in front of the door, the better to hear her restlessness. There were no sounds of thrashing bedcovers or of pillows being pounded, no hints of lonely distress or frustrated agitation; not even the absolute dreadful silence of rigid contemplation reached him. She must have gone to sleep.

Hippolyte got up off the floor and skulked out to the living room. The couch was appealing, but he was far from tired, and the odor of clams, onions, and oil hung heavily in the room. He raised the window and leaned out. Mixed with the warm night air was a touch of freshness that he'd been missing. "Ah, the call of the wild," he declared, grabbing the blanket and searching for his shoes. "I'll go sleep in the park." At the door he faltered, then went back to the living room desk. He slipped the ruler he'd spotted earlier into his jacket pocket and left the apartment.

The street was wonderfully quiet, with thick-leafed trees shading the sidewalk from the glare of the streetlamps. Plunging into the darkness, he began retracing the route they had taken earlier that evening. But when he came level with her car, he grinned. Extracting the pica ruler from his pocket, he proceeded to slide it between the driver's window and the side panel of the door. About eighteen inches long and wafer thin with a flange at one end, the ruler was normally used to measure lines of type. Within seconds he was bedded down in the backseat with the windows lowered and a cool breeze blowing through.

Hippolyte woke to someone prodding his shoulder and to the intense sounds of morning: a garbage truck, honking horns, a police siren. "How can you sleep through this racket?" Marie asked, leaning over the back of the driver's seat. "Come on, I'll take you to breakfast. You don't deserve it, but I'll be nice to you anyway."

Hippolyte crawled out, rubbed his face, smoothed his hair, and smiled at her.

Stuff it; it won't work on me, could be clearly read in her expression. "This way," she said out loud.

When they reached the café at the next corner, Hippolyte pulled a fancy hand-milled soap in faux-French packaging from his pocket.

"Gotta wash up." He grinned, knowing that she had identified the soap from her own inventory.

"How did you get into my car?" she asked when he returned from the restroom.

"What do you call this neighbourhood?"

"East Village. The car was locked. How did you get in?"

"I like it here; is it expensive?" He slapped the pica ruler onto the table. "I found this on your desk; it works perfectly."

"In the desk," she corrected. "You're nothing, if not resourceful. Does that thing damage the lock?"

You're terrific, thought Hippolyte. "Not at all," he replied. "But it doesn't work on all cars."

"There's that luck of yours again. Just imagine the odds against finding a suitable tool in *my* desk, using it to break into *my* car, which just *happened* to be susceptible. Are you always this lucky?"

Ask me why I slept in your car, he urged her silently. "How did you know where to look?" He accidentally bumped her leg with his shifting feet. "Sorry," he said.

She tucked her feet under her chair, otherwise not acknowledging the apology. "Don't flatter yourself. I walk past the car every morning to make sure it's still there. Being towed or having it stolen, it's all the same hell in this city. And it's better to find out sooner rather than later." She sipped her coffee. "I hate to change the subject, but the whole business about the boat is bothering me. It seems almost miraculous that you sailed so far with so little experience. Can't you supply more details? Particularly of your difficulties."

"Let's do something today."

"We will; we're going to work."

"You've got a car; let's go for a drive, play hooky."

"You're not doing anything except rewriting."

"Are you married?" Might as well hear it from the horse's mouth, he thought.

"Obviously, no. How much did the boat cost to charter per day? Then there's the Falklands. Is Stanley a very small town? Does it have an English feel? You're nodding. I think this is interesting, because I know that some people have the impression that it is more Argentine than English. Where did you stay? What are the people like? What did they think of you and your plans? You get my gist."

He borrowed a pen from a passing waiter and scribbled the questions down on a paper napkin. "I don't think it would be fair to write anything about anybody. I mean, they may not take it right."

"I'm not suggesting character assassination."

"I know, but sometimes people just take exception to being written about. And how much the boat cost. Peter would flip his wig if I published that. He'd either be accused of being criminally usurious or laughed at for being a sucker. There's no value in bringing up these details. Are you seeing anyone?"

"No. Anyway, think about it."

Marie paid the bill and they left the café.

"Where's your box?" she asked.

"Oh, I left it at your apartment."

Marie winced. "You can't stay there. You'll have to find somewhere else."

He dismissed her fretful voice; clearly he'd manage somehow.

Tested the camera again, don't feel super-confident since its last overhaul. Shot off a roll and got it processed at one of those one-hour joints. All looks fine. Relax.

2 February 2000
Saint Romualdo shrine, via San Borja, west of Estación Central, just off the Alameda. Wall about 10 metres long, 2 and a half high, smothered with plaques, small blue wooden altars filled with smoking candles and plastic flowers line the sidewalk. Bronze baby boots, faded photos dangle from the wall. What's going on here? "Graciàs Romualdito." "Thank you, little Romualdo, for helping me to conceive." Ah ha. No wonder it's so popular.

Rereading *The Count of Monte Cristo*.

Two-hour bus ride from Santiago to Valparaíso. Noticed road-side shrines. By Valparaíso counted 21. On the return trip (sat on the opposite side of the bus) counted 47. The highway's being revamped. Will they move the shrines or bulldoze them?

Actual colours

Av. San Diego: vendor selling pantographs. Will demonstrate— eagerly—but no takers

Entrance: 600 pesos

From "Your neighbourhood," an information booklet in hotel: "Slowly the area turns into a nocturnal and bohemian place with small hotels, meeting bars and women offering their services. Police enforcement released the illegal activities."

AVDA O'HIGGINS
Londres
Paris
San Diego

Museo Nacional Historia Natural (just off Plaza des Armes)
Spanish Vocabulary:
Pingüino = Penguin
pinipedos includes Lobos marinos, elepfante marino, focas, lobo común, lobo fino o dedos pelos

Maps: 1) "La America: Dispuesta segun las ultimas y nuevas observationes de las Accademias y de Paris, y de Londres." (n.d.) Shows I. de Sebalde, I. de Beauchene, I. de los Estados, I. de la Roca (S. Georgia?) and I. de Saxemburg?!
2) "A Map of Chili, Patagonia, La Plata and South part of Brasil." by H. Moll. Shows Falkland I. (limits not known) (n.d.)
3) "Kaart van Chili" (Dutch, n.d.) shows "Malouines Eil of Falkland."
Nothing goes far enough east.

Lemon slices wrapped in cheesecloth
Against wasps

Ribbon to hold it all together

Café con leche: from 600 to 700 pesos about #1.50

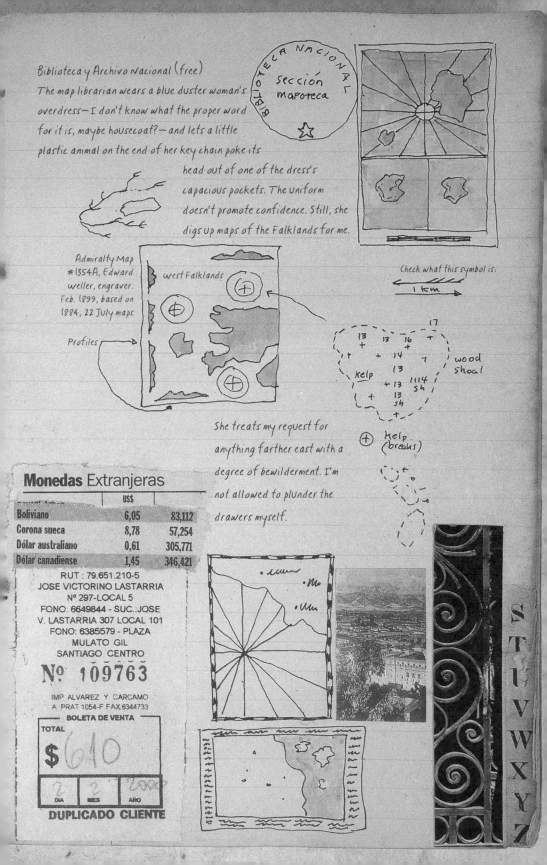

Biblioteca y Archivo Nacional (free)
The map librarian wears a blue duster woman's overdress—I don't know what the proper word for it is, maybe housecoat?—and lets a little plastic animal on the end of her key chain poke its head out of one of the dress's capacious pockets. The uniform doesn't promote confidence. Still, she digs up maps of the Falklands for me.

BIBLIOTECA NACIONAL
Sección
Mapoteca
☆

Admiralty Map #1354A, Edward Weller, engraver. Feb. 1899, based on 1884, 22 July maps

West Falklands

Profiles

Check what this symbol is:
1 km

17
13   13   16
+   +
+   +   14   7
13   wood
Kelp   +   13   1114   shoal
+   13   sh
sh
+

She treats my request for anything farther east with a degree of bewilderment. I'm not allowed to plunder the drawers myself.

⊕ Kelp (breaks)

Monedas Extranjeras

	US$	
Boliviano	6,05	83,112
Corona sueca	8,78	57,254
Dólar australiano	0,61	305,771
Dólar canadiense	1,45	346,421

RUT : 79.651.210-5
JOSE VICTORINO LASTARRIA
Nº 297-LOCAL 5
FONO: 6649844 - SUC..JOSE
V. LASTARRIA 307 LOCAL 101
FONO: 6385579 - PLAZA
MULATO GIL
SANTIAGO CENTRO
Nº 109763

IMP ALVAREZ Y CARCAMO
A PRAT 1054-F FAX 6344733
BOLETA DE VENTA
TOTAL
$ 610

| 2 | 2 | 2000 |
| DIA | MES | AÑO |

DUPLICADO CLIENTE

S
T
U
V
W
X
Y
Z

Nineteen

"WE MUST GO OVER MY SPECIMENS." Hippolyte looked around her office. It was surprisingly neat for all the work she was doing. The boxes he had sent earlier were not in sight; neither was the bag he'd stuffed under the chair; nor were the photos he'd left scattered across her desk. "Where's all my stuff?" he asked. "My duffel? And the boxes I sent by courier?"

"Later. Right now, I have more questions. Let's keep on track. When did you actually leave for the Falklands? I don't see a date in the manuscript."

"I need my duffel bag," he insisted. "All that information's in there."

"Don't whine," she chided. "We'll find it; when did you last see it? Was it at Jeremy's?"

A wave of relief swept across his brow as he remembered storing it in the lobby closet. He vanished momentarily and returned lugging the bag. From it he pulled a notebook. "It's in my travel diary. Here." He showed her the page, January 31st.

"Did you stay in Chile?" A nod, and a couple of pages later, Santiago appeared, annotated with addresses and sketches.

"Good," she skimmed the pages. "This will help. How about the other books in there?" She pointed to the bag. He shook his head and wound the rope tight around the duffel's neck. "Do you have your passport around. What does a Falkland custom's stamp looks like?"

The passport, which had been jammed in his back pocket, emerged. He showed her the stamps. "But you've only one entry and one exit stamp." She was scrutinizing the dates. "I thought you had to get your passport stamped when you left for the Auroras and again when you came back." He patiently turned the page for her.

As soon as she saw that all dates were accounted for, she lost interest and changed the subject. "I'm going to put you in another office." He picked up the bag. "Leave it there, for the time being," she suggested, pointing to the corner. "I want you to rewrite, starting with chapter one, an expanded description of how you traveled to the Auroras."

She guided him into a plush, windowless boardroom deep in Rumor's bowels and flicked on a reading lamp, its light cunningly placed as though to burn a hole through his manuscript already lying there. Either she wanted him to work, or she wanted to set his work on fire. A computer dominated the tabletop. It glowed maliciously. A couch beckoned from the far end of the room, but he sat down in the hard oak library chair and waited for her to leave. She hesitated, as if wondering what he'd get up to once the door was shut, then left. He doused the lamp and threw himself down on the couch. An intense afterimage of the bulb burned through his retina and prickled his thoughts.

Sighing, he dragged himself back over to the chair. Wriggling his bony bum on the puritanical surface, he regretted Marie's sufficient padding, which seemed to leave her numb to the discomfort of others. He winced when he saw what awaited him: lying on top of the manuscript was a densely typed foolscap sheet prepared by his overly industrious editor.

Enlarge on the history of the Auroras and provide detailed accounts of their sightings. Right now, aside from Bustamente and some rather spurious Spanish accounts, most of your references deny the Auroras. You need more information about Bustamente. In the library, I found a translation of Malaspina's voyage that includes Bustamente's search for the Auroras and have summarized what he wrote below. Go there and read it through yourself. The original document may be even more valuable.

Original account (Later edition): 970P M23vs: Malaspina, Alejandro [1754–1809]. *Viaje politic-cientifico alrededor del mundo por las corbetas Descubierta y Atrevida al mando de los capitanes de navio don Alejandro Malaspina y don José de Bustamente y Guerra desde 1789 a 1794, con una introduccion por don Pedro de Novo y Colson.* Madrid: Impr. de la viuda e hijos de Abienzo, 1885.

Translation: 970P M23p: Malaspina, Allessandro [1754–1809]. *Politico-scientific Voyage Around the World by the Corvettes Descubierta and Atrevida Under the Command of the naval captains Don Alexandro Malaspina and Don José de Bustamente y Guerra, from 1789–1794.* Edited by Don Pedro de Novo y Colson. Translated by Carl Robinson, 1934. MS.

You should state somewhere that Malaspina's expedition consisted of two ships, and that the *Atrevida* was surveying the Auroras on its own. What was the other ship doing at this time?

From the translation: Book 3, p. 164: Bustamente (B. from here on) refers to finding out information about the Auroras in Lima and then on p. 166 he comments about how the captain of the Princesa D. Martin Oyarvide gave him the information. I notice that you've referred to Oyarvide as <u>Manuel</u> de Oyarvi<u>do</u>. Confirm or refer to the discrepancy if you don't trust your original source. Follow up the reference to B. and Oyarvide's meeting in Lima. You make no direct references to Oyarvide's account. You'll find his description, in B.'s words, at the bottom of p. 166. He reports finding a shoal off of the Auroras that B. himself couldn't find. Consider looking for a primary source for Oyarvide.

p. 165: B. comments on an abundance of seaweed and a massing of gulls around the purported latitude of the Auroras. Did you notice this as well? You don't mention it. Also, B.'s longitude readings differ quite considerably from yours, as he measures from Cadiz (44°15′W) rather than Greenwich. Have you recalculated his readings, or have you relied on secondary sources?

p. 166: B's descriptions of the islands. Perhaps you could work his in with your own. This would show not only your greater familiarity with them but would also serve to confirm some of the details that you observed and give you a chance to explain the differences. Note especially that B. refers to one of the islands being covered in "a heavy mantle of snow" (pp. 166–67). He also refers to numerous icebergs; I cannot find a single iceberg reference in your manuscript. He was there in January when the weather, according to you, should have been even better than February, when you traveled. Was 1794 a colder than normal year in the South Atlantic or even globally?

p. 168: B. states specifically that he saw two islands, yet the map that you've supplied of his expedition shows four islands plus the symbol "+" (see Weddell, below). Explain this discrepancy.

B. frequently noticed errors when he took readings of his positions, and he states that the terrible weather—fogs, rain, squalls, strong winds—prevented him from approaching the islands closely. He also gives leagues for distance. The dictionary states that a league is anything from 2.4 to 4.6 statute miles. How many miles would a league have been in 1794?

Jeremy slid into the adjacent chair. "How're you doing there, Webb?" Hippolyte's concentration broke at the sound of Jeremy's voice.

"Terrible," Hippolyte admitted. "I'm having a hell of a time convincing Marie that I'm on the level. She thinks I've made this whole thing up." He poked his friend's arm. "Tell her that I'm incapable of lying!"

Jeremy stood up. "I'm staying out of it! I'll leave you to your work, unless you've changed your mind and want to come back home with me—" but the line of Hippolyte's shoulders, the angle of his neck, cut him off at mid-sentence. As though Hippolyte's need for solitude was expressed in posture. "Well," said Jeremy, "I'm off. See you!" He vanished only to reappear a second later. "You know, Webb," he grinned

uneasily, "I've missed you; no matter what happens with this book . . .
Let's put it this way, I don't want anything to jeopardize our friendship."

"What are you talking about, Jeremy?"

"Oh, nothing, just getting sentimental, I guess," and he disappeared again.

As for Hippolyte, he continued to read.

Regarding James Weddell. You have him listed in your bibliography, so I
trust that you have read him. His account of B.'s voyage differs so
extremely from B.'s own that I can't help but think that his source (not
listed) is suspect. Incidentally, Weddell doesn't refer to B., only to the
Atrevida. An example of the differences:

Bustamente (p. 166): "Scarcely had we time to make other arrangements
. . . when the sight of one of them at five of the afternoon came to
release us from our state of continuous vigilance. Luckily, in a clear
moment, we also observed the latitude of 53 deg. 40′ South and longitude of 42 deg. 24′.

'The Isle, seen at a distance of seven leagues and covered with
snow, made one doubt the truth of its existence. Under full sail we
steered toward it . . .' "

Weddell (p. 65, supposedly quoting from B.): " 'On the 20th in the
evening, after some hours of calm, and variable winds, it blew from
the S.S.E., and somewhat cleared away. We steered east, and on the
21st, at mid-day, found ourselves in latitude 53°40′S., and longitude
42° W. Cadiz . . .

'At 5 1/2 p.m. we perceived to the northward, at a great distance, a
dark lump, which appeared to all of us like a mountain of ice.
Notwithstanding, we bore away for it under a press of sail . . .' "

So many questions, but he saw her point. Aside from maps, he hadn't
done a very good job of providing convincing proof that the islands
existed. For instance, Oyarvido's/Oyarvide's description of the islands

could certainly have been used to greater advantage. He had mentioned the *Princesa*'s captain but hadn't linked his name with Bustamente's. Hippolyte reread Marie's comments and checked his watch; 4:30, too late to head to the library, of course; whenever he needed to go there, the library always seemed to be about ready to close. But he started scribbling notes and such answers as he could compose on the spot.

He wrote:

A league, as measured on land by the Spanish in 1794, was 2.63 miles. As for measuring distance at sea at this time, a league was the reach of a cannonball fired at a hostile ship, which was about three miles. We still use this to designate territorial limits offshore, although we don't call it a league anymore. A league is also three miles in the English-speaking world. We got it from the Normans, who got it from the Gauls, who got it from the Romans. In Rome, a league was made up of paces, 1500 of them, a pace being about five feet.

The weather question had always bothered him, but most of the maps he had consulted showed the Antarctic Convergence reaching to just south of where he had positioned the Auroras, meaning that climate was not as extreme as on islands within the Convergence and confirming his observation of relatively mild conditions. And as for finding records of the weather in 1794, he'd had enough trouble with forecasts for the year 2000. The iceberg thing was problematic as well, not to mention disappointing. He'd studied the terminology and had committed to heart words like bergy bits and growlers and found he had no use for them.

98°T/93°
100 kn

court agaun whil
ht it was a case wh
for the

spot

leave all public places—walking to a

d up, down and

FALKLAND CURRENT

1-4"

15°C

10°C

SOUTHERN OCEAN CURRENT

1-4"

5°C

80°   60°   40°

≥ 6m (≥ 20')
≥ 3.5m (≥ 12')

Twenty

"Where are you staying tonight?" Someone was talking to him.

"What?" Hippolyte dragged himself out of his reverie. "What?" he repeated, slowly coming to his senses. He'd been daydreaming, imagining himself back on the Auroras, watching a brig circle round and round as he ran along the beach, hailing it. He rubbed his face, sheepish, focused. On Marie.

"I guess the backseat wasn't so comfortable, after all! Were you asleep?"

"No, no, just lost in thought." He felt contented and hazy; he wanted to reach over and put his hands around her shoulders and hold her.

She glanced down at his work, scribbled over with notes, then to the computer screen pulsing with starfish. She sat down in the chair lately occupied by Jeremy.

"Where are you staying tonight?"

"I don't know. The park. Somewhere."

"Do you need anything in the box that you left?"

"No, not yet. I'll manage."

"I feel badly, not offering to let you stay at my place for more than one night." Warmth, not heard before, stirred her voice.

He absently laid his hand on her arm, a fragment of his earlier impulse escaping. "Don't be silly. I'll survive." Her flinch, expected he supposed, reminded him. "Sorry," he lied and drew back.

She stood up. "Here's more." Two pages fluttered to the table. "By the way, everyone's gone. The security guard will let you out. Just call down to the lobby. Good night."

Consolidate your information regarding previous attempts to find the Auroras. At present these details appear scattered throughout your journals. Please rewrite as one chapter or as a section of a chapter.

"I wonder if there's anything to eat in this place." He drifted down the hall of the now-empty Rumor offices. The first door he came to was Jeremy's. Not as deluxe as the boardroom, Jeremy's office was still a far sight more comfortable than the editors' cramped quarters. Hippolyte assumed the sober men's-club furnishings were leftovers from a previous command. If Jeremy's taste were allowed free reign, the walls would have been papered floor-to-ceiling with the Lone Ranger or Flash Gordon. There was certainly a king's ransom of spaceship wallpaper in Jeremy's kids' rooms, in spite of them all being girls.

A computer snoozed on the desk. He went over and punched a button; it sprang to life. Hippolyte scanned the screen until he came to a folder titled "H.W." He double clicked on it, opening it to a file called "Memos." He sank down into the leather swivel chair and double-clicked on the file icon. The program began grinding through the motions of opening up.

The short document consisted of memos pertaining to his book. The first one mentioned something about working on the book until August 30th, which didn't make any sense. Marie had told him it would take much longer than that. He scrolled down to the next about the title and frowned when he saw the reference to his suggestion as "a loser." The next, from April 11, describing his "fantastic story" was a boost, though he wasn't certain about the phrase "potential new author," since he'd already been given an advance and considered himself a "for-sure new author." The remaining memos were to the accounting department and revealed a great deal about how much Jeremy had had to fight for the twenty thousand dollars. Hippolyte thought about Jeremy's departing words earlier and resolved not to let him down. He returned to the beginning of the file and reread the first memo. Who was this McGovern? And what Givens letter was he referring to? Had they been in touch with Peter behind his back?

Where were these letters? He quit out of the program and began hunting.

The desk drawers divulged a bottle of scotch with an unbroken seal; he put it back unsampled. A package of gum lay in the top drawer; this he helped himself to. After a couple of chews, he tossed the wad into the wastebasket. In addition, there were several boxes of tissues, a file of press clippings, a binder of financial statements. It's all decidedly uninteresting, he assessed, finding no incriminating letters. As he turned to leave, he noticed the boxes that he'd sent earlier heaped in a corner and reminded himself to show their contents to Marie as soon as possible.

The lunchroom a little farther down the hall was scarcely more promising, with a coffee maker (but no coffee), packets of chamomile tea, and a box of crackled marzipan emblazoned with "Happy New Year! To all at Rumor! 1991!" Otherwise, there was a portable radio on the shelf and a drawer containing cutlery, crumbs, and a half-read Harlequin romance. A phone hung from the wall, directories lay on the counter beside it. He rang a nearby take-out joint, ordered pizza and a six-pack, and phoned the security guard to offer him some when it arrived. Then he went back to the boardroom, still bugged by the McGovern and Givens references. He sat at the computer and rested his fingers for a moment on the keyboard.

Okay, here goes:

Chroniclers who have undertaken to recount the many attempts to find the Auroras have been most guilty of perpetuating myths and falsehoods through the repetition of unsubstantiated and unreferenced accounts. At the risk of becoming a member of this club of rather lax historians, I will briefly summarize what is generally known.

We start in 1762 with the discovery of the Auroras by the Spanish ship the *Aurora,* * which had the distinction of spotting them a second time** twelve years later. In 1769, the crew of the

San Miguel, thinking themselves south of the Falklands, noted six islands, and later, when they realized how far off the mark they were, declared that they too must have seen the Auroras. In 1779 and 1790, respectively, the *Pearl* and the *Dolores* both reported spotting islands but failed to note their positions.

In 1790, Captain Manuel de Oyarvido (aka de Oyarvide or D. Martín Oyarvido, but get this: Poe called him de Oyarudo!), commander of the *Princesa,* reported seeing the islands and communicated his knowledge in 1793 to Captain José de Bustamente y Guerra (variously known as José Bustamente, José de Bustamente) when they crossed paths in Lima, Peru. Bustamente, along with the expedition's commander Captain Alejandro Malaspina, surveyed the coast of South America, and while thus engaged, specifically set out to survey the Auroras. From the 11th to the 20th of January 1794, Bustamente and the crew of the *Atrevida* made their way from the Malvinas (aka the Falklands) to the previously reported position of the Auroras. There they spent seven days seeking and finally locating three islands, which they identified as Las Islas de l'Aurore. The above accounts, including that of Bustamente, were related by the English navigator James Weddell in his book *A Voyage Towards the South Pole, Performed in the Years 1822–24. Containing an examination of the Antarctic Sea, to the Seventy-fourth Degree of Latitude: and A Visit to Tierra del Fuego, with a particular account of the Inhabitants* (1825).†† He stated that his information came from extracts translated from the "Royal Hydrographical Society of Madrid." *Memoria segunda, tomo* 1° pp. 51, 52.

Hippolyte's fingers froze as he heard a key turn in a lock somewhere in the distance. Then the distinct odor of pizza wafted down the hall. A gruff voice called out, "Where's the guy what wants the pizza?" And the security guard appeared, a solidly built, grizzling sixty-year-old, who looked as though he could eat an entire Italian restaurant on his coffee break. "My name's Ralph junior," he said by way of introduction. "The junior's very important; it distinguishes me from my old man.

Otherwise the only ways you can tell us apart is he's dead and I'm not!" He punched Hippolyte on the shoulder. "You owe me twenty bucks, fella!"

They demolished the mozzarella, olive, artichoke, and ham pizza, a respectable number of beers, the bitsy servings of coleslaw. "You can't order breakfast here without getting coleslaw," Hippolyte observed, his mouth full, then choked on Ralph junior's back-thumping guffaw. After wolfing down the last slice, Ralph burped and left, spiriting several cans of beer away with a wink.

Hippolyte reread his last line. He had written all of this before; why was he rewriting it? He skimmed through the opening pages in his manuscript; there it was, he'd already covered this early on, in chapter two. He read through it again carefully and could see what she was driving at; his description was spotty at best. But he had more details somewhere. He slapped his forehead. Of course, his duffel bag! All of his maps and reference books and photocopies were in there. He leapt up and raced to her office, grabbed the bag, and turned to leave, but was diverted momentarily by a letter sitting on her desk. "Dear Ms. Simplon," he read,

> It was a pleasure speaking with you the other day. I was glad to hear that book editors go through the same frustrations that plague us magazine types.
>
> Because you've never worked with Hippolyte or anyone like him before, I can understand your hesitations. I hope I can put your concerns to rest. I've been his editor here at *50° North* since 1997. (The fact that he was a co-founder of the magazine has nothing to do with my opinions. We call him one of the 'old guys,' and not always kindly.) At first I was pretty dismayed at the way he handed in material. Like you say, it's disorganized and messy. He once wrote a story on the back of dried-out leaves! *Ficus blancus* or something.

Christ, Johnny! how many times did I tell you it was *Heliconia barqueta*?

I almost gave up on him then and there, but he had intended that I run the story as is, reproduced on the leaves, so I did. It was a huge success and got a review in *Art Today*. Aside from that, I soon came to realize that no one else I worked with could deliver a story like he can. He won't buy a computer, won't admit that he can use one; I don't think he's had his telephone hooked up for the last year; he refuses to hand in nicely typed double-spaced manuscripts. What can you do?

For our part, we welcome anything Hippolyte sends. Although recent budget cuts have made it necessary to vet proposals first, for him I really only just go through the motions. Could you let him know that I'd still like to see his idea for the Aurora article? If it doesn't conflict with the book, that is.

Regards,

J Harada

John Harada

P.S. A copy of the *Ficus* article is enclosed.

The letter was dated 5 July. Today was the 2nd of August. That meant she'd had this for weeks without saying anything about receiving it, not to mention telling him she'd phoned the magazine in the first place. The McGovern / Givens letters were now making sense. She was checking up on him, was she? Good for Johnny, at least, for defending him. The desktop revealed nothing else pertinent, neither did the desk drawers. The filing cabinet over by the wall, the next best bet, was locked. Just whom didn't she trust?, he asked himself. He picked away at the lock; those letters are in there somewhere, he fumed, but it steadfastly resisted his attempts. He pounded the cabinet in frustration, then gave up and left, dragging his duffel behind him.

Back in the boardroom, he attempted to undo the cord. Something's not right, here, he thought, and looked closely at it. It had been knotted into a couple of tight overhands. Who'd done that? When he had tied it earlier, he had used a constrictor knot. He cursed as he struggled to undo the simple yet disagreeable knots, then finally succeeding, pulled the contents of the bag out book by book, box by box and spread them out on the table. There were his books, journals, maps, and photocopies. Nothing seemed to be missing, so with tacks scrounged from Janice's desk, he pinned maps and photos to the walls—the penguins alone stretched from one corner to the next—and stood back, pleased with the effect, naturally, since it mimicked his own living room. He remembered that it was his need for his reference books and journals that had set him off on the hunt for the duffel in the first place, so he found the appropriate material and settled back to write:

Weddell's account obviously impressed a lot of people, because we see it repeated almost word for word in Benjamin Morrell's story of his quest for the Auroras, as well as in numerous current histories.★★★ I personally have not been able to confirm the existence of Royal Hydrographical Society archives. Perhaps if the publisher were willing to fund a trip to Madrid I would be able to do so. Back to the Auroras:

Bustamente's own account, that is, unfiltered by Weddell, is close enough even if the actual wording is different. It can be read in Malaspina's *Viaje politic-cientifico* (1885). Bustamente's journey, as documented on the British Admiralty Chart 357 (A1) "A Chart of the Ethiopic or Southern Ocean," (W. Faden, 1 January 1808), shows the same configuration as an earlier version (1800) but with the addition of the Shag Rocks farther east.

We now move into more modern but no less confusing times. I have already referred to Weddell's¶ account of others' expeditions. His own began on the 27th of January, 1820 at Staten Land just off of Tierra del Fuego.¶¶ On the fourth day out, Weddell had reached the latitude and longitude of the Auroras as reported by Bustamente but could see no islands. They puttered about in the general area to no avail until the 7th of February and then gave up.§

Benjamin Morrell [1795–?], §§ a sea captain from New York, and, it turns out, one of the biggest liars and braggarts in seafaring history, undertook to follow in Weddell's wake. The resulting voyage, captured in his book *A Narrative of Four Voyages,* aka *Morrell's Voyages and Discoveries with a Sketch of the Author's Life,* 1841 (1st published 1832), is essentially a recap of Weddell. Leaving the Falklands a few weeks after the return of the *Henry* (see below), that is, on the 2nd of November 1822, Morrell headed southeast. He reports that he scoured the area for over 15 days "attempting to discover this *terra incognita,* and being now fully convinced that any further search would be equally fruitless"; he left on the 18th.

Morrell was not the first American to make his way to the Auroras. As I mentioned above, the *Henry* had already been. This was a schooner under the command of a Captain Johnson, who had laboured futilely for six weeks to find the Auroras, but was back at anchor in the Falklands by the 23rd of October, 1822. What do I know of Johnson? Not a heck of a lot. Morrell mentions him, then authors who read Morrell mention him, and so on.

There was also Captain John Biscoe, who sailed around the South Atlantic in the *Tula* from 1830 through to 1833. He's best known for charting Enderby Land and Graham Land. To tell the truth, I don't know if Biscoe was American or not. I can't find anything else about him. I'm not even certain about why he's said to have reconnoitered the Auroras, as I have read no first-hand reports by him. If any readers have information about Captains Biscoe or Johnson, I'd certainly be happy to hear from them.

A final sighting comes from a log entry from the *Helen Baird.* This has been reported by several sources† and, according to Stommel (92), is held at the Hydrographic Office, but they were unable to trace it for me, although they were helpful in many other respects. The unnamed captain of the *Helen Baird* wrote that on December 6th, 1856, the northernmost of the <u>five</u> Aurora islands was spotted at 52°40′S, 48°22′W. The whole grouping was partially snow covered and extended over 20 miles in length.

Auroraphiles will notice that I am omitting the Edgar Allan Poe story *The Narrative of A. Gordon Pym*. I described this earlier, and as it is fiction, it has no place in this summary. [Marie: This will be, nonetheless, a good place to stick my portrait of Poe.]

Footnotes:

★The *Aurora* apparently saw two islands. The westernmost was the largest, just over five miles in length; the one to its east was smaller but of an unspecified size. Lat. 53°15′S, 325°22′W from Tenerife.

★★During this sighting, the *Aurora* reported that the westerly island was about three leagues long.‡ The second island's extent was unspecified, though it was three to four leagues distant (E.S.E.).

††Of interest to book lovers: According to a bookseller friend, Weddell's second edition is actually preferred over the first one. The later edition incorporates a 48-page account of his second voyage and a chapter entitled "Observations." See photocopy of the title page.

★★★See Bibliography.

¶ Weddell (1787–1834) was a Master of the Royal Navy and a sealer. His name graces both the Weddell Sea *and* the Weddell Seal *(Leptonychotes weddellii)* [see sketch]. During his hunt for fur seals, he sailed to 74°15′S, farther south than any other explorer before him.

¶¶ Weddell's brigs‡‡ were called *Jane* and *Beaufoy*. Weddell himself commanded the *Jane*. I have no record of the name of the *Beaufoy*'s captain. Staten (or Staaten) Land is now called Isla de los Estados.

§ "I therefore considered any further cruize [*sic*] to be an improvident waste of time; and, to the gratification of my

officers and crew, directed our course to the Falkland[s],"
wrote Weddell (p. 72).

§§ Morrell also claimed to have searched for Saxenbourg
Island‡‡‡ but historians suspect he just made up the tale in
order to mask some other activity.‡‡‡‡ His reputation as a liar
was clinched upon his declaration that he not only spotted but
also landed upon "Morrell" Island and "Byer's" Island, two
non-existent rocks west of the Hawaiian Islands.

†See Stommel, Rhamsay, Gould.

Footnotes to the footnotes:

‡At 2.63 miles per league, this estimate would be 7.89 miles in
length. See my note on leagues, elsewhere.

‡‡This may be a good place to mention that the *Atrevida* and
Descubierta were corvettes. For a decent description of the
differences between brigs and corvettes, and schooners, clippers, and sloops, for that matter, please refer to *A Beginner's
Guide to Sailing*.

‡‡‡Saxenbourg is also known as Saxonberg and Saxemburg.

‡‡‡‡Morrell hid his wife Abby Jane on the boat when he
departed on a voyage in 1829. She subsequently penned her
own account: *Narrative of a Voyage to the Ethiopic and South
Atlantic Ocean, Indian Ocean, Chinese Sea, North and South Pacific
Ocean, in the Years 1829, 1830, 1831* (1833). Unfortunately, she
wasn't along for the ride during Morrell's 1822 expedition.

LOG OF THE Southern Saracen

Date: Thurs., 2 March 2000

Hours: 1430

Knots: 2

Fathoms: 6 to 10

Wind: None

Force: 1 / Light Air

Barometer: 30.10↑

Temp. Air: 10°C

Water: 10°C

Remarks: High cirrus, scattered cumulus, 3/10

Lat: 52° 35'S   Long. 47° 43'W   Var. 002°W   Course: 020°C

Princesa

⚓

Kelp

Dangerous along here with the northwest winds

Kelp

Atrevida

⚓

Probably why I was able to manage today

fresh water

↑

terrestrial

↓

supralittoral

mesolittoral

infralittoral

circumlittoral

aphytal (deep)

*Draft proper map asap

Have completed the first entire circumnavigation of my islands
and managed—at low tide—to land on both Princesa and
  Atrevida. It's been a very successful day, so far, but I just
realized, as I was coming along to where I'm now anchored, at the
north tip of Aurora, that something has been eating at me. I
map features, then can't find them again; I count birds, then they
disappear. I don't know what it is, but I get the impression
that I'm seeing things that aren't there.

The air is so warm, the ocean seems to be inviting me to dive in and
cool off. Its smooth glassy surface stretches out forever. To swim out
to the horizon looks like a trifling thing, merely the length of a pool. The
temptation is almost too great to resist, though I know the warmth is deceptive. But, still

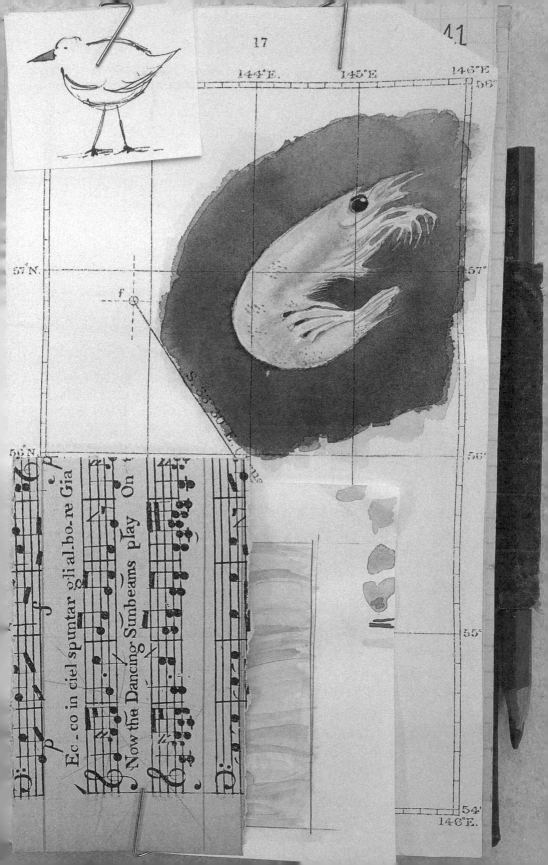

Twenty-one

WHILE HIPPOLYTE LABORED AWAY in the office over her notes, Marie was at home, sitting on her bed, picking at a take-out salad. An avocado pear plunked onto a mass of wet, limp lettuce had gone brown and mushy, and the shrimp—for this had been offered as a seafood salad—were minuscule and fishy. A sheaf of papers rested on her lap, ignored in deference to her efforts to find something edible in the plastic container. A red hardcover book lay at her feet, and manuscripts were stacked on the floor beside the bed. She sighed and pushed away the papers, rolled off the bed, and went out to the kitchen. There she dumped the salad into the garbage and opened the fridge. A half bottle of wine remained from the previous night's dinner, because, in spite of Hippolyte's professing to have missed wine, he had hardly drunk any, and she'd scarcely touched hers. Now pouring herself a large glassful, she went back into the bedroom and rearranged the papers, settling them back on her lap.

Not able to get comfortable, she fluffed the pillows and rearranged them against the headboard, then stood up and banged them one by one on the mattress and tried again, then sat up on the edge of the bed and stared down at her feet still confined by stockings. Sighing again, she wriggled out of her clothes, put on a pair of pajamas, then fell back onto the bed.

The papers were the bones of a book on etiquette she'd been neglecting; they cried out for attention but couldn't hold her. "Typical, acknowledged, nineteenth-century family social behavior," she read, "within the confines of the middle class, usually consisted of, not only—" she threw down the page and took a sip of wine. "Too much punctuation already!" she yelled. Commas danced in front of her; she took another sip and crumpled the page in her free hand before tossing it onto the floor.

"Damn him," she swore aloud. And swept books and papers aside. She got up and padded out to the front room, stood staring at the empty couch and the crate beside it. She kicked it with her bare foot. "Damn him," she howled and returned to her bed. She paused to consider the red book lying at the foot, then picked it up, turned it over, and set it down.

Two alarm clocks—one set to 8:30, the other, 8:45—informed her that it was too early to go to sleep, so she grabbed a novel from the floor and tried to read, but only heard his voice. What am I feeling so dreadful about?, she asked herself.

The answer, obviously, was Hippolyte. Everything about him bothered her. She could write a list of grievances. Why not? It might do me good, she muttered. For a start, he bounces around too much, won't stay still for a moment; he needs Ritalin or something to calm him down. He's always changing the subject, deflecting pressure, won't stay focused. And there's the way that he has of looking at you, like he already knows everything about you. That smile of his, when he flashes it at you, you'd swear he's looking ahead to the day when he'll break your heart. And I don't like the way he recruited Janice, treating her like an old friend when they'd only just met. And he's too confident, thinks he can just walk this book over everyone, have his way, especially with Jeremy, the poor sap.

How could she convince Jeremy that Hippolyte's story was a barefaced sham? Why would a man who had hundreds of real experiences fix on this obvious fable? She took another sip of wine, rolled the glass with its skin of condensation against her cheek, and tried to picture Hippolyte on a sailboat, squeezed into a tiny galley, dreaming of a bottle of wine. The picture wouldn't materialize, so she shifted to the boat's cockpit. She conjured him, sitting at the tiller, no, behind the wheel, the boom angled off to the right, wind filling the canvas. She saw him with a stubby beard—that was easy, he never was too far from that state—and with his thick brown hair longer, below his ears, but blowing back from his face. It was evening, cool, but he was in cutoffs and—a T-shirt? No, no shirt at all, like a real beachcomber. And he wore running shoes but no socks. Light spray came up over the side of the boat; his eyes squinted into the setting sun. Wrong, if he was still heading towards his islands, the sun would be behind him.

The boat skipped along the surface of the water, gulls shrieked. Hippolyte was sitting at a table, eating spaghetti marinara. Forget that, she scolded herself, that's the spaghetti from last night. And he wouldn't have a table. Okay, he was holding a bowl of one of his freeze-dried stews. She racked her memory for the names of the soups and stews he had bought, but for some reason imagined paella, a huge helping of steaming yellow paella dotted with enormous prawns. And craving cold white wine, like this Chardonnay, dry and tart and cold. She took another sip, allowed a smile. So far, so good, she congratulated herself, but she gradually became aware that the picture included her; she was on the boat, sitting opposite him. The image suddenly faded.

If he really did sail that boat, and even if he didn't, what drove him to wander all the time? She traveled occasionally, enjoyed getting away for a week or two, but wasn't compelled to sacrifice a home and her job for it. Her holidays were sane, comfortable. She frowned and dropped the subject of holidays; her last one had been three years before.

Another thing that bothered her immensely was the self-taught knowledge that he claimed to possess. She abhorred the way he dipped needlessly into foreign phrases when English ones worked perfectly well; she considered his references to classical mythology as pandering and cursed Jeremy for divulging her background. She resented the attention Hippolyte drew to himself, the time he wanted her to spend on him and his book. She couldn't make any sense of him; he was illogical and unknowable, and she loathed him for this.

Another editor should take it on. Lucinda would be a good bet; credulous and eager, *she* would be seduced by the story. Bad idea, Marie, decided, shaking her head; she'd be seduced by the author first.

Casimir would be better; he didn't have an ounce of nonsense in him, and, furthermore, had a business-like way of accepting the weirdest concepts. She'd tell Jeremy tomorrow.

With Hippolyte already hogging space in her thoughts, she reached down and picked up the red book again. She barely opened it, then slammed it shut. It was his log. He had told her that he'd lost it. There must be something in here that he didn't want her to read; therefore, she shouldn't be reading it. She opened it back up again. Nonsense, of course she should be reading it; she was his editor, wasn't she? She settled into the pillows, then sat back up. The bed was driving her crazy, so with his book under her arm, she dragged the quilt out to the living room couch. Before flopping down and tucking herself in, she poured the rest of the wine into her glass.

Turning to the first entry, she was immediately struck by the care Hippolyte had lavished on his logbook. Organized and orderly, it was so unlike the messy journals. She flipped to the next page and immediately realized that the opening was an anomaly; the rest promised to be as chaotic as anything else he touched. A few pages on, her own name caught her eye. She looked at the date of the entry, February 17; he'd written about her before they'd even met! Fascinated, she read through the passage about his musings on her name. So that's why he'd been so pleased when she had traced her family's migration for him at dinner the other night.

She went back to the beginning and read about how the boat was really called the *Seaspray,* not the *Southern Saracen,* and chuckled at Peter Givens taking Hippolyte to task for keeping a handwritten log. She and Peter would get along just fine, she figured.

God, she sighed, I don't know what to make of all this. If he's lying, why would he go to this extent and then not even show me this stuff? If anything would convince me that he'd really made the trip, it would be this book. Unless the whole thing's been artfully planned: the initial presentation of the inadequate manuscript, the so-called losing of the logbook. And if she hadn't swiped it from his duffel bag, would he have ever admitted its existence? She grinned at the memory of herself ransacking his bag; the glimpses of the red book had been too tantalizing to resist. And she'd done it so methodically, too, casually suggesting that he leave the bag in her office so she could get an uninterrupted opportunity to root through it, carefully untying his knot and doing it back up the exact same way. Her face burned suddenly; had she retied it the same way? She closed her eyes and tried to re-create the scene. Now she wasn't so sure; somebody had come to the office door just as she was doing it up. Forget it, she commanded herself; the bag will still be there in the morning, and you can redo it then when you put the book back.

She relaxed and returned to reading. Hand-drawn charts of the three islands were sprinkled throughout. Smears of watercolor contained in neat little boxes showed his attempts to capture the state of the clouds, the weather. Sketches of birds punctuated the pages.

Then she read of his accident, how he'd unknowingly cut his hand. Racing ahead to find out how he dealt with it, she learned that the wound had refused to heal. Is it healed now?, she asked herself. She'd never noticed his hands; she'd look next chance she had.

An entry near the end recounted the finding of the skeleton, the haphazard excavation. There were details that were missing from both his journals and the manuscript. The manuscript treated the find like an incidental event. She skipped back, choosing March 2nd at random, and read about Hippolyte's circumnavigation of the islands.

She was lulled by the description of the sun and the warmth until she came to where he dove into the water. An uncontrollable shiver passed through her. I'd never do that, she murmured. Then she read of his panic and his struggles when it hit him just how cold the ocean was. That's what it would be like, she nodded. What a foolish thing to do, all alone the way he was. Her heart was pounding, and she realized she'd been holding her breath. She exhaled deeply and read to where he lost the boat. And the islands. This doesn't make any sense; she shook her head. She reread the passage. There it was. "2 March . . . and when I surfaced, both boat and islands were gone." She shut the book angrily. What on earth was she supposed to make of that?

She found her place and scanned the entry again. Why hadn't he mentioned this? Was this why he had lied about the log being lost? He himself wrote that he was delirious. The whole thing made his voyage suddenly real yet, at the same time, more impossible than ever. What if he was deluding himself? Then what? Did that make all this more acceptable? And how far had the deception extended?

She grabbed a piece of paper and a pen and drew out two columns. In the first, she wrote "H's voyage is real"; in the second, "H thinks his voyage is real." She stared at the paper, then noticed that she hadn't drawn the third, the one she'd been convinced of all along, "H's voyage is a total lie."

Setting aside the paper, she continued to read through the log and the entry describing the injury to his arm, sustained in the disquieting hours following his swim. Against her will, a picture of the darkened cabin formed; she could almost hear the rustling of sails and rigging, the creaking of boards, and could well believe his mind creating a fearfully powerful unknown adversary. She reread the passage. When he tripped and fell, she jumped. As though he had just landed at her feet.

She closed her eyes, took a deep breath, then turned to later entries. There were references replicated in the manuscript: bird-watching, efforts to map, salvaging the leaking dinghy, but the account of the airplane had been left out. The idea that one could hear a nearby plane but not see it was completely incomprehensible. And the sensation of the ground disappearing! She dismissed it—using his own words written there on the page—as sheer hallucination. An absurd picture was forming of islands that were, yet weren't, of radios that inexplicably stopped working, of solid ground that virtually vaporized, and she saw it leading up to an unreasonably supernatural explanation of why no one else except Hippolyte was able to see the darned things. You'll have to do better than this, Mr. Webb, she said out loud, but she read on all the same.

When, on the day of his departure, the islands finally and absolutely vanished, she threw down the book in disgust.

Twenty-two

WHEN HIPPOLYTE WOKE UP THE NEXT MORNING, having fallen into a deep sleep on the couch, the sounds of a busy office could be heard beyond the boardroom door. Staggering over to the table, smoothing his hair, he noticed flags appended to his printed-out revisions. "Shit," he said out loud. Marie had come in, seen him lying there, his head no doubt thrown back, his mouth wide open, drooling and twitching in his sleep. Then she'd printed out and read through this latest work and was greeting his day with more questions. Endless questions. "Stop already," he pleaded.

H.W.:

—This is far too much detail, please remove the citations and references; they can be placed in the notes. Will you describe the Shag Rocks at some point? How relevant are they?

—Please discuss the original naming of the Auroras. Who first called them that?

—I should think you would be more sympathetic towards Morrell, considering that he, too, claimed to see islands that everyone else believes to be imaginary. Have you thought of turning him into an ally?

—Paragraph about Johnson, the *Henry,* and Biscoe. Delete this last sentence. In fact, you might consider deleting them altogether unless you find out more.

—Save the comment about the Hydrographic Office for your acknowledgments.

—Delete the reference to Poe.

—Footnotes are altogether unnecessary. Please either incorporate the information into the body of the text or omit.

—Footnotes to footnotes!?

Hippolyte ducked out of Rumor, then walked the ten or so blocks to the library as briskly as possible, pausing only to wolf down a coffee and a bun. As he fought against the tide of people streaming towards him, he looked across the street at the opposite sidewalk. How come I always seem to be on the wrong side?, he thought. No matter which direction I go in this city, I always seem to be struggling against everyone.

The sidewalk gave way to the library grounds. He managed to expel himself from the crowd and bolted up the stairs, propelling himself into the building, focused entirely upon Marie's questions, until the grandeur of the hall brought him up short. He stood, gawking like a child, feeling dwarfed and overpowered and at home.

Drifting down hallways, passing doors shut against the leaden, antiquarian thud of typing and others open to vast cabinets and shelves, Hippolyte promised himself an intense exploration of all the library offered. Another time! Coming to his senses, he made his way to the catalog and dove into the collection.

Bustamente was there in his own voice and in translation, just as Marie had promised. So were Weddell and Morrell. A search of subjects—South Atlantic, Falklands, Antarctica, South Georgia, Sealing—revealed an abundance of titles, including previously elusive ones and even unheard-of ones. He handed in his requests and sat down to wait, reading and rereading her queries, her hesitations. A challenge welled up in him, uncertainly at first and then with sudden force. He had to convince her! He had to find more proof! His numbers appeared on the board; he rushed up to claim his books.

The pile, gathered over the day, included information on the previously evasive Captain John Biscoe, who turned out to be a British sealer. Voyaging later than Weddell or Morrell, he set out on the 27th of September 1830 charged with finding the Auroras. Biscoe failed, however, declaring that the Auroras "must be either considered henceforward as not existing or looked for in some other position." He later discovered Enderby and Graham Land. Tough luck! Biscoe would have been good to have on his side.

An unlikely title, *Voyages Round the World; with selected Sketches of Voyages to the South Seas, North and South Pacific Oceans, China, etc. performed under the command and agency of the author* by Edmund Fanning, ended up being that day's mother lode.

Fanning, who lived from 1769 until 1841, was a well-respected sea captain, hailing from Stonington, Connecticut. In his memoirs, he recounted instructing his son William, who was the owner of the brig *Hersilia,* and its captain James Sheffield to search for the Auroras. *Hersilia* shipped out in 1820, though the account of the voyage wasn't published until 1833, six years after Weddell's account appeared and a year after Morrell's. According to Fanning, William and Captain Sheffield found the Auroras.

Fanning could well be the proof Hippolyte needed to convince Marie. Here was a sailor who had made many voyages to the South Atlantic, a successful sealer and discoverer of islands himself. He also had a great deal of confidence in both his son and Sheffield. Hippolyte immediately slid Fanning's account into his manuscript:

> Fanning, like Weddell and Morrell, was a sealer, but unlike Morrell he was beyond reproach. No stranger to the South Atlantic, he directed Captain Sheffield and his own son, William,★ to search for the Auroras, in the hopes of finding newer, richer sealing grounds. It's a shame he didn't go himself; he was bolstered by a good reputation, having discovered Fanning and Palmyra Islands in the South Pacific. Fanning based his belief on the Auroras' existence on evidence from Bustamente and the Dutch captain of the *Good News (Blijde Bootschap),* Dirck Gherritz. Now the *Good News* is news to me. This ship apparently sailed in 1599, and if I can find more information about it, that'll be more proof.★★★

Here are Fanning's own words:

"[The Aurora Islands] were . . . each in the form of a sugarloaf, but having no landing places, even for amphibious animals, on them. A number of birds about, with some shaggs [sic] and white pigeons in the clefts, were all the living creatures discovered on them. The brig sailed around and between these islands without discovering any danger, except a reef which put off southwest, a short mile from the southernmost island. The centre island they place in latitude 52°58´ south, longitude 47°51´ west."‡

Another quote, also from Fanning:

"[The Auroras] are three peaked mountains, lying in a triangular position from each other—a short reef runs out S.W. from the southernmost island, the latitude of them as laid down in Patten's chart is sufficiently correct but they are about 4 degrees to the Eastward from their situation on this chart. In nearly a direct line between the Aurora Islands and the Northwest Cape of New South Iceland [South Shetlands], lies Shag Rock Reef,★★ a most extensive and dangerous reef of rocks, some of which are above water and the size of a ship's hull, at about 54°45´S.‡‡

The *Hersilia* did not find seals on the Auroras, so they went on to the South Shetlands where they slaughtered more than 9000 of them and would have taken more had they only brought enough salt to preserve them.

By the way, here is the answer to your question about the naming of the Auroras:

I assume, like everyone else, that the islands were named after the Spanish ship the *Aurora*. Two other ships, also called *Aurora*, plied the South Atlantic but at much later dates. The brig

Aurora, an American sealing ship, sailed from New York harbour on 1 July 1820. Her captain was Robert R. Macy; she was owned by James Byers# and Associates. Damaged in a storm on the 6th of April 1821, she almost capsized, and was declared unseaworthy at the Falklands. *Aurora* was also the name of one of Shackleton's ships.

Footnotes:

*Fanning believed both Sheffield and William to be vested with "nautical talents" and called them "able lunarians." If you were to call me a lunarian, Marie, I should take it as a compliment.

‡Fanning, *Voyages & Discoveries,* p. 303

**This is proof that the Shag Rocks were not mistaken for the Auroras. By the way, Patten's chart is unknown to me; I'll try to find out something about it.

‡‡Fanning: *New England Palladium and Commercical Advertiser,* Boston, Dec. 5, 1820, quoted in Bertrand, *Americans in Antarctica,* p. 45.

#You'll remember that Morrell named one of his fictitious islands Byers Island, after this ship owner. I could name the middle Aurora island after you, Marie. Marie's Island. It has a lovely ring to it, hasn't it? By the way, his schooner was called the *Wasp.*

***I just reread the passage; Gherritz was referring to the South Shetland Islands, not the Auroras.

Hippolyte searched vainly for more information on the Spanish ships—the *Aurora, Princesa, Dolores, Pearl*—for their captain's names, their routes, any mention at all. Tackling the *Corona,* the name that he'd found etched into the driftwood and presumably that of a ship, he came up empty-handed, nothing in the indexes, nor in the catalogs, electronic or card; neither did the initials G.T. leap out at him from any pages. Still, he had found Fanning, and that made his day.

Slipping back into Rumor just before it was locked up, Hippolyte's pack bulged with simple delicatessen treasures: sandwiches, beer, potato salad, sweet buns oozing cream cheese, as well as coffee filters and a packet of ground coffee. A dimpled young man whose glasses were far too thick for the bridge of his nose was jangling his keys, getting ready to leave. "We haven't met," he snapped, as though it were Hippolyte's fault, but he held out his hand anyway. "I'm an editor. My name is Casimir. C-a-s-i-m-i-r." And with that introduction the two men were immediately sympathetic to each other, sharing the burden of unusual first names. "You," Casimir added, "I already know about. Otherwise, I would not be able to leave you here unattended." With that responsibility dispatched, he departed.

After locking the door, Hippolyte went to the boardroom and flung his repast across the table. Paper serviettes; plastic knives, forks, and cups; food! Marie had left him notes, but he shoved them aside, sat down, prepared to dig in, then bounced back up. Something was missing. Music! The lunchroom radio was seconded, the dial fiddled with until a station capable of penetrating the concrete walls was found; music and traffic reports straggled out between commercials. As he made his way down through the layers of his meal, he eyed his duffel bag, bothered by something he couldn't put his finger on. The knot was bugging him, he realized, but beyond that his disquiet had no discernible grounds. He stuffed a last morsel into his mouth and pulled Marie's notes over:

Don't make yourself too much at home here—I see you've put some maps up on the walls—we need the boardroom tomorrow for meetings.

—The on-line library catalog shows an article by Captain Biscoe in the *Geographical Journal* for 1833. (Month not specified). Please look up this article and fill in the missing details in the appropriate section.

—See attached notes regarding volcanic explosions in 1783 (Asama and Laki) and 1815 (Tambora) and the general trend of cooler temperatures that accompanied the opening years of the nineteenth century. These may help your research on the climate.

—Someone will inevitably raise the issue of ship traffic through the
area. You need a map showing shipping routes vis à vis the Auroras. I
should think that you'd have to contact the Falkland Islands Fisheries
Department, British Antarctic Survey, any cruise or tour companies
that make the trip between the Falklands and South Georgia, etc.,
unless you have this information already.

He'd show her maps; in fact, all she had to do was look on the wall
where he'd pinned charts of every kind of traffic. He had more maps
in his log; he must photocopy those; they would convince her! He
reached for the duffel and dug around for the precious book. It
wasn't there. Now that he thought about it, he couldn't recall seeing
it the day before. He plunged his hand in farther, feeling around
boxes and cases and other books. Then he emptied the bag item by
item. Things that he didn't need, that had been deliberately stowed on
the bottom were now near the surface; other items that he'd consulted recently were deeply buried. Everything was topsy-turvy, but
neat, too neat. Finally, in the nethermost depths, he found it and
sighed in relief.

He began copying pages, but the work was laborious and self-
defeating. He gave up and stared at the walls. She wanted answers. He
had to get them for her. There were his rock specimens, for instance.
Though not conclusive by any means, they would, with their evidence
of movement, immersion, eruption, and metamorphoses, silence any
challenge! And how would she be able to ignore all of the other
material he had collected? Time to spread it all out and show this evidence. Some of his boxes, he remembered, were in Jeremy's office. And
the crate as well, or was that still at Marie's? He turned Rumor upside
down and found the crate, a courier tag stuck onto one side, and
sundry other boxes in a store room. Reuniting them all, he spread
their contents over what was left of the tabletop, spilling them onto
the floor, the vacant chairs.

The music was filtering through his brain, and suddenly he realized that the notes were fitting together too well, it was too satiny, too

lulling. He gave the plastic case a bang to disarrange them, but the melody remained smoothly unobliging. He twiddled the dials till the blast of a tenor saxophone emerged. That was better. The instrument squealed breathlessly, invaded the office vibrantly. He jacked up the volume. More instruments joined in: a wailing trumpet, drums, cymbals, another saxophone. Shells, seaweed, rocks danced on the table; feathers flew; the room filled with a frenzy of crashing waves and howling winds. Hippolyte shouted over the roar, "Now tell me you can't see the Auroras!"

Blechnum
magellanicum
Blechnum penna-marina

Blechnum magellanicum

AW

Twenty-three

"I WANT TO KNOW MORE ABOUT THESE SHAG ROCKS." She stood at the door, holding a steaming cup of coffee, then walked over to the table and dropped his notes on Edmund Fanning in front of him, seemingly oblivious to the remarkable clutter strewn about, to the cacophony that had erupted the previous night. In a sober moment before he'd again bunked down on Rumor's couch, he'd left his notes on her desk, and she'd already read them over and was already responding with more questions.

He quickly scanned them.

—Please substitute the last sentence of the paragraph that deals with the Dutch ship *Good News* with relevant information, if you can find any.

—Work Fanning's quote into your own description of the appearance of the Auroras. Discuss differences, similarities.

—Are you familiar with Nathaniel Palmer's contradictory report of Fanning's account?

—There is a lot of irrelevant detail. Please omit, or explain relevance. And please restrain your use of footnotes. See my previous notes.

—You do not answer my questions about Shag Rocks. What are they? Why is this proof? Why didn't you go to the Shag Rocks, or did you?

"What is so important about the Shags?" he fumed. "They are three big rocks near South Georgia."

"How near?" She bunched up her mouth. "What's happened in here? It stinks like low tide."

"My specimens!" he beamed proudly. "We have to look at them."

"Didn't you read my message about the meetings? You've got an hour to put all this away." Yet she scrutinized each item, stalking something, circling round, touching shells, barnacles, dried kelp, her hand resting here on tussock, there on moss.

"Is there something in particular you're looking for?" he asked.

She frowned. Finally, she replied, "The giant squid tentacles."

He burst out laughing. "You believed that?!" Her expression—so serious, so incredulous—fed his laughter, but when her look became one of impatience, he settled on a grin and replied to her demand that he clean up the room, "I can't move anything until we go over it all. Everything's arranged in a very specific order."

"Okay, in a minute. How near are the Shag Rocks to where you claim the Auroras are?"

"You mean to where the Auroras are. They're about two hundred and twenty-five miles east of the Auroras. Or two hundred and fifty kilometres northwest of South Georgia."

"Why can't you coordinate your measurement systems?"

"Two hundred and fifty times five divided by eight. One hundred and fifty-six miles west northwest of South Georgia."

"Forget it. Kilometers, miles, whatever. Several experts say that the Auroras are without doubt the Shag Rocks."

"Let them. Weddell himself wrote that the difference in longitude between them made it unlikely that such a mistake could be made. But what do you think of the stuff I found on Fanning? It's so exciting! Fanning actually describes the Shag Rocks lying in the path between the Auroras and South Shetland. And imagine, I'd never heard of him before. By the way, thanks for sending me to the library."

"All the same, I want you to introduce the Shag Rocks. Describe them explicitly, explain why you think that it's impossible for them to be mistaken for your Auroras."

Annoyance grazed his face. "I don't think it's necessary, but if you insist. I thought you'd be interested in Fanning." He tore open the bag of cream cheese buns and pushed it over to her. "Help yourself. That coffee smells so good; is there any left?" Then he ran out, to return peeved, "Figures, doesn't it? It's why I don't work in an office. Nobody buys anything, then when someone does, everyone descends on it like vultures. That was my coffee!"

"Sit down and pay attention," she reprimanded. "Fanning isn't particularly relevant. If you'd read through that material thoroughly, you'd realize that he didn't find the Auroras himself; he is recounting a third-party story. I don't see that you can use that as particularly strong evidence. Then there is Nathaniel Palmer, a sailor who was on the Falklands at the time who wrote his own account. He categorically states that the *Hersilia* did not find the Auroras." She handed over a photocopy for him to read. "This is from a book on Americans in the South Atlantic."

"Where do you dig this stuff up?" he asked, but the admiring tone evaporated as he skimmed the words. "Marie! It says here that Palmer wasn't onboard the *Hersilia,* either! Why do you believe him and not Fanning?"

"Just find out more about him. But, on another matter, we need to talk about the skeleton you found. It's very important. I want you to move it up in the book, hint earlier at its possibility. You must have noticed the seal bones, for instance, a lot sooner." She watched him stuff a second bun into his mouth. "Are you sure you've got enough to eat?"

"You're in a good mood this morning," he snapped but put the bun down. "Fact is," Hippolyte continued, "I didn't have a clue about it. Odd, eh? I thought I'd combed the place over thoroughly, but it turns out I'd missed this site."

She spread out his notes. "I have to tell you that I have a couple of problems with your description."

"Like what?"

"Well, for a start, it's pretty extraordinary."

"Yeah, it is."

"I mean, I'm having a hard time believing it."

Hippolyte waited for her to continue.

"You haven't brought back any material from the dig. There's only the drawings, maps. There aren't even any photographs."

"The drawings are very accurate. I took great pains with the measurements. And I did bring back some pieces of ceramic, a clay-pipe fragment, and soil samples. But you know, I'm not a trained archaeologist, and it struck me as a bit presumptuous to raid the site of its artifacts and bones should there be a chance for a professional to go there. I'm also not stupid. Would you go through customs with human remains, even if they were a hundred and fifty years old? If so, good luck to you."

"But why, Hippolyte, why no photographs? You've got a thousand photographs of penguins. You could have taken those anywhere! Even one lousy photo of the site would put my questions to rest."

He nodded. "I know. It was towards the end. I blew all my film on those birds. That's why I took such care with my drawings, since there would be no other record."

Marie sighed. "I should tell you that I've sent copies of the plans and profiles to an archaeology professor and am waiting for her response."

"Great!" he exclaimed. "I wanted to do that but didn't want to ask anyone to analyze my data for free. Who did you send it to? Where did you hear about this person? Do they have experience in the South Atlantic or with sealing sites?"

"I'll show you her credentials later. In the meantime, have you had any luck identifying the remains, tracking down the initials?"

"None whatsoever. I've been trying to track down G.T. I'm presuming it's someone's initials and *Corona* must be the name of a ship, but it's like looking for a needle in a haystack. For a start, knowing whether she were Spanish, American or British would be a big help. *Corona* is Spanish for crown, but it would be an obvious name for English ships, too. They all sent sealers to the area." He rested his chin in his one hand and spun the half-finished roll round with the other. "Or my man may not have been a sealer. He could have been from another ship and got into an altercation, was murdered. He could

be Dutch or French. Maybe not even a sailor. Perhaps he was a passenger on the ship, heading out to settle—no, that doesn't make sense.
He might have been a naturalist like Darwin or Banks; no, there would
probably be gentlemen's effects with the remains. Unless they were all
stolen from him when he was buried. That would make sense, a little
grave robbing, sailors out on this lonely island, with little to call their
own. What good would personal belongings be to a corpse?"

"How are we going to deal with this then?"

He ignored her. "Of course, he could have been abandoned on the
island. The ship sailed without him and he died, but then how was he
buried? That was a definite burial; he wasn't just covered over by
blowing soil. No, he was with others when he died. Damn, I wish I'd
been able to take photographs. I can't wait to read what your expert
thinks. The femur was shattered in places, but whether or not that took
place before or after death is not in my area of expertise. And the skull,
too, it was crushed in the back. Through the occipital bone." He
rubbed his own. "Here. And here, as well." He touched his cheek. "On
the zygomatic. Isn't that a gem? It's got three descenders in a row—
like pyjamas—depending on how you write your zeds, of course. Or
zees, as you would say."

"Pajamas does not have three descenders."

"Where I come from it does," he retorted, but continued back on
topic, "then, I say 'he' as if it's a given. I assume it's a he, but I've no
way of knowing." He slid into silence for a moment, then spoke
quickly, "I did measure the bones. They'll be able to tell from lengths
and such."

"I ask again, how do you plan to deal with this?"

"What do you mean? Just the way it is. How else?"

"Do you really want to include it when there's no absolute
proof?"

"No absolute proof of what? Of what I recorded? First of all you
want me to move it forward in the book, then you tell me you're having an archaeologist look at it, now you're trying to dissuade me from
including it!" At that moment he never looked so much like truth.

"If only you had more artifacts!" she sounded desperate. "Those along with photos would have been enough!"

"Are photos really so important?" he asked. Up to now, he'd considered her resistance as a challenge that could be overcome, but the truth was dawning on him. "You don't *want* to believe me, do you?"

"I'm trying, Hippolyte. You're not giving me enough material. This is very difficult for someone who can't see the place firsthand."

"Photos can be faked, you know. I could have gone to some archaeology department and borrowed photos of an excavation. No one would have been the wiser. But I wouldn't do that; I'm confident in what I found."

"If you can't convince me, how will you be able to convince others?"

"The excavation is only a small part of the whole story. I don't think it's so important."

"Maybe so, but it's a part of a bigger problem."

"Are you saying that you don't believe a thing about my expedition?"

Marie chewed on her lip.

"You don't!"

She opened her mouth, then shut it.

Hippolyte stood up, gathered up the pages of the manuscript, shoved them into his pack, grabbed the jacket slung over the back of the chair, and walked out.

Plate I.

FUCUS.

J. Pass, sculp.

1. The Serrated Fucus. 2. Bladder Fucus. 3. Gigartine Fucus. 4. Necklace Fucus. 5. Kaliform Fucus.

London Published as the Act directs May 24 1800 by J. Wilkes

Twenty-four

ALICIA DUNSTEAD, Ph.D.
Department of Anthropology
Harvard University

20 July 2000

Marie Simplon, Editor
Rumor Press
10 West 52nd
New York, NY 10019

Dear Ms. Simplon
Re: Aurora Islands

As requested, I'm putting the results of my examination of the notes
and plans produced by your author in writing for your records. It's
been a pleasure to review this material. Though he was clearly not
well equipped, he has, on the whole, done a fine job for an amateur.
I wish some of my students took as much care with the recording of
details.

I should qualify that, not having any idea as to the location,
beyond that of a South Atlantic island, without detailed analysis of
the soil composition, and lacking historic context, I can only go by
what has been provided. Specifically, regarding soil, for example,
where your author has written "ash" or "charcoal" I have no choice
but to believe him. You mention that he brought soil samples back
with him. If you find that my report is inconclusive, you may decide

to send them to a geology lab. I also take on trust the measurements, both of site topography and of the skeletal remains. I doubt they are precise; however, as neither show unusual extremes I believe we can use them with some confidence. I would have wished for tighter topographic control, but singlehanded mapping is difficult.

The site, located on the edge of the terrestrial zone of a coastal environment, overlaps the supralittoral. The adjacent sandy beach, consisting of fine-grained white sand, accounts for sand deposits observed in sub-surface levels of the excavations. Judging from the location and distribution of test pits, the site appears to extend north/south for about 100 meters and east/west for 20. The width corresponds to the limits of flat terrain on the east and the edge of the beach to the west. The north/south extent could actually be much greater.

Artifacts fortunately include clay pipe fragments. I gave the drawings and the one example to Professor Susan Lightfoot, a clay-pipe expert. She tells me there are three variations of pipe bowl indicated, dating from 1720–1820, 1780–1820, and 1820–60. Therefore, she hazards a guess of around 1820, 1821.

The ceramics are English, of a very common type produced from the late 1700s until the mid-1920s. Shards like these litter hundreds of sites in Britain and North America. The leather appears to be from a disintegrated boot or shoe. The metal fragments are from a large pot, most likely a try-pot, which was used by sealers for boiling elephant seal blubber.

The driftwood is possibly the most interesting artifact, supplying us with a vessel: the *Corona;* a place, St. John; and initials, G.T. Historical research is not my bailiwick, but there are any number of people who might be able to unearth the significance of these names for you. I would suggest calling the history department and getting a list from them.

The animal remains indicated are almost all of seal, possibly *Arctocephalus tropicalis gazella,* or South Georgia Fur Seal, although there are some bird bones scattered about. My knowledge of fauna is alarmingly inadequate, and I'd encourage you to send the sketches to the zoological department for further analysis. I can, however, say that the site appears to be that where seal slaughter took place.

The human remains were interred; the pit profile shows definite disturbance of the surface and sub-surface along with the inclusion of surface material (seal bones mainly) within the back-filled soil. With regards to the skeleton: I referred this to my colleague, Dr. Michael Tsolinas. These notes are a summary of his findings. The remains appear to be of a man, 5' 8" in height, 30 to 50 years of age. The wounds in the occiput and the zygomatic bone may have been caused by a blow. However, without having the skull in hand, this is just conjecture.

One is tempted to hypothesize. Could this man have been struck on the head with a club? Clubs were the weapons used by sealers to kill the seals. But why?, one would ask. Did the crew run out of food and attempt to reduce their numbers by murder? Or was this a result of a quarrel that broke out over food? These scenarios seem unlikely given the abundance of seal bones. Seals were regularly eaten by sealers and were a good source of nourishment. If the seal bones were left by earlier visitors and, at the time of our man's death, there were no seals to be found, birds such as penguin or albatross and their eggs could have been eaten. These have been a much-treasured foodstuff even during times of plenty. I would have to conclude that death was not the price paid over a battle for food nor was it due to starvation.

It is not possible to tell if the fracture on the femur was from a pre-death injury. The missing phalanges could have simply rotted; noted soil discoloration is consistent with that possibility.

I hope that our conclusions do not strike you as too obvious. Photographs would have been a great asset. If the author returns to the site, you might suggest that he take some. Once again, it's been a pleasure to review this material, and if you have further questions, I would be glad to discuss them with you. I have enclosed all of the original material, along with a list of sources and addresses that might help should you decide to pursue your inquiries further. Yours sincerely,

Alicia Dunstead

Alicia Dunstead
cc: Michael Tsolinas

Marie threw down the letter in disgust. It didn't tell her anything that she wanted to know. Why couldn't this Dunstead, Ph.D., see the excavation notes for all they were? Crap crap crap. And where was Hippolyte for Christ's sake! He'd been gone for a whole week! She blasted out a terse memo to Jeremy.

MEMO
August 7, 2000
To: Jeremy Gould, Publisher   From: Marie Simplon, Editor
Jeremy:
If you are wondering why you can't use your own boardroom, it's because your author debunked, leaving all his crap behind. Did he tell *you* when he'd be back?
Marie

"Mr. Webb to see you, Miss Simplon."

"Thanks, Janice. Send him right in." Marie hung up the phone, breathed deeply. How could she face him? She'd lashed herself a hundred times for admitting her doubts to his face; and she'd done it awkwardly, cruelly. A knock. Then the door opened—just a fraction— and he peeked through the crack.

"Come in," she called out, and in he slouched, but not without a sly grin. "Where have you been? I've been worried." Not wanting to admit this, it emerged unguarded. She would have clapped her hand over her mouth, and not for the first time, but it was too late.

"That's the only nice thing you've ever said to me." He sprawled in the chair, outstretched legs crossed at the ankles, and whistled softly an indefinable ditty. He clung to a grimy bag on his lap and clasped a large roll of paper under his arm. Still the grin.

"You've swallowed a penguin. What's so funny?"

"Nothing funny." He considered her at various angles. "But I found some things."

"What, for Heaven's sake?"

"A map. A ship."

"The driftwood ship? The *Corona?*"

"Yes. Yes, indeed. The *Co-ro-na.*" He continued whistling.

"Stop that puffing and tell me more!"

"First the map." He released the bag—it slipped off of his lap—then unrolled the map, laying it on the floor. "Hold this corner with your foot," he directed. He pointed to a dashed line that traversed the South Atlantic, then zigzagged like an Etch-A-Sketch around the Auroras. "Bustamente's route, from the 1800 map. From the Library of Congress. They printed out the whole thing for me."

"Very nice. We already know about Bustamente's route."

"Yes, but I didn't have the map. It cost ten bucks. Can I get reimbursed?"

"No." She lifted her foot an inch. The map sprang back into its tight roll. "What about the *Corona?*"

"You won't believe me if I tell you." He stretched out, easing himself farther down into the chair, then sat back up and pulled paper out of his bag, sheets stapled together. "But you can read about it. Here's a new chapter." The page whizzed across like a skipping stone and landed on her desk. He got up.

"See ya." He sauntered out, whistling.

The Corona

In 1820, the brig <u>Fortuna</u> (not to be mistaken for a later
ship of the same name) was bought by a Mr. Adam Forsyth
of New York. Forsyth was an acquaintance of James Byers,
owner of the sealing company James Byers and Co., also of
New York, and, impressed with the profits that Byers was
reaping from his sealing enterprises, decided to send a
ship in competition. The <u>Fortuna</u> was in poor condition;
already having seen much service in the South Atlantic,
the previous owner considered her too costly to repair.
Forsyth reoutfitted the ship, renamed her the <u>Corona</u>, and
put her under the command of Capt. George L. Thomas. In
September 1822, she left New York, bound for Staaten
Land, an island just off the coast of Patagonia. Corona
arrived in November 1822, then headed east to find new
sealing grounds. In February of the following year, she
anchored off the Falklands for several weeks and then
returned to New York. The revenues for the year were
spectacular--the catch having been some 10,500 seals--and
contrary to those of other vessels who had noticed a
marked decline in the seal population.

A year later Forsyth hired an entirely new crew,
except for Thomas who remained as captain, and in October
1823, she again sailed to the South Atlantic, this time in
the company of another ship, <u>The Delight</u>, under the command of Nathan Stafford Farnham. Forsyth did not indi-
cate where the bulk of the seals were caught in 1822, and
as he hoped to increase his profits, he must have thought
it prudent to keep silent. The ships landed in St. John and
then headed for an undisclosed destination somewhere to
the east, but only 3 or 4 days out were separated for the

duration of the voyage. This time, when the _Corona_
returned to civilization, she was sorely disabled with a
serious hole in the hull ("miserably patched," according
to one observer); and worse, she was missing half her crew,
including the captain. The survivors, after describing the
accident--a collision on a reef--spoke of a marvellously
rich island five days' sailing from the Falklands.
Unfortunately, no one thought to check the captain's log
or the ship's charts for the location of this island, and by
the time the ship had limped back to New York, the crews'
effects were dispersed. I could not find the names of the
sailors, beyond that of the captain.

Forsyth did not attempt to repair the _Corona_. There is
no record of her fate.

The _Corona_ was a 140-ton, 70-foot-long brig with a
breadth of 23 feet and a depth of 11 feet. Owners were
listed as Mr. Adam N. Forsyth and his son Mr. Samuel R.
Forsyth. George Thomas had previously been the master of
the _Eliza_.

It's interesting to note that Forsyth was an acquaintance of Edmund Fanning (qv), and may have been beguiled
by Fanning's account of the Auroras.

Sources (Unpublished material):
Byers, James. Correspondence relating to sealing
activities, August 1820. National Archives, Microform
series M-180, Roll 20.
Forsyth, Adam N. Personal papers housed at the G.W. Blunt
White Library.
Forsyth, Samuel R. Letters to Adam Forsyth. October 1822
until April 1824, G.W. Blunt White Library.

Marie looked up from the paper and swore under her breath. Hippolyte was no longer there; he was going to make her chase him to the boardroom. But he wasn't there either. "Where is his proof?" she muttered as she marched down the hall, out to reception. "Where's Hippolyte?" she demanded.

"He left," replied Janice, "five minutes ago." Then, taking a deep breath, she added quietly, "If you speak to me like that again, I'll quit."

"Was he alone? What did you say?"

"Yes, alone. Nothing."

"And Jeremy? Did he leave, too?"

"He's not back from lunch." They looked at their watches and simultaneously scowled in disapproval; it was three o'clock, after all.

Marie turned abruptly and stormed towards her office, then changed her mind and went back to the boardroom. She ransacked the room, searching for what she didn't know. Something that would give Hippolyte away. Something that would scream out, "Here's my reason for lying to you!" or better yet, "Here are my lies!" She found the field book in which the test excavation was recorded and devoured each word, each sentence, each diagram, juggling them, attempting to decipher in futile fits any cryptic message hidden therein. But no plainer words could be found than those on the page. No subterfuge existed unless it were that produced by her own raw cynicism.

How angry she was! And it burned, this testing and retesting of her credibility. "I am not an idiot," she declared, tossing aside the book.

"What on earth are you doing?" Jeremy stood in the doorway.

She was so startled, she almost burst out crying but suppressed her agitation and took a deep breath. "You frightened me," she admitted. "Thank God you're not Hippolyte," and handed over the new chapter on the *Corona*.

"Wow!" Jeremy exclaimed as he skimmed the notes. "Wow!"

"I was afraid you'd say that."

"What do you mean? This is absolute proof that Hippolyte's islands exist."

"Do you really think so? I don't." Her hands were trembling; she hid them behind her back. "It's entirely possible that he had this information all along and sketched the wood sign to fit in with the story of the *Corona*. Did I ever tell you about the wood sign? Doesn't matter. Or he might have made up all this new stuff on the spot. He brought back only these notes; I can't find any photocopies; there's no real proof. And why couldn't he have made it up? What are the odds, after all, that I or any other editor, for that matter, would go to," she consulted the sheet, "to the Blunt library, whereever that is, to check out the sources firsthand. I mean, don't you see how convenient it is?"

"Are you serious? You make this sound like deliberate fraud!"

"That's what I think it is. We either turn this book into a novel or we drop the whole thing." She so badly wanted to show Jeremy the logbook, but how could she do that without giving herself away?

"You promised to wait until the thirtieth; it's only the fourteenth."

"He knows my opinion already."

"Have you told him what you think of this new material?"

"No, but I'm about to." She left Jeremy with his head sunk into his hands, as though willing Hippolyte back to the Auroras.

Later that day Marie found Hippolyte in the boardroom, like a little boy, possessively inventorying his stones and bones. She'd squandered hours wrestling with her conviction; and though her anger still flared like vagrant flames of a doused fire, she'd lost the words that went with it. She tried to reconstruct what she had to say and found the sentences sticking, lumpish, in her throat. Which she cleared.

"The table got messed up a bit, otherwise nothing is missing!" he announced, turning around, obviously expecting her. "Come and have a look. Do you have time?"

She drifted to the table, the fighting mood not only less belligerent but less urgent as well. In fact, in the few short steps from the doorway to his side, it evaporated altogether, as if she had parked it in the hall, leaving her exhausted and sad. She stood and listened to him eagerly describe the different kinds of limpets and what they indicated, how an *Adelomelon ancilla* had strayed from warmer Patagonian waters and confounded him, how there were an astonishing two hundred kinds of coral in the South Atlantic waters, but he had managed to get a sample of only one. He bemoaned his deficient collection, swore he'd go back someday and complete his work. His hands carefully cradled dried kelp tubers, fronds of seaweed. He took her by the arm as though she too were precious and led her over to the other side of the table where she watched him untangle ferns, mosses, tussock grasses.

Granite, basalt; sandstone, flagstone, and mudstone; rocks that, according to him, proved the geological legitimacy of the Auroras weighed down the table. "You see, don't you, that because the rock formations are so similar to the Falklands and Patagonia, that they could be part of the Gondwanaland supercontinent?" he asked. He held up the stones for her approval. She nodded. Biting her lip, she leaned on the table for support. The force that drove her and that shielded her from him was gone.

"What's the matter?" he asked, meticulously replacing the stones. He took a step closer to her, and though his eyes still shone with pleasure, his scrutiny was unnerving.

"I read your logbook, Hippolyte," she admitted.

The animation in his face was supplanted by a look of wariness. "Oh."

She hesitated. "I had a problem with the story before—you must have sensed that—now I don't even know what *you* believe!"

"You know what I believe."

"Then how do you explain your initial problems finding the islands? It's as if they really, truly didn't exist. Then, somehow, you were able to see them."

"I can't explain it."

"You can't just ignore it."

"Why not?"

"It's too important. For instance, maybe there's some phenomenon that accounts for nobody else being able to see the islands. Have you thought of that?"

He glared at her.

She persisted. "Then there's the account of your swim."

"You had no business reading any of that."

"What about your injuries, the cut on your hand, your arm?"

"They were silly accidents without lasting repercussions." He glanced at his hand, then offered it for her scrutiny. "See. All healed." She held it in hers. The hand itself was broad and square with blunt fingers, tanned and callused, so very large and rough compared to her own. They were ridged with layers of scar tissue from burns, cuts, scrapes. "I'm trying to believe in you," she admitted, "but—" They'd never been so close.

She knew he was watching her as she inspected the scars, as she ran the tips of her fingers along the surface of his skin. She could feel her face blotching; it was declaring unguardedly all of her doubts—not only of him but of herself as well. He unhooked his hand from her grip and pulled her to him. And he held her for that moment of defenselessness as though he wanted nothing more in the world than to drown himself in the waves of her hair. Drained of resistance, her arms responded, and they couldn't have held each other tighter if they'd been lovers. Then he let her go. Without looking at her again, he methodically packed up the specimens, his eyes unheedful of her, his body tense, his silence more eloquent than words would ever be.

With the last box closed, the Auroras no longer claimed their space. She had shared his silence but now could speak again. "We're giving it, that is, Jeremy would like me to work with you until the end of the month."

His eyes tore into her. But his voice, his actions were gentle. "I hardly think that's possible."

"I promised him I would," she protested. Suddenly, irrationally, she wanted to save the book. "To see if there's anything more you can find that would convince me. It's just me, really. Jeremy believes. Strongly," she almost accused. As if Hippolyte had told Jeremy some secret that she'd been left out of.

Then Hippolyte was gone, for the second time, and possibly for good.

PART FOUR

SIGNS OF LAND

SECTION VIII.

SOUTH ATLANTIC OCEAN ;

COASTS OF SOUTH AMERICA,

With the West Coast of North America and adjacent Islands.

Twenty-five

"I've split my books up between Lucinda and Casimir," Marie informed Jeremy. "It'll mean tough loads for them, but it's time they got used to it."

"I don't think you've ever talked about taking a holiday, never mind actually taken one, since I started here." Jeremy was very sober. He turned his back to her and looked out the window. "An author, no, a dear friend, that I counted on; an editor, another dear friend, that I still count on. And you're both gone or going. What can I say?" He pulled out his handkerchief and blew his nose. "You're coming back, aren't you?"

"Oh, Jeremy, don't make me cry! I've messed this up miserably for everyone; I can't stay here a minute longer. Don't worry though," she took his hand, rolled it around in both of hers—he stared in disbelief— "I'll be back in a month. Maybe less. I'm sorry, Jeremy. It doesn't seem worth it for a book to have torn up everyone so much."

"Where are you planning to go?"

"I don't know yet. It's kind of a sudden decision. Maybe someplace tropical where I can drink myself silly."

Although Washington, D.C., was hot, it hardly qualified as tropical. Marie's decision to take a holiday and forget her troubles was as short-lived as the time it took for her to return to her apartment and pack. She threw her small suitcase into the trunk of her car, crumpled up the new handbills that had accumulated on the windshield, and tossed them onto the floor on the passenger side. She headed through town nervously, barely able to negotiate the tunnel. How long has it been since I've driven this car more than two blocks?, she asked herself. Just before the Jersey Turnpike, she stopped at a gas station to fill up and discovered that most of the oil had drained away and that one of the tires was nearly flat. While the attendant tried to rehabilitate the poor vehicle, she bought road maps for New Jersey, Pennsylvania, and Maryland and worked out a route to Washington, D.C., some 200 miles south.

The highways were miserably jammed; it was rush hour, and there were agonizing bottlenecks everywhere. As she plowed through the heavy traffic, she cursed herself for taking the car. The trip was only three hours by Metroliner, and she would have been spared the hassle of both driving and parking.

Late that night she checked into a hotel in Silver Spring, Maryland, six miles north of Washington's center, and the next day made her way into town and the offices of the National Archives via the Metro.

"Yes, I think the Byers papers were consulted a week or two ago," the librarian at the National Archives told her. "I could confirm that, if you need the information." Her tone implied that she'd rather not.

"That's not necessary," Marie replied, "but may I see the papers?"

"Certainly, just fill out the request form." Fifteen minutes later, Marie was struggling over the handwritten correspondence of James Byers and Co. of New York City. Because of the old-fashioned penmanship, the occasional blobbed ink, and the faded writing, she read with difficulty about the business transactions of the day. The purchases of salt and provisions, the hiring of sailors, the making of promises to shareholders, the extraction of money from debtors. All very interesting, but where was mention of Forsyth, the owner of the *Corona*? There wasn't a word about him in these records.

"Excuse me," she interrupted the librarian again. "Do you have anything about an Adam Forsyth? Or Samuel?" She was directed to reference catalogs, given suggestions for alternative search categories: *Corona,* Fanning, *Fortuna,* Mercantile Activities, New York City Harbor, Sailing, South Atlantic. But she came up with nothing.

That afternoon, her search spilt over into the Library of Congress, where she followed Hippolyte's tracks to the map department.

"I remember him," said a bespectacled librarian. He assisted her through the signing-in procedure and effortlessly re-created Hippolyte's Aurora request. "It was a gentleman, very enthusiastic, if I recall. We all got quite caught up in the search. You see, he asked if we had a British Admiralty map of the South Atlantic for 1808, and we ought to; we have it listed." He vanished for a moment, then reappeared with a small catalog. "Right here." He pointed to a scribbled notation on the side of a page listing map acquisitions. "But we couldn't find it. He wanted to see another one, a Spanish map from 1800, but we couldn't find that one either. He was ready to give up, when," the librarian chuckled with pleasure, "wham! I remembered where it was. He told me that it was even better than the 1808 map. We ran off a copy for him. On the big printer over there." He pointed to the far wall.

"Can I see that map?" she asked. He brought her "Carta Esferica del Oceano Meridional Desde el Equador hasta 60° grados de Latitud y Desde el Cabo de Hornos hasta el Canal de Mozambique." She grasped the heavy paper, testing herself, trying to understand what he would have felt when he spread it out in front of him. It didn't work. This map told her nothing she hadn't already seen on the copy. Bustamente, that poor deluded fellow, thought that he had surveyed the Auroras. But he was three hundred miles out. That she was sure of.

"Were there no other maps? None that you were able to find of the South Atlantic?"

"We went over many maps," replied the librarian, "but they were all too recent. Your chap seemed content with this one. Would you like a copy? It's ten dollars, but you have to pay by check."

"Sure," she said, dutifully writing one out. She wasn't sure, though, what use it would be.

Hippolyte had done nothing else traceable at the library. The next logical stop would be to check the Forsyth papers at the G. W. Blunt Library, whereever that was. If she was lucky, it would be right here in

CARTA ESFERICA
DEL
OCEANO MERIDIONAL
DESDE EL EQUADOR
hasta 60. grados de Latitud
Y DESDE EL
CABO DE HORNOS
HASTA EL
CANAL DE MOZAMBIQUE
CONSTRUIDA DE ORDEN DEL REY
EN LA DIRECCION DE TRABAJOS HIDROGRAFICOS
Y PRESENTADA Á S. M.
POR MANO DEL EXCMO. SEÑOR
DON ANTONIO CORNEL

Secretario de Estado, y del Despacho
Universal de Guerra, encargado del
de Marina, y de la Direccion
general de la Armada.

AÑO DE 1800.

M A L U I N A S

ISLAS

I.ª FALKLAND
C.º Perciball

C.º Merredih

B.ª S. Felip

Fru. Pepys

Pto. Egmont
I.ª de Borbon
C.ª Leal
Br. del Aguila

I.ª Las Salvages

C.º Corrientes
Pto. de la Soledad
I.ª SOLEDAD

I.ª Beauchenes

Muchas Bancas de nieve

Muchas Bancas de nieve

I.ª de la Aurora

Advertencia.

———— Derrota que hizo el Conde de la Perouse en 1785. en busca de la Isla Grande de la Roche.

- - - - - Derrota del Capitan Jorge Vancouver en 1795. con igual objeto.

.... Derrota de la Corbeta del Rey Atrevida en 1794. para reconocer y situar las Islas Auroras.

Washington. She dialed information. "For what city?" the operator asked.

"How about Washington," she suggested. When the operator told her there was no such library in Washington and asked if she wanted to try another city, her mind went blank.

She phoned the office and got Janice working on it. And she couldn't resist asking if Hippolyte had come back. The answer was no. Calling the office again an hour later, she was told it was actually the G.W. Blunt *White* Library in Mystic, Connecticut. She cursed Hippolyte for his mistake—it undermined her perfection—then checked her notes. It was her error. Connecticut. Back north. Well, she was pleased for one reason, the car was finally getting a workout.

That night she had dinner at a bookstore café just off Dupont Circle, one of the few places in which she remembered feeling comfortable eating alone when she'd been to Washington on previous trips. This evening was no different, and she smiled to herself as she looked at the other patrons, mostly women, dining with only their books for company.

Getting an early start the next morning, Marie was able to avoid the worst of the traffic and crossed the line into Connecticut by four that afternoon. Following I-95 through Stamford and Westport, then passing New Haven, she arrived in Mystic by six that evening and by lucky chance found herself a bed-and-breakfast with a vacant room.

The Blunt White Library was filled with maritime data, accounts, ephemera. It was no wonder that Hippolyte had headed here in his search for an uncelebrated ship's captain; if any record of Capt. George L. Thomas existed, it would be here. But Hippolyte had not written in his notes the catalog numbers for the papers he had consulted, and no one, unfortunately, remembered his visit or could help beyond making general suggestions. Marie found herself greatly hampered by the vagueness of her request, by her lack of research credentials. It felt as if she wouldn't be able to do more than scratch the surface, that she'd never be able to dig through it to find what

Hippolyte claimed to have found. Little details gratified her momentarily, though; she learned, for instance, that the *Hersilia* had been built in Mystic in 1819.

A frustrating weekend intervened. Saturday, with the special collections department closed, she sat by the water with nothing to do but listen to gulls and tourists and become annoyed by their leisure. Recalling that Edmund Fanning had resided in nearby Stonington, she killed a couple of hours there that afternoon and discovered that it had also been home to Benjamin Morrell and numerous other scalers. Back in Mystic by Saturday evening and tired of twisting her ankles in her city shoes and holding her skirts against the ocean breezes, she bought light cotton trousers and a pair of running shoes. On Sunday morning she watched waves of ice-cream lickers and wondered how Hippolyte could have tolerated the mock antiquity overlying the genuinely historic town. Where had he stayed? Surely not in the bed-and-breakfasts filled to the attics with lovers cooing over ruffles and potpourris. In the afternoon, she fell asleep in the sun and woke with a sunburn. In the waning hours of the day, she shook off her shoes and dangled her feet in the water, spotting here and there white clam shells and blue mussel shells momentarily exposed by the low tide. Squatting down in the shallows, she let the water lap at her legs and run over her fingers. She splashed her burning face with the coolness and wondered about swimming and being lost in water. It was no good, she shook her head; she and Hippolyte were worlds apart.

Monday morning, not convinced it wasn't a workday, she pulled on nylons, stepped into her tailored linen skirt, yanked it up over her hips, then stood, clutching the fabric. Sun streamed through lacy curtains. The dappled reflection in the full-length mirror—of her sunburn, her hair that not even a washing could scrub Sunday's wind out of—was of someone else, not her. Was the mirror to blame or was it the red face and the wilderness of curls cascading over her shoulders? Or perhaps a loss of something that was expressed in her eyes, her mouth, her stance? Or was fault even the issue? She let the skirt slip back down her legs onto the floor and tore off the stockings, retreating to the slackness of the trousers, the ease of the canvas shoes without even socks to compartmentalize the feet. And sighed in relief.

As soon as the library doors opened, she was applying to the special collections for access to their manuscripts. But by the end of the day, she was afraid she was going to wear out her welcome before finding anything relevant to South Atlantic sealing, never mind specifics like information about Capt. George L. Thomas. Why am I persisting?, she asked herself dementedly. Here I am in a maritime library, squandering hours looking for something I don't believe in when I could be taking this precious holiday someplace soothing, someplace where I'd be happy. And just where is that magic place of joy?, she wondered but could not answer. She was back in the library again the next day and the next. The staff became accustomed to seeing her, and rather than eject her as she had feared, went out of their way to help, though they were hardly optimistic. "You know, dear," one sympathetic librarian cautioned, "those sealers were a mighty secretive lot. They had to protect their sealing grounds from others, so very few logbooks or other records of where they went have been preserved."

Marie phoned Rumor daily, extracting a promise from Janice not to tell Jeremy she was calling. But she had to know. Had Hippolyte come in? Had he called? No, she was told, every day.

By Friday, Marie was at the end of her rope. She was going through desperate measures now, reading through file folders stuffed with invoices, letters, crew lists. When she was just about cross-eyed and ready to give up, but by no means prepared to do so, the name Nathan Stafford Farnham caught her eye. He, she recalled after double-checking her notes, was the captain of the *Delight,* the ship that had sailed alongside Thomas's *Corona* in 1823, until either the *Corona* or the *Delight* had gotten lost. There was nothing else of interest in that particular file, but she noticed that a slip of paper had been taped onto the cover of the folder. "Runford Coll," she read, and asked the librarian what it meant.

"The Runfords are an old family, going back, in these parts, to the 1760s," she was told. "Their papers and other effects were in the hands of two different, I guess you'd say, factions, of the family. The one side, where this folder comes from, they donated everything to the museum mostly. Sailors' gear: uniforms, medicine chest, paint boxes, medals, compasses, some books. I believe this folder contains the only written records they possessed." He looked at the tan card of the file and frowned. "Hasn't been cataloged yet. Anyway, the other side of the family—and that really just consists of one man, Jonathan Runford—he's hanging on to the documents. He says it's only 'til I croak,' then we're welcome to come and, these are his words, mind, 'rob my grave.' Since he's almost ninety-six, I expect that'll be any day."

"So, Jonathan Runford lives around here?"

"Yes, but that doesn't mean he's easy to visit."

"Could you tell me where to start?"

Robert Runford

Corona

Twenty-six

Iⱽ MARIE HAD BEEN WORRIED about how she'd spend another week-end in Mystic, she shouldn't have been. Armed with a romantic tale about her own great-grandfather, possibly great-great-grandfather, whose name she had supposedly found amongst the Runford papers, she was received by the Runford clan with generous curiosity. Skillfully turning her story into a request to visit old Mr. Runford, she was handed along the coast, from one Runford to another—nieces and nephews, not so young themselves, and their children—as they debated what to do with her and her inconvenient demand.

"My dear, Uncle Jonathan is not seeing anyone these days."

"Lemme tell you something, young lady, Jonathan that old bastard barricaded himself into his old shack in 1989 and threatens to shoot anyone who comes within fifty feet of the property."

"Uncle John, poor soul, is on his deathbed."

"Jonathan? Didn't he cop it just last year? Mavis, whose funeral was it we went to last summer?"

And finally, "I think I can arrange something, if you don't mind being patient for a few more days."

This last was from a woman in her late twenties, Heather Runford, the granddaughter of Jonathan Runford's grandfather's brother's son. Or something to that effect. "He likes me," she confided, "because I'm the only one of our whole extended family who declares an aversion to sailing. Crazy, huh? Of course, I said that when I was nine; I probably just picked up on something he said and repeated it like a typical kid. Truth is, though, I love to sail."

"Is he so very against the sea?"

"I don't believe it's that; probably, it's more to do with his grand-father who went completely lunatic because of something that happened at sea. It had a devastating effect on their immediate family." Marie opened her mouth to interrupt. "Don't ask me," Heather cut her off, "exactly what that was. He won't talk about it though I have heard rumors. But I'll find out if we can visit. I'll call you in a day or two."

Heather picked up Marie early on Monday morning and glanced approvingly at Marie's feet. "We'll have to do some walking," she said.

"Are you sure this is okay?" Marie asked anxiously. "Aren't you missing work? Are you sure you don't want me to drive?" To herself she fretted about having lied, about keeping up the pretense, about wasting Heather's time.

They rolled down the windows to let the moving air cool them. "I hate air conditioning," Heather confessed, as though admitting to a crime. Bugs spattered the windshield, the car smelt of summer asphalt and ripe vegetation. An hour's drive inland they turned off the high-way onto an unpaved road. After passing a couple of rundown cottages, the road dwindled until it petered out into a mass of weeds. They pulled up under a gnarly fruit tree; there wasn't a house in sight. Heather unpacked four brown paper grocery bags and handed two to Marie.

"I'd have never found this on my own," Marie marveled.

"We're not there yet," Heather replied.

They headed off past the tree, which was heavy with already fermenting, wizened little apples and swarming with early wasps. The tops of long weeds brushed Marie's hands, burrs attached themselves to her clothing, flies and wasps flew into her face. And it was hot. After fifteen minutes they arrived at the perimeter of a scraggly yard, fenced in with barbed wire.

"Uncle Jonathan!" Heather yelled. "It's me!" Then they waited.

The old man, contrary to Marie's expectations, did not greet them with a sawed-off double-barreled shotgun. He shuffled out, a straw hat his only weapon. Possibly once a tall man, Jonathan Runford had accordioned in on himself. His belly bore the brunt of the collapse, and shredded suspenders were his trousers' only defense against gravity. He seemed tickled to be visited by two women. "Got's so's I appreciate anyone younger than eighty," he chuckled. Then he frowned at the bags and patted his stomach. "Hettie, you know your fancy food wrecks my digestion." But he took the bags anyway and glanced into them furtively.

The cabin revolved around a large open kitchen. Three doors led off the room; one was the one they had come through, another led to a darkened room, probably a bedroom, and the third led to a field that she could see out back. Marie wondered where the bathroom was, then decided not to think about it. In the kitchen, a roughly planed wooden table was set for three, and greasy black tea was already cooling in thick white mugs; store-bought biscuits, more crumb than cookie, were daintily arrayed on a cracked earthenware plate. "Hettie, here, is my favorite, aren't you?" he patted her head playfully. She rolled her eyes at him, re-creating without realizing it her nine-year-old self, and polished off the plate of dried-out cookies. "Outdone yourself, haven't you, baking day and night, just for us!" she teased, and downed the tea. "Delicious," she smacked her lips. Marie could barely sip it. She had nibbled a cookie politely and tried to ignore the big gray fingerprints on the rim of her mug and the tea-leaved scum floating on the surface. And she tried to will Heather out of her childhood, to get her to the point faster, but in the end, gave up, suspecting that Heather knew her relative best.

"You," Jonathan said, pointing to Marie, "are a lucky lady. There was a fellow up this way just yesterday, asking the same questions about Robert Runford."

"Oh, come on now, Uncle Jonathan," protested Heather, "I was here yesterday!"

Marie's brain was at once torn apart: she felt even worse for all the bother she was causing Heather, who, it now appeared, had had to drive up on purpose to ask her uncle permission to visit. And who was

Robert Runford? Why did Jonathan assume she was asking about him?

"Oh, okay," Jonathan's concession disrupted Marie's thoughts. "Maybe it was a week ago. Anyway, not so very long. I told this fellow—"

"What was his name?" Marie interrupted, all of a sudden aware that this "fellow" must have been Hippolyte.

"How the hell—excuse me, I forgot my tongue." He began again, "I didn't find out what he was called, but he was a nice young man. Actually, now I remember, he came around two times. Funny this sudden interest in my great-grandfather." His voice dropped, becoming mischievous, "Now there was a nutcase for you. And folk think *my* porch light's dim!"

"Robert was your grandfather, wasn't he, not great-grandfather?" Heather asked.

Marie was only half listening; how could Hippolyte have found Jonathan all on his own?

"What's it matter?" he retorted, "the old coot's dead, in't he? And well out of it, too, I might add. I'll be joinin' him soon," he winked, "they say there's a special place for us," he touched his finger to his forehead and laughed. "But you don't want to hear me going on." He levered himself up and off the chair. "Wait here," he commanded as he left the tiny kitchen.

"Robert Runford was his grandfather," Heather quickly filled in the details. "I don't know if it's Robert's papers you've come to look through, but I think you'll find his story interesting all the same. If Uncle Jonathan will tell it to you. I mentioned about him being called a lunatic. He died in 1913 at the age of—ninety-five, I think. Same age as Uncle Jonathan; no wonder he's talking about popping off. Anyway, the story—or what I've heard—is that Robert Runford was a sailor, but when he came back from a sailing trip—it had been his first voyage—when he was sixteen years old, he started talking funny; I don't know what it was about. He left again the following year and went back to sea, but had taken to raving so badly that he could never get another job onboard a ship again. At least I think that's how the story goes. Anyway, Uncle Jonathan, who was born in 1905, ah, here you are," she broke off at the return of her uncle, "what's in that box? You've never shown it to me!"

"No, I never have, you little smart-aleck. You're too young. Now this lady," he graciously nodded to Marie, "is also young, but far more mature than you'll ever be." The box landed on the table with a dusty thud.

"That fellow that came here, he got me thinking. I didn't show him the box neither at first, but I told him about Grandad. All that I could remember, that is. I never told you, have I, Hettie? I forgot about these letters. They went clear out of my head until the fellow was gone, so it was a good thing he came back. Seemed to appreciate having a look see. Here," he pushed the box towards Marie, "I'm getting too old to be ornery about all this. If you want anything, just take it."

"Uncle!" Heather exclaimed, "you know you promised the family's documents to the library!"

"Don't worry," Marie cut in, "I won't take anything, I just want to look at what's here." And she began to dig while Heather and Jonathan went off to repair some fallen part of the old man's world.

At first the dust annoyed and inhibited her; she'd pause to wipe off accumulations from her hands. Then she ignored it, letting it discolor her fingernails and palms. She dug through letters, bills, mortgages, deeds, and wills, searching for a sign, any sign of the captain of the *Corona*. Finally, she unearthed a scabrous little booklet, handbound with hemp string, tanned brown by age and acid, labeled with the name of Robert Runford and dated 1823. She turned back the cover and her heart stopped. Forget Capt. George L. Thomas. Or rather, don't forget him, here he was, described by Runford's quick eye and quicker pen.

December 5th

—the first mate Mr. Gunner still experiences difficulties with his foot. He begs off his duties to such an extent that Captain Thomas has, in moments of bad temper, threatened to leave him at the next port of call. We are not inclined to take Captain Thomas seriously as he is a good and kindly man and has not suffered any of us to undue hardship. There is a certain amount of discontent, though, amongst the men, as we have not yet approached any sealing grounds. They grumble about uncertainty of wages.

December 6th

We have lost sight of our sister ship, the Delight. Perhaps she went off course sometime during the night. Otherwise, Captain Thomas is in a vigorous mood, owing to the brisk winds and clear skies. We pray to God this fine weather holds as tales abound of the dreadful seas in these latitudes.

December 7th

10½ AM. The Captain has cried out for the ship to heave-to and the men have been ordered to prepare the longboats. We are bewildered as we are not in sight of land. What can this mean?

11 AM. Wishing to keep as complete a record of my voyage as possible, I have asked Mr. Gunner what our latitude and longitude is. As his foot continues to impair his mood, I received a slap on my ear for my impertinence. He too is disquieted by the Captain's orders. The boats are ready to be lowered ; and I have taken myself from underfoot. A lookout has been sent up to keep an eye out for the Delight.

11½ AM. Four longboats with eight men to each have set out to the east. Captain Thomas is in the first, Mr. Gunner is in the second. My good friend Martin Sanderson is also in the second boat. They are equipped as if to make for sealing grounds close-by. We are, all of us who are left onboard the ship, fearful of what will become of these thirty-two men. I loaned Martin my mother's handkerchief, embroidered with her intitials E.R., as good luck.

12 AM. A miracle has just taken place. In front of our very eyes, the first boat pulled up on to a shore that was heretofore invisible to us. The men have disembarked and are hailing the others. The island, of which it is no doubt, seems to have appeared as though out of a fog, though no fog exists. All four boats are now landed and the men stand firmly on land. Martin has signaled to me with the handkerchief!

5 PM. Mr. Gunner and two of the boats are back, already fully loaded with fur-seal skins. He is excited to the extent that he has forgotten his bad foot and has left off abusing us. Still, as we assisted in the unloading of the skins, there are mutterings of much unhappiness. Some may think that Captain Thomas is in God's hands, but others believe he works at the side of the Devil. I have resolved to take advantage of Mr. Gunner's improved disposition and ask to visit this miraculous island.

December 9th. I am much in awe. I have stood on this land that we could not see. Indeed, I think at times it dissolves beneath my feet and the sensation leaves me quite breathless. When I am in Captain Thomas's presence the island is as firm as my own homeland; as soon as he is out of sight, the sensation of disappearing recommences. When we row back to the ship, we see the land vanish with an abrupt certainty, as though it doesn't want us to return. The men continue to grumble, though very quietly ; they are also grateful for the quantity of seals. Our wages are most certainly guaranteed.

I am now in possession of the latitude and longitude. The island, which Captain Thomas calls The Auroras, though we see only one, is at 52°37′S. latitude and 47°42′W. longitude. Martin tells me that he has seen the chart and states that there are three islands drawn thereupon.

I would have Captain Thomas show all of us this chart as dissent is rising. Perhaps those who would claim that we are destined for Hell for our work with Satan would be convinced of the veracity of the land if they were to see it on the chart. For, as we all know, the charts have been made by honest men.

The island is very bleak by way of vegetation ; there is not one tree nor even a shrub, but tall thick grasses through which one cannot walk but with much difficulty. There is, however, an abundance of animal life ; I would not claim to have ever counted so many birds and seals. Penguins abound in the hundreds and are very tame. Too tame, in fact ; many have been killed and, like the elephant seals, are being rendered for their oil.

December 12th. Three thousand skins have so far been stowed onto the ship. A delegation of men has approached Captain Thomas to beg that we leave off and be contented with this number. The Captain refuses ; and says we must continue until we have fulfilled our requirements. I am afraid for him. He, too, is disquieted, though, as there is still no sign of the Delight. He has carved a piece of driftwood with the name of our ship, his initials, the date December 12th, and our next port of call, St John on Staten Land and before he set the sign upon a tall pole fashioned from a broken oar he handed it to me, asking me to paint in the letters in some bright manner. This I did by grinding the island's red soil and mixing it with seal oil to bind it. We wonder that he expects Captain Farnham of the Delight to locate this board, as we have grave doubts that Farnham will be able to find the island upon which it stands.

December 14th. We have now taken nearly five thousand skins. The men labor like fiends all through the day and night.

December 15th. 4½ PM. The worst has happened. Captain Thomas is dead. The men demanded we be allowed to depart, for many are truly frightened. They say that when they row away from the island to transport the skins to the ship, they can no longer see the land. It vanishes behind them, and this, they declare, can be none other than the work of the devil. The captain refused their demands, voices were raised, a struggle broke out and in the panic the captain was bludgeoned to death. Mr. Gunner came to his defense and has also been killed as have several other men, ensign James Turvey, second mate Erasmus Simms, deckhand Isaiah Jervis. I was loathe to join the men in this dreadful deed, but also, to my shame, I did not defend the lives of those who have died. May God forgive me.

They have been buried. The signpost for the Delight has been broken up, lest it tempt other men to these evil shores.

December 16th. We leave this God Forsaken place and have directed a course west for the Falkland Islands. The command is shared between the mutineers. Without Captain Thomas to guide the way, as he was the only man who could see that which confronted us, the ship struck a reef and more lives were lost in the saving of it. Our progress is much reduced owing to the heavy northwesterlies and to the damage to the hull. God speed us back to safety!

I must not be caught writing ; I have hidden my words from all eyes, even from Martin. We have been sworn to secrecy, and the logbook has been thrown overboard.

Marie read on, through the repeated attempts to patch the hull, the landing at Port Soledad in the Falklands, the lies. The remaining crew testified that all of those dead perished when the ship struck the reef, and they were allowed to limp back to New York, having saved at least the financial intent of the voyage. Forsyth was reluctant to accept that no one on board could pinpoint exactly where the tragedy happened nor could they confirm where the skins were taken. The secret of the Auroras effectively died with Captain Thomas.

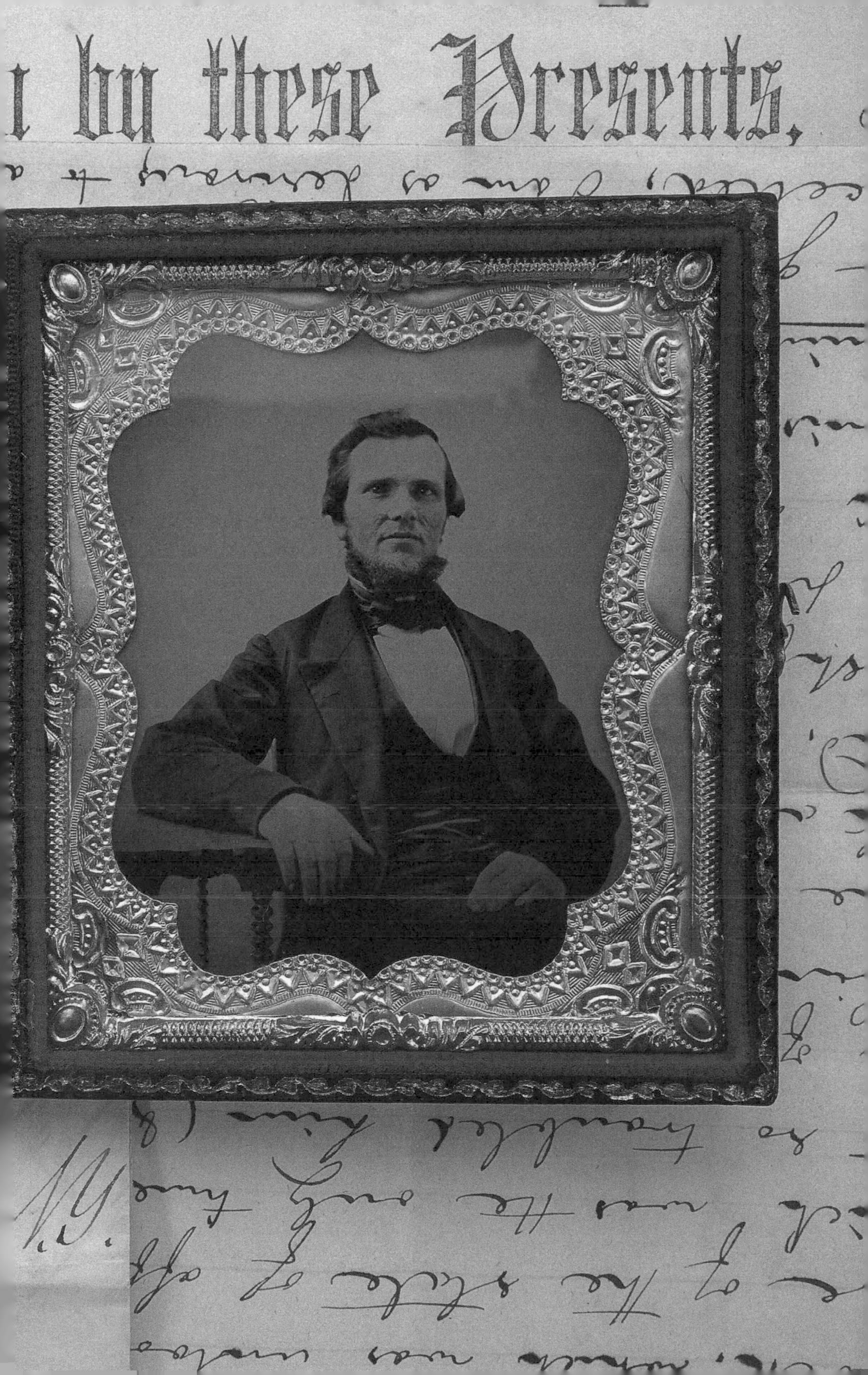
by these Presents,

Twenty-seven

WHEN HEATHER AND JONATHAN CAME BACK into the kitchen, they found Marie searching frantically through the box. "There must be some other sign of the *Corona*," she announced, handing them each packets of letters which they leafed through in visible confusion. There were documents that confirmed Runford's unsuccessful stint on the *Delight* the following year, correspondence between family members concerned about his descent into what was called lunacy, and most tragically, many missives that he had written in the empty years following, to politicians, navy headquarters, newspapers, about the mysterious islands and the dreadful event that had taken place on them.

Jonathan found and opened a small black case, revealing the portrait of a young man who, at first glance, looked you in the eye, but on second glance, stared far beyond. "That's him, that's Robert," he declared, tapping the glass with his finger. "Crazy bugger."

Marie took the portrait and stared at it. She then snapped the case shut and gave it back. She was afraid that she'd see Hippolyte in Robert's drifting eyes. But she would not be parted from the journal, promised that she would return it, clutched it to herself.

Jonathan had decided on food as salvation and cut them thick sandwiches filled with fat-streaked ham and green-fringed cheese that Marie wolfed down, oblivious to her earlier revulsions. She demanded more tea and swirled the warm tannic-stained water round her mouth to dampen the dust. While they ate, Jonathan recounted the story he'd told Hippolyte and added more.

"From before I can remember they set the old fellow to minding me by way of making him think that he had some important occupation," Jonathan remembered. "So for my first eight years—he died when I was eight—I listened to his perpetual mutterings. You might say I was weaned on the magical island that was there yet wasn't. He'd sit and jaw away—at times I could barely hear him—then he'd burst out angry and shake his fist. Caught up in nightmare or something along those lines. Sometimes he shrieked that the ground was giving way and that he was going to drown, other times he'd relive the seal slaughter. He was just a young fella; it must have been something to see all those seals being clubbed and skinned. Did you read that bit where they were taking a thousand seals a day?

"Anyway, when he shouted out angry-like, I always was afraid he was mad at me, but when I asked he'd come to like he didn't even realize that I'd been there, listening to him. When he wasn't talking he was writing those letters. Before she died (that was before I was born) he gave them to my grandmother to post, and though she said she did, she never actually sent any. Mortified, she was. And intimidated the rest of the family, visitors, maids, to also agree to accept them but to not actually send them. Never getting any replies, he naturally grew suspicious of her and offered bribes to whoever. Of course, once I was on two feet he started on me. I carried on the tradition and was a traitor to my grandfather, but what could I do? My grandmother's voice commanded me from her grave. Which is why I've still got them all.

"It was enough to drive a boy up the wall. I never appreciated at the time what he was trying to say, and I'm not sure even to this day if I believe his rantings. Course I don't know what that book has to do with your family, but if you had an ancestor on the *Corona*, God preserve your peace of mind."

Peace of mind was one thing, presence of mind another, and Marie could barely muster enough of the latter to remember to ask about the man who'd returned to go through the papers. "What did he look like? Please try to remember when he came here the first time? When did he come back? How long did he stay? Did he say what he was looking for? Or why?"

"Just who are you trying to find," Jonathan asked, "this fellow or your relative?" He laughed when Marie's steady interrogation faltered; his question had hit its mark.

Marie was convinced in the end that it had been Hippolyte, that he'd returned for more proof after she'd so thoroughly rejected his story about Thomas and the *Corona*.

Heather drove her back into town and dropped her off at her B&B. They exchanged addresses, phone numbers; Marie allowed herself to be hugged. Then she drove back to New York.

Marie tossed Robert Runford's journal onto Jeremy's desk. It landed with a thud. "There!" she cried out, "You win!" She picked the journal up again and this time placed it on the desk gently. "You win, Jeremy," she said, appeasing. Then she picked it up again and held it up to display, saying nothing but arching her eyebrows meaningfully.

The drama of this scene was much diminished by the fact that she was alone; Jeremy was nowhere near his office at that moment. Marie continued to practice how to concede this battle, but she remained dissatisfied; nothing expressed the conflict that she was suffering. Nothing made allowances for her skepticism, her right to disbelief. Only in Hippolyte's continued absence could she find comfort, and distress.

She turned the journal over and over in her hands. The soft kid of the cover was pliable and so very real; the pages within were dog-eared and stained, much read by their own author and corrected and—oh, she knew she was letting her imagination run with too much slack— possibly wept over.

Jeremy walked in an hour later. She was still in his office, slumped in a chair, the journal resting on her outstretched leg.

"Hello!" he exclaimed. Her trousers seemed to startle him. "Are you starting a new trend?" But he must have realized the levity was misplaced, for his second question quickly overlapped the first. "Where have you been?"

Marie forgot her premeditated dramatics; instead she simply leaned forward, placed the journal onto the desk, and said, "Sit down and read this." While he read, she stared at her bare ankles, the lacings of the running shoes, the seams of the pants.

Jeremy closed the book. "Amazing. Too bad it's too late."

"Too late? What do you mean?"

"I dropped the book. Naturally."

"What do you mean, naturally? We didn't talk about canceling it! We were going to wait until the thirtieth!"

Jeremy looked at her in disbelief. "You can't mean to say that when Hippolyte left, when you left, that you really thought we were going to hang on? And by the way, today is the twenty-ninth."

"You're right," she was chastened. "I didn't. Truth is, I guess, I never thought it would ever get as far as it did. But, you can see that's all changed, with this journal. All along I was getting in the way of something I didn't understand. I still don't understand, but I'm ready to suspend—belief. We should go ahead."

"Without Hippolyte? You know, he came over shortly after you left."

"But I told Janice to tell me—"

"To the house, not to the office," Jeremy cut in. "He hinted at this," he pointed to the diary, "but said that, short of you going to the Auroras yourself, nothing would convince you. And so agreed with me to drop it; he himself wasn't prepared to continue under the circumstances."

"That doesn't seem possible," Marie protested.

He handed her a letter. "This came a couple of days ago."

Dear Jeremy and Marie:
Not being the type to feel sorry for himself, I won't ask if you're happy now that I'm out of your hair. I'm naturally disappointed that my book, whatever it would have

275

ended up being called, is not going ahead. I hope you don't self-inflict the same amount of pain with all of your projects.

Marie, thank you for putting up with me as long as you did. I have to admit something: I read a letter on your desk. From Johnny Harada at 50° North. At first I was a bit miffed that you didn't pass along the message from him about them taking the article, but no matter; I've made arrangements with him to publish part one. Now that there's no book, I can't see that you'd have a problem with that. Anyway, don't feel too badly about reading my log-book; we're even.

Jeremy, I'm sure we'll keep in touch better in the future. I'll call you when I'm back.

Regards to you both,

Hippolyte

Marie was on the phone before she'd finished reading. "Janice," she barked, "find the number for *50° North* for me. Please." She hung up the phone, and they waited, both staring at Hippolyte's letter.

The phone rang, Marie snatched up the receiver, scribbled down the number, then dialed. "John Harada, please," her voice became professional, mellow, but insistent.

"Hello, Mr. Harada. It's Marie Simplon from Rumor Press."

"Hello, Marie. I half-expected you to call. It's about Hippolyte, right?"

"Yes, it is. What's this about an article on the Auroras?"

"He's given us his manuscript, so we're publishing a condensed version. In, let me check, in the November issue."

"I have a letter from him that says it's to be part one."

"That's right. He'll be bringing us part two when he gets back."

"Back? Back from where?"

276

"The Auroras, of course."

"The Auroras!?"

"Yeah, he wants to get more evidence. Apparently you really held a gun to his head. Good for you!"

"You sound as though you believe the Auroras exist."

"I do, actually. In a weird kind of way."

"Has he left already?"

"Apparently."

"But it's too early! It's still winter there."

"He's driving. Said he always wanted to do that. Expects to get to Patagonia in October."

"Will you do me a favor?"

"If I can." The three words were tinged with suspicion.

"When you publish the article, could you add a line at the end?"

"Maybe." He sounded even more cautious. "What would it say?"

"Have you got a pen? Write this: Excerpted from the forthcoming book, called"—she snapped her fingers soundlessly, shut her eyes as though a title was floating in the darkness behind her eyelids—"called *Hippolyte's Island*. Got that?"

"Okay, I can do that." The suspicion in his voice gave way to relief. "I have a message for you, by the way."

"From Hippolyte?"

"Who else? He asked me to tell you—but only if you phoned—that you're welcome to join him."

"Join him!?"

"Yeah, and he asked me to make sure you know that he means it."

Marie laughed. "Maybe I will!" And she meant it.

Bibliography

Marie: Some of these were more useful than others, but
I've included the works anyway.

Bertrand, Kenneth J. Americans In Antarctica: 1775-1948.
    Special Publication No. 39. New York: American
    Geographical Society: 1971. I wish I'd seen this one
    earlier; it would have saved me a lot of footwork.
Biscoe, J. "Recent Discoveries in the Antarctic Ocean from
    the log-book of the brig Tula" Geographical Journal,
    1833. This is the one you found, Marie. I never did
    look it up.
Cawkell, M.B.R., D.H. Maling, E.M. Cawkell. The Falkland
    Islands. London: Macmillan, 1960. Useful overview of
    the history of South Atlantic discoveries.
Darwin, Charles. The Voyage of the Beagle. London: J.M.
    Dent, 1955 (1st published a lot earlier). Always of
    great interest.
Fanning, Edmund. Voyages and Discoveries in the South
    Seas: 1792-1832. Salem, Mass. Marine Research Society,
    1924 (1st published as Voyages Round the World: with
    selected Sketches of Voyages to the South Seas, North and
    South Pacific Oceans, China, etc. performed under the
    command and agency of the author, 1832)
Farnham, Moulton H. Sailing for Beginners. New York:
    Macmillan, 1967. This is the one that saved my buns.
Gould, R.T. Oddities, a Book of Unexplained Facts. London:
    P. Allen, 1928.
Gurney, Alan. Below the Convergence: Voyages Towards
    Antarctica: 1699-1849. New York: W.W. Norton, 1997.
    This, like Bertrand, was very useful.
Harris, Graham. A Guide to the Birds and Mammals of
    Coastal Patagonia. Princeton: Princeton University

Press, 1998. I'm glad I was able to take this book out
of the library, do you have any idea how much it costs!

Headland, Robert. The Island of South Georgia. Cambridge:
Cambridge University Press, 1984. Extremely useful,
but dismissive of the Auroras.

Kendrick, John. Alejandro Malaspina, Portrait of a
Visionary. Montreal: McGill-Queen's University Press,
1999. Also useful, but I wish someone would write a bio
of Bustamente.

Malaspina, Alessandro 1754-1809. Politico-scientific
Voyage Around the World by the Corvettes Descubierta
and Atrevida Under the Command of the naval captains Don
Alexandro Malaspina and Don Jose de Bustamente y
Guerra, from 1789-1794. Edited by Don Pedro de Novo y
Colson. Translated by Carl Robinson, 1934. MS.

Malaspina, Alejandro 1754-1809 . Viaje politic-cientifico
alrededor del mundo por las corbetas Descubierta y
Atrevida al mando de los capitanes de navio don Alejandro
Malaspina y don Jose de Bustamente y Guerra desde 1789 a
1794, con una introduccion por don Pedro de Novo y
Colson. Madrid: Impr. de la viuda e hijos de Abienzo,
1885. It goes without saying that this book and the
translation were the mainstay of my research.

Maury, Captain M.F. The Physical Geography of the Sea.
2nd ed. New York: Harper and Brothers, 1855. I still
think I could have got the Brooke's device to work if
I'd had a bit more time.

Mitterling, Philip I. America in the Antarctic to 1840.
Urbana: University of Illinois Press, 1959. Even better
than Gurney and Bertrand.

Morrell, Benjamin. A Narrative of Four Voyages aka
Morrell's Voyages and Discoveries with a Sketch of the
Author's Life . New York: Harper and Bros., 1841 (1st
published 1832). There's a fantastic portrait of
Morrell in here, but I couldn't get my hands on it

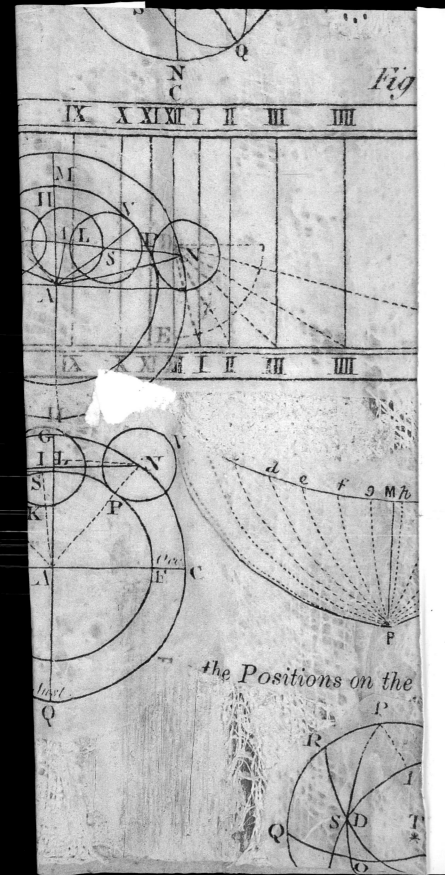

without buying a copy for several hundred bucks. I
still could, if Rumour would pay for it.

Ocean Passages for the World. Taunton, Somerset:
Hydrographic Dept., Ministry of Defense, 1987.
Absolutely essential for sailors.

Poe, Edgar Allan. Narrative of A. Gordon Pym. In The
Complete Tales and Poems of Edgar Allan Poe. New York:
The Modern Library, 1938. I've put this in reluctantly,
but I have quoted from him.

Ramsay, Raymond H. No Longer on the Map: Discovering
Places that Never Were. New York: The Viking Press,
1972. He had a teasing reference to a shipwreck,
confirmed by the fellows in the pub in Stanley. I never
did find out anything more about it.

Reeves, E. A. Hints to Travellers Scientific and General.
Ninth edition. London: The Royal Geographical Society,
1906. Don't leave home without it.

Stommel, Henry. Lost Islands: The Story of Islands That
Have Vanished from Nautical Charts. Vancouver:
University of British Columbia Press, 1984. I would
like to meet Mr. Stommel and thank him for setting me
on this search.

Weddell, James. Master in the Royal Navy. A Voyage
Towards the South Pole, Performed in the Years 1822-24,
Containing an examination of the Antarctic Sea, to the
Seventy-fourth Degree of Latitude: and A Visit to Tierra
del Fuego, with a particular account of the Inhabitants.
London: Longman, Hurst, Rees, Orme, Brown, and Green,
1825. I don't know what to say about Weddell, except
that he was an honourable man and reported what he
saw. That he was wrong does not affect my good opinion
of him.

Credits and Acknowledgments

Source material for the location of lost islands on the "Chart of Magnetic Curves" (facing
  page 10) is from *Lost Islands* by Henry Stommel (see bibliography).
The photograph of Charles Darwin (page 46) is from *Darwinism and Human Life* by
  J. Arthur Thomson. London: Andrew Melrose, 1909, frontispiece.
Source material for the diagrams of sea mammals (page 57) came from *Whales, Dolphins and
  Porpoises* by Mark Carwardine, illustrated by Martin Camm. Toronto: Stoddart, 1995.
The navigation examples (page 74) have been adapted from *A Complete Epitome of Practical
  Navigation* by J.W. Norie. London: Imray, Laurie, Norie & Wilson, 1900, p.63.
Source material for the watercolor sketch (page 81) came from *Antarctica: The Last Frontier*
  by Richard Laws. London: Boxtree, 1989, p. 121.
The *Odontocymbiola magellanica* (page 112) is redrawn from an illustration by James Nicholls
  in *The Larousse Guide to Shells of the World,* by A.P.H. Oliver. New York: Larousse & Co.,
  1980, p. 251.
The engraving of Edgar Allan Poe (page 158) is from *The Works of Edgar Allan Poe* by
  Richard Henry Stoddard. London: Kegan, Paul, Trench, 1884, frontispiece.
Source material for the maps of the South Atlantic (page 200-01) came from *Ocean Passages for
  the World,* 4th edition, published by the Hydrographer of the Navy, 1987.
"Section VIII, South Atlantic Ocean" (page 251) was reconstructed from the *Catalogue of
  Charts, Plans, Views, and Sailing Directions* by R.B. Bate of Poultry, London, Admiralty-
  Office, 1832-1836, in the holdings of the Library of Congress.
The map of Bustamente's voyage to the Auroras (page 255) was adapted from the 1800
  "Carta Esferica del Oceano Meridional," in the holdings of the Library of Congress.

I'd like to thank the following people and institutions for their much-appreciated help with
this book: Editors Sarah Malarkey and Beth Weber, for their care and enthusiasm; Todd
Belcher, for his invaluable assistance with the photography; John Kendrick, author of
Alejandro Malaspina: Portrait of a Visionary, for advice on sources for Malaspina and
Bustamente; Christine Adkins, acting curator, Cowan Vertebrate Museum, U.B.C., for allowing me to photograph the collection; Tim and Pauline Carr, curators of the South Georgia
Museum, for the helpful response to my inquiries, and to the many others who provided
assistance, including Liz Darhansoff, Chuck Verrill, Sarah Williams, Charlie Haynes and
Doug Johnson. Thanks as well to those on the Falklands who so generously helped me during my stay: Corrinne Parkes, International Tours and Travel; Mr. and Mrs. Hadden; Bob
and Celia Stewart; Rob McGill; Neil Rowlands, Hebe Tours; Phyllis Rendell, Department
of Mineral Resources; John Smith, curator, Falkland Islands Museum; and the staff at the
Harbour Master, Fisheries Department; Falkland Islands Customs and Immigration; and
Falkland Islands Weather Service.

And special thanks to David, for his unflagging support; to Dave Gay, for taking me out on
his boat and for patiently answering innumerable questions; and to my father, Stan
Hodgson, who cast his critical eye over my sailing blunders and who methodically and
wisely corrected them.

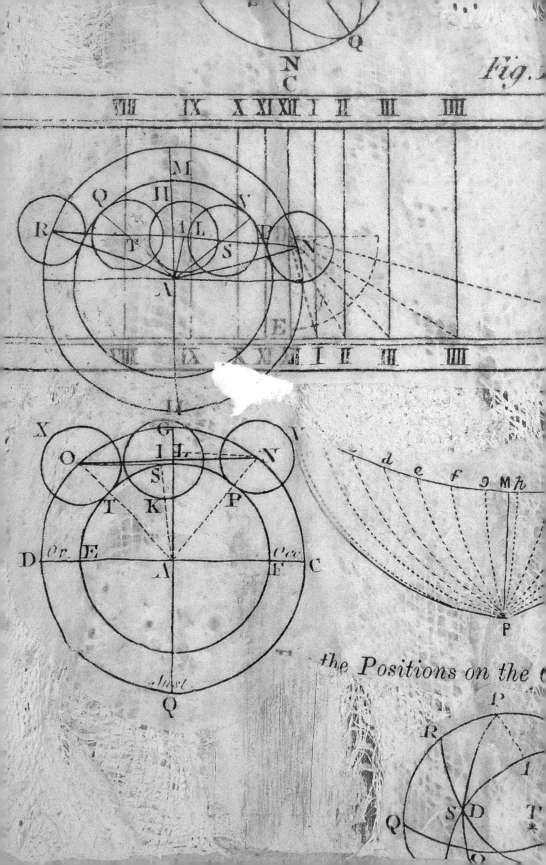

Fig.

the Positions on the